Eve of Snows

Sundering the Gods: Book One

by

L. James Rice

Eve of Snows is a work of fiction. Names, characters, places, and incidents are the product of the author's imagination or are used fictitiously. Any resemblance to actual events, locales, or persons, living, dead, undead, possessed, or anywhere in between is purely coincidental.

No part of this book may be reproduced in any form or by any electronic, mechanical, or magical means, including information storage and retrieval systems, mind melds or other psychic means, without written permission from the author, except for the use of brief quotations in a book review or seance.

Edited by Dorrie O'Brien
Cover design by Damonza.com
Cartography by Jenna Jing Rice

ISBN: 978-1-7324083-1-9 paperback
ISBN: 978-1-7324083-0-2 e-book

Join my newsletter list for updates, promotions, and exclusive short works at:
sunderingthegods.com

Dedicated to my lovely wife and two beautiful daughters;
may their inspiration live forever.

TERRITORY OF THE CLAN CHOERKIN

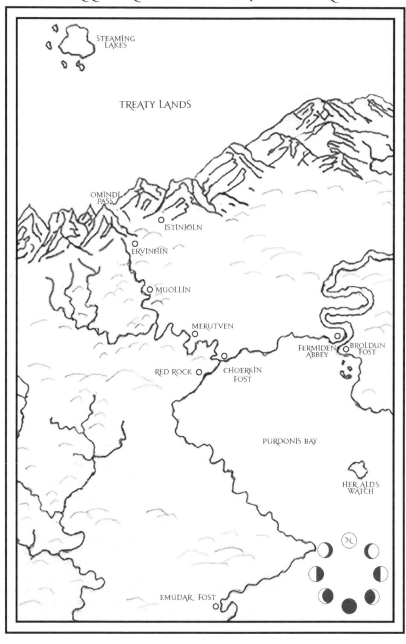

STEAMING
LAKES

TREATY LANDS

OMINDI
PASS

ISTINJOLN

ERVINFIN

MUOLLIN

MERUTVEN

FERMIDEN   BROLDUN
ABBEY   FOST

RED ROCK   CHOERKIN
                FOST

PURDONIS BAY

HERALD'S
WATCH

N

EMUDAR FOST

A FORGOTTEN VOICE

"It will ease your worries to know you aren't dead, but it shouldn't. Whatever end your destiny holds is neither so simple, nor pleasant, nor is it now.

"You will find yourself on the island of Kaludor, a frozen rock with a mountainous spine, ruled by seven clans for the Seven Heavens. This is as it should be, as it has been for as long as time remembered, but it is not as it has always been. In the beginning, in an age when the gods were invited by their adherents to war with the gods of other nations, the Silone clans bent their knees in obeisance to the king priest, the mortal voice of Sol, king of the Silone gods.

"This Age of God Wars is past by a thousand years, its end not in blood but a rending, a shift in the universe. The world shattered, banishing the gods from the world and stealing the memories of the mortal peoples in an event known as the Great Forgetting. Debate with the First Dragons if you will whether this change was for good or ill, what matters is its enfeebling the tether between mortal and gods, empowering the clans to rule without a king priest. Likened by some as a body without a head, this hierarchy is an abomination in the eyes of those who dwell in the Conqueror Heaven where Sol's throne trembles in the raging grip of a pensive, angry king.

"The Sister Continents have calmed, stabilized for half a millennium. The Forgettings have left mortals without a memory of why the gods went to war, why the world shattered and returned in pieces. It is a thing best left forgotten, but the gods remember and will never forget. They destroyed the world once for a glimpse of the truth; they will risk everything for a second look, the chance at grasping the source, but for this a head must return to the body, and the body must find its home.

"You will forget me and all I have said, but like your history, some hidden portion of consciousness will remember these truths and the necessity to survive.

"You will learn who you are and someday learn again who you were.

"Enter.

"Forget.

"Open your eyes to blue."

ONE

Bones for Songs

Tarry thy thoughts, Harry thy thoughts!
Ha ha ha ha!
Only a mad man notes his own laughter.
So they say, so They say, so they Say.
I do not believe them. Do you, foolish reader?
Who do I fool? Only fools who believe me mad will ever read this.
Better a Mad man than a Dunce man.
So prove your worth, oh, Worthy!
Go! Laugh, laugh Out Loud!
And take note of it.

—*Tomes of the Touched*

Seventeen Days to the Eve of Snows

Robed figures huddled in an oasis of flickering brazier light as bones hit the cave floor with a clatter and bounce. Pips flipped until coming to rest, the dice totaling sixteen. Monks and priests hollered and groaned, their voices a discordant symphony echoing in the hollows of the cavern. Tokodin clenched his jaws, saving his curses for the next roll if it came in over seventeen.

Hawk and Snake, a game of over-under chance, and Tokodin's weakness. He anguished over his coins falling into other people's

3

pockets, but relished the rushing breaths and churns of his gut. He leaned, knuckles grinding into the cavern floor as Meliu blew on the dice rattling between her slender fingers.

The two of them had grown up together in Istinjoln Monastery, but within months of pronouncing her vows of priesthood, she'd traveled to serve in the libraries of these Chanting Caverns. It'd been over a year since they last spoke, so for the past two weeks they'd much catching up to do, which included her taking a healthy chunk of his coins. "Not today, girl. Not today."

Meliu swiped auburn curls from her eyes and blew him a kiss, winking before snapping her wrist.

Numbers tumbled, three white dice and one black, keys to a small fortune for a poor monk.

Too nervous to watch, he looked to Angin, the game's overseer. The man stood a shave under seven feet tall and would ring the scales at fifteen bricks if anybody bothered to weigh him. Combined with a nose flattened between sagging, lopsided eyes courtesy of a horse's hoof, Angin scared the wits out of any gambler who thought to cheat.

The dice clattered to a stop and Angin called out, "Seven days and two nights, for a total of nine. Pass the bones and ante up!"

Tokodin pumped his fist and shot Meliu a smirk. She curled her lips and stood to stretch. Five feet nothing and petite, she could make Tokodin's eyes droop like a hungry puppy's with a smile and a flutter of her lashes. No matter, the girl didn't look twice at him with his fat round nose and squinty eyes, and scars marring his face. If he'd earned the priesthood, maybe she'd have taken notice, but failure had sent him on the monk's path.

Angin shoved songs from the Hawk and Snake lines to the pot, and Tokodin eyed a couple glints of silver amid the copper. The bones were his now, and odds favored the roller.

He snatched the dice from the floor, tossed the ante of two songs into the pot and warmed the dice in his hand with a breath. If it weren't sacrilegious he'd pray for all ones or sixes, an automatic win on any roll. He rapped his knuckles three times on the ground and slung the dice.

The three white dice yielded eleven and the painted black die a four.

Angin called out, "Eleven days and four nights, fifteen's the target."

Gamblers mumbled and coins jingled, but Tokodin focused on the beat of his heart. The rhythm spoke to him: *Three snakes.* He dug his fingers into his pouch to find coins scarce, but he put everything remaining on the three mark of the snake line.

"You're due for some luck." Meliu grinned and matched his bet on the third snake.

"Hope so." If he had to share a win with anyone, Tokodin would prefer it be her or his closest friend.

He glanced at Loepus as the man contemplated his wager. As first-year postulants they'd shared a cell at Istinjoln Monastery, and despite Loepus making the priesthood they were best friends to this day, but damned if that blond bastard didn't put his copper on the fourth snake, with a grin his way. Loepus counted on Tokodin's luck to be good, but not good enough.

A win that stuck it to his chum would make the jingle of coins all the sweeter. Tokodin tapped his knuckles once and rolled. If he hit the target on any roll, he won. Instead of reading the dice, he waited for Angin's call.

"Seven days and three nights, totaling ten, the game goes snake."

Tokodin exhaled and slapped the ground before sweeping the bones into his hand. "Snake, snake, snake," he muttered for the dice to hear. He struck his knuckles twice, and dice hit stone.

Angin called out, "Eight days and one night for a total of nine, two snakes and counting."

Tokodin rocked on his knees, whispering to the dice. "Get me drunk, my little darlings." With this swollen pot, even split, he'd be drinking the same ale as the priests, not the watery swill impoverished monks endured. He swore even the hangovers were better. His knuckles struck thrice, dice flicked from his fingers.

"Eight days and six nights totaling fourteen, three snakes and counting."

Tokodin muttered under his breath, "Gods and hells, gods and hells." A roll over fifteen and he'd fill his purse. He needed to piss. No, just nerves. "Gods and hells." Four raps of the knuckles and he let fly.

He couldn't look.

Gamblers chortled, groaned, and cheered as Angin called, "Three days and two nights totaling five, four snakes and counting."

His spirit sank so deep his bladder went away, and Meliu buried her face in her hands with a groan. If the night die had been a one, the whole pot would jingle at his hip. He groped the dice, slow and depressed, glared at the pips. His darlings had become sons of bitches.

Loepus lay an arm on his shoulder, his eyes aglow with more mirth than Tokodin could stomach. "Three ones and a two, the night die taunts you."

Tokodin smirked at his friend, the dice might still teach him a lesson. "You're wrong, every damned one taunts me." He kissed the dice, hope remained. "Fifteen or four of a kind, you worthless bones." He cast the dice with a rattle and his forehead clunked the stone floor, pain enough to prove the dice hadn't killed him outright.

"Fourteen days and six nights for a total of twenty! Four snakes is the winner!"

Tokodin glared as Loepus hooted and butted heads with Pindin, the other man with money on the fourth snake. Loepus was a good friend, but right now Tokodin loathed him. A priest's stipend was four times a monk's. He tried not to hate him for achieving the priesthood while Tokodin failed, but jealousy was a hard flea to shake. As Angin collected side bets and divvied the pot, Tokodin's eyes slipped from the celebration and into the blackness of the cavern. *Gruel and water for me.*

Meliu stood and passed him, gracing him with a smile. "I'll be back soon, you get 'em on the next round, you hear me?"

"Next round." He didn't have enough coins for an ante. He watched the sway of her hips as her form faded into the shadows outside their braziers.

Guntar, the bearer whom he served, slapped him on the back. "I hope your luck on the trail is better than your dice." At least he feigned sincerity.

Tokodin rose to his feet with a groan of stiff muscles and agonizing loss, wandering from the halo of brazier light surrounding the dice game. More fires burned near a priest who stood watch at the Crack of Burdenis but the murky dark suited Tokodin's mood. He stopped and looked up, but the cavern's ceiling hid in deep shadow. The dark hollow appeared infinite, but like life, somewhere above, it, too, met an end.

He had never seen this cavern lit by the troughs of oil carved in the walls, but folks told him pyrite streaked the ceiling, earning it the nickname The Fool's Haul for those who thought it gold. Tokodin figured it was better to chase false gold than to throw away real copper. But he knew the moment a few songs jingled at his waist the optimism would return and he'd be back throwing the bones. Optimist or fool?

He grinned, deciding what he really needed was a stiff pour of whiskey to drive away the hurt those dice put on him. Tokodin huffed, adjusting his plain gray robes hanging limp from his shoulders. They wouldn't serve him any drinks down here anyhow, songs or no.

He meandered to the ring of braziers surrounding the Crack of

Burdenis, a deep hole in the world. Named after the Patron God of Snows, the chasm hid the fifth shrine of Burdenis, younger brother of Sol, King of the Gods. A hundred strides long and twenty across at its widest, the Crack mirrored the ceiling: so deep you couldn't see its end.

Gods and favored priests like Meliu were the only ones who knew what went on in the hidden caves below. There was only one way Tokodin and his dingy monk's robes would earn a visit to the floor of the Crack.

"If I threw myself down this hole would I come up fifteen?"

Tikotu, Third Priest of Burdenis, was in his fifties and his gut suggested they feasted well at the Crack when there weren't guests to feed. "With your spit-poor luck I'd say you'd come up dead by the third stair."

Tokodin chuckled, throwing the priest a smirk. "Your holy compassion soothes me to the marrow." His humor ended when he gazed at the steep, zigzagging stair carved in the wall of the chasm and nauseous waves passed through his head. He counted twenty torches set into the descent before darkness consumed their meager lights in its depths.

The old priest suffered a phlegmy cough and spat. "You didn't even lose a poor man's fortune. And if you had, who's fault but your own?"

A poor comfort that a poor man's fortune had been his own. "I had fifty songs, you should know, for walking escort."

"Gutted and bleeding out from a Colok's claws, would you think it a fair wage?"

Tokodin squirmed, the sentiment was a lifetime from Guntar's rousing recruitment speech. "Colok are stupid animals, nothing more."

Tikotu guffawed, chins shaking. "Dumb beasts, sure. Who run in tribes, forge weapons and armor, and pray to false gods for power."

Loepus called out. "Tokodin! You in the next round?"

He raised his pouch and gave it a silent shake before slumping to sit at the edge of the Crack, leaning his shoulder against the pulley-post, making sure not to jostle the bell dangling from its arm. He peered into the bucket hanging from the pulley's rope, a method for transporting messages faster than the fifteen-hundred steps to the bottom, and found it empty. What the hells did he expect, a song to buy a pint?

Tokodin rubbed his eyes and gazed into the black hole. A dim pulse of light shook his malaise, and a rumble echoed the lower caves. He glanced to see if anyone else heard and found Tikotu standing over his shoulder and the game of Hawk and Snake strolling his way.

His body took a chill, goosebumps pimpling his arms. He jumped to his feet and prayed for heat.

Loepus thumped his shoulder, breaking his prayer's concentration; no warmth came and his goosebumps multiplied, the reason he'd failed the priesthood. The power of the gods required focus, even for a lord priest.

"What'd you see?" Loepus asked.

"A flash of light, deep enough to be bottom."

Another flash, brighter, and followed by a rumble deeper and more powerful, shook the caves. The quivers beneath his feet reminded him of a rumored collapse in the Ihomjo mines, only a wick or two of a crow's flight from where he stood right now. These caverns might have stood for millennia, but a jab of claustrophobia squeezed the beat of his heart.

Guntar edged through the press of milling adherents. "We should head down."

Tense but composed, he had a way of appearing at the brink of fisticuffs on a happy day. Now his teeth ground, spoiling for a fight.

Tikotu grumbled. "You go rushing down them steps and half of you'd be dead from the fall before you got there. We wait."

Guntar's jaw muscles flexed in clenching pulses near his ears, and Tokodin feared the man's words. Guntar carried a temper, and as a bearer for Istinjoln, charged with delivering important messages, his status in the Church lay beyond his years.

Guntar's diplomacy suggested the answer to who bore the weight of authority. "I bow to your wisdom, of course."

A pulse of light and another rumble echoed from the deeps, interrupting the power play. In the bass of the echoing thunder, a subtle, higher-pitched shriek caught his ear. Could humans scream so loud? A chill prickled his skin, pervasive, unfading even in the ensuing silence.

The chasm went black and silent. Monks and priests meandered from the Crack, muttering reassuring words as time passed. Tokodin could not. He stood pensive, staring, ears strained for any sound.

A quarter candle later the notion of screams hiding in the rumbles still haunted his ears. "What were they doing down there, Tikotu?"

The older man scrunched his face and rested his arms on his belly. "I haven't the slightest pissin' idea." He chortled, his eyes nervous. "But don't ever believe our betters don't come up with damned fool notions." The priest's eyes scanned for listeners. "I did hear—"

The pulley bell clanged four times, echoing through the hall, and explosions followed. Flashes of white as intense as a thunderstorm crackled across the depths of the Crack and streams of fire lended hues of orange and yellow and blue. This time the screams were of men dying.

Tokodin's fingers tingled in panic, chest pounding faster than the rhythm of the thunder below. "Twelve Hells."

Tikotu hefted a lead brick, trembling fingers fumbling its weight until it dropped in the bucket, and it plummeted into the abyss. Adherents swarmed the edge of the Crack to gain a view as the rope whirred, but the pulley jerked to a sudden stop. The post strained as a fishing pole that'd caught a whale. The oak cracked then snapped, its tip and pulley spiraling into flashes of fire and lightning.

Guntar fumed. "We're headin' down."

Tikotu clutched the bearer's robes at the chest and shoved him backwards. "Down is dead! Gather your faith and prayers. Spread out. Anything that pokes its head from the Crack that ain't a man, you burn it to the Forges."

Guntar found his footing and stared hard at the big man, but he didn't make a move. "You heard the Third Priest! Fan out and hold faith in Sol."

A gong sounded in the cavern, deafening Tokodin to further commands; he knew the reverberations in his ear from training, and they straightened his spine with a tingle. The call to battle, to defend the Church with prayer, steel, and blood.

Tokodin rushed to snatch his staff amid others scrambling for weapons and gear. The nine hands of oak reinforced with iron caps stood a finger or two taller than him, and its heft in his hands lent small comfort. He trotted back to the Crack and edged close to Tikotu as the gong's echo faded. "What the Twelve Hells is going on?"

The priest glanced for eavesdroppers. "Them dice may be the best part of your day."

Tokodin stared, stymied. "Colok?" The beasts had slaughtered priests on hallowed ground before, but not a major shrine so well protected.

"No." The man gnawed his lip. The old priest wanted to let slip the secret, but Tokodin never expected the man to break. "Shadows from the Stone, that's what we call them."

"Shadows? Stone? What the hells does that mean?"

The priest shook his head with a snarl followed by a panicky laugh. "You'll regret finding that answer." The priest pushed him back and faced the top of the stairs.

The Crack of Burdenis returned to darkness and remnants of thunder trailed into silence.

Guntar shoved past him, his shouts booming. "Focus. Prayer. The gods will listen and answer."

Tokodin found Loepus and stood by his side. "Not liking this."

His friend sported a nervous grin, and he cleared his throat after his voice cracked. "Well, we didn't join an escort to meditate."

They waited in the dim light of braziers and torches, the only sounds their breathing and shuffling feet. Too quiet, too long. The adrenaline of a game of dice couldn't compare to the chilled blood in his veins as time drug on. Nothing was coming up those stairs, friend or foe. Eyes meandered from the Crack, looking to each other for answers or questions, perhaps reassurance or inspiration. But no one dared utter a word.

A soft sound came from the chasm with a stuttering cadence, and all eyes retrained. Waited. Gasping breaths and the slap of leather soles and hands on stone. A priest struggled from the stairs and collapsed to his knees, his chin sagging and rising from his chest with every desperate breath. His words were a fight for air as he raised a quivering arm with tubes clutched in his fist. "Diamond failed. Hells're comin'."

Tikotu grabbed two scrolls from the man's shaking hand, opening the one unsealed. His eyes flicked across the page as Guntar stepped to kneel before him. The Third Priest exhaled a deep breath and handed the bearer the scroll sealed in a leather tube. "To Istinjoln with haste." The big man leaned to the bearer's ear, but his nerves made his whisper loud enough to hear. "No aid from Istinjoln, and every soul here is forfeit."

Guntar took the tube and bowed his head, his voice determined. "On our lives, we swear it." He leaped to his feet and raised an iron-clad staff over his head. "Ready escort!"

Tokodin trotted to the gaming braziers with a snort and snagged his dice from the floor before grabbing his pack. He tested the buckle strapping snowshoes, a shovel, and a hatchet to its side, and made certain his jerked deer and canteens lay buried beneath his fleece-lined trousers. The latter in case the weather took an unseasonable turn. Wool wax coated the soft-soled elk hide boots and wool robes he wore, to repel snow or rain, but extra gear never hurt in unpredictable mountain weather. He yanked the drawstring and pulled its straps over his shoulders, praying he wouldn't need any of these things.

Priests and monks rushed into the cavern from several directions, answering the gong's alarm, but the auburn locks he sought were nowhere in sight. He banged the butt of his staff on the floor in frustration and strode toward the bearer. He'd dreamed of important missions when he clasped arms with Guntar and pledged his life, but with the moment upon him, his stomach knotted.

"Leaving so soon?"

Lovely Meliu, such a relief to hear her voice.

He turned, caught by a hug. He smiled despite his terror. "Whoa, girl, no time for that. Well, all right." He grabbed her hand and dragged her several feet into darkness before she pulled free and slugged him hard enough to sting.

"Naughty boy."

The humor faded and his grin died as he looked into her eyes, wishing there were more light to see their soft beauty. How many monks and priests served this shrine? How many were friends? Everyone's lives were in danger. Meliu's life. "Shadows from the Stone?"

She shot him a cockeyed glance, her mouth opening and closing without a word before she planted her feet. "You shut up about those, you hear?"

"I hear you." A dead subject, whatever those words meant.

"No time for kisses, monk!" Guntar and the remaining escort stared, waiting on him.

He ignored the bearer at his peril. "You'll be safe?" Her prayers were those of a scholar, not a killer.

She fidgeted and giggled, forced a smile. "I'm damned good at hiding, if it comes to it. Next time you're here, stay longer."

He wanted to kiss her, but a lack of courage turned him to stone. No need to prove himself a fool. "It's come to it, wherever you think is safe, go now." The smirk on her face hammered his confidence in her. "The diamond failed, and the hells are coming." She blanched. Tokodin didn't know what these words meant, but she sure the hells did.

She shrugged her shoulders and righted her habit before tromping up to and right past Guntar. "Shortcut. Follow me."

Guntar bellowed, "You heard the priestess."

Tokodin swiped his forehead and exhaled with a moment of relief, knowing she was with them for a stint. His eyes focused ahead but his ears listened to the caterwauling from behind.

The clamor of coming battle mangled shouts and screams into a cacophony, but a few rang distinct over the din. "Ignite the fires! Slings with oil!" The voice belonged to High Priestess Endelu if he wasn't mistaken. Her reputation left no doubt to the power of her prayers, but the pitch to her shouts left no doubt of the edge her emotions walked.

The cavern narrowed as they traveled with hurried steps, and as the tunnel turned thunder bellowed and a breeze swept over the back of his head, warming his ears. He stopped, afraid to look back even as the bearer's torches disappeared around the bend. Tokodin never had faith in the gods to answer his prayers, but he kissed two fingers and touched his forehead before he turned.

The cavern's walls blazed in ribbons of fire, lightning crackled and sparked, and smoke roiled in billows, as robed priests formed a wall facing an unknown foe. Angin's hulking form stood out from the rest, whirling a staff wreathed in flame. The holy held their ground against evil by the grace and with the power of the gods, and for a flicker he held hope. Then Angin froze, his arms splayed, his staff dropping from his hands and growing dark, his mass of flesh and bone lifted from the ground, stiff as a straw doll before slammed into the stone floor by an unseen force. Tokodin's hope drained with the blood from his face, and he ran until catching the escort, panting, unable to bring words to his tongue.

Guntar asked, "What'd you see?"

Flames and sparks and smoke and death, but the words stumbled and tripped before reaching his tongue.

The bearer slapped him in the side of the head. "What'd you see?"

An oracle, poet, or minstrel might find words for the terror, but there was a deeper truth to utter: "We need to move faster."

Two

The Lonely Scar

In darkness a light, fleeting and desperate.
In Darkness there is no light nor flight, but there is desperation.
My wings refuse to unfurl, I fall, but go nowhere.
The laughter is mine, but the Voice is not.
Who am I? I am not. Never was. Never will be.
Not until tomorrow.

—Tomes of the Touched

Seventeen Days to the Eve of Snows

Eliles' eyes twitched beneath drooping lids, deep breaths easing her mind and soul against the tension surrounding her in the Hall of Trials. Imaginings of a pastel blue sky streaked with yellows, pinks, and oranges in sunset pulled her into tranquility, rounding her shoulders with a deep exhalation. A dozen snow buntings lifted from Istinjoln's cobbled courtyard with breezes warmer than a breath in cupped hands sweeping beneath their wings. The flutter of their heartbeats beat in her chest and her eyes raised to the sky as if she could join in their flight of freedom.

The slap-crack of a whip shattered her peace, resounding through the deep caverns beneath Istinjoln Monastery. She straightened her back and opened her eyes as a dozen voices rose in a droning chant, the prayer's energies summoning a spectral shaft of Light. A circular dais of white marble blossomed into a brilliant glow, highlighting silver-and-gold streaks in its polished stone.

A horseshoe of priests in black robes stood on the edge of the aura across from Eliles, solemn, heads bowed, and hands hidden in the deep bells of their sleeves. Three dozen, maybe, were Masters of Fire and their underlings, each here to witness their students in the Trials, but the rows of faceless robes counted far greater than those instructors.

Many were here to see her.

Eliles kneeled at the head of the row of twelfth-year postulants, those here for their final and most difficult trial before priesthood, and she'd be the first to kneel in the circle of blinding light.

Liermu, Mistress of Trials, stepped from the shadows and into the Light, a snake whip curled into a tight loop in her right hand. Her form cast no shadows as she walked, for the Light of the Gods enveloped all, disallowing darkness. Her black robes brushed the stone floor, her cowl thrown back to reveal its blood-red silk. Liermu's dark brows were thicker than her narrow eyes and she wore a twitchy smile that suggested she enjoyed swinging the whip known as the Maimer's Lash.

Liermu said, "The final trial of priesthood is to ignite with prayer seven candles for the seven heavens." She pointed to a candelabra hanging from the ceiling and then to twelve candles ringing the room. "And these twelve candles, representing the hells we must cross on the Road of Living Stars in order to stand beside our gods."

A high priest with gold silk rimming his robes at the sleeves and hood, took a single step forward. His face hid in his dark cowl, but the voice was deep and mellow, distinct. "Begin." Woxlin was a pup amongst old dogs. Surprising he'd receive the honor of commencing the trials after four months in the high priesthood.

Liermu spun on her heel, locking eyes with Eliles. "Maevu, ward and postulant of Istinjoln, and seeker of the Flames of Sol, come forward."

Eliles stood before she realized her name wasn't called, and a squeak came from the back of the row. "Me?"

"Come forward, postulant. Prove your worth before Sol, King of the Gods."

Eliles slumped to her knees, gazing over her shoulder at the terrified girl who rose and inched toward the Light. Maevu should've been the last of the twelfth-years to face the whip. She would lack focus; they were throwing the most vulnerable into the Light to bleed first. In her twelve years of servitude, Eliles had never heard of such a break in tradition.

Maevu trembled as she reached the circle's center, untying and slipping from her robes, dropping them in a heap around her feet. The girl was naked, showing humility before the gods, and her long black hair was tied in a bun to reveal the forty or more white scars crisscrossing her back, glowing white in the Light.

"Kneel and face the Trial of Nineteen Candles."

Maevu steadied herself with her hands as she lowered her knees to her robes, the only comfort in these chambers.

Liermu said, "What is easy in practice, with solitude and patience, may prove impossible beneath the stare of hundreds of eyes and in the face of time."

A trial-candle ignited. The standard timing-candle held forty-eight conjoining wicks, and twenty-four candles burned end-to-end marked a day. The flames of the wicks alternated between yellow and orange, and flared blue as wicks transitioned. Trial candles flared every quarter-wick.

Maevu bowed her head, focusing. Muttered prayers murmured from her lips.

Eliles' fingers dug into her own thighs, hoping the girl's count of scars ended here. Maevu was the lowest ranked postulant, Eliles couldn't imagine what she'd done to deserve this pressure.

Mistress Liermu sauntered to stand behind Maevu as the candle approached its flare, unraveling the whip to twirl its tip on the floor in a figure eight.

Maevu's prayers intensified, and the candelabra above her head lit for the Seven Heavens. The wicks representing the Twelve Hells smoked, glowed orange, but refused to ignite. If Maevu pushed too hard, she'd melt the candles, a flaw punishable by an extra whipping.

The trial-candle flared blue with a hiss.

Liermu intoned, "Facing the wars of gods and mortals, a priest must overcome not only the pressure of peers and haste, but the reality of pain."

The whip fell with a crisp snap and a fine streak of blood welted on Maevu's back. The blood flowed a moment only before congealing, the split skin knitting with unnatural speed toward what would in a half candle be a perfect scar, but experience taught Eliles that the pain intensified even as it healed. Priests spoke of the Maimer's Lash with reverence, a vestige of the Age of God Wars, but Eliles knew it for what it was, a torturer's device, a slaver's cruel joke incapable of killing anything but the victim's will.

Mistress Liermu snuffed the candelabra with a whispered prayer and a wave of her hand, and the trial continued.

Eliles' heart beat thirty times before the next flare.

Liermu stared into Eliles' eyes and smiled. "A priest's own life as well as the lives of their peers will rely upon their ability to focus one's devotion to prayer in the most trying circumstances."

The snap of leather left a second stripe down Maevu's sweating back, and the Mistress of Trials' twisted lips told Eliles the truth:

Whipping this poor girl was a game, a torment from this torturer meant to rattle Eliles' nerves. Eliles shut her eyes and breathed deep to retain her calm. She fidgeted beneath her robes; she wanted to scream, run, disappear. No, what she wanted was to end this charade by setting the Mistress of Trials ablaze.

The candle flared, and Liermu said, "When Jæmex of Ilbor was dying, her flesh flayed and her limbs stretched by rope, her prayers immolated herself, and her enemy, to save the lord priest's secrets. Could you match this feat?"

The third crack of the whip split skin and Maevu screamed.

Eliles gnashed her teeth. Whether she surrendered or fell unconscious, Maevu would fail the priesthood.

Another flare. "A priest unused to suffering will prove unable to summon a prayer to survive or destroy." The Maimer snapped an X across a healing wound, and Maevu shrieked. She continued her prayers with tears flowing down her cheeks, dripping from her chin like the wax down her candle.

Please quit, please.

Eliles chewed her lip, wanting to help the girl, but if a single priest noticed her calling Fire without prayer she'd expose herself as defiled, cursed with the feral magic of Vanquished Gods. It was a heretical and unholy practice punished by torture and death. She could save this girl from the whip, or doom herself trying.

The candle flared. "Failure is not shame, donning the monk's habit is not a disgrace."

"No," Maevu blurted, her shoulders tense and swollen red.

Leather snapped and the girl's sobs forged Eliles' will into iron. Damn these priests to their hells, Maevu deserved the priesthood more than most here with her overlapping scars.

She focused on Maevu's muttered prayers, they were chaotic and difficult to understand, but words were powerless. The discipline of prayer was training the body, the will, and the soul to inhale and shape the energies of the gods with ritualized focus, and then release the prayer in a moment called the Dispersion. Eliles watched the muscles in Maevu's shoulders tense, followed the pitch of the prayers as they rose.

Even before Eliles' first trial, her master had worked with her on leashing her feral magic. Whether the trial was to light and extinguish a single candle, to set a cloth ablaze, to summon Fire into a ventless globe, to build a wall of flame, or one of a hundred other tasks, they strove to perfect her succeeding while building the illusion of effort.

Mistiming the call to Fire could bring an inquisition Eliles wouldn't survive. She closed her eyes as a flare approached and imagined the candles smoldering, glowing orange, then fluttering into flame.

Maevu's tone climaxed.

Now. Her tiny, unseen friend caressed her skin with flickers of warmth and Eliles opened her eyes.

First the candelabra, then the twelve remaining candles ignited, sputtering and imperfect, but they lit. The priests and postulants in the chamber gazed at the wicks, smiling as they nodded with approval and relief. Maevu's tear-streaked face betrayed bewilderment with wide eyes and slack jaw as she stared at the flickering wicks, and a monk rushed to apply salves to her wounds.

Eliles grinned and ducked her head.

Mistress Liermu twirled her whip in a spiral on the floor, her lips straight and eyes cold. "The gods have blessed your perseverance, child. Your strength is commendable. Stand, servant of Sol, and leave this chamber so you may be judged."

Maevu stood, stiff and sore despite the salves, and the monk helped with her robes. The girl kissed the tips of her fingers and pressed them to her forehead in thanks to the gods as she strode from the room hunched and sobbing.

Liermu said, "Eliles, come before the nineteen candles."

Eliles strode to the center of the room, chin high, and sucking a deep breath to calm the gloating rhythm of her beating chest. She wanted to smile, but didn't dare.

Liermu's passionless lips turned into a crooked grin beneath squinty eyes, and Eliles wondered if this woman dreamed of striking her. She lowered her gaze, untied the sash of her robes, and lifted them from her shoulders, dropping them into a bundle on the floor. Her face burned red with shame.

She stared down the length of her nakedness, her skinny legs and knobbed knees, her breasts not so developed as some other girls, but what blushed her cheeks to rose she couldn't see: a lone scar on her left shoulder.

A four-inch welt of porcelain white.

Priests tallied scars much as a warrior recounting battles, and in Istinjoln the fewer the marks the greater the pride. Less than fifteen was a monumental achievement of skill while over forty meant you were tough as an axe head. For two hundred years the holy number twelve was the record, until Ulrikt took only three lashes on his fabled path to lord priest of Istinjoln.

Ulrikt still ruled, the most powerful lord priest on the island of Kaludor, the chosen one whom the oracles proclaimed a future leader before he'd turned twelve. Eliles was a nobody, a fishmonger's orphan whose oracle bones bore no witness to an esteemed fate. Her single scar was a slap to the tender egos of her peers, and a slight to her elders' beloved lord priest. Many praised her with smiles and shamed her as she walked away. Eliles wanted neither, she wanted to be free.

"Eliles, orphan, postulant, seeker of the fires of Sol, nineteen candles await the fire of your prayers." Liermu's whip slapped the hard rock floor. "By decision of the Council of Masters, because pain is the greatest teacher, and you have suffered so little, you will begin with three licks of the Maimer's tongue."

Eliles twisted her body, gazing back at the woman and her demon's smirk as the whip's tip danced circles on the stone floor.

Three scars, giving her four, one more than this devil's lord priest. It made a sense that twisted her guts into a knot until she wanted to puke. Her eyes darted into the hooded and shadowed faces, hoping someone would speak for her, but not a one stirred.

Eliles spoke as calm as her rigid spine and rapid breaths allowed. "I demand confirmation from the full council."

"Number four, for daring to question the council's decision."

The slither of the Lash's twirling ended with a wisp as it rose from the floor, and every muscle in her body tensed.

"No." The word was deep and carried the power of prayer, the power of law in Istinjoln, and the whip slapped stone. "The council has overstepped its authority."

Lord Priest Ulrikt stepped from the crowd of priests and into the shadowless light wearing a plain black habit instead of the gold-threaded robes of his station. He eased his cowl to his shoulders, revealing a handsome man in his sixties with an angular face and a straight nose, but what stood out so close to the Light was his silvered hair, aglow as an aureole in paintings of the gods.

Her tongue dried in her mouth as she stared into the eyes of her savior. She'd never been so close to the man; his eyes were kinder, a softer blue, than she would have imagined from a man with the blood of innocents soaking his hands, a man who preached fire and doom for children born like Eliles.

"Continue."

Liermu's voice shook. "Yes, My Lord. What is easy in practice, with solitude and patience, may prove impossible beneath the stare of hundreds of eyes and in the face of time."

Eliles forced her eyes from Ulrikt as the trial-candle lit.

This was her one-hundred and forty-fourth trial in twelve years, in a place she gave the blasphemous nickname of the Twelve Hells. In the eighth year postulants faced the whip for the first time. Courage or naïveté gave her the strength to take a lash while trying to light and snuff a single candle with a single prayer. Over the years her master had tried to convince her to take more scars, the better to hide her feral magic, but she never found the strength.

She mumbled her prayers, as she always did, hoping the gods would answer, as she always hoped, but knowing they ignored her. With Ulrikt so near, might the gods listen to her pleas? Flickers passed, and the memory of the Maimer's pain still burned within, stretching through the healed gash in her back and into her lungs.

Her heart beat faster with half of her time remaining, and Sol denied her Fire. Forsaken by the gods, but hidden amid their faithful. *Please.*

She continued her whispering prayers, but the candles remained dark, and her will to trust the gods faded as a familiar heat warmed the breath in her lungs, spreading to her heart to follow her veins.

The wick burned short, but the mistress wouldn't have her blood this or any other day.

The warm caress on the back of her hand came as it had since childhood, beckoning her to summon its power, and though she dared not smile, she felt a joy in the creature's touch. She clenched her eyes, and the room appeared in her mind, empty but for the white candles. She imagined them burning.

And when she opened her eyes, they were.

Gasps echoed through the chamber and someone whispered too loud, ". . . gentleness, as if they were already lit."

Her gut tightened, and she fought to keep her face placid. She'd gone too far, made a trial that sent energies in nineteen directions look easy.

Eliles met Ulrikt's gaze, and the man nodded with a smile, as if an oracle had told him what to expect, before turning and walking away. When Eliles looked to the Mistress of Fire, Liermu's hideous smile had been replaced by a stricken, blank expression, with every muscle in her face gone limp.

"Stand, servant"—the words struggled from her lips—"of Sol, and leave this chamber so you may be judged."

Eliles pulled her white robes over her shoulders, covered her head with its hood, and shuffled from the room in silence. She couldn't smile, she couldn't cry, she couldn't laugh, even the stone face she forced herself to wear would draw someone's ire.

She'd arrived at Istinjoln at the age of five, expecting to face beatings and a branding iron, then execution by fire or thorns, but the torture here was more subtle: Isolation, jealousy, fear, awe, her punishment for being different.

She stared at the stone floor while exiting the Chamber of Trials, marching silent through the rows of postulants. She entered the maze of tunnels beneath Istinjoln without a one raising their eyes to her as she passed, and she knew they'd whisper of her as soon as her shadow disappeared around the corner.

A tall man in black robes fell in step beside her and a sonorous voice as familiar as her own came from beneath the cowl rimmed in red silk. "Sol answered your prayers with strength, my child, and beneath the most holy judgement of Lord Priest Ulrikt himself. You should be proud your prayers were answered with such strength. Walk with me."

Master Dareun's voice remained cool and steady; she understood the undertones well. Eliles tucked her chin to her chest. She was in trouble and hoped the walk would soothe her master's anger.

THREE

Unseasonable Snows

Obsidian sockets in fleshless bone sobbing tears of diamond and sapphire,
rubies not blood, in Mortal sorrows shed for the imMortal,
those living in universes breathing lip to lip, hand in hand, never eye to eye,
eternal Lovers with a mortal affair doomed to Die.

—*Tomes of the Touched*

Seventeen Days to the Eve of Snows

Cold breezes slipped up Tokodin's sleeves, driving icicles into his arms as they approached the cavern's exit to mountain skies, but there was a deeper chill in his soul. The depths of the world were safe most times, but today the warmth and security of being in from the weather had turned into a miserable march through winding, drip-slicked tunnels.

When they reached the final rise before departing the Chanting Caverns, the party stopped, and Guntar spoke to a priest Tokodin didn't recognize. He slipped between bodies and cocked his head for a listen.

The priest's tone was tepid. "An autumn squall blew through two days back, left us a couple hands of snow, but drifting pushed spots above your head."

Tokodin's eyes rolled, the dice were just the beginning to his luck. The whole damned year had been unseasonably cold, but this was the first mountain snow.

Guntar asked, "I'm on foot, then?"

"We've had teams out since, cleared the trails down to the Omindi, salting the worst parts, and word is it's clear enough. Mountain pony should keep its feet for you."

Guntar nodded and waved his guards up, but Tokodin lingered as Meliu stepped in his path and hugged him; the embrace grew too long, more than the ordinary goodbye, before she wriggled from his arms. Her smile belied the tension. "I'll see you soon."

"You're not going back down there."

"You know I am, there're more than lives to be lost."

"What the hells is that supposed to mean?" The smirk reminded him of what a scholar valued most. "Don't you go dying for some damned books."

She rolled her eyes and strode past him, walking backwards into the dark to face him as she faded in the shadow. "Worse things to die for."

He watched until the light of her torch disappeared, mumbling to himself. "Foolish woman, anyhow." But staring into the dark worrying after her wouldn't save her life; getting Guntar to Istinjôln might. He spun for the exit with a new determination.

Blinding sunshine speckled by shimmers of snow falling and rising with swirling winds greeted his cave-accustomed eyes as he stepped outside. Tokodin covered his brow with his forearm, listening to the clop of hooves on stone as his vision adjusted. They had a solid three candles before dusk.

He gazed over the sturdy mountain pony's withers as his eyes strained into focus, taking in the ring of mountains surrounding the cavern's mouth. A fortnight past, only peaks and high ridges wore crowns of white, but now snow covered everything but the most severe outcroppings, and the green pine forest hugging the lower reaches of the valley stood frosted and gleaming.

Snowy mountains, white-capped seas, and ladies in white, Tokodin's father had always said they were the three most beautiful and dangerous sights in the world. Tokodin had never seen the sea, and women in their postulant robes had battered his ego more than a few times, but of the mountains, his father was right.

Mountains killed men in a hundred ways, but the risks of an avalanche, tumbling from a cliff, or freezing to death, these dangers were mitigable; they weren't random. Colok were more akin to the dice in Tokodin's pocket.

When man and beast met, it meant death. No prisoners, no survivors, and a year ago the Colok had eaten their human kills for the first time. Whether he was dinner for vultures, wolves, or Colok, it didn't sit well. Travel to the foothills would be half the speed they'd make on open ground, at least four candles, but once on the winding downhill they should reach the village of Ervinhine in a half candle or so. Istinjoln was a longer but secure journey from there.

It wasn't as cold as it might be, the days were long this time of year. He pulled gloves from his pack and slipped them on, but several men went without.

Guntar swung onto his mountain pony and strapped himself to the saddle with leather lashes and steel buckles; even if Guntar died, the pony would take the message home to Istinjoln. The remaining priests and monks surrounded Guntar on foot as escort.

"Loepus, Tokodin, scout the lead, stay in earshot."

Perfect. Scouting the trails meant them scaring up any fever snakes. The deadly creatures weren't common, but the way his bad luck was piling up today, he didn't like it.

Tokodin turned and strolled ahead, eyes dancing between boulders and brush for signs of ambush. They spent a quarter candle walking a rocky goat trail two men wide, with a jagged-fall precipice on their right hand. Violent winds rocked his steps without warning, and patches of ice hid in shadows the sun and salt didn't find.

When they reached the Omindi Pass Tokodin kissed two fingers and pressed them to his forehead. *Thank you, Burdenis, thank you.*

Loepus grinned at his display of faith. "Don't let no Colok eat me, now."

Tokodin smirked and faked a laugh as they slid down a slope of scree to Omindi Pass. If Colok attacked his weak prayers made him fodder, not savior.

Guntar and his pony followed, guided down the loose rock by a monk on either side of the pony's withers and flank. The Omindi was broad here, and the party spread out, their eyes on the walls of the trail despite it being an unlikely place for an attack. The Ambush Chokes, the most dangerous stretch of the Omindi, were a candle's walk north, opposite their heading.

As promised, the pass was clear of snow, but there was a trade-off for easy walking. The sound of the pony's clopping hooves kept time as they passed through open valleys and narrow gorges, announcing their arrival as sure as a drum.

The damned pony needed softer shoes.

A chill ran the length of Tokodin's spine, but not from the bitter winds and pellets of ice in the air. Fear. Foreboding. Dread. A presence? He pulled his wool cloak tight, peering from beneath the hood for movement on the icy slopes of Omindi Pass. Colok were famous for ambush, their pelts perfect camouflage in snow, rock, and shadow.

A Colok roar echoed through the valley, an eerie blend of elk call and wolf's howl carrying on the winds, but it was distant.

Tokodin muttered a prayer to Sol for warmth, and a comforting heat rose in his heart, spreading through his veins like warm molasses. A simple but blessed prayer on a frozen day.

A rock tumbled from the cliffs, clattering to his feet.

Tokodin crouched and whipped his staff off his back. He stood, chest heaving, ready for a fight, but nothing came.

"A little jumpy, aren't you? That rock remind you of your dice?" Loepus' eyebrows danced to a smart-assed tune.

Tokodin smirked, as close to a smile he could manage without poking his friend in the nose. He scanned the cliffs, spotted a switch-back trail crossing above. Tokodin remembered passing it on the way in, a miner's path, he figured. He squinted. High above, dangling over a rock, what might be a hand.

Loepus leaned in. "What the hells you looking at?"

He pointed. "Somebody pushed that rock."

Loepus squinted, muttered a prayer. "Mercies be kind, it is a hand."

"Move along!" Guntar shouted, only twenty strides away, but his voice was faint over a surge of wind. Tokodin signaled with two sharp whistles and pointed at the trail with his staff.

Tokodin faced Guntar's scowl, glanced at Loepus. "If we don't look and we get ambushed—"

"We make it quick." Loepus raised his staff and nodded to Guntar.

Guntar waved his arm, giving them permission to explore.

Tokodin slipped his staff into its harness. "Let's go."

"We waste Guntar's time or get ourselves killed, he'll be pissed."

Tokodin reached into his pocket. "The target is sixteen, Snake we stay low, Hawk we go high." He held the dice in his palm: eighteen. He'd hoped for Snake, but the dice passed judgment.

"Considering your luck, we should stay low."

Tokodin snorted and climbed the trail, slow and steady, slipping off his gloves to grab shrub Junipers for a better grip on the slope. Rocks skidded beneath their feet on the steep, narrow trail. They pulled their hatchets from their packs and used the pick side in slick spots, climbing on all fours. Picks clinking. Fingers scratching. Knuckles bleeding. Eyes wide unless chill winds forced a squint.

A ravine cut through the mountain at the top, a well-used trail leading west. To the Ihomjo mines? Dark mounds scattered the ground fifty feet away, likely bodies and gear, and a mule stood in the distance, still alive. The hand belonged to a man, arm outstretched, a crawling pose, and they rushed to his side.

Dead, but not for long. A bloody trail stretched behind him; he'd dragged himself this far before expiring.

Death wasn't a stranger, but Tokodin swallowed back bile and covered his mouth. With clothes sliced, ripped, and torn the man lay damned near naked. Scratches and teeth marks marred his skin, half of his right thigh gone, eaten.

"By the gods, it's true. The Colok ate him."

Tokodin glanced at his friend. "You're good with your prayers, but you'd make a damned poor hunter. Colok have claws, they would've split him open like a sacrificial goat. The scratches, too small, man-sized." He stretched his hand over scrapes down the man's back, his fingers matched. "And these." He pointed at teeth marks. "Think a baby Colok did this?"

"You're saying a cannibal?"

"If the killer were starving, why leave the damned mule alive?" Could cannibals gain such a taste for human flesh? Campfire tales of cannibalism in the mountains frightened and educated postulants, but those were desperate people in dire straits. This looked like a hunt, but so much wasted meat—his stomach turned. He rolled the man over. "Ah, hells."

Loepus vomited too close for Tokodin's taste, but his eyes didn't leave the dead man's face where dark bruises and blood surrounded empty sockets. *What? How?* The answer brought him to his feet.

Something had sucked the eyes from the miner's skull while still alive; there wouldn't have been bruising if the man had been dead.

"Get the hells out of here," Tokodin whispered.

They scrambled down the mountainside, sliding on their asses to reach the Omindi and ran to Guntar.

"Miners, all dead. Not just dead, eaten, his eyes," said Loepus, panting. and out of breath

Tokodin added, "Not by Colok, either. Fresh kills."

Guntar squinted at him. "Not Colok, then what?"

A damned fine question, and Shadows from the Stone danced on his tongue before he bit and swallowed them. Shadows couldn't eat a man, could they? "Never heard of nothing like it. We need to get out of here."

They traveled fast, his thighs burning as they cleared a steep rise and turned downhill into a section of pass with sheer walls. They were at least halfway to the foothills and they'd make good time downhill, but as they rounded the next corner, his heart palpitated.

Snow slide. Thigh-high with drifts above his head and stretching several hundred paces through a narrow gorge, the mountain pony wouldn't make it through.

Loepus glanced his way. "Screams ambush, don't it. There any way around?"

Only one came to mind. "There's the Beroy Branch, but it'd add three candles and no promise it isn't blocked too."

Both men glanced back to the priest who'd decide.

Guntar bellowed over a gust of wind: "Monks to your shovels, priests in a circle. Slow and steady gets us through this."

Tokodin shoved his staff into its harness and yanked his shovel from his pack, digging as Loepus strapped on snow shoes and strode atop the drifts, watching the heights of the gorge.

The snow was a fine powder that collapsed back in on them as they dug, adding to the torment, but perseverance made headway.

The sun was slipping behind the mountains to the west and the temperatures dropped fast with the growing shadow. Tokodin's throat and lungs burned with every heaving, frozen breath. He wanted to collapse, but clear trail lay a dozen strides ahead. Muscles burned and shook with every step, and he dropped to his knees as he struggled onto bare stone with several monks following behind.

Loepus slapped him on the back. "We're almost out of here."

Guntar and the remaining priests entered the canyon of snow.

A bellowing roar louder than a bull elk's call and far more terrifying ripped his sense of accomplishment to shreds; Tokodin had never heard a Colok so close.

Ambush.

The pony's shrill whinny brought him to his feet. A boulder crushed a priest's chest at the back of the party, burying him in the deep snow. Lightning answered a priest's prayer, a series of flashes striking the walls of the Omindi with pulsing thunder. The deadly energies crackled in a terrifying display, but the attack was too slow. The enemy no longer hid in the nooks and crannies the lightning sought; Colok leaped through the air, landing in the midst of the holy men.

The bear-like creatures were over eight feet tall and wore bits and pieces of armor covering portions of their striped and whorled fur. They were powerful, lithe, and the snow didn't slow them, while the priests slipped and slid to find their footing. Clubs, spears, and pole-axes thrust and whirled in the beasts' powerful hands. Blood sprayed, and the holy fell screaming.

Guntar yanked his mount's reins, an able rider, but the pony reared and spun with terrified eyes. If the priest steadied his mount, he'd be able to focus his prayers; hope remained, but the pony went wild, and only the leather straps kept Guntar in his saddle. Monks and priests didn't lend the bearer a hand, they fought for their lives.

Tokodin stared at the scene, dumbstruck by fear and exhaustion. Courage and duty didn't drive him to take the Oath of the Guardsman, a few extra coins and a roll of the dice had. Instinct begged him to stay on open ground and run; reason told him hope rode a pony, hope for them, and everyone at the Crack.

His legs drove him into the ambush. A rock twisted under his ankle and he plowed into a drift face first. He scrambled to his feet and brushed freezing snow from his cheeks and nose. With a duck and dodge, he slid between two Colok, collided with a priest and stumbled, snatching the pony's reins to keep his feet.

The critter reared, its hooves missing his face by a finger. He yanked the animal's head to its chest, and they spun in an uncontrolled circle, threatening to drag them both to the ground, but man and pony kept their feet. It was enough.

Lightning crackled from Guntar's hand, striking a Colok square in the chest. The creature blew back from the thunderous force, opening a hole in the wall of battle.

Tokodin planted his feet and steadied the pony best he could, gauging the battle from the eye. Loepus held his ground, but of those on their feet, he was the exception. Another bolt of lightning screamed into the battle, saving a priest's life, but for how long?

Chickens with their heads cut off, standing, fighting, but dead all the same. Hope deserted him. Everything was backward. The bearer protected them when they were his escort. His message must reach Istinjoln or an enemy he couldn't fathom would slaughter Meliu and everyone at the Crack.

Tokodin grabbed Guntar's arm and yelled. "Ride! Ride out of here!" Guntar's infuriated eyes bore into him. Surrender and flight weren't in the man's nature, but Tokodin matched his gaze. "Go! Or they're all dead!"

A moment passed, time enough for the mission to overpower the man's temper. Guntar nodded and spurred the pony.

Lightning flashed as he drove through the fray, but Loepus lay knocked to the ground, freeing a beast to attack. The Colok struck Guntar in the chest with a club, throwing man and mount to the ground, the pony's shriek echoing as it slid on its side into the snow. Another blow hit Guntar's back.

Tokodin focused his mind and screamed a prayer; fire raged, enveloping the monster's head, searing the Colok, and its club swung wide.

The creature dove into a drift to quench the flames, giving the pony time to scramble to its feet. Guntar clutched the animal's neck and mane as it whinnied and bolted, leaping from the vestiges of deep snow to run free. The pony's clopping hooves meant Meliu might live.

Tokodin watched the rider with pride before pain erupted in his left shoulder. He spun and collapsed into a boulder. A Colok brandishing a club the size of a small tree stalked toward him through trampled, blood-stained snow. Howls, explosions, and screams echoed, but for Tokodin the moment froze in time. Saliva flowed over yellow fangs set in a black bear snout, and bare skin pulsed red beneath deep-set yellow eyes, a terrifying trait men called the blood rage.

He prayed for fire, but the pounding pain in his shoulder fractured his focus, leaving him bereft of the power of the gods. He drove his back into the boulder, pushing, struggling to regain his feet, but snow, ice, and a ruined shoulder felled him.

"Loepus." No one could hear such a pathetic cry.

Screams and intermittent explosions of a prayer's might echoed between gorge walls, but he abandoned hope. Exhaustion and the excruciating pain in his shoulder defeated any chance of powerful prayer. His doom strode to him at its leisure, testing the heft of its cudgel and licking its fangs with a bestial smile.

Loepus leaped to his side, a prayer weaving fire between his hands. Flames seared the creature, patches of fur turning to a cloud of reek.

Tokodin tried to smile, but his hope was brief, as insubstantial as the warmth of a kiss on a winter's day.

A glaive's strike came from the corner of his eye and left his friend of fifteen years standing without a head. Blood splattered Tokodin's face and robes, and he vomited through his pain as Loepus crumpled into a headless heap.

Tokodin fought for breath, retching, spitting, coughing, and by the time he regained control of his body the last echoes of battle had faded. The Colok who broke his shoulder rolled in the snow, snuffing its smoldering fur, and in the distance a pony whinnied. He wished Guntar well. If the bearer got his message to Istinjoln, it earned Tokodin's soul favor with the gods as he strode the Road of Living Stars in search of the heavens.

He slumped against the boulder, staring at the blood-and-filth-soaked snow between his legs. The Colok approached with heavy steps crunching snow, the creature's black claws digging ice and stone for traction. Tokodin refused to lock eyes with his death.

The silence of the Omindi Pass meant defeat. He muttered a prayer under his breath, but no power came, his prayer beseeched a merciful death.

A Colok growled, and hidden in the reverberations of the snarl he imagined the word "weakling," and at this, the last moment of his life, denying the accusation was impossible.

The glaive tapped beneath his chin, and he felt blood trickle, pooling in his jugular notch.

The beast growled, long and guttural . . . trying to speak? He didn't understand until:

"Choerkin."

The word hid in the back of the beast's snarl, easy to pass off as his imagination, but the impression was too strong. Why the Twelve Hells did the beast speak of Clan Choerkin?

The blade slid from his throat, and a great paw grabbed his robes. The Colok lifted and flung him over a shoulder, pain ripping through his torso. He screamed. His heart pounded slow in his chest and he grew faint. Then, darkness.

FOUR

Third Son of the Second Son

*Upon the Creation of the World, the First Dragons cast their seed
in the light of a Sun and a Thousand Suns,
beneath the Moon and a Thousand Moons,
on a World and a Thousand Worlds.*

—*Tomes of the Touched*

Seventeen Days to the Eve of Snows

The body of Ivin Choerkin's mother lay reposed in the burning logs of the great hearth's morning fire, her golden hair and pale skin untouched by flame, flawless in all the ways only a memory achieved perfection. It had been twelve years since Peneluple's soul strode the Road of Living Stars and her body turned to ash on Pyre Rock, and still the images haunted his wakened eyes.

Ivin figured it was a sign of weakness, a flaw that an old pain could still bring sorrow, but some days, her vision didn't force him to fight tears. On rare days like today he could gaze upon her face in the fire, and if not smile, at least recall some pleasant memory. Hints of lilac amidst the musk of her perfume, imported from the Crown Islands of the Luxuns, cracked his lips with a smile this morning, but he knew not to linger long else sorrow would follow.

He shut his lids and took a breath to dissolve the illusions, and trained his gaze elsewhere when again they opened.

The great hall of Herald's Keep stood fifty paces long and thirty wide, capable of entertaining great parties beneath hand-hewn beams of a girth to have served as masts on mighty ships. Seven candelabras hung from the ceiling, great oak wheels carved with fanciful hunting scenes, but dust covered their candles and hoods since the lady of the tower strode the Road of Living Stars. Light here was no longer to accentuate detailed moldings and other millwork, it was for heat; any beauty hid in shadow.

His father sat at the end of an oak table suited to seat thirty, but today there were only three, the old man and two of his boys. Lord Kotin squinted as he perused a vellum scroll, shifting it in his fingers as he read by the dim light of the hall's hearth, but any message from Kaludor these days was worthy of strained eyes.

Ivin asked, "Any helpful word?"

Kotin might as well have been an island away. Ivin glanced past the hearth and its roaring fire to his brother, Rikis, who sat hunched and silent. "You've lost your tongue as well?"

Rikis snorted and smirked, dipped a spoon in his stew without a word. The eldest son wasn't just the spitting image of their father, with dark eyes and unkempt beard, he'd spent his entire life perfecting the same gnarled attitude.

Ivin fidgeted in his seat, gazed at the great hall's ceiling, and drummed his fingers on the table. It was his day to be off this rock of an island, but he was as far from the docks as he could get without climbing the highest tower of Herald's Watch. And if that damned note pertained to him—

Vellum crumpled louder than the crackle of the fire, and Ivin's eyes drifted back to his father.

Kotin said, "Burn this damned thing." The balled scroll sailed through the air, hitting a bumbling scullery boy square in the nose.

Joslin scrambled under a chair for the message like a kitten for a ball of string and bounced to his feet with prize in hand. "Aye, my lord." A boy of ten, whose parents both worked in the kitchens of the main keep, he was used to the Choerkin lord and his tempers.

Ivin grinned. "Don't punish the boy for another man's words. Is there trouble at the Fost?"

Kotin snarled through his beard, his feet rocking the table as he kicked them up for repose. "A man might as well yap with an oracle, if you want to take blind shots at interpreting blather. No word on help from Istinjoln, not sure if the messages aren't reaching the lord priest, or if they're gouging our eyes. Godsdamned lord priest's always got his nuts in a clamp over somethin' we done or said. A score of souls might well walk the stars with him dragging his toes."

They'd gotten word of a cave-in at the Ihomjo mine five days past, trapping at least twenty miners. In times past the priests of Istinjoln were quick to help, but the Ihomjo was a new and rich vein of gold on ground Istinjoln claimed holy. By both tradition and law, the claim was dubious; if nearby ruins ever belonged to the church they were centuries removed from use. A legitimate claim would've given mining rights to the church, or at least, they'd have been due a share of gold, but the Choerkin denied the claim outright and reaped the benefits of taxes. There was no doubt in Ivin's mind why the lord priest ignored their demands, it was one part pride, and one part greed. Lord Priest Ulrikt would dance around every excuse to make a point.

"If you'd listened to me and had the miners pay a tiny stipend to ease the egos in Istinjoln, we might save those men."

Kotin's right eye squinted with a glare that made Ivin swallow. "Lovar heads the Clan Choerkin, not me."

"Your brother, and he listens to you."

"Your uncle, and he makes his mind on clan matters without my word or yours. All the best, on the latter."

"A failing of both brothers, never listening."

Rikis guffawed but choked his humor back as the other men stared. "My pardons, choked on a tater in my stew."

Kotin's eyes returned to his youngest boy with a smug smile. "It's thinking like yours that got us here, boy. It's the Choerkin who command these lands and tolerate the church's holdings, not the other way 'round. I'll take orders from the gods when I'm good and dead, not a flicker before. Every time we loosen the reins the further those holies stray."

"Everyone knows who rules, but whether we rule with an open hand or a balled fist is our choice. The price of peace is generosity, and the price of gold is blood." Ivin knew those last words were a mistake before they finished from his tongue; a religious quote from the *Book of Leds* would set a fire, not put one out. It didn't help one spit that the book specialized in how a mortal's soul earned its way into the hells.

"You'd see your old man to the Hoarder's Hell, would you? The price of letting your enemy regain his feet is steel in the belly. Fairness and blood, what the hells does a boy know of these things?" His face turned red through his beard as he laughed. Kotin snatched the goblet in front of him to find it empty. He shot a glare at Joslin and the youngster scrambled to refill. "Any further wise words for your poor deaf father before you sail?"

Ivin's cheeks burned, and he stood, the feet of his chair squawking on the maple floor. He kept his voice flat, but his words held an edge. "I'll head for Skywatch to consult with the oracle."

"Breaking bones with that whore-witch? I forbid it!"

"I sail for Kaludor to ride with the Estertok Wardens, by your biddings, and you forbid me the oracle of the gods?" Ivin met his father's wide-eyed snarl the best he could, then turned to leave. He reached the door and snagged his heavy cloak, wrapping the bearskin over his shoulders as he wandered into the hall.

Pounding steps echoed in pursuit behind him and Ivin hurried to the tower's exit. He hadn't planned on breaking bones with the old priestess before traveling north, but he sure as hells was going to now.

Winds whipped the door from his grip and slapped icy rain in his face as he stepped from Herald's Keep. He squinted into the tempest as he pulled his hood tight to his face and descended granite steps to the cobbled street where a cart rattled past. It was petty and childish, and he'd feel guilty later, but he left the tower door open and predicted the count: *One, two, three.*

A gust banged the oak door against the tower wall. His father huffed and slammed the door shut, snarling a curse familiar to any of Kotin's three sons. "Godsdamned boy."

Ivin turned, locking eyes with his father's glower. Taunts and curses tempted his tongue, but Kotin thrived on bickering, egging his boys into fights; escalation into a shouting match meant an argument lost. For years, every time Ivin had mentioned visiting the oracles, he'd allowed his father to shame him into not going, disrespecting Ivin's faith.

Ivin kept his tone tame and recited a line he'd practiced a hundred times. "The right of divination may be denied by the gods, not men."

Kotin loomed on the high step with fists struck to his hips. He was a grizzly of a man with ominous eyes. Wrapped in thick furs and fog clouding every angry breath, it was easy to see how a blooded warrior might piss his britches. "To have your head filled with lies? What's the point, boy? The only truth the priests ever spoke to me was that forward is the path to everywhere, but no bones will show the path to you. A truth they withheld until your mother's pyre burned."

Ivin's heart pounded. The child inside wanted to surrender to the imposing gaze, but today he used his most barbed weapon. "I will honor my mother, in whatever heaven she may reside. Hate the priests all you like, but I will honor her memory and her faith today."

The old man's shoulders slumped and his iron jaw softened. Everyone on the island knew the Lady Pineluple was the old man's weakness, but few dared use her against him.

Ivin's victory wasn't sweet, but still, better than walking away as a kicked cur. He turned into the wind with a steady gait. A grunt of disgust and soggy footsteps proved his father followed. "Stubborn about all the wrong things, that's your mother's blood."

Ivin trudged on. No argument ever convinced his father a trip to Skywatch was better than a waste of time. Kotin was by clan-right Lord of Herald's Watch and by self-proclamation Lord of his Own Opinion, and only death would relieve him of either title.

The island of Herald's Watch was Kotin's kingdom, a barren rise of stone in Purdonis Bay transformed into a fortress by forgotten generations and tended by the Clan Choerkin for the past five hundred years. Miles of steep roads crawled from the sea to the towers high above, winding like drunken snakes between gray stone buildings.

They passed through the gate of the inner bailey, entering the holy ward where the path split in twain. He chose the short route, skipping the temptation to torture his father with an extra thousand strides past the Shrine of Nameless Slaves.

The streets grew broader and more traveled as they approached town. Ivin had run on these roads with abandon as a boy, learning every in and out, and meeting more than a few bricks nose to stone as uneven pavers caught his toe and sent him sprawling. As Skywatch came into sight, he recalled one such run: Seven years of age and scared witless by his first fortune. His legs carried him all the way to the tower, chased by his father's echoing laughter. His mother died not long after. He remembered how the priestess had intimated such a thing happening. Ivin took on his mother's faith in the gods, while Kotin blamed them and their priests.

The squat, domed building known as Skywatch stood out from the plain gray granite of other buildings on the island, a polished marble bubble in the midst of gray corners. He stepped to the building's single door, took a breath as if about to fish for pearls, and stepped into perfect night with his father on his heels.

Skywatch greeted them with a cloudless sky full of stars where the ceiling and walls should be, the eternal heavens depicted with precision. The sun never rose here, and turning a circle revealed nothing but standing in the middle of emptiness in an eternal night, except for the faint outlines of the entry. Here, the oracles watched the skies and their passing seasons day and night without cloud nor sun to obscure the view, and gleaned from it glimpses of the future. The Great Forgetting had erased the names of those who erected Skywatch and its enchanted sky, but most folks believed it dated from the Age of God Wars.

Skywatch appeared empty, as it always did.

High Oracle Meris' voice boomed from the heavens, the tone projecting power. "It has been long years since you graced our hall, Kotin. Your arrival is a welcome surprise. And you, Ivin, you seek the oracle of bones?"

Nerves sent Ivin's stomach into a twirl. He swallowed and cleared his throat, and still his words came muted and weak. "Yes, servant of Bontore, and his father, the ever-mighty Sol. I seek the oracle of bones."

Kotin huffed with disgust beside him, but held his tongue.

Footfalls crossed the heavens, each step a ringing chime echoing as they crossed above their heads. Moments later Meris emerged from the dark, walking to them with outstretched arms. The withered old priestess hunched at the shoulders and her feet scraped the floor as she walked, but her face was little different from the woman Ivin remembered from fifteen years ago.

The oracle clasped Ivin's hands, and he dropped to his knees. Meris offered her hands to Kotin and received a cold stare. "The unforgiving man shall never be forgiven."

Kotin snorted. "The unrepentant are unforgivable."

Ivin bit back his annoyance with the duo. The feud between clans and church dated back to the War of Seven Lies. The church had remained aloof from the warring clans in the chaotic and bloody years following the Great Forgetting, but in the fourth year of Remembered Time, as the clans settled their disputes and stitched their wounds, Lord Priest Imrok Girn and his followers struck while the clans were weak. Thousands more died, and the church came close to wresting power from the clans, but instead of hoisting the crown of a king priest, Imrok found himself burned alive outside of Choerkin Fost a year after starting his holy war.

The clans crushed the holies beneath its collective boot and mandated the Church's power severed into seven heads. A subtle struggle ensued, flaring now and again into bitter conflicts over souls and gold (mostly gold), but after Peneluple's passing, Kotin's animosity grew into bloodshot hatred, and Meris was his focus. Ivin wanted no part in the dispute, whatever its cause, and kept his tongue where it belonged, sealed between his teeth.

Meris grinned at Kotin as she knelt before Ivin. "It is good to see you again, Ivin, son of Kotin, of the Clan Choerkin." Meris pulled the scapula of a bear from her pack. The cleaned bone bore a multitude of tiny holes on its surface with several carved symbols for each hole. "How might this humble servant of Bontore serve your needs this day?"

The ice in her pale blue stare and the grinding gravel in her voice always injected a mote of terror into the beat of Ivin's heart. He took a deep breath, reconciled his mind to the possibilities of his future, and relaxed.

"You've heard of the Ihomjo mine collapse?"

The old priestess gave a curt nod. "The stars are not without mortal rumors."

"I will travel north to find aid in Istinjoln. Will we be able to entreat with the priests of Istinjoln for aid? Is there hope for a solution to this disputed territory? Will we find survivors?"

Kotin muttered, "A waste of our time. You dragged me beneath these cursed stars for this?"

Meris ignored the elder Choerkin and stared into Ivin's eyes. "Much of what you ask relies upon the will of man, and not the gods. Your questions are fulsome with noble intent, but any answers are dangerous if trusted, for they are in flux with the whims of emotion, not set in the stone of holy destiny."

Ivin nodded. "Those are my questions."

"So be it. Be still and await the reply of Bontore, the Fatespeaker."

A slender needle of steel appeared in the priestess' hand. She laid it flat in her left palm, then covered it with her right. Her eyes closed, and they twitched as if a bug skittered to and fro beneath her lids. Prayers droned from somewhere deep within the priestess as though some creature lent a second voice. The old woman rubbed her palms together until a soft glow emanated from between her fingers.

Opened hands revealed the piece of steel gone from gray to radiant silvery-white, a shiv of star fallen from the sky. Meris raised the metal above her head and plunged it into a small hole in the bone. A crack resounded, more powerful and sonorous than the voice of the oracle when speaking from the stars.

"Bontore has spoken with us, young Choerkin, look as I read to you his words."

Ivin gazed at the bone. A myriad of cracks stretched from the sliver of metal. He'd never seen so many fractures. He wanted to touch it, to trace the lines passing through his future, but his hand trembled by his side.

"The gods have spoken to you, but I fear they speak little to your concerns." Meris pointed. "Here a crack runs through the Heart of Januel. Our Goddess of Love will pull your soul to another's, young Choerkin, but the split at the end foretells uncertainty. And here the bone speaks of danger near the Heart, so be wary of false love. This danger will bring an end . . . but not to your life, your search? There is blood in the dark, death in the Ihomjo mine, perhaps. And darkness beneath the sun. This crack passes the Sails of Zinmil, suggesting you will travel far by sea." There was silence, then in hushed tones: "This crack by the Sword of Anzelok, the way it circles, it's hard to decipher. It is war, or battle." Meris looked up. "This is all the gods will say."

The uncertainty in her words, the uncomfortable flutter of her eyes, he'd never seen the old woman flustered. "What aren't you telling me?"

"A hundred cracks might mean a hundred things of which I will not speak, full of contradictions. It would take days to decipher." Meris stood, replaced the bone in her pack. "Leave now, young Choerkin. The bone speaks volumes which would serve to confuse and muddle your thoughts."

Ivin knew better than to press further.

Kotin's tone was placid. "Enlightening as you ever were."

"I welcome a return to view your future, Kotin."

Kotin spun on a heel and marched to the door with a laugh, the sound of his voice taking on a power to rival the oracle's. Ivin followed him into the overcast light of day with a snarl on his face.

The pair stood in the rain as the door closed behind them, the smile on Kotin's face wearing Ivin's nerves thin. Ivin said, "I love the rain."

"As do I."

The Watch's horn wailed across the small island, bugling low twice, followed by a high note, alerting everyone to an incoming Choerkin ship.

"Your cousin must be arriving." Kotin took several steps down the steep, winding road to the docks. "We should see whether Eredin brings your new lady friend."

Ivin's head rolled back to stare into the rain, muttering to himself: "The bastard won't ever let me live this down." He'd brought it on himself and any word in his defense would fuel laughter. At least his brothers weren't here, and with luck he'd be on a ship before they heard.

He lurched as a hand thumped him in the back and he turned to find Rikis with a smirk splitting his beard. He didn't let an opportunity to take a jab at his little brother pass. "What's this about a girl? I'm jealous."

Ivin raised his hands toward the sky, beseeching mercy from the gods, and followed his father.

"Easy, brother." Rikis chortled as he trotted to catch up.

"I see now why our father hates oracles." A lie, but at least it changed the subject.

"They're witch-kin and worse, ask any Choerkin aside from yourself. Not like they're much fond of us, either."

When Ivin was seven years old, his mother carried a daughter, and both had died during labor. Twelve years later, Kotin still slept in the same bed, always alone, or as some whispered, slept nestled beside cold ghosts. Everyone knew Kotin blamed Meris, but no one knew why.

Peneluple's final visit to the oracle was a popular guess. "What might a divination say to make father turn his back on mother's faith?" Ivin asked.

"Are you certain you want to know if the secret is so dark he lost faith in not only oracles, but the gods?"

This wasn't a question Ivin had considered before, but it didn't change his mind. "Damn this weather."

"Aye, damn this weather."

The rain turned to a light drizzle, and the gale faded to a breeze. The men glanced at each other.

Ivin chuckled. "We should've tried that years ago."

The brothers strolled the winding street to the docks with their father long disappeared ahead. Ivin had spent most of his life on this water-bound rock. Island, fortress, home, the ground on which the ashes of his mother and sister were scattered, it was where his life began. He'd never been away more than a month in his life, so the prospect of a year or more on Kaludor fell on the wrong side of an emotional eternity.

They rounded the storehouse at the corner of the wharfs and Eredin stood halfway down the gangplank of the Sea Owl. Kotin blocked his path with legs planted and a parchment in his hand as Eredin's arms waved as if trying to explain away bad news. Roplin, the middle brother, kept his distance, not wanting a part of whatever had set the old man off.

Eredin looked more Ivin's brother than either Rikis or Roplin. Ivin and Eredin were the tawny lions in a family of bears, slender and blond. Their resemblance more than anything else had brought the two together as young boys.

"My hand on the Heart of Januel, Ivin. I had no idea what was in the message until I got here," Eredin said as soon as they arrived.

"What are you—?"

Kotin interrupted with a snarl. "Lovar wants the ship to turn sails immediately." His venomous tone whipped back to Eredin. "My brother best know what the hells he's doing. First, he takes my youngest, now he gives me no time for a proper send off?"

Cold drops of fresh rain hit Ivin's face like flakes of flint, each a bit more painful than they should be.

Kotin crumpled the parchment and tossed it into the bay before wrapping Ivin's neck in the crook of his elbow, leading him to the side with Rikis and Roplin trailing. Gulls squawked, cussing the human intrusion as they took flight.

Something was amiss.

Kotin spoke under his breath. "We've word of a wagon load of Broldun priests rolling toward Istinjoln."

A blood feud between Clans Broldun and Choerkin simmered and flared over the past sixty years. Ivin rubbed his chin. "So close to the Eve of Snows, what's the worry?"

"These aren't some holies chanting down a road on ponies or mules. A little bird sings that these holies are from Fermiden Abbey." The Abbey seated one of seven lord priests and stood a candle's ride outside Broldun Fost.

Rikis' bass voice interrupted in a rough whisper. "Traveling for the Eve of Snows isn't nothing new."

Kotin said, "These are covered wagons, escorted, and left Fermiden in the dead of night. High priests for damn sure. By Lovar's word, it's been damned near two decades since Fermiden sent a ranking priest to Istinjoln."

Ivin said, "Lovar's worried about Istinjoln cozying up to Fermiden and the Broldun?"

"I don't know my brother's mind. If you're askin' me, it smells of consolidating power… or a rift in the ranks, here or the Abbey. If there's trouble in either, might go half way to explaining why they haven't sent no one to the mines. When you reach Istinjoln, listen, pay attention, nod polite like, but don't you go trusting a single holy word, any one of them bastards is liable to stick a dagger in your gullet." With those encouraging words Kotin addressed his older boys. "Get your brother's arms. Go."

Ivin exhaled, watched as his father stalked back to Eredin, his growls and snarls continuing the façade. He leaned on a dock post, grumbled as he brushed fresh gull droppings from the sleeve of his cloak.

Diplomacy and politicking weren't Ivin's strengths. His training was a warrior's, but Kotin had taught him that negotiations were similar to any fight: you earn victory by seeing and seizing opportunity. But whatever the hells was happening between Istinjoln and Fermiden, he still needed to secure aid in opening up the Ihomjo mines. The maneuver would be a complicated dance while trying not to stomp on crystal toes.

His brothers brought Ivin's longbow, spear, and arming sword, as well as his helm, gambeson, and mail. Ivin first thought they'd forgotten his shield, but Kotin presented him with his grandfather's targe, a round shield smaller than most clansman carried. Bullhide wrapped its wooden core, and while its center bore a brass boss, black steel rimmed its edge. It wasn't the fanciest targe the family owned, but Ivin would be the first Choerkin to carry it since grandfather died when Ivin was a baby.

Everything came so fast that reality blurred into heads of ale, beefy spices rich on his tongue, and molten honey-butter on fresh bread, without time for sorrow over the past or to worry on the future, exhausting every excuse to delay departure before his kin took turns pounding his back with hugs and muttering their farewells. Until he set foot on the swaying deck of the Sea Owl, and the world stopped with a surge of clarity.

In a frozen moment he took in the concern on his father's wrinkled brow, and his brothers' awkward unease. The Estertok Mountains were plenty dangerous without conspiracies in Istinjoln. The Sea Owl bucked on a wave, and his heart lurched. This might be the last time he'd see any of them.

He smiled and mustered his most bellicose voice. "You look like women about to blubber! Get your asses back to that tower and knit something!"

The brothers laughed and Kotin locked the head of each in an arm, hugging his boys in his own bearish way, as the boat cast off. Oars creaked and splashed as they moved from the rocky island, its steep winding roads, and the great central tower his family called home.

Eredin sighed, drained the last drops of ale from his tankard and tossed it into a pile of canvass sacks. He took Ivin's shoulder and directed him sternward. "For a moment I thought he might drown me in the harbor to make it more real for any holies watching."

Ivin glanced askew at his cousin. "You knew?"

"Names of the Slaves, cousin. Some secrets are best kept."

"Years of study in the holy scriptures and that's what you took away?"

Souls who served as slaves in penance, between hells and heavens, never spoke their names, lest they fall into the Vainglorious Hell.

Eredin shrugged, pulled a bottle of whiskey from his cloak. "The wind's against our sails, so we've a journey ahead." He popped the cork. "I would have brought a woman or three if I'd thought to get away with it."

Ivin mulled his cousin's words as he leaned against the rail and took the bottle. "What am I missing?"

Eredin rolled his eyes. "Details, maybe, details I'm not privy to. But birds are singing all across Kaludor. Something foul brews in the Twelve Hells. The Wolverine's sure to know more."

Pikarn, the Wolverine, had commanded the wardens for longer than Ivin drew breath, and it was his patrol he'd be riding with. It felt as if the story was incomplete.

Ivin cocked an eyebrow. "Names of the Slaves?"

"I've told you all I know. I swear. Sit. Drink." His cousin's sideways grin was infectious. "There's no use to pondering the future without a swallow of fire in the belly to battle the ale."

Ivin took a pull on the bottle, a smooth burn with a hint of oak in his throat. Wind, waves, and whiskey, standing wasn't an option for long.

FIVE

Guests in Darkness

Diamond lies from Golden tongue whispers Air to speak from your lungs.
Tongues. Entwine. Slippery vines with taste of wine,
Slithering deep, throat, heat and moist in your drums,
Erasing the cacophony prattling in your Skull,
the shucked and hollow Hull,
'til you bellow sweet anythings for who to hear?
Do not fear! Your words fall through disappeared ears
from your dead Lips.

— *Tomes of the Touched*

Seventeen Days to the Eve of Snows

Eliles had never been happier for the distance between the Chamber
of Trials and her master's cell. By the time they'd ascended three levels
and trekked the long hall where the masters of fire resided, they'd
walked a quarter candle in silence to cool the man's mood. They
passed through squared tunnels, chisel-and pick-hewn by untold candles of labor, and lanterns hung every ten paces down the halls, telling
time by the color of their flames.

The fires flickered in transition from deep yellow to the light red of
the nineteenth candle when they reached Dareun's cell. Eliles followed

Master Dareun into his chambers and closed the door. Dareun's study was a cramped space with feather-ticked bed, four plain and uncomfortable chairs, and several round oak tables that held thick tomes for instructing postulants. Lanterns for reading outnumbered everything in the room save for shelves of books in an alcove.

Dareun tossed his hood back, revealing a man in his seventieth year. Maybe handsome once, the wrinkles and long ears grown hairy over the years marked those days as past. It didn't matter; he was still her sweet master, her mentor and savior. He'd taken Eliles beneath his wing after her arrival at Istinjoln Monastery and concealed her curse from his peers and defended her from jealous words and prying eyes.

His face pinched to a scrunched nose and pursed lips as he turned his gaze upon her, and his gentle, soulful eyes squinted in a glare.

"What, by the Vainglorious Hell, were you thinking? Can't take a blow from the Maimer? I understand, by the gods, I do—but twelve years! Twelve years we've worked on making your trials appear the same as other postulants."

"I waited until the last moment—"

"Showmanship! Not a voice dared claim otherwise! Can you? Oh! It was like you threw twelve years of trials in everyone's face: 'See? See me, I've toyed with you all along.'" Dareun poured himself a mug of mead and slurped.

Her master might be right, a childish desire to show off could lurk in her soul. She could've had them flicker as she did for Mavu. And in front of Ulrikt, no less. "I didn't mean to."

"Liermu herself would struggle to achieve such subtle plays of fire!" His fingers drummed the arm of his chair. "And Mavu?"

She considered lying, but her master was aware of her every tell. "She practiced the ritual a hundred times and succeeded most."

"Girl be damned, that isn't the point! A single hiccup in timing . . . by the Mercies, girl."

Forgetting wasn't possible. If her trick revealed her, she died. Sometimes she managed to neglect this complication, but she never forgot. "I'm sorry."

"If the girl's prayers had stopped a moment before your fires lit? An inquisition would discover your truth, and neither I nor that poor unsuspecting girl would have escaped whatever doom Lord Priest Ulrikt prescribed."

"I said I'm sorry."

"Sorry is a stale and worn word between you and me; this was reckless." Dareun massaged his wrinkled brow until his berating stare turned to an exasperated chuckle. "Oh, my girl. You're my blessing and my curse. My headache. We're so close." He drained his mug and refilled.

Her spirit wilted further. In just over a fortnight she pronounced the vows of priesthood, their goal for the past twelve years, but what came after was a mystery.

"Something else troubles you, what is it?"

Their years together made feelings difficult to hide, but she wasn't in the mood for hiding today. "I've finished my training. So what do I do, where do I go?"

"I'm certain you'll do whatever it is you wish to do, as always." She pinned his eyes with her glare, in no mood for humor at her expense. He redirected with a smirk. "If you were a normal student of such exceptional ability, I should recommend staying at Istinjoln to educate the next generation. Replace me, maybe." He waved for her to sit. "Who am I fooling, you'd be a high priestess in a decade, heading a major temple or shrine. Maybe you still could if you avoided antics like this evening. If not for your mouth, you might be lord priestess one day."

She appreciated the old man's attempt to humor her fears. "I'd be better off in the brewhouse. I'm defiled, an abomination before the gods. I need a clear path, a clean cut from Istinjoln."

"You aren't thinking of faking your death again?"

At twelve, after taking her only lash from the Maimer, she'd decided to escape, but Dareun put an end to the ill-conceived plan that would've ended with her buried alive and not faking at all. She blushed and smiled. "No."

His lips pinched with a smirk. "Good. The currents in the River of Time pull us in one direction or another; we swim with them or against them. There are many who believe Sol chose you for a reason. That breeds not only jealousy, but the aim to use you for mortal purposes in the name of the gods. We've kept your divinations vague, thus far."

"Vague will be useless when the high priest asks my intentions." Eliles slumped in her seat, glancing to a book sitting on the table beside her.

Its cover depicted the silver spear of Bontore, the son of Sol, and the God of Knowledge and patron of oracles. When young Dareun had trained in the ways of breaking bones and reading their cracks to guess the future, and this book detailed a part of those teachings in its hundreds of pages.

When she'd arrived at Istinjoln as an outcast child, the potential for the Oracle of Bones to reveal her curse had terrified her. Dareun had assured he would hide her, and as a game they'd opened the book to a random page, discussing the meanings of symbols and signs, making light until she smiled and forgot her fears. They'd continued this tradition until she outgrew the need for reassurance. Tonight, the child within needed to grasp for that comfort.

She flipped the book open and rose to look at the pages. An elegant drawing of a symmetrical maze, representing the Road of Living Stars and the Twelve Hells, greeted her. The souls of the dead needed to step from star to star without falling into one of the Twelve Hells to reach the heavens. Whether they had lived in piety or sin determined the difficulty of the crossing.

Finding levity in this dismal book wasn't easy, but she tried. "Well, at least there isn't a specific hell for those defiled by the Vanquished Gods." The Liar, Malignant, Heathen, Heretic, or the False Prophet's hell, any of them might house her soul well enough.

Dareun stood with a smile and took a deep drink of his mead before closing and reopening the book. A star sat on the page, eight rays reaching from its center to represent the pursuit of righteous knowledge. It was another of Bontore's symbols and called the Wanderer's Star. Dareun chuckled and was about to say something when he stopped, squinting at her. "The Traveling Wisdom."

Eliles blinked, it wasn't amusing, and she didn't recognize the phrase. "Master?"

His finger tapped the star. "It frustrates the oracles to find no higher calling in your bones when they've deemed you born for some great purpose. We need to provide them with a road to your divine destiny."

"Destiny? A destiny written by the Vanquished Gods will send me to the hells, or worse."

"You will seek the Traveling Wisdom, as did High Priest Xivcok."

The name Xivcok was familiar, a noted high priest who lived in the second century of Remembered Time, a missionary to the common folk, if she recalled. "The Traveling Wisdom?"

"You will travel the whole of Kaludor, beyond if you wish. Enshrine the words of Sol in the hearts of the people, bring them deeper into the folds of the Pantheon."

Skepticism oozed through her tone. "A missionary? I'll be a priest-ess in name, not deed."

Dareun waved her words from the air. "Missionary, pah! The Traveling Wisdom is so much more. Xivcok didn't preach to convert the doubters; he sought to enhance his holy knowledge with the common wisdoms of . . . . But that's of little consequence. Once you step beyond Istinjoln's gates with the lord priest's blessing, never look back. Go, find the current which leads to the waters you are destined to swim. Your robes will open every gate on the island and there isn't a one you'll need to open unless you wish. Or you could throw those robes to the Ten Winds and live as common as you desire."

"Lord Priest Ulrikt won't question this?" Ulrikt ruled Istinjoln with an iron fist and a thousand watching eyes; she wouldn't pass through the gates without running for her life without his say so.

"Throw in some gibberish about weakening the clans and strengthening the pantheon in the hearts of the people and a few might collapse prostrate in a devout froth." He laughed. "Add my manipulating the bones a touch or two, and we'll see you safely out of these walls. I promise."

A piece of her doubted he'd bring her this freedom, but she needed this faith. A smile spread across her face, for the first time in months she had hope. But, hope carried a price.

"I couldn't have had a better father than you. I will miss you."

"And I you, my girl . . . most times. I won't miss needing to explain away your miraculous gifts as part of my grueling candles of training." He chuckled into his emptying cup of mead. "Away with you. An old man needs his sleep."

A tear welled in her eye as she kissed his forehead. "Sol bless you, my master."

He waved her away with a smile.

She strode into the hall and stood in silence beside a red lantern, at a loss for what she should do. The prospect of parting from

Master Dareun saddened her, but leaving Istinjoln gave her thrilled goosebumps.

The celebration of the autumnal equinox on the twenty-fifth of Yistole, known as the Eve of Snows, would mark her entrance into the priesthood. In eleven days the Oracle of Bones would reveal her future, and another five days before she declared her freedom on the Eve of Snows. The dank tunnels, the half-concealed sneers and contempt, would be behind her. She'd find a new life, find her happiness. She wanted to celebrate, steal a bottle of wine, but such exuberance was premature.

She swept the giddy thoughts from her mind, deciding on a breath of fresh air. Celebration enough to see the stars. Hurried strides carried her to an exit chamber, one of several sitting beneath the buildings of upper Istinjoln, but this one sat nearest to the stables. A monk stood beside the ladder with a grin on his face.

Jinbin had spent ten years studying the ways of Light before failing the priesthood and taking the monk's habit. Only a year older than Eliles, they were passing acquaintances then, but now that he guarded her favorite exit into the world above, they'd become friends. Or at least she liked to think so.

"Greetings, One Lash."

His smirk was unbearable; he knew how much she hated the nickname many muttered when they thought she couldn't hear. But it was the fact he stood underground rather than in the building above which irritated her most.

"Bad news?"

"The Guard is running drills from red through deep red tonight. No one's allowed outside."

Eliles groaned. "They had drills two weeks ago."

"Twelve days."

She rolled her eyes, then glared at the light-red flames burning in the room; she had time. "I'll run straight to the wall and I'll be back whip-quick."

He folded his arms and stared. "If you're out there and get hurt, I'll be scrubbing every garderobe and pisspot in Istinjoln for a week. A month."

It was a famous punishment, and one that forced her to up the ante. "Dareun's in charge of final inventory for the Eve of Snows." She grinned and walked her fingers up an imaginary ladder.

"A travel cask of ale?"

A ten-marked keg wouldn't be easy. "I can manage at least a half."

His feet shifted and shuffled before sighing. "You've a half candle before full red, after, the price is a full cask. Two if I have to dump a single pisspot."

She followed him up the ladder into a stone building lit by a single lantern and small enough that three people lacked elbow room. Jinbin stepped to a monk guarding the door leading outside. "She's a message for the guards at the gate."

Eliles didn't know the other monk's name, but he was more senior than she'd expect to be guarding doors. He cast her a wrinkled squint and a solemn nod as he opened the door. She bustled through as if in a hurry.

Recollections of shame and guilt faded with a deep breath of fresh air as she strode into streets lit by stars and scattered lanterns. A chill north wind filled the hood of her robe as she turned west down a road folks called Cricket's Way, but the shiver running down her spine was welcome beneath heavy wool robes. Her cowl fell to her shoulders, and she reveled in the brisk wind.

A handful of guards walked rounds and stood their posts in Istinjoln's streets as they always did, their postures relaxed. It was more quiet and ordinary than she'd expected with rehearsals for war in the offing.

Her steps slowed to a casual gait as she weaved her way west through winding streets, and she gazed at the sky instead of her feet. The evening was clear but for wisps of clouds blowing toward a horizon in sunset. For Eliles the beauty of the world lay outside Istinjoln's walls, away from the great tower and its keep, and the squat maze of buildings appearing to kneel before it in prayer and servitude. Everything these walls contained was an ugliness making the outer world so much more beautiful.

She reached the western courtyard with the main gatehouse straight in front of her, its gates closed, but swerved toward the stables. A set of stairs scaled the wall on either end of the stables, which held stalls for over two hundred horses, if it housed less than a quarter of that these days. She loved the stables, the smell of grass hay stored in the loft and the neighing of the mountain ponies, so she always climbed to the wall's allure from here.

She topped the stairs of the northern wall and a guard glanced at her as he leaned against a battlement, but paid her no more mind than to give her a nod of recognition. She passed him and several more, wondering how they were so relaxed with drills less than half a candle away. They mustn't be taking part, holding their positions on the wall.

She leaned against a parapet and stared north to the mountains, their snow-white peaks and evergreen forests. Snow blotted the green of the trees, a gift from an unseasonable storm in a year colder than any she remembered, but here in the foothills the deep snows that bent branches with their weight a morning ago faded with warmer days.

A strong wind curled through the buildings of Istinjoln and swept up the wall to bring shivers. She willed warmth into her flesh, and a pleasant heat swelled in her heart, flowing through her veins until the world was pleasant as a spring day.

With a wind in her face that no longer felt cold, she closed her eyes and focused on her breath, losing track of self and time until family slipped uninvited into her consciousness. Once free, she should visit them, make sure they were well. She opened her eyes, angry for allowing a pleasant moment to sputter. Her mother abandoned her in the woods, to hide her from father and the inquisition, but she couldn't forgive her.

The memory of her mother's swollen eyes wrenched her into melancholy. She slouched against the parapet, watching as darkness conquered the sky and revealed stars. The constellation known as the Heart of Januel hung to the left of a valley leading into the mountains, a set of stars love-struck couples prayed to each year, hoping the goddess heeded their prayers.

The eight stars formed an inverted arch in the sky, its shape representing both her aspects: love and war. A bowl representing her endless capacity for compassion as well as bringing two distant souls together, and a convex wall to safeguard her people from enemies. The Heart of Januel, bringing two souls together and protecting them through all of life's battles for eternity.

She gazed at the Heart and prayed now and again, prayed she would find love in this life, but so far Januel showed no signs of having listened. Tonight she did not pray. All she needed was to gaze at the heart above the mountains and marvel at its brightest star.

"Gates of Istinjoln, open!"

The cry broke the night's silence, followed by the grinding iron gears of the rising portcullis. Eliles gazed at the gatehouse along with every guard on the wall. A ponderous, covered wagon with lanterns hanging from its corners rolled into Istinjoln with an escort of riders. Such wagons might bear cargo or passengers, but if it carried supplies it would've stopped for the night in the village of Petrin a candle's walk south, or found the gates closed until dawn.

The realization she'd lost track of time lurched her heart into a frenzy. By now the fires burned red, but guardsmen didn't swarm the streets with shouts and commands. There was only this wagon.

She leaned against the parapet with her head cocked. The drills were a lie, and she didn't know why that surprised her, falsehoods filled these caverns and walls. No, they'd closed upper Istinjoln for an important arrival.

Her heart warned her, but her curious mind and feet already had her on the move. She descended the nearest stair and did her best to pass without notice through the scattered outbuildings, getting closer to the wagon and its escort. She stopped outside earshot in deep shadows, close as she could get and still feel safe.

The lead rider greeted a priest of Istinjoln. Darkness hid their faces and ranks, and their conversation was too quiet to catch a single word. Creeping closer to eavesdrop on her betters wouldn't sit well with Dareun after his recent reprimand, and while she toyed with pushing her senses to hear the conversation, that'd risk more than mere sneaking. If she pushed her hearing too close while eavesdropping, people sensed her; it was safer to use in crowds.

The driver of the wagon jumped from his perch and went to hands and knees. Moments later a rotund shadow draped in black robes stepped from the wagon and onto the driver's back before tromping the ground. She wasn't close enough to see the color of his cowl's lining, nor any markings on his sash, but as far as she'd seen only high priests demanded such respect, but this priest wasn't of Istinjoln.

Despite several strong appetites among the high priests of Istinjoln, none bore the weight of this man. It would take three sashes from average men to tie his waist. In her years here she'd witnessed high priests arriving from other regions a handful of times, often around the Eve of Snows, and always with fanfare and greeting parties. To arrive after dark and without heralds was downright scandalous.

The driver stood, brushed his knees, and climbed to the wagon's seat while thirteen figures robed in plain gray slipped from the wagon and fell in line behind the high priest, their shadows dancing in lantern light. Unloading last came a man without robes, dressed in a black tunic and leggings, and as his sleeves fell back while lowering himself from the wagon, silver bracelets caught lantern light.

An inquisitor.

Peculiar didn't begin to describe the situation. A foreign priest arriving with an inquisitor after dark was one thing, she could brush it away as a matter of timing, an accident, but the false drill to seal lower Istinjoln from this courtyard spoke of secrets. Who was this man?

Her thoughts snapped in twain: The priest's company headed in her direction. She could've stepped from the shadows with her hood pulled and passed the party with her eyes to the ground and they might never say a word to her, but a wiser voice in the back of her head stopped her. It was a bad idea, she guessed that witnesses to this priest's arrival were hand-selected. She skulked deeper into shadows and crouched.

The group passed so close she recognized the priest of Istinjoln as Woxlin. An esteemed guest to warrant a greeting from a high priest.

Woxlin's voice was low, but the winds helped carry his words. "I'm certain Lord Priest Ulrikt will be pleased to hear of your arrival. At your will, I'll alert him immediately."

The ranking guest answered in a voice more used to preaching in wide halls than clandestine sneaking about, and with a heavy Broldun accent. "Yes, mmm. Good, very good. I would like to meet with him as soon as is convenient, mmm." The group passed into a small building where a monk began his bow, hesitated, then prostrated himself on the ground, kissing the dirt instead of the deep bow a high priest required.

Eliles' eyes flew wide as she sucked her breath. A meeting with Lord Priest Ulrikt, and a monk prostrate. Lord priests drove monks prostrate. Lord Priest Dunkol of Fermiden Abbey. Dunkol and Ulrikt were famous for butting heads over politics and theology, but here the man stood in the dead of night. If discovered, the lord priest of the Broldun clan sneaking into Istinjoln would enrage the Clan Choerkin. If the Choerkin hated anything more than a priest, it was a Broldun priest, and that's why he'd arrived in secrecy.

If anyone found out she'd witnessed his arrival, her scar would have companions.

She closed her eyes and leaned against the wall, waiting for time to pass. Whatever she'd stumbled upon, it was monastery intrigue she'd be better off forgetting.

The lord priest and his procession had long since entered the tunnels of Istinjoln, but she didn't budge. She crouched in the shadows until the wagon creaked and groaned to the stables and there wasn't a soul in sight, except guards of Istinjoln who paid Eliles no mind. She passed between buildings, one shadow to another, until she grew certain of her safety and stepped into the open.

For a flicker she forgot how close she came to a frightful punishment and allowed herself a breath. A hand grabbed her throat, crushed her into a wall, and stole that air.

The voice was raspy and quiet, with a Broldun accent. "Your name?"

Images of fire burst into her mind as her nose and cheek raked across rough stone. She came within a moment of summoning flames to discover what one of her little friends could do to a man before yielding to greater wisdom. "Eliles, postulant of Istinjoln."

"Seekin' a breath of fresh air, I s'pose."

She nodded, and he ground her face into the stone. "Yes, air."

"Now I know your name, be sure I do not hear it again, nor see your face where it should not be." She couldn't see his face, but the jingle of his silver bracelets left no doubt who held her.

"Yes."

The inquisitor released her and disappeared into the dark, leaving Eliles to slip to the ground. Feral magic roared within her, begging for vengeance. She quenched these raw desires with the will Dareun had taught her and rose to her feet. She calmed her breath and made her way into the subterranean halls, the lanterns having turned to a blood-red flame.

She sulked back to her granite cell with her cowl pulled snug over her face. Sleep didn't come until she lay beside her little fiery friend, who warmed her scratched cheek and kept her company as it had since she was a child. Twice the size of a candle's flame it floated several fingers from her nose. Silent, flickering, warm, it bore no judgment nor ill will. The flame was her peace. As her eyelids gave way to the weight of sleep, she wondered if this was the same flame as always arrived to her call. Her oldest and most faithful friend, this tiny flame. When a child she'd believed the being protected her from harm.

As an adult, she prayed the child was right.

Six

Hallowed Bones

Some dead remember, some dead forget,
Some dead are forgotten, some Dead are known only after Dying.
Death is a mystery with marvelous many endings to the Living.
The Enduring. The unending Ending.
But what can be learned from knowledge only knowable when Gone?

—*Tomes of the Touched*

Fourteen Days to the Eve of Snows

A ball of brilliant white Light hovered above Dareun's head as his fatigue-blurred eyes gazed at the hole in his inventory list: Five missing kegs of Thonian whiskey. If he'd licked the toes of the right people and spoken the right words, he might've achieved the high priesthood decades ago, and now be curled in his blankets dreaming of quaffing rare, imported liquors instead of searching for them.

He stretched and glanced down a warehouse row, a hundred paces of crates and barrels stacked from the floor to well above his head, full of beer and whiskey and wine . . . thank the gods for the girl who found the final cask of wine—if anything was pricier than Thonian whiskey, it was the wine. He glanced to four young monks who too would rather be asleep and felt bad for making them move half the stores in his fruitless search.

He rolled his list and rubbed his temples as he yawned. "You boys head to your dormitory, but meet me in the upper warehouses after morning devotionals."

The monks and their strong backs bowed and bustled from the chambers, leaving him to stare at the mass of supplies. He'd taken final inventory of this warehouse for a decade now, and he'd lost nothing more than a few bushels of wheat, but this year's supplies doubled the usual count, so there was plenty to hide between and behind. Thonian whiskey, an expensive favorite of Lord Priest Ulrikt, wasn't a thing a man wanted to lose.

It was late, and finding the whiskey would have to wait, there were more pressing matters: The bones of divination were sorted and shelved after months of preparation, and there shouldn't be any attendants to note a late-night visit. He strode between the walls of crates and oak casks, the ball of Light following him until he stepped into torch-lit halls, where he released the energy of his prayer. He turned and made his way to a stair that led to another stair and yet another. His destination was deep in the ground, far away from this storehouse, with a single winding route with a multitude of wrong turns for the uninitiated.

Everyone in Istinjoln knew of the place, but only those with a reason learned the way. Many called it the Chamber of Bones, or the Cave of Mysteries. In Dareun's opinion, albeit a well-guarded one, the Pit of Deception rang truer.

After winding his way through a rising and falling maze with more than a score of potential wrong turns, he paused beside a non-descript passage to regain his breath and listened to make sure no one approached to witness his entrance. He slipped into the cramped, rough-hewn hall which led him to a steep descent.

The twisting and uneven stairs, worn rounded by centuries of trickling water from these caves, as well as the thousands of adherents who trod them, collected treacherous mold-slimes slick enough to send a man tumbling. Old and brittle, an injurious fall might kill or leave him unconscious, crippled, or dead in a place he shouldn't be. In the strictest terms, he wasn't forbidden to make this journey, but his presence would raise questions he wouldn't be able to answer well enough, and he wanted nothing to jeopardize Eliles' future, let alone reveal his role in hiding her.

He reached the bottom of the stair with tentative and thankful steps and slipped beyond the feint lights of the scarce lanterns in this region. He leaned against the wall, relaxing for a moment in abject dark, a blackness to which eyes would never adjust without aid from the gods. He mumbled a prayer to enhance his vision and the empty abyss shifted into grays, with shelves and tables and bones igniting into glowing whites, their edges sharpening into crisp lines.

The Pit was a storehouse of bones bleached by the sun, washed in the sands of the surf, then polished by the hands of priests, and arranged on rows and rows of shelves. Divination bones ranged from cattle to dolphins, each with its own specific use and reasoning, many beyond his knowledge. Dareun had studied the ways of divination in his youth, enough to realize it wasn't his calling.

This marked his twelfth journey to the pit since Eliles had infiltrated his life, once for every year he'd known her. The girl had appeared at the gates, five years old. She was an orphan with eyes so similar to his dear sister's he took her in rather than turning her away, even when he discovered her feral magic. She wasn't an orphan, and her eyes didn't bear a resemblance to his dead sister's, those were dweomers, auras of feral magic manipulating his vision, connecting Eliles to his own memories to build a sympathetic attachment.

Whether he believed in the Vanquished Gods or their curse didn't matter; the Church believed, and they didn't tolerate those defiled by the heresy of feral magic. If the Oracle of Bones had revealed her secret she would've been "cleansed" of feral magic's taint by an inquisitor, which Dareun supposed was a euphemism for tortured until dead. What became of the children was a mystery, rumors spoke of a deep oubliette layered with bones, but whatever the truth he couldn't allow it to happen to his girl.

Most who sought an oracle prayed anticipating an honest fortune. Dareun was either fortunate or unfortunate to know the truth. At age eight he'd found himself assigned to polishing bones, a slow and tedious chore, but from this hated task he'd learned a greater truth than most ever received from their divinations:

The future was a lie.

They called it Smoothing the Carve, and the priests had shrugged at his youthful concerns over the practice. Then threatened to clean the skin from his bones with a cat-o'-nine-tails if he spoke of it. Dareun had always been bright, so his mouth smiled and praised the wonders of the oracle. As his reward they allowed him to train in carving the bones and how to alter them to the designs of the ruling priesthood. He kept his promise of silence, so when his strengths proved to be in another direction, his elders had allowed him to pursue instruction in the ways of Fire. A rare honor to change paths.

After decades without an honest use for the bones, a quirky knot in the strands of fate had given him a dishonest one: Eliles. He couldn't allow a truthful prophecy, one which could reveal her secret, but this time the smooth would be specific and directive, not obfuscation.

The familiar and disturbing scents of glues and oils struck his senses as he entered the Hall of Bones. A putrid mix of musk and spice, kerosene, and something caustic assaulted his nostrils and left a foul metallic twang on his tongue. These were the tastes and smells of lies. His face wrinkled as he tugged his nose and snuffled, getting reacquainted with the odor.

The shelf which held the bones destined to provide readings for the eldest postulants rested in a distant corner of the Pit. Dareun found Eliles' bone after a few wicks and passed his hand over the surface with a silent prayer.

At first he detected nothing unusual, with glues used to strengthen much of the bone's surface. This was the first and crudest method to altering a bone's prophecy, but hidden beneath the surface of the bone and its carvings lay the greater lie. Prayers created hairline fissures guaranteeing the locations and lengths of the cracks to achieve the desired divination. One passed through Bontore's Wisdom, an attempt to keep her in Istinjoln, and others teased the possibility of love and glory in the name of Sol.

Dareun prayed, his eyes slipping closed. He placed his thumb over the Feral Tooth and hardened the bone all around as he'd done every year. Such strengthening was impossible to detect, far as he knew, but what came next worried him. In the past he'd kept everything simple, increasing cracks he approved of, reducing those he didn't like, but tonight he took the unprecedented step of adding his own fissure.

He opened his eyes and stared at the tiny symbol of the Wanderer's Star and its eight waves radiating from its center. He prayed, his finger tracing a line straight through its center, felt the tiny tremble of the bone. He took a deep breath and inspected his work: The line was strong, but still weaker than Wisdom.

He sighed, fretting over this detail, and instead of working his own line a second time, he healed Wisdom instead, figuring the alteration would be harder to detect. There was no way to know if it was perfect, but it would have to suffice; anything more would complicate matters.

A single important crack would free her from the vows of Istinjoln, nothing else mattered. His father had taught him as a small boy that simplicity is best when practicing deception. A hard lesson learned at the end of a belt after a complex string of lies. He replaced the bone to its seat, pleased with himself, but he froze on his first step to leave.

In all the candles he'd spent in the Pit after midnight, he'd never seen another soul. Tonight, he had company. The soft slap of shoes on stone wouldn't have been audible if there was another sound, but in the silence, they were as loud as a lash of leather on flesh.

The footfalls came his way, too close. His heart pounded in his chest so hard he feared it might betray him. What would become of him? There was no precedent he'd heard of for his meddling. Thrown to the thorns seemed a reasonable bet. A brutal and popular punishment under Lord Priest Ulrikt, being cast from the monastery walls and into the briar. Being sundered from the gods wasn't outside possibility, either, a horrific ritual which would leave his soul wandering the mortal realm until fading into oblivion.

The shoes of the priest passed without pause as they headed straight for a section of bones considered sacrilege to smooth. These were honest bones, those reserved for the high and lord priests.

Dareun braved a peek around the corner, struggling to keep his breath silent with a pounding heart. In the distance, a hooded figure passed his hand over what he suspected was a bear clavicle. Dareun's breath stopped and his mouth dried. The prophecies of lord priests used bones of bears in Choerkin territory.

Any attempt to smooth the purity of this bone should cause it to explode, killing the sinner. Tezlonu would claim their soul from the Road of Living Stars and condemn the violator to an eternity in the Slave Forges. Courage, audacity, or foolishness, what would drive a priest to such madness?

The sanctity of the lord priest's divination could be a lie, smoothing could be commonplace. Body and soul, he wanted to believe this, but it wasn't true.

He drifted into a dark corner, prayed for shadow and silence, and didn't move until long after the priest's flapping soles passed from the Pit. If he told anyone of this sin, he'd incriminate himself. He sat in pitch-black terror, taking deep breaths. There was one exit, and the sacrilegious priest could be waiting. He resolved to sit for a while and yawned as he counted to give the priest time to be plenty ahead of him.

One thousand.

Stiff, weary muscles brought him to his feet with an agonized groan. The journey from the Pit to his chambers felt longer than ever before, and the security of his bed far greater. He did his best to forget the priest and the holy bone's desecration. A meditative prayer cleared his thoughts and eased his conscience as he fell into slumber, but no prayer protected him from dark dreams promising blood and eternity in the Slave Forges.

SEVEN

Dead Man's Message

There is a Light darker than the Dark, a living not alive,
Just as Fear is not alive but forces us to Live.

—*Tomes of the Touched*

Thirteen Days to the Eve of Snows

Bells of the morning vigil passed her door, awakening Eliles before dawn, and she went to the First Hall for morning prayers. Hundreds congregated in this massive cavern every morning, and with its acoustics, they heard the speaker's intonations from anywhere in the chamber. A hundred lanterns and a score of braziers standing between rows of kneeling faithful provided the light.

Chanted prayers droned, enveloping the body's senses beyond the ears. Eliles had never felt the powers of the gods when praying, but from bass to soprano these gathered voices brought drifting energies to wash over her skin, the unison vibrato easing the warmth of the gods into muscles and bones to relax the body and soul. It was a peace difficult to deny, to not fall in line with.

She sang with distraction these past three mornings, fighting the chant's tranquility, her eyes searching every hood for a face, but she'd yet to spot a stranger in the congregation. The lord priest's entourage could hide in their cowls, no doubt, but every face she spied was familiar.

The droning prayer echoed to an end and High Priest Woxlin stood, taking center on the dais, a spear plated with red-gold in his hand. "As you walk your devotions this morning, ruminate upon the pilgrimage of Meridi of Modon, who lost her faith and four children, before rediscovering the truth in Sol's Fire."

The congregation spoke, "Sol's fire and devotions."

Woxlin stepped from the dais and disappeared behind a tapestry with a string of priests in his wake. With the morning's sermon ended most of the adherents didn't kneel long, and the hundreds turned into a couple dozen within a handful of wicks.

Eliles remained kneeling, taking any glance into hoods she got, but didn't see a stranger's face. She wrinkled her nose and sighed, curiosity about the Broldun lord priest ate at her, but being too nosy might reacquaint her with the inquisitor, a price unworthy of any reward. Still, the kitchens might be a good place to listen for rumors, and an inquisitor wouldn't show his face in such a lowborn place.

The swish of robes across stone came from behind, and someone kneeled so close they brushed her shoulder with their arm. "Ruminating well?"

She recognized the sardonic voice and stifled a groan. Rovol was a priest in his third year, still in his brown robes, who served as an archivist in the book vaults. He was also a notorious cad renowned for trying to talk the robes off every attractive postulant in Istinjoln. "I was ruminating on Meridi of Modon's rebellion and how well that worked out for her, crushed beneath a portcullis."

He dropped his cowl and flashed her the smile that reputedly worked on a lot of girls. He was handsome, she supposed, with a broad-round face and dark eyes, but how any girl saw past the two hairy caterpillars nestled above his eyes Eliles couldn't fathom. Even then, his cocksure attitude made her want to vomit.

"I've a couple candles before I need to be in the library, and you've not been assigned any duties since passing your trial—"

"I need to walk my devotionals." She stood and turned her back on him, but he was slow to take hints and followed.

"I'm devoted to you, does that count?"

She never quite decided whether he was attracted to her face, or if he was in it for the fame of being the man who blooded the sheets of One Lash. "Go away, Rovol. And if you won't do that, at least shut your mouth."

She kept walking, but despite his obeying her second command, he stayed on her heels. She led him on a winding trail through lower Istinjoln to the Shrine of Burdenis, God of Winter and brother of Sol, and was disappointed to find they were alone.

The alcove stood ten paces wide and twenty deep, and in the back stood a boulder of white marble carved into the likeness of a mountain with a swooping eagle soaring over its peak, and at its base was a carved bowl filled with water. Eliles dipped two fingers in the water and pressed them to her mouth for a kiss before touching her forehead.

Rovol moaned at her kiss and she wanted to punch him, but she kneeled to pray. "Mighty Burdenis, may your winds be calm this year, and your snows light." With their first snow already fallen in a freakish autumn storm, many priests were promising a bitter winter from this god. "But if cold it must be, may you freeze Rovol's manhood off so he might never pee standing again." She kissed her fingers and pressed them to her forehead as she stood and started to walk away.

But a hand snagged her shoulder, pulled her into his chest. His smile was angry, and his brows bunched together. He was about to say something but feet came running, and a man's voice echoed down the hall. "A dead bearer and wardens. Up top."

"Guntar." Eliles ripped her arm from Rovol's grip as three postulants trotted by and she fell in behind them, relieved to be away from the librarian, but worried who might've been killed. Guntar was one of her few friends in this horrid place and a bearer, and he'd ridden out a fortnight ago.

She followed the others for a quarter candle before peeling off and taking a different route. She climbed into an empty building, the monk who should be guarding the door missing.

A chilly morning greeted her as the sun edged over the eastern horizon, casting her shadow long in front of her as she jogged through the streets. By the time she arrived in the courtyard, a hundred or more adherents stood on its edges, mingling and staring.

She craned her neck, spotting three horses with two riders, Estertok Wardens, judging by their heavy bear-skin cloaks and armament. She shuffled and nudged through the milling crowd and covered her gasp.

A mountain pony pawed the cobbles with a dead priest draped over its saddle and leather straps dangling to the ground. She'd hoped the others had been mistaken, but the dead man was a bearer, and her hands shook.

The bearer's face remained hidden, and fear nibbled at her patience. Eliles spotted a familiar group of priests and postulants who mingled a polite distance from the riders, and she slipped among them. "What word?"

Sufelu turned to her with swollen eyes. "Guntar is dead."

Eliles slumped, her air escaping her lungs and not wanting to breathe again. She had known Guntar for as long as she'd studied at

Istinjoln; he'd been a postulant under Dareun before she'd arrived and had gained the priesthood only a few years ago. "How? When?"

"I… I heard Colok, already four days past." Sufelu appeared ready to say more, but she fell silent, as Woxlin entered the courtyard. The high priest crossed open ground with hasty strides to stand before the wardens. Their mouths moved with animated words and a nod passed between the men before Woxlin stepped beside the pony and yanked on the scroll tube strapped to Guntar, shaking the body to and fro. The high priest checked the message's seal, nodded to the wardens, and headed back to the tower.

Eliles didn't hear a word, but she was aghast. This was the welcome for a murdered priest of Istinjoln upon his return? She expected Woxlin to demand answers, to call for monks to take the body away, something. Instead, Guntar remained tied to a horse's back while a hundred or more people stared or milled about.

What in the name of Sol?

Eliles took advantage of the uncomfortable silence and slipped from the group, making her way into the tunnels beneath Istinjoln. She wound her way to a secluded alcove dedicated to Etinbin, Patron Goddess of the Dead, depicted here as an ivory skeleton with beckoning arms extended, and a black skull with eyes filled with crystals. She paced between two bowls, the fire of life and the water of eternity, light to see and reflection to learn. The pain she felt at the loss of a longtime friend withered beneath the anger growing within her.

How important must a message be to warrant such a dismissal of his remains? And four days dead, it was wrong for the wardens to hold the body in such a manner, without prayers to guide his soul along the Road of Living Stars.

Four days. The seventh of Yistole.

Lord Priest Dunkol arrived the night Guntar died.

The notion of a connection felt faint at first, but grew by the flicker. Guntar was a respected bearer, he didn't carry love notes or trivial disagreements over canon. The lord priest of Fermiden arriving at Istinjoln was important, but more important still, whatever brought him here to meet with Ulrikt. The murderer could come from within the Church, if the two sought to settle a canonical controversy. Would the Choerkin have killed him only to return his body? Many in Istinjoln would accuse the clan of any heresy or sin without a second thought. If it was political, the Broldun themselves were suspect.

They're connected. Her conclusion eased the rhythm of her thoughts, but didn't soothe her curiosity.

She kneeled before the skeletal depiction of Etinbin and prayed. Her eyes flew wide. She realized she prayed for answers rather than her friend's soul. Humbled and embarrassed, she bowed her head and muttered a more appropriate prayer.

"In honor of Guntar, Bearer and Servant of Istinjoln. May Etinbin see your soul across the Road of Living Stars. May Rettinu greet you in the Heaven of the Faithful, and provide you guidance unto and beyond the heavens of the Wealthy, the Loved, the Serene, the Provider, and the Wise. May the Queen of the Gods, Elinwe, greet you at the gates of the Conqueror Heaven where resides Sol, our heavenly king, and may you earn his forgiveness for any transgressions, and may your voice speak strong of your accomplishments and faith. May Sol accept your humility and pride as a man of faith and honor, so someday you may fight by his side.

"In the name of Sol, may you live forever in his light."

She stood, pulled her cowl over her head and climbed back to the surface. Two monks tended the body, and the crowd had dispersed. The morning carried a chill she hadn't noticed earlier, and a few flakes of snow drifted in from the heavens. Guntar wasn't the first friend carried to their slumber in the catacombs beneath Istinjoln, but his was the first violent death.

If Dareun stood beside her he would slap her for a fool after a single glance and rebuke her for every notion flitting through her head. Fortunate for her he was deep in prayer by now.

Searching for answers was a dangerous game if she played it wrong, but she needed to find out how the message and the lord priest's arrival connected. She considered the inquisitor in black and his threat; she couldn't let herself get so caught up in the hunt she'd do something foolish.

Woxlin was the connection, but getting close required careful thought.

Subtle and savvy, these two qualities would keep her from the ledge Dareun always said she danced beside. Her master's voice echoed in her head, "And remember, a ledge may give way any moment; if falls were predictable they'd kill nobody."

EIGHT

Frozen Repose

A fire in the liar,
a thorn in the briar,
welcoming blood of lovers and victims,
feeding on flesh and decay
of jumpers and thrown.
Thorn thorn beware be aware
of your nature used against others.

—*Tomes of the Touched*

Thirteen Days to the Eve of Snows

No Choerkin lost their liquor on board a ship in three generations, or so spoke family legend, but Ivin couldn't be sure he'd maintained the streak. The storms passed a candle out, and clear skies brought weak winds. A journey which could've taken a day took more than three, and there'd been nothing to do but drink. In the midst of his memory haze he recalled leaning over a rail, but didn't know whether from retching or laughing.

Something cool and wet pressed to his lips. "No, no. No more." Laughter erupted around him, and a horn sounded in the distance.

"It's water."

Ivin opened his eyes, his head pounding in the sun's morning light. Behind the water-skin an oarsman's toothy grin.

"Thank you." He slugged water down until he gasped for air and rose to his knees.

Ivin struggled to focus, but there was no denying the bad news: The *Sea Owl* was near docking at Choerkin Fost. The Fost's trade and town districts rose from the bay, protected from storm and surf by a triple ring of concentric walls constructed of granite boulders and rubble that horseshoed the harbor. Within this secured bay a score of docks jutted into calm waters where trading vessels were tied off. Later in the day fishers would swell the number of boats, creating a racket as mongers dickered over prices and weights. Homes and businesses grew dense as you moved inland from the quays and reached a stark cliff face rising four hundred feet above sea level.

The crowning glory of the Fost rested atop these cliffs, a fortress of white stone with high towers overlooking the city and bay. Supplies took two routes to the castle, pulled up the cliffs aboard what locals called the flying boats, or a long, winding road that led out of town before returning to the main gates.

When Ivin first set eyes on the walls of the Fost as a boy it had taken his mother's hand to close his gaping mouth, but even as a man who'd seen its wonders half a hundred times, the gleam of those walls and towers under a bright sun never failed to impress.

The ship passed the breakwaters into the protected harbor and sailors cast mooring lines to rowboats to help guide the *Sea Owl* to dock. Eredin stood nearby in the mast's shade. "I'm never drinking with you again."

Eredin peered at him from the slender shadow. "You said something similar last Eve of Snows."

"I may never drink again."

Eredin threw his arms in the air. "Your birthday, two years ago."

Ivin climbed to his feet, his head reeling as he wobbled. "Damn it! I'm still drunk."

"On the bright side, it might make dealing with the Wolverine more pleasant."

Ivin glared at his cousin's smile and cursed himself for a fool. He splashed his face with water, ran his fingers through his hair, and chewed on a hunk of beru-root to kill the taste and smell of whiskey. By the time the ship docked he felt himself presentable, considering having slept drunk on a boat.

When they disembarked Ivin took a step toward town, but Eredin tapped him on the shoulder and pointed. Ivin followed the finger and grimaced. "Twelve Hells."

The Wolverine sat on a bench at the end of the dock with his horse tied off beside him and an orange harbor cat napping in his lap. They walked his way, and if not for the sway of his jaw, a bull chewing cud, Ivin would've sworn the man was asleep. They had the horse's attention more than Pikarn's.

Ivin cleared his throat. "Commander Pikarn."

His right eye squinted open. "Drunk. Damned near four days on the water and you come in drunk."

Ivin's shoulders slouched. *How the hells did he know that?*

Pikarn eased the cat to the dock's planks and groaned as he stood. A bearded axe dangled from either side of his belt, their hafts long enough to use them as walking sticks in the mountains. The man was barrel-chested, with legs thick as trees. Despite the advantages of youth and towering over the man by a foot or more, no way Ivin wanted to tussle with him. Wolverine fit him well. "You slurred. And you came in with that one; the boy's a walking still."

85

"He's got me there," Eredin said, "but most find it an endearing quality."

"If I were your father, I'd take a strap to your hide."

"It's good your children are bastards, then."

Ivin watched as the two glared. He coughed.

Pikarn swallowed whatever he chewed. "Get your soft ass back to your father, let him know your cousin's heading north." He turned his back on them both, cinching the saddle tight.

Eredin clasped Ivin's forearm and yanked him in for a head butt that rang Ivin's whiskey-spun head. "You be careful out there. There are worse than crotchety old men."

"Aye, I'll be careful."

Eredin strode the dock, hailing several sailors by name as he went. Ivin admired his cousin for his bravado and easy-going nature, how he got on with people. They looked alike, but when it came to social banter they were stamped on the opposite sides of a coin.

Pikarn swung into the saddle with surprising ease considering his stature, then spat into the bay. "When I heard I was getting Kotin's youngest, I wondered what sort of spoilt turd I was getting. Prove you're less your cousin and more like that rock you hail from, and we'll do well enough, you and me." The man eyeballed him. "So, boy, what's your plan?"

Ivin licked his lips, hoping to conjure a semblance of wisdom. "We speak to Istinjoln, convince the Church to assist in saving the miners."

The Wolverine's deadpan stare froze Ivin's lips. "A better answer woulda been 'Whatever the hells I'm told.' But please, do go on."

Ivin straightened his shoulders, determined. "I will bring cooperation between Istinjoln and the Choerkin."

The Wolverine's face didn't so much as twitch as he reined his horse, backing and turning before clopping down the dock. The horse's tail raised and Ivin stepped over a steaming pile of dung; apparently man and beast shared a low opinion of his goals.

"Straightaway to Istinjoln, then?" No answer, so he walked in silence for a quarter candle, until they reached a small stable used by the wardens. A few boys tended a barn a quarter full with a red roan mare saddled out front.

Pikarn motioned him to the horse. "Mount up." A split flicker later. "You know how to ride, else-wise they wouldn't have sent you."

Ivin was a quick learner: The Wolverine didn't appreciate hesitation. He slid his spear and bow into their respective scabbards, attached his quiver to the saddle horn and leapt into the saddle.

The Wolverine rode past him without a glance, he was quieter than Kotin and at least as surly. With light pressure from his heels and a shift of weight his roan followed the commander. Pleased with the quality of his horse, he patted the mare on her neck and scratched the ridge of her mane.

Ivin vowed not to say a word until spoken to, but as they exited the town gates and climbed the steep road to the top of the cliffs, he couldn't take it anymore. "Where're the rest of the wardens?"

"Ahead."

Brilliant. Ivin wanted to prod, make demands in the Choerkin name, but Pikarn had run with his Uncle Lovar and Kotin as boys and later at war with Clan Broldun. Stories spoke of him saving both of their lives more than once. Respect was mandatory.

They reached the top of the cliffs and passed the castle's gates in silence. A granite boulder blackened by fire stood at the side of the road with a hole chiseled in its top, its face carved to read "In fire may loyalty be reborn", a famous quote from the *Book of Leds*. Priests preached this to mean that the blasphemous dead who suffered the wrath of the Fire Lion, a manifestation of Sol, while serving penance in the Heretic's Hell could prove their loyalty to the King of Gods and rise to the Seven Heavens. At the end of the War of Seven Lies, the Choerkin gave the words a more worldly meaning, strapping Lord Priest Imrok Girn to a stake on this same stone, setting him ablaze for the crime of rebellion against the clans. Every year since, a bonfire marked the occasion here and throughout the clans. This blackened rock, its words, its yearly fire, helped keep the wound between Church and clans raw. It was a tradition Ivin would end if given a choice.

The road beyond was bare rock rut-worn by wagon wheels, with sparse pines and shrub juniper, as well as patches of sedge lining their journey. Ivin spotted a hare now and again, but snow buntings with their trilling songs were more constant companions.

Pikarn broke his silence several miles out of town. "We'll meet up with the wardens at Merutven, then head for Ervinhin by way of Muollin."

Ivin had visited Merutven once, an outpost with a stable and a small but impregnable tower, at least to a youngster's fancy. Any other day he would look forward to this stop, with pleasant memories of a childhood summer, but Ervinhin dominated his thoughts. "Kotin mentioned a messenger."

Pikarn pulled a stretch of jerky from his saddlebag and tossed it to Ivin. Ivin's whiskey-stricken belly growled as he stripped a length to chew on.

"We *were* headed to shadow Istinjoln next week while hunting Colok. Then the mines crashed down; now, we got dead holies."

"Dead priests? Shadow Istinjoln?"

Lovar said you were a religious boy, taking after your mother. You should know these things." Pikarn grinned, specks of meat and spice in his teeth. "The Eve of Snows is coming. Lots of high and mighties coming in for the celebration. We already lost holies from Istinjoln.

Don't want no cursed Broldun holy losing their damned head and them muddlers blaming us, do we?"

"No." Wardens were common in the area, and it made sense, but he didn't swallow the hook whole. "A Colok attack?"

"Aye. The beasts slaughtered 'em all right. Poor bastards, one body wasn't even found, as I hear it. A rider came in from Ervinhin, he traded mounts and rode straight through thirty-six candles. Dead holies put folks in a tizzy like that." Pikarn chortled and spat. "Enard heads the Wardens in Ervinhin and he's holding the messenger's body long as he can to give us time to get close, but your poor winds held us back." The clop of hooves quieted as they moved from stone to dirt road.

"I heard the Colok fed on a band of priests last winter."

Pikarn grunted, pointed at the jerky. "Exercise your mouth with that, boy."

Ivin bit into the hard meat, twisting and ripping. He hoped the rest of the wardens were more talkative. They wouldn't arrive in Merutven until midnight, if then, so it would be a long stretch of silence. Or so he thought. His jerky finished, the Wolverine broke into a series of bawdy tavern songs that reminded Ivin his head pounded. He prayed for silence before the third verse, but the gods weren't listening.

They arrived at Merutven after shadows and dark ruled the land, and after a few candles' rest in its lone tower, the wardens rode out before dawn on fresh horses. Thirty-two, including Ivin, rode in the company. The Wolverine rattled through most names with the speed of pounding hooves, but slowed when he got to those who rode closest.

"Modan Hiklar, my fist. You'd recognize him better if'n he bathed and shaved more than once a year."

Modan replied, "I'll shave and bathe twice when you stop shrinkin' from age. He used to be tall as a Choerkin y'know, about a hundred years past." Pikarn's second winked as he shook Ivin's hand, a gesture unsuited to greeting Choerkin-blood, but Ivin sensed only one man's rank mattered here.

Behind the dirt and bushy black beard sat familiar blue eyes, he might've met the man at the Fost once or twice, but he knew his reputation: A stalwart of the Wolverine's who turned down a promotion to head his own Warden Patrol. His notoriety also lay in spearing a priest who defied arrest on accusations of rape.

Pikarn pointed to the only woman in his patrol. "Puxele, we call her Little Sister, so no one gets the wrong-headed notion to try'n take a poke. Last one who did will limp 'til his end, and the other we buried."

Petite, with a crooked nose and brown hair bundled above her round face, she smiled and rolled her eyes. "He weren't dead when you stuck him in the ground."

"Buried him all the same. Over there is Rinold, best godsdamned tracker this side of the Road of Living Stars. We call him the Squirrel. If'n you've lost your nuts, blame Puxele, and ask Rinold to find them."

Short and thin, with a twitch in his right eye where an ugly scar marked him, Rinold laughed harder than the rest. "Good to meet you, Choerkin."

"The big ugly bastard riding like a sack of potatoes is Suvarn. You might call him tater, but we ain't found a name as sticks right yet."

The man's bulk was enough to give Kotin a wrestle; with cauliflower ears and a nose crooked in two directions, no doubt the man didn't back out of fights.

Ivin said, "Call him Slick, then."

Suvarn shrugged. "Nah, Slick done got himself killed last year, wouldn't wanna take the pretty boy's good name."

Ivin found it fascinating most bore a nickname, yet everyone in the Fost and beyond knew not to call Pikarn the Wolverine. Then he feared what nickname he might earn, considering the spoilt turd comment.

Ivin rode on Pikarn's left owing to his birthright as a Choerkin while Modan took the right flank. He felt them questioning his worth when he looked into the wardens' eyes; the Wolverine had slotted him into the uncomfortable position of third in command without a day's ride in experience. Nobody said a word, least not within earshot, but no doubt several eyes on his back figured another deserved his spot of honor.

They traveled at an ambling gait, stopping twice to graze the horses and refresh themselves before and after noon, and just after nightfall they arrived at Muollin, a village protected by a ditched palisade.

They dined on turkey stew and spelt bread, and slept on straw-ticked mattresses. Never had such basic food and a lumpy bed tasted so good and commanded sleep so deep. Modan awakened him mid-snore and before sunrise with a blow to his foot. The man's gap-toothed smile surrounded by ratty beard gazed on him with twisted pleasure.

"You're piss poor in the saddle, but you snore with the best of them. Breakfast, then on to Ervinhin."

That meant fewer miles but harsher road.

Ivin rolled out of bed, ate turkey stew and spelt bread, which wasn't quite the delicacy he remembered, and swung into the saddle of a fresh mount as the sun peeked over the horizon.

The Estertok Mountains grew as the day passed, great peaks of stone and snow looming over his future. The company pushed into the foothills midday and an icy rain fell long enough to soak a chill into their bones. Another day they might've taken shelter, but the Wolverine pushed on, determined to reach Ervinhin before storms destroyed any trail. The pace was brutal, but the horses ambled all day without a care for the rises and falls of the land. They reached their destination well after dark.

Ervinhin was a black splotch twinkling with scattered lights amid a dusting of snow on the ground. The palisade walls were pine poles sticking five paces from the ground. The people took Colok raids as a serious threat this far north.

The stables were a welcome sight just inside gates. Ivin handed his reins to a stable girl, eased his right leg over his saddle and dismounted, damned near falling flat on his back. His ass and legs were numb. "Son of a bitch."

The girl giggled. "Need anything from your saddlebags?" Ivin shook his head, and she led his horse into the stable.

Ivin followed his comrades into the dinner hall, steps high and stretching to regain his land legs. Supper came and went, but tonight the Wolverine kept him and Modan at the table instead of letting them find their beds. A boy poured mugs of mead, watered but still welcome, and they stretched in front of the hearth.

Pikarn finished his mug and ended the awkward silence. "Drain your drinks, boys, ugly work ahead." He groaned to his feet and led them outside with a lantern in hand. The wind howled through the town's dirt roads as they walked to a dark storehouse. Inside, the Wolverine lit a twist of straw with his lantern and ignited braziers hanging around the room.

Bodies lay displayed in the cold room, most wore robes denoting their holy status, but across the room stretched corpses clad in mountain gear, trappers or prospectors. Miners. A woman's skull was caved in, and several eye sockets were black holes. One lacked a head, others their arms or legs, but every one lay as a remarkable display of sanguine brutality.

Ivin reminded himself to breathe before he turned blue. Dead people he'd seen, men killed in battle, a drowned woman at the pier, his own mother, but it failed to prepare him for this carnage.

The Wolverine pointed at holy corpses. "Eighteen bodies, plus the messenger we sent on to Istinjoln. Meaning?"

The quiz caught him offguard, it took a moment before he stammered up an answer. "We're missing one; messengers travel with nineteen guards, one for each god of the pantheon."

"The last time Colok struck a messenger's group was a year back, same damned thing. Wrote it off, seeing as Istinjoln didn't act like they were missing no one. Twice makes for a hell-kissing coincidence."

"A captive, or they let one go on purpose?"

"Can't say as I know." Pikarn knelt and pulled back a robe. The dead man's thigh lay ripped open, hunks of flesh missing. "Somethin' ate on this one."

Ivin muttered, "Godsdamned Colok."

"Let's see your arm, Modan."

The man pulled up his sleeve to reveal a nasty set of bite scars. He put his forearm next to the dead man's wounds

"My scars are Colok. This man's wounds are too small," Modan said.

Ivin scratched his ear. "Then what?"

"Care to test your chompers?"

The implication took a moment to settle. "You're saying a man did this?"

"No bleeding at the bite marks, you notice. These gentlemen, and lady, were dead when eaten. Colok killed 'em. I don't know what the hells done ate on 'em, but it's much like a man."

Life on a tiny island was more sheltered than he'd thought. "Wakened Dead?"

"We thought the same first time 'round. But the Wakened Dead are dumber'n eating water with a fork and easy to track. Plus, they don't go eating folks already dead and cold." He spun on his foot and pointed. "Now those miners, they've been eatin' on while alive, and one poor bastard's eyes got sucked out. Ever hear of a man capable of that?"

What the hells could do such a thing? No rival faction in Istinjoln, for certain. Still, if they found what creature mutilated these people, the situation led to clan and Church fighting a common enemy. Nothing would bring two foes to the table quicker. The Dævu were creatures of ice and snow who wiped out encampments without so much as a drop of blood left behind. "Wouldn't be Dævu?"

Pikarn chuckled. "Who's to say those things even eat? No, now you know what we're facing: Nothin' we ever heard of afore. The old man didn't mention that, eh? But don't go blaming him, some things a man gotta see himself."

"Another name of a slave." Ivin understood the result, but the perpetrator of such atrocities? He needed answers in order to put the pieces together and use them to his advantage. "Whatever they are, they need to die."

The Wolverine laughed. "Now you sound like a Choerkin."

Modan said, "The miners were killed a quarter-candle's ride from the Ihomjo mine, folks helping in the rescue, and the priests weren't far south of there in the Omindi, twice the chance to catch a trail."

Meaning the hunt was on come morning. His heart fluttered with fear and excitement, a thrill similar to facing a skilled opponent in a dual, only here the blades wouldn't be wasters. "I've never been more eager for the dawn."

Nine

Faces

We tickle and we talk,
our lives gears in a clock.
Wink, blink, sink, and rise.
Wisdom wingless and yet it flies.
not You again. You aren't here, no, no, not yet
but Do go away astray away anyway.
You aren't here today
But yesterday, part of my tomorrow's forever next.
damn your Craven Raven eyes.

—*Tomes of the Touched*

Thirteen Days to the Eve of Snows

Meris sat cross-legged amid the stars of Skywatch, afloat in the universe, pondering the hairline fractures in the bear scapula she'd used for Ivin's divination. For the past four days her thoughts couldn't escape the web of these cracks. The fortune should've been clean. It should've been simple. It should have been boring.

The bone spoke of many things, but nothing with certainty. The Choerkin would be at war soon, but with whom? The fissure in the bone that might have given an answer as it passed through war god Anzelok's sword took a sharp turn into uncarved bone. Divinations

95

didn't do that, but this one had. It meant something, but it was impossible to decipher an answer from a blank code.

"Flummoxed, Meris?"

The voice boomed around her, echoing through the heavens with a power greater than her own. She scowled as she glanced across the empty stars, angry to be startled in her domain.

"Where are you?" She should be alone among the stars, with other oracles at the temple in prayer. No mortal should be able to sneak up on her, not here, in Queen Elinwe's stars. For a moment, she considered that a god might have spoken to her.

"What about the bone gives you pause?"

The voice was mortal, she knew this as truth. The gods hadn't spoken directly with their faithful since the Age of God Wars and their violent banishment from the world. Her vocation within the Church, reading the words of the gods in bones, rested on this truth. Still, no man should have been able to set foot in these stars without her knowing. Lord Priest Ulrikt himself might tread the sky without sounding chimes, but, he was in Istinjoln.

"Everything."

A figure materialized in the unnatural distance of the open sky, walking, but it made no sound. Impossible in the stars where every step played a note of the universe's song. She tapped the night sky with her fingers and bells chimed at her touch, escalating in pitch, their notes more perfect than any mortal instrument. This man must be a figment of her aging imagination, or a ghost. When the cowl covering the person's face dropped, she realized it was neither.

An indistinct and shifting face gazed at her, a reflection in slow-moving ripples of a flesh-tone pond. Eyes, nose, and mouth curled and waved, changed colors and shapes, never feminine nor masculine in a pure sense.

Every Barefoot Postulant in their first year of studies for the priesthood heard the rumors of the Lord Priest's Face. A man or woman so gifted with the arts of Fertility God Tulule's Prayers of Life that they forsook their own features, living their lives in the guise of others. The Face could be anywhere, molding their features into anyone to watch and listen.

Forty years ago a group of high priests had plotted Lord Priestess Sadevu's fall. Testimony at their trial proved the group had been noose tight, speaking to no one outside their circle, but a nameless spy revealed their plot. Inquisitors tortured the conspirators and the lord priestess Sundered their souls, cursing them to walk the world until fading into oblivion. Tongues that dared speculate spoke of the Face, some even claiming to have seen a conspirator's double. If indeed this was who stood before her, its appearance boded grave tidings.

Her saliva may as well have been a stone sliding down her throat. She stuttered. "Face of Ulrikt." She prostrated herself on the floor of the heavens.

The Face's chuckle shifted from masculine to feminine and back again. "Rise, Meris. I am neither a god, nor your lord priest, worthy of your groveling obeisance. We've met before, and I bowed before you, wearing a different smile."

Meris rose to her knees, tried to look the Face in its eyes, but it unnerved her, and her gaze wandered to a distant constellation in the sky. "What can I do to serve you, Lord Face of Ulrikt?"

The person's face contorted into what might have been a smile, for a moment at least. "All service to me is service to Lord Priest Ulrikt, and to Sol himself."

"Of course. Understood."

"Please, hand me the bone." The Face took it from her outstretched hands and studied it. "This was smoothed?"

"Yes. I'm always prepared if a Choerkin desires a reading. It should have said nothing out of the ordinary."

The person held it up to the stars, and Meris guessed he, or she, was looking through the holes and cracks. In her decades of divinations, this technique for reading a bone was foreign.

"Bontore did not send this message."

"But—"

"Tsst!" The Face glared at her, or maybe it did, as a swirl of flesh later the expression more resembled crying. "It was not sent by Bontore nor was it meant for the Choerkin boy. This message is for you."

"My Lord, that's not possible, I've never heard of such a thing."

"My words carry the weight and will of Ulrikt. Do you question my wisdom?"

Meris shook her head, and the Face took a seat in the stars with the Fire-Lion's constellation framing his head. "I've been observing your sky for weeks. What do you see behind me?"

Weeks? Meris' heart jumped and wavered. What face had this person been wearing? What secrets might it know? Had he witnessed Ivin's reading? "The Fire-Lion, to his left the Winged-Viper—"

"What is out of place? You have stared at these stars too long if you do not see."

Out of place? Stars are never out of place. A twinkle of light caught her eye. "A comet?" Its appearance was a mystery, she'd never seen its like before. A new star didn't make sense. It was an impossibility that hung in the night, a ball of light, smaller than most stars, to the right of the Fire-Lion. "It has no tail."

"Not a comet, not a star, a Messenger from the Celestial, a harbinger for great change. Upon the Eve of Snows it will sit as the eye of the Fire-Lion, and the followers of Sol will rejoice like never before. It is written that the Road of Living Stars will align, and the gods come to rid our people, the Silone, of their enemies."

"What enemies?"

The lips twisted, narrow then pouting, fading to pale blue. "The bears, the elk, any foolish animal which will not bow before their rightful king."

Confusion mangled Meris' thoughts, then fear. The Choerkin Clan would be the bears, and Clan Emudar the elk, and Lord Priest Ulrikt the king. She hadn't studied the prophetic scriptures for fifty years or more, preferring the immediacy of cracks in bones to scrawls on a sheep's skin, but one thing was clear, the Face spoke of forbidden texts she had never set eyes on. He spoke of the Codex of Sol and its mysteries, of Holy War. Rumors of the tome spoke of dozens of contradicting prophecies, and she hadn't a clue of which one the Face spoke, but she feared to show her ignorance. Meris straightened her jaw and met the Face's disturbing gaze. "I see, My Lord. And why reveal this to me? Am I to observe or cast bones?"

"You will travel to Istinjoln for the Eve of Snows."

The last time she'd left the Watch was for a wedding in Choerkin Fost twenty years ago; she couldn't recall the last time she'd traveled as far inland as Istinjoln. "My Lord, I will be ninety-five in a matter of days. I-I—"

"Come spring you will be a young girl again, bathing in the fires of Sol. Lord Priest Ulrikt commands your presence to break bones for the great celebration, and feast to celebrate a glorious future."

It didn't ring true, and she proved she still possessed nerve. "There is more?"

"There is." The Face's visage twisted into a silent, gape-mouthed scream, but said nothing more.

"What?"

"You will know."

"And if I don't? If I fail?" Suspicions and doubts pounded blood through her veins, and she hoped she didn't look as terrified as she felt.

"Failing me is to fail Lord Priest Ulrikt, and Sol himself. You will live the eternity in the fires of the Slave Forges with no faith in your heart, for I will have smitten it from your breathing breast."

A serious threat to her soul coming from the Lord's Face. Meris trembled. She'd suffered threats such as these decades ago when training at Istinjoln, and though frightful, they never carried this venom and weight.

She answered the only way she could muster, uttering a phrase of devotion from her acceptance into the priesthood. "I am hardened in the forge fires of Tezmanu and quenched in the salted waters of Zinmil, my metal is not to be questioned. I will know."

The voice became feminine and sultry, lacking the threatening quality of moments before, but it sickened Meris to the depths of her soul. It was the voice of the Lady Pineluple Choerkin, Kotin's wife, who'd died in Meris' arms during childbirth. "Even to the doom of my sons?"

Meris fought anger and disgust, and did her best to stare unflinching into the face of a woman long dead, a woman she'd befriended.

And murdered.

"My metal is not to be questioned."

TEN

Afloat in an Ephemeral Sea

You complain of not remembering, whilst I complain of not forgetting.
How I wish I could forget what I see each day I Awake!
Tremble. Scream. Rage.
I have gazed into the eyes of the First Dragons
And they into mine,
And it was for me that they wept,
He who will never forget.

—*Tomes of the Touched*

Thirteen Days to the Eve of Snows

*O*pen *my eyes to blue.*

His thoughts echoed the fading memory of a deep, yet feminine, voice. A flicker later he awoke to a universe of brilliant undulating blues marked by streaks and swirls of shading grays, the colors washing over and through his body and soul in stringy waves of energy like cool, wriggling worms. No sun. No moon. No stars. The light of this universe was soft and sourceless.

His feet rested one upon the other with straight legs, and his arms stretched perpendicular from his body. He tried to look at his toes, but found his head immobile, only his eyes moved. Fingers and toes wiggled at his command, but they tingled and felt disconnected from his being.

Am I dead? Am I alone? Deep in his gut resided a confidence which dismissed both these possibilities. He released a deep breath to relax. There was exhalation, but his chest didn't move, as if experiencing breathing as memory instead of reality.

"Might you be dreaming, my love?" Feminine, sultry, and passionate, the voice came from everywhere or nowhere at once.

"No." His voice too came from an unknown, haunting origin as his mouth didn't move.

"You are wise, my love." Despite the proclamation, he realized love wasn't a term of endearment, but a phrase without emotional attachment.

"Who am I?"

The presence swallowed him. "Wouldn't you rather know where you are?"

"Where I am doesn't matter without knowing who I am."

Awareness of the omnipresence became acute, smothering, as she spoke again. "You are Solineus Mikjehemlut, of the Clan Emudar, a Silone warrior in a long line of warriors and sailors." The voice coalesced in a dance of eight white sparks funneling to a single point.

His memory was vacuous, it denied every word. "I've never heard the name."

"Irrelevant, my love." The man who now thought of himself as Solineus was in awe as an indistinct haze shifted and flowed, molding into a woman more beautiful than he conceived possible. Her eyes read the depths within his soul, but they didn't pierce, they took him in, soothed his being until snuggling into every thought.

"You are Solineus Mikjehemlut, of the Clan Emudar, a Silone warrior in a long line of warriors and sailors."

Solineus struggled against the warmth of the woman's gaze. "Where am I, then?"

The woman smiled with teeth of polished ivory. "You are afloat in Purdonis Bay, territory of the Clan Choerkin. You were upon the *Resten* when it struck ice and sank two days ago. Soon, you will wash ashore, upon the island of Kaludor."

Kaludor, the name felt familiar. "I am dead then?"

"No, my love, death is not for you."

"Then where am I?"

"I am sorry to confuse you in these ways, my love. You are now upon a rocky shore, safe. The waters are cold, but cold you will survive."

Attempting to shake his head resulted in frustration. "No, my consciousness. Me. Here. Where am I?"

"I will not confuse you so much, so soon." She leaned in, the warmth of her being palpable so close, and kissed him on the forehead.

❄ ❄ ❄

Solineus awoke with a chill in his bones and a lip-shaped burn upon his brow. He'd never felt so cold, with icy waves slapping his bare feet and calves. His breath came with a start, and his eyes sprang open to a world more gray than the one he left, the cloud cover hazy and absolute.

He rolled from his back on the rocky surf, propped himself on his elbows. His body was stiff and sore, and he groaned from the exertion to stand. He stared at bare feet, wiggling his toes, then his hands, making fists.

Giggles caught his ear, and he raised his head. Two young girls stood side-by-side, clad in roughspun robes, carrying baskets of clams. From their blue-gray eyes and long, straw-blond hair to matching hand-on-hip postures, he decided they must be sisters.

He did his best to smile and spoke, hoping they shared a common language. "Greetings."

"Hello," the eldest girl said, speaking the same language as he spoke, the same language as the woman from the dream-state.

The younger chose blunt words. "You're naked," she said as she pointed at him.

Naked? The concept struck him as outrageous, but when he looked he realized more than his feet were bare. He blushed, a sensation so foreign it felt the first time he'd done such a thing.

Wide-eyed and embarrassed, he covered himself the best he could as the elder girl removed her scarf and tossed it to him. He snatched the rough wool from the air and wrapped it around his waist. "Thank you."

"I'm Alu, and this is my sis, Kinesee." She smiled, expecting him to say something.

He stared at the girls with a blank brain, stared too long, as they grew uncomfortable with his gaze and silence. "My apologies." He shook his head and released a breath. "I'm Solineus Mikjehemlut, I sailed upon the *Resten*. We struck ice, and she sank, and I find myself washed ashore. I fear my memories are a bit . . . confused."

The sisters relaxed, but they stayed silent until young Kinesee chimed in. "If Father were here, he'd invite him to sup."

Alu nodded. "But Father isn't here, and we don't know to trust him." She appraised him with a squint. "Still, we shouldn't leave him to nature this way. If we lead you home, do you swear to stay thirty paces behind us the entire walk?"

"I swear, with gratitude for your kindness."

Alu took her sister's hand and led the way while Solineus fell in a safe forty paces behind. "You're Silone?"

Kinesee laughed. "Of course, silly."

And Alu hushed her little sister.

Solineus cursed himself under his breath. "I meant, of course, Clan Choerkin? My brain is still cold and slow."

"Yes, but we ain't clan-blood if that's what you mean." Alu glanced back. "What clan do you hail from?"

"Emudar."

"Father says the Emudar are good and honorable to trade with," interjected Kinesee.

Alu was having nothing to do with her sister's platitudes. "I know nothing of them." She glowered at her sibling.

Solineus kept his mouth shut and his eyes anywhere but on the girls so they didn't catch him looking. A gray sky, a gray surf, and gray rocks interrupted by evergreen shrubs and patches of tall grass. Not a single landmark was familiar; however, such a stark and simple landscape, it didn't seem foreign, either. He spoke their language, he looked like them . . . would two young girls accept him as one of their own if he wasn't?

He rubbed his head in search of a welt or bruise and found pain. Could the woman from the swirling pale and his lost memories result from a blow to the head? Logic suggested one conclusion: He was Solineus Mikjehemlut, of the Clan Emudar, a Silone warrior from a long line of warriors and sailors.

Nothing else made sense.

A thin trail of smoke rose above a ridge to the north. They climbed a winding trail up a short bluff and the children's home came into view. Round, single storied, and constructed of the region's common gray rock, it stood in the midst of a wide array of greenery, including bloom-ing purple monkshood and sunflowers. A broad, single door faced the sea and a massive chimney rose from its peaked center. Chickens ran free, feeding on sparse vegetation, and a few hens peeked from a coop nestled on the conical slope of the home's roof.

A woman spotted him behind the girls and ducked into the house. He stopped and waited for the girls to tell his story.

A bearded man walked from the home, a knife at his belt and a triple-barbed spear more for fishing than war in his hand. The man spoke with the girls then walked Solineus' way, stopping a safe distance in front of him.

The man appraised him with a squint identical to Alu's, a family trait he guessed. "Should I fear an unarmed, naked man?"

"Solineus Mikjehemlut, indebted to those girls for a simple cloth." He gave a modest bow.

The man raised his voice to make sure his youthful audience would hear. "They are good girls who've normally the wits to not bring strangers home. One is near twelve but you'd guess her half that from her stubbornness, while the other is fourteen and thinks she's the elder of this home. If they don't mind my words, they'll be sleeping with the chickens." He cast the girls a glare and pointed to the house. They darted through the door.

"I hope my people would do the same for you and yours if fate were so unkind." Truth, even if he didn't remember his people.

The man grinned and nodded. "Fate is kind and cruel, to throw a man into the icy waters of the Strait, and still see he survives. Most would be dead. Yet here you stand, without a chill, wrapped in little more than a loincloth."

Solineus struggled for a convincing answer and stammered. "I can't explain my luck, either good or bad."

Alu trotted up with woolen tunic and pants. "Here, Father."

He took the clothes and offered them to Solineus. "To the fire, Alu."

The girl trotted back to their home, dragging her sister inside with her.

The scratch of wool was foreign but its warmth welcome to his bare skin. "My thanks."

"I'm Iku Koest, father to these girls, and Second Voice of the Fire in our home. You are welcome, by my word, so long as you guest with honor."

"I appreciate the hospitality; maybe someday I can return the kindness."

Iku gestured to the door. "Join me by the fire." The thick oak door was reinforced with iron and led into a corridor, marking the walls several paces thick. Wide open space greeted them, except for wood and fur structures pressed against the outer walls, through the flaps of which a few curious eyes peered at him. In the center of the home sat an open stone hearth with a fire.

Iku led him to the fireside and sat on a simple, three-legged stool. The man didn't invite him to sit.

Solineus said, "An impressive home."

"Our family is fortunate to have shelter where we may stay safe and welcome strangers." Solineus acknowledged this with a nod. "What ship were you on?"

"The *Resten.*"

Iku's face fell into solemnity. "I've hailed the *Resten, a* fine vessel and respected crew."

"I reckon I'll miss many, once my memory returns."

"A man's memory, a blessing and sometimes a curse," said a hoarse voice from behind him.

Solineus turned, catching the gaze of a frail woman hunched by her years. Her leathered face bore decades of wrinkles, and her ears and nose were too large for the rest of her face, but her black eyes remained keen. She walked with a staff carved with owls and vines, and which stood two feet above her brow, its fur-wrapped base silent as it plied the floor.

Iku gestured. "Ielu the Matron, First Voice of the Fire, this is Solineus Mikjehemlut of Emudar."

The woman shot Solineus a cockeyed squint. "Do you know what year it is? It is the five hundred and second year of Remembered Time, over five centuries since all the world's peoples lost their memories. The Great Forgetting, our priests call it."

"What's this to do with me?"

"Some say it's an auspicious honor, bearing a moniker beginning with our Lord Sol's name. We of the Choerkin do not believe this. My people believe it is arrogant, insulting." Ielu ambled to the fire and took a seat, her eyes pinned on him. "Pray, what were the parents of a man thinking to name their child so?"

"I can't say."

"It is not a sailor's name, Solineus." She stressed the Sol until her voice slid into a deep bass. "Sit. Warm yourself."

Solineus stepped toward a bench, but she corrected him. "On the stone and dirt. You have the welcome of our fire, but not our wood. Not yet."

So he sat cross-legged on the floor. "I never claimed to be a sailor."

"You are no sailor, I already told you. Your wits are gone with your memory? No. A boy with such name is clan-blood or the child of a famed warrior. Both. Your parents were prideful, or their priest convinced of your greatness."

Iku moved to sit beside Ielu. "I've heard of chieftains who consult oracles on the birth of their children, breaking bones to discover the child's name."

"I wish I could tell you."

Ielu smiled with crooked teeth. "Some say the Great Forgetting was a punishment, others say a cleansing of the sins of mortals."

Solineus put the weight on her scales. "What do you say?"

Her wrinkled mouth curled into a smirk. "I say nothing. I accept the Great Forgetting, but leave the moral judgment to my betters. A fool looking to impress might choose a name such as yours when pulling himself from the waves, adding memories lost to forget and cover their sins. Are you such a fool? Desperate to impress? Were you punished or cleansed?"

Solineus appreciated the way this woman did battle with words despite being her target. "I might be a fool, but I feel no need to impress. Nor lie."

Ielu stared with a blank expression, but her mouth retained an unnerving smile.

He cleared his throat, uncomfortable in the silence.

"If your name is true, you are either a man with a future deemed blessed, or the son of braggart fools who is a fool himself, and maybe a liar. I heard of a man born and named Solik. The bones declared he'd rise to rule. He wailed as an infant about his destiny until the stake burst from his throat. His blood watered the grass and stones, the true destiny bones didn't reveal."

"My name didn't spare me from the Strait, nor did it find the shore. Luck is the more likely culprit."

"So much luck makes for destiny, maybe. Or divine luck is fate? I didn't witness your survival, so which and whether I do not know. It speaks of you and who you are, but I don't know what it says."

"I could lie, say I awoke in the arms of the captain's daughter after striking ice, clung to a piece of the *Resten* while watching others freeze and sink into the strait. The currents carried me until I reached shore where the girls found me. A knot on my head explains my lack of memory. But, I know none of this, so they would be a lie. I do not lie."

"So tell me then, he named after the king of gods, how is it you know your name, your family, and the ship you sailed upon?"

Solineus hesitated. Could it hurt a man claiming no memory to be labeled crazy? "A voice in my head told me. A woman's voice. Before I awoke on shore."

Ielu cocked her head and clucked. "A woman in your head. Mmmm. More men, maybe, could use a woman in their head. Warm your belly with the food of my family, but you sleep beside the night fire until you've proved your worth. Yes?"

"Thank you."

Kinesee appeared from behind a fur wall with a wooden bowl and ladled soup as the Matron disappeared into a nearby alcove.

Kinesee smiled. "What was the dream woman's name?"

"She didn't say. Next time we speak I'll be sure to ask."

The girl giggled and handed him the bowl. He ate his first hot meal in what may as well have been forever, with one young girl staring at him with a child's enthralled smile, the other rolling her eyes at her sister's infatuation, and the father's gaze full of suspicion. How many other eyes watched him sip from the bowl he didn't know, but he felt them.

ELEVEN

Lesser Evils

I dreamed tomorrow of yesterday,
As I slept in Eternal Wakefulness,
needles beneath my nails to keep lucid.
Lucidity? Lucidity is brief and uninspired amidst the cries for answers.
Who are you? What have you done? Who is the meaning of you?
They demand answers for a sane world.
They do not realize there are either No answers, Or insane Answers, or answers not at All.
They believe I have answers.
Perhaps I do, but I do not know the truth within the visions of Madness.
The Truth, however, does know me. Nothing should terrify a sane man more.

—*Tomes of the Touched*

Twelve Days to the Eve of Snows

Tokodin regained consciousness blind and unable to move his arms. If this was the Road of Living Stars, it sure wasn't what his elders told him to expect. For one thing, it hurt like the hells. Second, no stars.

Turning his head sent pain surging from his shoulders to crash into his skull like surf pounding a beach. He groaned at the head-splitting pain and tried to roll over, but bindings kept his arms pinned to his sides and his knees and ankles locked bone-to-bone.

"Best to move as little as possible, for your own good, son."

111

The voice echoed as if in a cave and was so weak he felt it might be from a dream fading as he awakened.

Tokodin struggled to quell the agony assaulting his senses and waited for the roar of blood in his ears to fade. "Where am I? What day is it?"

A laugh sputtered into an ailing cough and wheeze. "The Twelfth of Yistole. I kept you sleeping the past several days to assist my prayers. As to where, high in the Estertok Range. Someplace very high and very cold."

"The Colok left me? You saved me somehow?"

The voice skipped laughter and went straight to a lung-ripping hack. "No, son. We're both their guests."

Tokodin's mind raced, pain making it difficult to piece together. "Colok don't take prisoners."

"Right, which is why we must be guests." The mystery man damned near amused himself to death judging from the sounds of his coughing and wheezing as he laughed.

Tokodin wriggled, pressing against a rock, leaning to stare blind into the darkness where the man must be. "Am I blind?"

A fire ignited in a small cook pit, revealing a man either old or grizzled to the appearance of age by his hardships. A gray beard hung unkempt to his chest, and his hands bore scars and wrinkles.

"Who are you?" Tokodin asked.

"Mecum, or so I was once called."

The name haunted his memory, but his head hurt too much to organize muddled thoughts. He looked around the best he could, the light of the tiny fire unable to reach the walls of what must be a cave. "Well, Mecum, could you cut my tethers?"

"I could feed you, maybe." The man shuffled to him with a heavy limp in his gait. "If you've got the strength to eat, that is."

"Water would be great."

Mecum clapped his hands. "Water, yes. Of course. Water!" The man stepped from the light of the meager fire and into the pervasive dark. He returned moments later with a canteen and held it to Tokodin's lips.

The icy water hit his parched throat; he coughed, swallowed, and choked.

"Sorry, so sorry." Mecum withdrew the water and sat beside him. "Let me know if you're thirsty again."

When the realization struck him, Tokodin didn't know whether it should make sense, or if he should be shocked. "Mecum? You were with the Yantin Party, ambushed north of Ervinhin, outside the Omindi Pass, right near where we were."

"We were more northerly."

"They thought you were dead. I went to your funeral."

"Was it nice? The funeral, I mean."

"It was . . ." His mind seized upon an incongruity. "Yantin and his people died near the Ninth Marker. We weren't even out of the Omindi. And how would you know where the Colok attacked?"

Mecum sulked, staring at his meager fire. "I don't know where they took you, I just know we were north of that."

"That makes no—"

"You're thinkin' too hard." The old man's cheek twitched. "They took me in the Treaty Lands."

Tokodin squirmed in his bindings. For over four hundred years, a treaty signed by the seven clans and the Church had designated the tundra north of the Estertok Range a free territory to which none laid claim. The frozen waste was barren and dangerous, but legend spoke of treasures.

"Why would you be so far north? And why would they lie?"

The old man's gaze held a hint of mischief. "They'd lie because they didn't want you to know the truth, and as for why we were there? The answer is something I was never privy to."

"But the Treaty Lands—"

"Shush. I answered your questions, now answer mine."

Tokodin scrunched his brows and stared at the man.

"My funeral. How was it? Lots of people? Was Nelu there?"

"It was nice. I suppose. As funerals go." This man's obsession with his own funeral puzzled him. "I've no idea who Nelu is."

"No, I suppose you wouldn't." Mecum smiled. "A nice funeral, good. Yes, a man should know he's to have a nice funeral when he goes. Comforting."

"But you're not dead."

"A matter of time, a matter of time, as with us all. I fear I've little of that remaining. The funeral was early, but that's fine so long as it was nice." He looked Tokodin in the eye with a disturbing calm. "I'm dying, unable to travel, so they went to fetch you."

Tokodin's heart raced. "What?"

Mecum fumbled with a copper pot and filled it with water. "I will make us some tea. It's terrible . . . but hot!"

"What did you mean, fetch me?" He struggled against his bindings, pain shooting through his shoulder until he figured his head or his heart would burst. He relaxed, surrendering to the rope.

Mecum's next words were under his breath, as if he hated to admit them. "Not you in 'ticular, you see, they just needed someone. They'll need a new speaker and a guide." Mecum's eyes sagged and went to the fire. "They've learned to speak with us."

"Colok can't talk!" He almost blurted out they were animals, but Mecum hushed him. Even as he fell silent, he recalled hearing the name "Choerkin" in the monster's growl. A delusion. "This is madness."

"They captured me, like they did you. I was a bearer." He set his pot in the fire to bring it to a boil. "They nursed me back to health, best ways they could, anyhow. Their chieftain, Grolkan, is very smart."

"Impossible, this is impossible."

A low rumble sent Tokodin's skin to ice. "Fire."

Mecum bowed his head in a quick prayer and torches ignited throughout the cave. Tokodin blinked in the strength of new light, his eyes adjusting to a world with several Colok sitting around them. His heart raced, and he did his best to squirm free, but it ended in pain and frustration.

In one Colok's hand was the long-handled glaive that Tokodin would never forget, the weapon that took Loepus' head.

The creature strolled to loom over him, dipped the glaive until a notch at the tip hooked Tokodin's bindings. Another growl, through which Tokodin struggled to understand the clan-speak. "Name."

"Tokodin."

The Colok lifted Tokodin by his ropes with a single hand on his weapon, but only a few fingers from the cold floor, as the glaive's edge sliced the bindings with a razor's ease. He sat to find he had only one good arm.

Mecum said, "It'll take many prayers before your arm is serviceable again, I fear."

Tokodin stared at the Colok, defiance rising within his soul. "You are Grolkan?"

"Grolkan. Yes." In another place and time, the long growl would've fascinated him.

"Whatever it is you want from me, I will not do."

The great mannish bear's black snout wrinkled. "Respect." His hand thumped his chest twice. Grolkan took a deep breath and the next growl was very long. "Own good. You talk. Respect." He pointed at Tokodin, then himself. "Respect. Talk. Choerkin."

Tokodin pieced it together the best he could. "You wish to speak with the Choerkins?"

Grolkan nodded. "Choerkin. Respect. Three day."

"Why?"

"Talk. Choerkin." With those words Grolkan turned and walked from the cave with his warriors falling in step behind him.

"Your people fed on Mecum's people! Killed them and ate them. Now you want to talk?" The exertion of yelling spun the world, and he wobbled.

Grolkan turned, looked Tokodin dead in the eye. "Kill, yes. Eat, no." He pointed his glaive to Mecum. "No eat." From the disgusted curl on Grolkan's lip, Tokodin decided to believe him.

The Colok lumbered from the cave with a single word hanging in the air. "Respect."

Alone, or so he presumed, the two men stared at the pot, silent in their thoughts until it boiled.

"Why does he want to speak with the Choerkin?"

Mecum puffed steam from the pot's spout. "Have you any Choerkin blood, wrong-eyed kin even?"

"A Choerkin bastard? No. Not that I know, anyhow."

"Unfortunate. An introduction would've been easier that way."

"Does this have something to do with the Treaty Lands?"

Mecum shrugged as he poured the foul-smelling tea into a dented cup. "I told you, I don't know why we were there. So how could I possibly know if they're connected?"

His elder avoided the question. He knew but wouldn't say. Tokodin took the cup from the man's outstretched hand, gazed at the murky, steaming liquid.

"He used the word respect several times."

"He respects your decision and wants you to respect he's giving you three days to decide. But don't worry, if you stick to your word, your end will be clean and swift. Then they'll find another."

Clean and swift. How noble. The remainder troubled him more. "They'll take another?"

Tokodin fumbled with his cup, trying hard not to burn his one good hand. He sniffed the tea, and his nose curled. To aid these creatures who had murdered so many of his people or to subject another to capture. He sipped and found the tea as vile as it smelled, but it wasn't as distasteful as his decision.

TWELVE

Caution in the Ten Winds

The compass Winds carve desperate lines
in the fury, for the leery, humble and dreary.
Gears locked grinding precise. Pattering sands in glass.
Granite marked by the passing shadow.
Lover. Killer. Giver. Thief.
This monstrosity we Create but cannot Defeat,
A Forgotten Wind more than Ten, so many, so much more.

--Tomes of the Touched

Twelve Days to the Eve of Snows

Eliles kneeled alone before the shrine of Elinwe, wife of Sol, fiddling with her sash and staring at the Goddess' fanciful mural instead of praying. The wall was a curved plate of silver, twenty hands high and ten paces across, polished to a sheen and encrusted with precious stones to honor the Queen of Gods. Adorning the center was a lion's paw, Elinwe's most famous symbol, fashioned from hundreds of golden heliodor that shimmered in the eternal Light of this shrine.

A ten-pointed star surrounded the paw, each of the triangular points filled with powdered gems: Diamond, sapphire, ruby, pezzottaite, jeremejevite, zircon, aquamarine, topaz, kyanite, and phenakite, ten gems, ten colors, ten winds, representing the Elements of Power with which the Gods gifted men through prayer.

Life, Water, Fire, Air, Stone, Cold, Heat, Spirit, Light, and Dark. I am a child of ruby, the destroying Fire of Sol, and topaz, the replenishing Spirit of Elinwe. Am I the destroyer or the savior? I've never destroyed much more than a candle, and I've used Spirit to manipulate and eavesdrop, saving only my own skin. But no wonder her magic was different, her powers didn't come from Sol nor Elinwe, they came from the Vanquished Gods and their feral magic.

Footsteps padded to her side and her gut tightened, she couldn't bring herself to look. Adherents joining her at a shrine was common enough, but after her run-in with Rovol yesterday, somebody finding her alone made her queasy.

"You owe me ale. A travel keg, for sure."

She relaxed with a sigh, then twisted her neck to stare Jinbin in the eye. "You didn't clean a single chamber pot. Half, and I'll get it to you before the Eve of Snows."

He stepped in front of her, put his hands to his hips. "When did you make it back in? I never saw you." A brow raised over a squinting brown eye.

"I took another route." She hesitated, but she'd already trusted Jinbin with her secret exit. "There weren't any guard drills."

"There had to be, of some kind. Why else shut off upper Istinjoln?" The monk shifted his weight, but his eyes remained straight and steady, she didn't think he lied.

But admitting this tidbit of what she learned through her tardiness was as far as she would trust him. She wanted to tell him about the wagon, the lord priest and his strange procession, and in particular wanted to mention the inquisitor, but her heart pounded at the mere thought, and she couldn't. "I don't know, but I didn't see a thing. I was out there a long time, nothing at all happened."

She kept her gaze strong as he stared until his eyes drifted to the floor. "Hells if I know. Canceled? But hey, I didn't track you down for ale, word is an inquisitor is bringing a plucked falcon up through Petrin, could be reaching the gates any time."

Plucked falcon was a derogatory name given to children defiled by the feral magic of the Vanquished Gods, for the leather hoods tied tight over their heads, much like a falconer's bird without plumage. Jinbin had caught her watching the death march of feral children several times over the years and asked why. She concocted the fable of a defiled child setting the family home on fire, killing her parents, and it made her feel better to see the cursed herded to their deaths. It was a youthful lie, and good enough to cover her tracks, but now he let her know every time he heard an inquisitor's arrival.

He offered his hand, but she stood on her own. He was cute in his way, but she was tired of flirty men. They walked together through tunnels deep beneath the eastern edge of Istinjoln's walls, and the shortest route to fresh air opened with a view of Jinbin's favorite shrine: The brewhouse. The two-story brick and mortar building sat nestled with its back to the eastern wall, so esteemed that it had its own set of gates and four senior guardsmen on duty.

Jinbin planted his feet and stared, arms crossed. "I always imagine, when the guards have drills, that the brewhouse is their final redoubt." He grinned. "If I'd made the priesthood, I'd have been a brewer for sure."

Eliles snorted and walked toward the wall. Competition to work in the brewhouse was fierce, the most prestigious goal for any priest with modest talents, or as Dareun said, the best of the worst became brewmasters. "They may have let you strain the mash."

"Aren't you the hissing cat this morn."

Her brows scrunched, irritated with herself. "I'm sorry, you would've made a fine brewer."

"Godsdamned right, might not be much left! But it'd be good while it lasted."

They climbed to the allure. "Just how much you think you can drink, anyhow?"

He hooped his arms in front of his gut. "Don't underestimate me, girl, I swell like a tick. Swell. Like. A. Tick. And I don't go falling off the hound when I get full."

She giggled and shook her head. The man was foolish, but his humor was useful considering the torture she was about to put herself through. They rounded the wall's walk to the north until they stood a dozen paces east of and overlooking the stables, and took a position between two guards, leaning on the parapet. The bells of the gates rang as they arrived and Eliles' stomach tensed.

Over fifty years ago, in the four-hundred and fiftieth year of remembered time, Lord Priestess Sadevu decreed a reward of five-hundred songs for those who turned over any soul defiled by the Vanquished Gods. After attaining the mantle of lord priest, Ulrikt doubled this handsome bounty. The bounty her father thought to fetch upon discovering her powers.

The fate of the defiled children after entering the Tower of Sol was a mystery, but a good many spoke of it, anyway. The priests preached of cleansing these children of their taint, but no one could say for certain they had ever met one of these saved souls.

One woman in the kitchens claimed that Lord Priest Ulrikt cleansed her with his touch, but Eliles could sense her lie: She was a nobody seeking to stand out, to be special in any way she could, and Eliles couldn't fault her. Most agreed that those children whose souls were too darkened by the feral magic to be cleansed were killed, but the horrifying stories of this road to death varied from one person claiming knowledge to another.

They spoke of tortures, whips and fire, flesh-eating beetles and barbed iron, tongues and eyes scorched and mutilated, castration, the list flashed through her memories as her breath shuddered. Most stories agreed upon only one thing: Inquisitors cast them into a deep oubliette, their falls broken by the remains of those who'd gone before. The fortunate died without making a noise, the rest suffered. Wailing, screaming, praying until their bodies became the next layer of bones.

Eliles had heard their screams in more dreams than she could count. She ran, trying to find them, save them, but every nightmare ended the same: A long fall broken by bones and rotting flesh, surrounded by centuries of their collective screams. She could hear the haunting cacophony now, and she closed her eyes, inhaling deep to silence the phantoms.

"I'm not sure why you still do this. How many times, how many children?"

She returned to reality and shrugged at Jinbin's questions, but she knew the latter answers: Thirty-four and forty-two. But the why eluded her. The first time had only been a month after arriving to Istinjoln. After testing her feral magic on Dareun and getting caught he had dragged her out here to watch a hooded and bound child herded across the courtyard, to disappear into dark rumors from which no one returned, a stark reminder of her tenuous position among the devout.

Those first years every feral child who marched through Istinjoln was a reminder to be thankful for being alive, but in later years they became sources of sorrow, excuses to weep in the dark and lament the curse of the Vanquished Gods she suffered.

Now, they were just another burr in her boot to prove why she hated this place and these priests. She didn't need reminding of the evil and dark that hid in this house of the gods, she lived it every day, but here she stood again watching as an inquisitor garbed in black sauntered through the gates, his silver bracelets flashing in the sun as he led a rope tied around the hooded throat of an innocent youngster.

The child the monster led was no more than six, judging by height, and worse, wasn't alone. A second, and then a third, leather cowl followed, each with their hands bound and if tales were true, their tongues removed beneath those hoods. It was a banner day for this inquisitor. Eliles had never seen more than two children marching before and she forced her eyes closed, her fingers fidgeting, and her lips quivering.

Jinbin's hand squeezed her shoulder, and her eyes opened to stare at his boots, sorrow and anger choking the words from her throat. "Let's go."

He took her hand, and she followed without an argument.

Jinbin said, "I guess even revenge has its limits."

"Yeah. Yeah, I suppose so." But there would never be revenge, there was only survival.

THIRTEEN

The Baroque Pearl

Dozing numb steps on the tundra,
The merciless tyrant howls without lungs
And blows without mouth.
The wind? Why do I speak of the wind, you wonder?
A fine question, if only it were the wind of which I speak.
The tyrant long dead stands in vapors, blowing smoke
From long dead fires, seeing a future false,
Of rising again to conquer not one world, but a world caught
In a dizzying multifaceted gem.

—*Tomes of the Touched*

Twelve Days to the Eve of Snows

It attacked without warning, alighting upon Solineus' chest to interrupt his snore, its feet like rocks as it snuffled his fur-wrapped head. He eased blankets from his face, blinking into a morning sun that peeped through a gap in gray clouds while a small black goat pranced on his belly. The horned beast stared at him, then put teeth to the fur of his blanket to graze.

"Bad goat, bad." Kinesee grabbed the critter's horns and eased the animal to the ground. "This is my goat, Tengkur. She's a bit friendly. And hungry."

He glanced around, noted several men with nets slung over their shoulders in preparation for the day's fishing, while others hefted their dories over their heads to shamble toward the bay. Falling asleep while wrestling his lost past had been torture, but once sleep took him, it carried him to dawn. Solineus sat with a yawn and stretched with a groan, salty air filling his nose.

Kinesee patted him on the shoulder with a touch more gentle than she stroked her goat. "Gran'ma will let you sleep inside soon. Two days. A week at most."

"I reckon I should appreciate your optimism."

The youngster smiled. "I brought food, been waiting for you to wake up." She reached into a pouch at her hip and pulled out a bundle of boiled leaves. She unwrapped the contents with painstaking care, no matter that it'd been crushed.

He couldn't help but smile as he accepted the crumbling biscuit sandwiching fried eggs and took a bite. His eyes wandered as he chewed, watching as members of the family, men and women alike, carried fishing boats and gear to the sea.

The sun disappeared behind heavy clouds as he ate, and Kinesee prattled on about goats and chickens, but he paid little attention except to nod or smile now and again. His gaze shifted to the goat, and her slitted pupils captured his stare.

Tranquil moments passed without a thought until he caught himself muttering, "So who do you think I am, wee Tengkur? Holy man or trickster?"

"Sometimes we bring back clams and find pearls." The girl hadn't heard a word he said, and he was grateful. "We don't get to keep them, except the most baroque. That means oddly shaped. Papa lets me keep some of those! I've a secret stash."

Solineus smiled. "Pearls? Beautiful, no doubt."

She leaned in, glancing around to make sure no one listened. "I've got a special one. Don't tell Papa."

"I won't."

She whispered, taking pride in their clandestine conversation. "It glowed. When I rubbed it. Wanna see?"

He returned the favor of a whisper. "A magic pearl? Of course."

"Solineus! Help me with my boat?" One of the last to head for the Bay, Iku stood beside his dory, beckoning.

"We'll look at the pearl later." He leaped to his feet and rubbed the girl on the head, to the consternation of the goat, and trotted to help. It took five of them to carry the hand-hewn dory to the rocky shore and the weight of its planks made his shoulders ache and his thighs burn.

They flipped the craft into the water and Iku laughed as Solineus settled to the pebbled shore for a seat. "You're certainly no fisherman, but you'd grow used to the load in time."

Solineus rubbed his shoulders, grinning. "You should keep the boats closer to the water."

Iku shrugged. "Better to carry a dory than build a new one. Storms, thieves . . . and Migu Tortoise are thick in these parts. The males seem to think our boats are competitors for their breeding territory."

Solineus nodded rather than question the turtle story, but the look on his face must've betrayed his ignorance as Iku chuckled. Was he the victim of a joke, or not remembering a simple truth?

The men chucked their spears and nets into the hull. "We'll be out much of the day, unless the fishing is good."

"I'll sit here a moment, enjoy the sun."

The fishermen laughed, and Iku said, "If you know where the sun's at in those clouds, your eyes are better than your memory. Now help us shove off."

Solineus waded back to shore moments later to watch the dory bob into the bay. A tingle darted up his spine, and his heart raced. He surveyed the region. Peaceful. A dull knife struck his gut. He buckled and grabbed his belly, but there wasn't blood or blade.

Something's wrong.

He turned to the family home, his walk shifting to a dead sprint. "Kinesee, where is she?"

No one knew, and the dagger of premonition probed deeper into his intestines until he found Alu.

"I haven't seen her." The girl shrugged. "She wouldn't be far."

Solineus stared, panting in agony, and it unnerved the girl, her eyes growing wide as she backed from him.

"Her treasure. Where're the pearls?" The girl stared, and he realized he must appear a mad man. "Something is wrong. Run to the surf and yell for your father, but tell me where she hides the pearls."

"In a small cave in the roots of an oak by a stream, thousand strides or more northwest. There's a deer trail, follow it."

"Thank you." The pain faded. "Go get your father."

Solineus ran, scrambling over a steep outcropping to wade through waist-high grasses and brush. Bushes and small trees gave way to woods a hundred strides downhill, and he spotted a path. He hit the deer trail at a sprint, swiping branches from his face instead of slowing to duck and weave.

His senses heightened with the rush of blood through his veins, the fear of what he might find. Reality became a dazzling onslaught of waving branches and falling leaves, bird songs and fluttering wings, the scents of cedar sap and something days dead over a rise to the north. He caught every detail, a small footprint in the dust, a broken branch, and his ears zeroed on a gasp over the thundering beat of his heart. He stopped. She was close. He snagged a long branch from the ground and broke off a four-foot section over his knee.

The crack resounded, and a cry rang out in response. "Help!"

"Kinesee!" Stress and fatigue faded as he ran, the universe a vision of peculiar and impossible clarity. Her footfalls were drums in his ears, running his way as she screamed his name. She was not alone. The odor of sweat assailed his nose, and his ears caught the rushing breaths of runners in pursuit of his girl.

A headlong blond blur in wool came into view with dark shapes in pursuit. Blood streaked her face, but only scratches, and her hood hung from her cloak by a scant few threads. Solineus slid to a stop, and the girl hid behind his legs.

Four pursuers slowed and fanned out. Armed with a couple battered daggers, a sling, and a cudgel, they wreaked of whiskey-sweat and campfire. The bandit who stank least stepped forward.

"Lookee here, gents, someone else caught our bird."

Solineus' heart slowed. It was as if he hadn't been running, that he wasn't facing four armed men. The rhythm of his pulse told him he may as well be sleeping, but the world was life and death.

"See now, you can have fifths with our bird there, but we saw her first. Ol' Jolly here, he likes the jakes and the jennies, he don't care much. But you, you seem a man with girlish tastes."

The whir of the stone spinning in the air caught his ear, and he could've counted the silver speckles in its spinning face. Solineus slapped the sling-stone with a swing of his stick, sending it clattering through distant branches over the heads of the bandits.

"You should leave before the girl's father gets here."

The leader nodded. "The girl's father, yes. I suppose, a very dangerous man, yes?"

The bandits rushed him, except the slinger who kept his range.

Ten flickers of pure instinct.

He waited for the first to close, with his branch pointed low to the ground, until the timing was perfect. He came up and stepped into the blow, a heavy punch of jagged wood straight to the man's nose and face that left jagged slivers. Blood sprayed as the thug flew from his feet to land square on his shoulders.

Solineus took a half-step back and swung. The second man's dagger sailed from broken fingers as Solineus stepped into his path, locking his arm with his own as the branch deflected a timid cudgel strike. He wrenched the one man's arm breaking the elbow backwards, drove him to the ground, and struck a vicious stomp to his throat. The bandit with the cudgel struggled for footing in the undergrowth and Solineus' branch cracked his head, tumbling him to the turf.

He turned to the slinger with the branch held above his head in what a trickle of memory called the Sun Guard.

The ruffian blinked once and bolted.

Solineus looked to Kinesee. "Are you hurt?"

She shook her head with glazed eyes, stunned by the last few moments, and he didn't blame her. He wasn't sure what had happened himself, but whatever it was, dirty work remained.

One man lay unconscious, which became two with a solid rap to his head, but the leader . . .

"You"—he pointed his bloodied branch—"you should've listened."

The thug lay in the dirt, wiping blood from his eyes and fingers groping a shard of branch lodged in his cheek. He spit blood, frantic glances plying the woods. "Don't kill me, Lord of the Forge, please."

Solineus drove the branch into his chest, crushing the air from his lungs, then grabbed him by the ankle and dragged him to a log.

"Don't seem right to kill you, a raper of small girls. Rob a father of the chance to look you dogs in the eye? No. Look away, Kinesee."

When she averted her eyes, he lay the man's leg sideways over the log and drove the thug's calf into the dirt with his foot. The knee-joint crunched, and the leg didn't straighten again.

The man quivered and gasped, his eyes rolling into his head before falling unconscious.

Solineus collected the weapons and stood beside Kinesee, who sat with her back to the men, knees hugged to her chest. He sat cross-legged beside her without a clue in the world of what to say. Comfort? Reassurance? Concern? He found it discouraging that he understood how to hit people with sticks better than how to talk to a young girl.

"I'm sure your father will be here soon." She stayed silent. "Then you can go home, pet your goat, sit by the fire." She nodded, but it was her only reaction. He stared at his feet and rubbed his chin, stymied for words. "They didn't get your treasure, did they?"

"No, I got my pearls."

He clapped his hands, jubilant. "That's great! May I see them?"

She opened her clasped hands and revealed a leather bag, dumped pearls into her palm. "Papa gives them to us, the odd ones." A dozen misshapen pearls. She rolled them around with her fingers, showing them off.

"Those are beautiful! You have a great papa, Kinesee. Let's see if I can pick out the magic one." She grinned for the first time, and he leaned in close, squinting. Not a one looked so different to make it stand out, but he pointed. "This one."

Kinesee gasped and punched him in the shoulder. "How'd you guess?"

He lied. "I didn't guess, it's magic." He picked it up, tossed it in the air, caught it and rubbed before opening his cupped hands. His heart skipped a beat: The oblong pearl glowed. So much for lying.

"See! I told you! What kind of magic is it? Do you know?"

He stared at the dim pearlescent glow highlighting the cracks and creases in his hands. How his mind lost every damned moment of his life, and yet he understood this pearl vexed him to the core. It held no particular power, this glow nature had bequeathed, but it was a power he would mold.

He closed his hands around the pearl, concentrating, feeling the light of the pearl grow into warmth. A vision of him and Kinesee holding hands grew crystal clear in his mind and he sensed the impression sealed within the pearl's essence. The energy tugged on him, linking their souls.

"It is a very special pearl, Kinesee. If ever you're in danger, rub this pearl, and think of me, I will know to come. If I'm able, I will."

"Kinesee!" Iku and several men with spears in hand barreled into the clearing. The girl ran to her father and leaped into his arms.

"These men tried to take me. Solineus beat 'em with a stick!"

Solineus stood, the wonder of the pearl having made him forget that three men lay splayed across the clearing.

Iku glanced from the bloodied men, to Solineus, the bloodied branch by his side, and back again. "You took three men with a branch?"

"There were four! But he ran!" She giggled.

Solineus walked to Iku, and slipped the pearl into the girl's hand. "It's a fine stick."

Iku grinned, but his face turned sour when a bandit groaned. "They're alive? What should I do with them?"

Solineus took Kinesee from her father and held her tight. "I'll get her home safe, you do what your heart tells you right, to men who'd rape your daughter." He sensed the man's heart clutching and heat rising.

Iku nodded, and Solineus pushed the girl's head into his shoulder as he carried her home.

FOURTEEN

The Bloody Scholar

Dragons recognized Light the moment their eyes opened.
Its sight, its bite, its temper in the stoneless glow
Forged without hammer or tong
In the Foundations of Creation, speaking to the mighty to come, to see,
But Man? The mortal bones with sighted eye
Must live in Darkness abject before recognizing Light.

—Tomes of the Touched

Ten Days to the Eve of Snows

Morning in Ervinhin saw the first day the wardens donned their full armor. Ivin slipped on his wool gambeson and mail, and while most wore simple iron skullcaps with dangling nasal guards, Ivin settled a steel helm with solid nose and cheek guards over his head and a gorget around his neck. He secured his grandfather's targe with steel rim and brass boss to his back, tightened his sword belt, and stuck a long-hafted axe Pikarn gave him through its loop. The axe was similar to the pair the Wolverine and many of the wardens carried, with a bearded head and a steel spike at the end of the haft, which could serve as a weapon or a walking stick in ice and snow. The quality of his panoply was only rivaled by the Wolverine's, but when it came to keeping him alive, he didn't mind standing out.

They rode through the town's gates as the sun lit the horizon and it took a candle's ride between the rocky walls of the Omindi Pass to reach the sight of the killings, marked by a red steel post driven into the ground. Winds howled through the craggy ravine, kicking up a snow devil between two steep slopes riddled with shrubs, crevices, and boulders that afforded hiding places for ambush.

The patrol dismounted, half scattering up and down the road with bows in hand, while the remainder circled the perimeter. When retrieving bodies, earlier wardens had cleared a snowfall, and the winds had kept the floor of the ravine clear since, but patches of snow caked the cliff walls.

Pikarn said, "Keep your eyes open, look for anything out of the ordinary."

Ivin stayed at Pikarn's side as the man studied splashes of red paint, marking where the bodies fell. A garish map of death. Eighteen dead, one missing, while the dead messenger made it to Ervinhin to receive an escort home. One boulder sat marked by blood, but no paint.

"Our survivor fell here, maybe." Pikarn gazed at the scene, rubbing his bearded jaw.

Ivin said, "Likely enough."

The Wolverine turned, staring up at Ivin. "Think you're gonna see something I miss? No? Then get off my tail and look around."

Ivin slunk from him, picking a sheer face of rock to examine while pretending to know what he was doing. Sure as hells, it was stone all right. What, by the gods, was he supposed to be looking for? He made a swath as high as he could reach, brushing snow from the wall into a sun-twinkling cloud that speckled his face with nips of chill.

He squinted through the frozen cloud: Vertical scratches ran the length of the face. His fingers stretched to match the marks, but as large as his hands were, they didn't match. A Colok slid down the cliff, its claws slowing its decent, before moving in to kill the holies. With grim curiosity he swiped at the rocks with his cloak, higher, lower, and to either side. He found only the one set of marks.

He continued along the cliff face, wiping away snow, stopped. The uneven, pockmarked stone of the cliffs showed indentations he couldn't call natural. He matched his fingers to the dents, then removed his cloak and jumped, whipping it against the wall's heights.

He felt someone behind him. "What're you looking at?" Pikarn asked.

"I don't know." He pointed. "See those scratches over there?"

"Aye, rockslide maybe."

"They're like fingers scratching down. And over here, there're pocks in the walls, spaced to fit a man's hand. If my arms were longer, I might be able to climb up this face using these."

"A coincidence of nature. Nothin' more."

Ivin put his fingers next to one set of marks, pointed up. "There's another set up there, and over there. Left hand, right hand, left hand… like something dented the stone as it climbed."

The Wolverine laughed, but there was an unease in the tone. "Nothing could do that. Rinold! Look at these here dimples in the stone."

Rinold studied the rock face and rubbed the scar crossing his eye. "Even if a Colok made them scratches, them pips in the wall, no. Daevu wouldn't leave a mark." He grunted. "My guess is natural, but we're hunting somethin' we don't know already."

The company searched other escarpments but found nothing to tilt their opinion in either direction. Without additional clues to guide them, the Wolverine threw up his arms. "Rinold, anything you see I'm missing?"

The tracker spat. "Nah, hells, chances of finding any tracks here ain't good. Lotta wind and a scattering of snow over the last few days, looks to me."

Saddle leather groaned as the wardens mounted. "Take us to the second site, then."

"Long road or the goat trail?" Rinold grinned at the Wolverine's hard stare. "Someday you'll get adventurous; long road it is."

Rinold rode ahead, his head on a constant swivel from the ground to the stone bluffs, stopping here and there to dangle from his saddle, inspecting a mark or stone. After a while he veered onto a winding trail out of the Omindi. The climb was narrow and treacherous with rocks under hoof, switchbacking into the mountains, begging the question of what Rinold called a goat trail, but the horses navigated it well enough.

At the top they came to a miner's road, cleared of trees and boulders, and followed it northerly before it split and they took the path less beaten. Twenty wicks later they spotted a red stake poking from drifted snow filling a ravine.

"Son of a braggart-whoreson." Pikarn gnawed his jerky as he stood in his saddle, gazing west. "Winds and snows done us in here. How 'bout the mines?"

"Quicker maybe to backtrack, take the other fork, instead of fighting drifts."

The Wolverine grunted and reined his horse, turning back, but the choice proved a wise one. The western trail was windswept-clean, bare rock leading them as straight as a snake's wiggle to the Ihomjo mines. Several small buildings, tiny but sound enough to withstand snow and wind, stood beside the rectangular adit leading into the mountain. The camp looked abandoned at first, but several heads peeked out of doors to the clop of their horses' hooves.

A man with a broad smile met them. "Godsdamned glad to see you wardens, sure as hells. Fig Lundin's m'name."

Pikarn eased from the saddle, shaking the man's hand. "What word you got for me?"

Fig's smile faded. "We're alive, better than I can say for most everyone else."

"What happened?"

"We were deep in the mine, chipping stone, tryin' to get to them trapped, well, time came our supply train dried up, we had no idea why. We comes out to find every damned . . . everyone dead. Some fled for the Omindi and not a one made it, I hear."

Ivin asked, "Anything unusual since?"

"Nah, not that's killed no one, at least. A little priestess stumbled into camp two days back, half her scalp ripped from her head, and we nursed her back to health best ways we could. Meliu she calls herself, but the girl ain't right in the head, you ask me. Godsdamned haunting screams from the mountains now and again, but we ain't seen nothin'."

"A miner I know was working this hole in the ground, name's Ungar. Know him?"

"Aye, sure, but he weren't one of the lucky ones that been found."

Pikarn ripped a hunk of jerky with his teeth. "Take us to this holy."

Ivin, Modan, and Puxele joined the Wolverine in a sturdy shack lined with heavy furs and warmed by a smokeless fire, while the rest of the wardens took the horses into the mine's stables.

The priestess was near his age, Ivin figured maybe twenty. She huddled next to the fire in slashed robes, hair matted with blood. The miners did their best, but it was hard to hide the raw flesh where something tore her scalp back from her skull. Hands, knees, face, all bore bruises and scratches.

Pikarn nodded and Puxele slid beside the girl while taking a salve from her own pouch, then greased the girl's wounds with the yellow concoction. "Meliu, ain't it?"

The girl glanced at Puxele with glassy eyes before her gaze slipped back to the fire.

Puxele took the girl's hand, rubbing ointment on a cut. "Who did this to you?"

Meliu's lip trembled. "Angin."

Puxele pulled needle and thread from her pouch. "I can stitch you up better, the salve should dull the pain. A man did this?"

"My prayers will kill any pain." Her head bowed to let Puxele work. "A man once, but Taken by the Shadows."

"Awakened Dead?" Ivin asked.

"Not Awakened, possessed, by the Shadows who bleed from stone."

Possession stories were cautionary tales told by parents to keep children in their beds at night. No wonder Fig figured she was touched in the head.

"Bleed from stone, what's that mean?"

"When the Taken die the Shadows linger in the body, trapped. Not for long though. They seep into the stone with the blood, like water into dirt, then the blood bubbles back up, and the Shadows . . . they're free again."

Ivin's breaths were shallow and his gut tense enough to ache. "You priests couldn't kill them?"

"Some prayers killed, but not my prayers . . . not my prayers."

The Wolverine asked, "There was a messenger. Were you with him headed for Istinjoln? We counted nineteen dead."

"No." She kissed two fingers and placed them on her forehead. "I'm a scholar at the Crack of Burdenis; the Shadows attacked there. Guntar, the bearer, he made it, then?"

Pikarn said, "His pony brought him dead to Ervinhin, we counted him in the nineteen."

"Twenty left the Crack."

Ivin glanced to the Wolverine and Puxele, sharing a nod as they confirmed a missing holy, but the name, Crack of Burdenis, was something he'd never heard of. Whispers of a shrine hidden in the Omindi region weren't uncommon, but most passed it off as fancy. If true, it explained why Istinjoln fought against local mining operations. The notion of letting miners die to keep a shrine secret sickened him. "This Crack is a fifth shrine to Burdenis?"

"Yes."

"Hidden shrines and missing holies." Pikarn rubbed his face, staring with unreadable eyes. "Just where the hells did these Shadows come from? What are they?"

She shrugged. "I heard they appeared at the Crack's shrine deep in the caves a few weeks ago, but the priests contained them. Shadows, demons, don't matter where they came from or what they are, it's what they do. They take bodies and they kill. Kill that body, the Shadow comes back and takes another. The books, I left so many books behind." Tears welled in her eyes.

Pikarn snorted. "You need to take us to this shrine. There any priests left in this hole in the ground?"

A cackling, mirthless laugh erupted from the girl's throat, short-lived before she stared into the fire. "When I got out of the caves, I didn't see a soul, neither priest nor Shadow on my way out. I'll take you there on two conditions: Any books we find are mine, and you don't let the Shadows take me. Kill me first."

Her conviction to die before possession convinced him of how real and terrifying old fire-side tales had become.

"What do you think, Choerkin?"

Ivin met Pikarn's gaze, heart racing. Leaving might be the better choice, but there was an opportunity staring him in the face. "I'm with whatever you decide." He didn't doubt which direction the Wolverine would take.

"You'll lead us there tomorrow."

Meliu smiled at Ivin. "Worst case, I guess, is I die while feeding a Choerkin to Shadow or Taken."

Ivin grinned, hoping not. Best case, he found a common enemy to unite Clan Choerkin and Istinjoln.

Pikarn grabbed his shoulder and took Ivin outside, huddled against howling winds. "She don't like you much; normally I'm the blood they want. What's your take?"

"We want mining rights and cooperation; they want this shrine's location kept quiet and safe. Might be we find a fulcrum for leverage here."

"You're a godsdamned optimist like your mother."

Ivin wondered if he was as much like his mother as folks said, or if it just sounded good. "Something's making me twitchy, too. Demons and possession and death, but she's right willing to lead us to the Church's secret for what, a book?"

"Your old man's blood. I was thinking the same: What's she really after?"

Ivin shook his head. "She's going back for a book. Question is, what kind of book makes a person risk death or worse to retrieve it?"

"I ain't givin' two shits for no book, but we need into those caves."

Ivin glanced at the Wolverine, an inflection in those words left him wondering if the old man withheld the Name of a Slave, then wondered if the slave's name was Ungar. Ivin opened his mouth, but licked his lips rather than speak, deciding to leave the man's secret at peace.

Pikarn offered him jerky after snatching a hunk with his teeth. "You believe this horseshit about demons taking folks' bodies?"

Ivin declined the meat. "After what you've shown me, yeah, I'd say I have to take the girl at her word. Either way, we'll know tomorrow."

FIFTEEN

Archival Con

Fading pages in the storehouse of time,
Drowning wisdoms in waves of self-preservation,
Saving by destroying, for a time, a time sublime.
Will Lime cover the stench of death
Before the Brimstone of living uncovers the end again?

—*Tomes of the Touched*

Nine Days to the Eve of Snows

Eliles focused her thoughts on Guntar and the oversized priest, distracting her from the screams of the defiled in her dreams. The bearer was beyond any help outside of prayer, much like the feral children, but her curiosity was fierce and it gave her restless mind a mission. It'd been three days since the inquisitor's threats, time enough for the bastard to maybe forget her a little, and time enough for rumors to swirl.

With a lord priest as large as their visitor, she started in the kitchens. The hall stretched forty paces, with vaulted ceilings twenty high, and housed ten hearths chiseled from the world's stone with their smoke rising through bedrock to pump through chimneys in Istinjoln's outbuildings.

Cooks and servants scurried between tables and cauldrons, going about their chores in the heat of blazing fires. The yeasty scent of fresh-baked bread was a favorite since childhood, so her presence here brought greetings rather than questions. She sat beside a fire, using the light to pretend to read a book while snacking on a buttered roll.

Rumors were a kitchen staple like potatoes and pork, and as often overcooked. She'd heard tales ranging from husbands who strayed to the stockyards instead of the neighbor's wife, to heinous murders covered up by the highest powers of the Church, not to mention whispers of a girl with prayers so powerful the gods must've blessed her in the womb.

She couldn't guess how much grain alcohol a man needed to mistake a cow for a woman, and monks did disappear without a trace (she assumed most fled this horrible place), but the girl chosen by the gods she knew was a lie.

The cackle and banter of cooks and servants, all of whom lived in a small village a half-candle's walk from Istinjoln, always changed with the coming of the Eve of Snows, but this year they had a dead priest, a bearer no less, to prattle about. Many spoke of war with the Colok and how the wicked man-bears took to eating people. The snaggle-toothed cook and his wife said there'd be no end to the feast now they got a taste for man.

The message might concern Colok, so she noted it, but it didn't explain the Broldun.

Most gossip centered on the celebration itself. The amount of provisions had the kitchen-folk in a snit. Half a hundred kegs of ale— cleaning up after so many drunken holies assaulted their imagination with mops and vile reek. Four score of hogs; there weren't enough spits. The fires would burn nigh every flicker of the day to bake the bread, wasted kindling. with winter coming on. These holiday chores piled on top of the normal day-to-day tasks were a thankless burden.

Not to mention, where the Twelve Hells were guests enough to eat this bounty going to sleep? Let alone draw hot water for baths? The question lurking behind every complaint: Why was this Eve of Snows special? No one recalled so many guests before.

Every tidbit raised Eliles' suspicions, but answered nothing.

Lord Priest Dunkol didn't escape without hushed words and jokes, however. They labeled him a high priest in error, and when maids first took food to his chambers they witnessed the priest and several young servants disrobed.

Those were the polite words, anyway. Since then the rotund Broldun sent his people for food and wine while the entire kitchen sniggered at the low priest and his tastes in food. The ribald and oft times sacrilegious comments built until the kitchen burst into thunderous laughter that made her blush. Whatever important matters might be at hand, she couldn't conceive of how they had to do with candelabras and mouse pie, so she tried her best to bury her nose in her book during these moments.

She did learn the lord priest stayed with his entourage in the southern wing of the keep. The well-traveled tunnels she knew risked running into the inquisitor. The Keep's tunnels, expansive and littered with stairs and alcoves, offered her the chance to get close without arousing suspicion. But for what gain? Confirmation of his sexual appetites? He wasn't the only adherent who enjoyed carrots and cake, in the words of the rumor mill, and it mattered naught to her.

She was two weeks from escaping this dreadful place, to risk dying for a glimpse of a giant, naked… She giggled at herself. The kitchen banter had worn off on her.

She slipped from the kitchens with a grin despite her frustration. Whatever direction she took, safety was her priority. Dareun had acknowledged the visiting lord priest, but her prying earned her a "Januel's wit, girl. Stay away from those people," followed by his fatherly cluck. When she mentioned Guntar she had received a hug, not information.

One object in the monastery held the solution to the mystery she'd built in her head: the message itself, and it wouldn't care one lick about giving up its secrets if only she could get her hands on it… if it was still in one piece. Fire was a great keeper of secrets.

Woxlin splashed into the whirlpool of her thoughts; he might still hold the scroll.

The high priest worked to impart the impression as a kind man, handing out treats to young postulants on holidays, but she knew nothing of him, except he'd achieved the high priesthood young, and disrespected her friend's body. A callous behavior, but he was under orders and in a hurry.

Was she making excuses for the man? Sometimes she made herself mad that way. He wasn't a good man. No one ascended to the high priesthood/priestesshood as a gentle soul, not even the pretty Demilu. Many young postulants simpered after her charming smile to find themselves humiliated. Honif followed the woman's every prayer session like a pathetic hound before earning five lashes for sniffing around the wrong places.

Wait. Sniffing around the wrong places.

Woxlin was a high priest only ordained a few months back; Lord Priest Ulrikt would receive important messages worthy of ignoring her friend's corpse. If true, archivists preserved it for history in the libraries, like transcripts of prayer sessions headed by the lord priest.

She tucked her book under an arm and walked with a mission. The library. And in the library, Rovol. The hairs of her neck raised on goosebumps; she wanted nothing to do with the cretin after their last run-in, but as she'd heard many a time in the kitchens, a man with his brain dangling between his legs can be useful.

Eliles couldn't help the smile lighting her face. Snooping might be more fun than she ever imagined, in particular if heaped with an extra helping of payback.

The first chamber she passed was the Hall of Scribes, which held rows of desks where monks buried their noses in tomes, copying texts all day so books from this library might travel to other holy sites. She didn't envy these poor folks, but it wasn't the worst task in Istinjoln. She figured that honor went to the muckrakers, who not only cleaned the dining halls, stalls, and privies, but turned the steaming compost piles. Scribes were bored, but fat and happy compared to those folks.

Directly past the arching entry to the Scribes stood the library postulants browsed, a small chamber with a dozen rows of shelves filled with innocuous books, full of accepted teachings and histories, fables to instruct the young. She eased past the rows, glancing down each to make sure she was alone, then headed for a square-legged desk in the back of the library where Rovol stood alone.

She sauntered to the archivist's desk and leaned on the polished cedar, her hood pulled low, forcing Rovol to lean in to see who she was. The man's brows were so bushy it was hard not to look at them instead of his dark eyes.

At the sight of her, the caterpillar on his brow creased into an ugly "V" rising above a smirk. "Eliles. You come to say you're sorry?"

"I came to let you apologize." She smiled, and as she did, she wondered what he saw. What changes to her features did the dweomer cause? When she allowed feral magic to flow, people saw in her a reflection of a woman for whom they bore a weakness: a daughter, a wife, a lost love, or whatever opened their emotions and pinched their vulnerabilities.

The wicked in his grin softened with mirth more than kindness. "You're a bold tease."

She leaned in and spoke in breathy tones to accentuate his vision while hoping it wasn't his mother he saw. "I've got an itch of curiosity, one I'd like you to scratch." She took a deep breath and went full kitchen banter on him. "Rub my belly and make me purr, and I'll do more than forgive you."

He eyeballed her, uncertain what the hells she was up to. He wasn't turned stupid yet, but he weakened. "I'm listening."

"I purr, you purr, we meow like cats in the stable until morning prayers." *And chase rats for breakfast? What is all this foolishness?* She giggled to herself while keeping as sultry a look as she knew how.

He licked his lips as he flushed. "Ah . . . hells . . . just what is this itch?"

She giggled. Men. Where was the challenge? "Are important messages sent to Istinjoln archived here?"

"Only the lord priest's. You mean the lord priest's?"

"I'm a real naughty kitty."

His head rested in his hand and he slumped so low he looked up at her. Time spent in the kitchens paid off. Well, that and feral magic. She whispered, her intent to force him closer more than secrecy. "The message Guntar carried, is it here? I'd take a little peep, nothing more."

"Oh no, no. I can't take you back there, they'd flog me or throw me to the thorns."

She recognized the trance fading and pulled out the verbal molasses. "Oh, sweetie, no. I wouldn't ask that. Never." Not that a few thorns in his ass would hurt her feelings any. "Just slip it out, a glance is all I need."

The look on his face said success, she thought, but no, she was wrong. "I'd have to slip through your chastity before I'd even consider it."

Tales from the kitchen had prepared her for this, but her stomach squirmed at his words even as she played it off. "You can slip anything you want if you copy it for me. Please?"

His eyes glazed, and she swore he drooled before swiping his lip. "Okay, right, sure." He searched beneath the desk until he came up with a stretch of parchment and a quill, stuffed them up the loose sleeve of his robes. "I'll be right back, honey-cat." He disappeared into the dark recesses of the library with a life to his step she'd not seen before.

She giggled behind his back, and muttered, "Honey-cat? Goodness." A part of her wanted to pity him a smidgen, but his vulgar behavior didn't allow it. She pulled her hood over her face and skulked to the shadows. She wanted only Rovol to see her because he wouldn't remember for long.

The archivist returned, sliding the rolled scroll across the table with a lascivious wink and smack of the lips. "Not much to it."

"You're positive it's the right one and complete?"

"As right and complete as you and me gonna be, honey-cat."

She wanted to set his nose on fire, but she smiled and pulled her hood so tight he wouldn't see her face. "Mmm, perfect, sweetie. Now, forget my being here, our entire conversation, and everything on this scroll."

His face went pale and blank as she turned and walked away.

He called out behind her. "Could I help find something for you?"

She shook her head and kept walking, not stopping until she reached an alcove dedicated to Januel, one of Eliles' favorites, with diamonds set in the ceiling to mimic the constellation of the Heart of Januel. It lay deep in the caves, yet was always well lit for the studious. Rovol's hurried writing was atrocious and hard to decipher.

Your Eminence, Lord Priest Ulrikt,

This morning advanced our knowledge of the Fire-Lion Gate, but the results are less than hoped. We lack the Devotion to force our prayers through the Gate while the Shadows remain. They are dark and deadly, taking the killed to live and die again. Without the Power, true success could bring disastrous failure.

The Codex spoke of knowledge from the Sunken Catacombs to achieve our goal, but time runs short. Another artifact arrived from the Ximfwa mausoleum while they explore the Cimdine as we speak. But word is the unnamed crypt, the last of those suspected to hold the Sliver, is blocked by the Wakened Dead. We will attempt the Gate again soon. Our numbers dwindle as we contain the Shadows, but we are hopeful the prophecy rings true, that this artifact will empower our prayers with knowledge and faith to reach Sol with our collective voice.

We have failed. They've breached the Gate. Destroy this place. The Shrine of Burdenis is our tomb.

Eliles read it a dozen times, the words made sense, but what they spoke of eluded her. First, she suspected code within the passages, a common practice. The constellation known as the Fire Lion shown in the sky now as a symbol of Sol, but in hundreds of candles of studies, she'd never heard of a gate named after the constellation. A gate associated with Sol next to a shrine to Burdenis, the Patron of Snows, was nonsensical. Shrines often had gated entries, but never named for another god. It meant something else, she was sure.

As for the Shrine of Burdenis, a rumored shrine stood near Istinjoln and spoken of in hushed tones. They studied the locations of one hundred and twenty-two major shrines to the Pantheon of Sol, but the Crack of Burdenis, which held the Fifth Shrine to this god, remained hidden. Some claimed it was a repository of forbidden lore involving foreign gods while others claimed it was the private retreat of the lord priests of Istinjoln. Either way, the location was a secret few knew.

The Wakened Dead made sense, but Shadows? Nobody knew what power restored the dead to walk the world, whatever it was it wasn't visible, not a shadow. Possession? Rare and frightful tomes spoke of this corruption, but if true, the Fire-Lion's Gate was a celestial gate opened into the heavens, or from the sounds of it, some place far worse. Celestial gates were forbidden by the Church, Master Dareun spoke of them as unintended for the mortal realm.

The slap of leather shoes echoed in the hall so she rolled the parchment in haste, stuffed it in her cloak, threw her hood back, and opened her book. A cowled priestess walked past with a glance and nod, but didn't take a second note of her.

Did she dare show the scroll to her master? No, she should destroy it. The prudent choice, but she couldn't force herself to do it. Hide the parchment, hold it safe, just in case. *In case of what?* she chided herself. *In case they need more evidence to sunder my soul?* No one knew, not even the fool who copied it. She was safe.

Sixteen

Lesser Theologians

Frozen toes burning low,
Frostbit bone sling slung sing and sung,
A desperate weapon, a rapier carved from your leg
Lunged through the heart of your enemy,
A stiletto from your rib plunged from your lover's heart
But you never die, at eternity's infinity end,
Your death a splintering into lives you'll never remember.
Forgotten.

—*Tomes of the Touched*

Eleven Days to the Eve of Snows

The first day, Tokodin determined he'd die instead of helping the Colok. The searing pain radiating from his shoulder factored into the decision more than noble sacrifice.

The second day he became convinced he'd live forever and soar above the mountains alongside the great eagles. He gnawed on too much Pimun Bark that day while trying to kill the pain, feeding hallucinations which didn't fade until evening. He vomited for a couple candles after, black and greasy, and the pain returned with a vengeance.

The next time he woke, he wasn't sure what year it was, let alone which day. He coughed and belched when he sat up, and terrified, ran for a corner of the cave. Dry heaves.

Mecum's lips screwed tight. "I warned you not to chew so much."

"It hurt."

"Worse than now?"

It was funny, hungover and miserable he often wished to die, now the opportunity was real, he wanted nothing more than to live. He spit in the chamber pot and sauntered back to the fire, trying his best to walk with a straight back. His head thrummed.

"Third day, isn't it? I'll tell you what,"—he grabbed a cup of noxious tea, slurped the lukewarm concoction—"I'll choose to live if you tell me what the Twelve Hells this is about."

"Choose to live, and you find out. Elsewise, ask your guide upon the Road."

A frustrating old man, that's what Mecum was. "Dice for it?" He pulled the bones from his robe pocket, shifted them in his left hand and squeezed. The dice clacked as he exercised his grip and dexterity, rotating them in his palm.

"Even a sucker fish needs better bait."

The night die slipped past his weak pinky and bounced across the rocky floor, coming up six. He swept it up with his right hand. "Damned to hells." The hand showed improvement, but still had a long way to go.

He considered throwing the dice again, to determine his fate, but reprimanded himself. He tried to let the dice decide a hundred times, but no matter their answer he wasn't happy with it. Live. Die. Day. Night. Over. Under. The pips only teased him.

His father had beat fear out of him as a boy, from the age of five he no longer feared the night or death. Istinjoln beat terror back into him. A bump in the night could be a *cithræl* coming to feed on your flesh, to take your body while sending your soul to one of the Twelve Hells. He'd more than once witnessed the body of a villager whose spirit had traveled on, rise to take revenge upon the living, a sign the soul had fallen to the Malignant's Hell while walking the Road.

The Wakened Dead were a strong reminder that death wasn't always an escape from the pain of living. And if he died here, in some dark cave, he'd doom another. What fate would await him while walking the Stars?

"The Slave Fields? The Twelve Hells?" Mecum's perplexed gaze assured Tokodin that the priest wasn't a mind-reader. "If I choose to die, which do I deserve?"

"Ah! I see. Not a bad theological debate." He scratched his chin. "The Third Hell, I'd imagine."

The old priest had gone too far. "The Coward's Hell! I—"

"Cowards and those unwilling to sacrifice, you recall. Arguably you'd fit both."

Mecum's tongue darted between his lips and he smiled, too satisfied with himself for Tokodin's taste. The Coward's Hell was a place of tortuous horrors to harden the soul before eventual atonement in the Slave Fields, his spirit rent and fed in pieces to the Nine-Faced Hound for a thousand years; the notion made him queasy.

His father would look low on his fear of death, the more so the fear to live. If here he'd add more scars to his face.

"I'd argue the path of conviction across the Stars. Dying to not aid the enemy."

Mecum smirked. "It might be argued, if the Colok are the enemy."

Tokodin bit the not-so-subtle bait. "If those threatening my life aren't the enemy who is?"

"Live and find out."

"There's a hell for the curious, too."

Mecum coughed, struggled to speak through the phlegm. "Only if"—he spat—"the curiosity results in sin."

Tokodin stared at his dice and gave them a toss. The Four-eyed Snake, a gambler's term for four ones, stared back at him. It had to mean something, didn't it? That was the problem with signs from the gods, they relied upon mortal interpretation.

"Life, it is."

The words echoed once before a Colok landed in front of him, damned near scaring his decision to a moot point. Tokodin stared into the darkness above. How many more Colok were up there?

"Good."

The growl still unnerved him, but he tried to keep his calm in the face of Zjin, Grolkan's son and apparent heir. He was at least nine and a half feet tall, with white fur patterned by gray swirls similar to a snow leopard. Tokodin mused that he would make an exquisite rug.

Zjin handed him a scroll. The broken wax seal, a black six-pointed star, indicated it'd been intended for Lord Priest Ulrikt.

"What's this?"

"The scroll I carried. Go ahead, read it. I won't live long enough to tell anyone of your sin." The old priest laughed.

Tokodin's heart quaked as he unfurled the aging vellum.

Your Eminence, Lord Priest Ulrikt,

Progress into the Lumhare crypt has been slow, while continued exploration of the Simdobwa Wing proved fruitless, despite discovery of false walls. We flooded this failed wing soon after, as Wakened swarmed from an open burial site. Entry to four additional crypts that fit the Codex's description has been secured. How many dead we might encounter in each horrifies us. Swarms can count into the thousands when they rise from the waters. We've no option but to fall back until they recede and hope our dead aren't already walking.

The crypts are marked Ximfwa, Cimdine, Komdwom, and Extek. A fifth is unmarked by a name, and the dead are numerous and sentient. We'll need additional priests and supplies to make headway in this quarter. The Golden Conch may be our best and only hope. If there is any chance of its retrieval, an agreement, perhaps? That might prove our success and victory.

Our scholars grow confident the Sliver of Star is somewhere in the aforementioned crypts. If the city of the dead is calm, we hope to walk from here well before Year's Turn of 501.

This place is a favored piece of the Malignant's Hell.

The message went on to name deceased guards, monks, and priests, over fifty, then transitioned into a requisition list, including rope, lanterns, bolts of cloth, weapons, axes for hewing wood, and unusual quantities of oil.

He recognized several names of the deceased; official word said they'd left Istinjoln to attend a variety of holy sites. Lies which kept those who cared for the deceased from praying for their souls.

Tokodin glared. "Plundering graves and hiding the deaths of the faithful? What the hells is this all about?"

Mecum couldn't look him in the eye. "I started running messages from the Steaming Lakes in the Spring of four-ninety-eight." He coughed and spat. "There've been expeditions up there for decades looking for artifacts and treasure, but in four-ninety-eight they set up a permanent camp. I didn't know it then, but they looked for this Sliver of Star, whatever the hells that is."

"You're going to sit there and tell me you know nothing?"

"Shut up and listen, boy. I don't know much, but it's more than you're gonna find anywhere else. I caught snippets of conversations 'tween High Priest Bulsvon and his lessers. What I heard I kept to myself; it sounded exciting at the time, but after what I've seen? Anyhow, it all ties into the Ailing Stars Prophecy and the Codex of Sol."

Tokodin swallowed hard. He'd grown up believing the Ailing Stars Prophecy a legend, or a lie fabricated by Lord Priest Imrok Girn in the Fourth Year of Remembrance, four-hundred and ninety-eight years ago. The Prophecy spoke of the gods returning to the world in order to establish the Church as a theocracy destined to rule the world.

"Nonsense."

"The Ailing Stars, the Dark Sword, two prophecies claiming the Church will establish a Pantheonate. You ask me, Ulrikt is working damned hard to make these come true."

Would it be so wrong? Shouldn't the priests entrusted with the word of the gods be in charge of the lives of their faithful? But the cost in lives, a Holy War would bleed the island of a generation or more.

"What's all this to do with the Shadows from the Stone?"

"Ah! You've heard of them, have you? Shadows don't kill, they possess. They aren't Wakened. Their hearts beat Shadow-blackened blood, they die much like men, but the Shadow returns to take another."

"These possessed, they feed on the dead?"

Mecum grimaced. "Even on each other. Grikarn took me to see, the things sat around gnawing on each other, themselves."

Tokodin's stomach turned. "They want me to betray the Church. Tell the Choerkin, why?"

"They call it Zwimfokum. They fear Ulrikt will summon this beast from the land of Shadow."

Tokodin remembered the bodies in the Omindi, the empty sockets of the miner's eyes. "If you're so convinced, why didn't you go to them when you were healthy?"

"With one scroll and conjecture, what proof? They'll take you to the Steaming Lakes, so you can see the camp yourself, maybe get a glimpse of something you can use." The old priest hacked and gurgled, the sound of drowning in his own phlegm.

A dark-furred Colok trotted into the cave, excited. Snarls, growls, and hand gestures passed between the newcomer and Zjin.

"What's happening?"

"Shush, I'm trying to figure it out."

Zjin turned to them, a snarl twisting his lips. "Time."

Mecum bowed his head. "We've run out of time. The scout says they're breaking camp at the Steaming Lakes."

"They've found the sliver?"

"Seems so. When the Colok locate wardens, they'll take you to 'em."

Tokodin slipped from his stone perch to the ground, burying his face in his hands. Defying the Church could condemn his soul to the Slave Forges. But what if Ulrikt betrayed the gods in the name of personal power? How many lives could he save?

Zjin and the other Colok walked from the cave, speaking to one another and Mecum's eyes darted and he ducked, reaching into a boot to produce an engraved silver flask. He handed it to Tokodin.

"What's this?"

"It's poison. Shush. It ain't my idea to help the godsdamned Choerkin. Maybe the Colok are right, maybe not."

"What—"

"Shut up, you peccant mooncalf. It ain't much, but it'll kill you if need be, you get me? I don't need no help getting out of this world no more, but you might. Turns out you're betraying the will of the gods…" He nodded with a wink.

Tokodin slipped the flask into his cloak next to his dice and squelched any questions as the Colok returned.

The notion horrified him, but he understood his predicament. Better to die able to navigate the Road of Living Stars than betray the gods and plummet into the hells. He stood at a moral impasse, to die rather than betray his gods, or live to stop a revered lord priest from doing the same.

SEVENTEEN

Sling Swing Wasting Whiskey

The righteous song rings sure in the ears,
the certain believer, the severe beleaguered.
Do your eyes believe what your ears tell you?
More a fool than I. No small feat.
Trust not the song your eyes see in the chamber of echoes.

—*Tomes of the Touched*

Nine Days to the Eve of Snows

Solineus' soul rolled on pellucid blue waves like a stretch of seaweed riding the surf. The roils warmed and soothed, lulling him into meditative peace.

"Hello, my love."

"You warned me?"

"Saving the girl earned the family's trust." The woman's smile was an ideal of beauty and sincerity. "Our presence resulted in her risk—"

"'Our' presence?"

"I am with you always, in my way."

"Then we got three men killed."

Her smile turned sardonic. "No men, those, and hardly missed. The girl is important, or she will be."

"You know the future?"

Her long blond hair danced in the swirling blue universe. "There are likelihoods."

"The surviving raper—"

"Is not a concern." The lady appeared in front of his face as the distant vision faded, and she lay a finger to his lips. Her touch was hot, yet sent chills down his spine. "You will receive a gift. You must leave this family and reach Istinjoln before the Eve of Snows."

Eve of Snows, a celebration on the autumnal equinox coming up on the twenty-fifth of Yistole. He'd heard of this while staying with the family. "On your word alone?"

The woman's smile curled. "I gave you a name, led you to rescue the girl, and still you do not trust me?"

"Tell me your name."

"For the girl or for you?"

The woman knew his promise to Kinesee. "You want me to trust you."

"Travel to Istinjoln, or stay. Only by leaving can you save these girls. Do as I ask, and the girls have a chance, and someday you may tell her my name."

He wanted no part in this woman's plan. "I'll consider whatever you have to say."

"There is a road to the north, journey there and wait for Ears the Elder to carry you to Istinjoln. Once there, you must kill Lord Priest Ulrikt before the Eve of Snows. Fail, and we must find another way."

Solineus awoke with a start, eyes locked on shadows dancing on the ceiling in the Koest home. Kill a man he'd never heard of to save the girls. *I'm not an assassin.*

It was dark outside but the hearth in the family home burned bright. Solineus sat with a yak-pelt from his makeshift bed wrapping his shoulders. Iku prodded the flames with a stick, and satisfied, tossed it into the embers.

Iku said, "You are leaving us. A woman whispered it so, in my dreams. You truly are God-touched."

Solineus scoffed, but right or wrong the conclusion became harder to dismiss. "She spoke to you?"

"She said you'd save my daughters, and even if you could not save me, you will free me. Do you know what she meant?"

"No." Solineus leaned into the fire until the pleasant warmth became hot enough to sear away the cobwebs of sleep. "She told me to find a place called Istinjoln."

"A monastery, farther to the north than I've traveled. Be wary." Iku snorted at the choice in destination. "I've a gift for you." He lifted a longsword clad in a plain leather sheath from the ground. "My great-grandfather fought beside the Choerkin and they honored him with this weapon."

"I don't deserve an heirloom."

Iku tapped the guard. "If he ever knew how to use a sword, not a soul in this family has a hint these days. It may as well be a stick. Though perhaps I always underestimated sticks." He offered the hilt, and when Solineus hesitated he struck the hammer blow. "Save my girls."

Solineus smiled and took the sword, flattered but uncomfortable with the man's confidence. *Am I a father, too? Do I have children, missing me?* No other words were acceptable for a father. "I will." The simple wire-wrapped grip fit his hand well, but instead of examining the blade he slung the belt over his shoulder. "I should wait, say my goodbyes to the girls."

Iku shook his head, handed him a waterskin, a sleeping roll, and a sheepskin haversack. "Hard rolls, jerked chicken, enough to see you through a couple days. I don't want to tie my girl down to keep her from following you come dawn."

The lady played her game well. He didn't understand every ramification of killing a lord priest, but one would be a price on his head. The task sounded daunting, if not impossible, but if indeed the lady knew the future, he needed to try.

They clasped forearms, mutual nods their final communication before Solineus walked into the chill predawn air. He wanted to turn around, to wake the girls and say his farewells, but their father was right. A cloud of breath caught the moon's light as he huffed and turned north, long strides hastening an end to the urge to double-back.

The moon traveled the sky and disappeared before sunrise. He came upon a wagon-grooved dirt road a half candle after dawn. It cut through tall brown grasses and spruce shrubs and sported battered thistles on the strip of dirt between ruts. He took a seat on a rock too small to be comfortable, but preferable to the ground.

The sun was full on the horizon when the clangor of metal on metal rattled him from his thoughts. The surprise brought a chuckle. Large ears appeared over the rise of the road, giving way to a shaggy two-donkey team pulling a wagon, its bed converted into a box to store goods. Whatever the wagon held banged and rattled with every bump and sway.

Solineus hailed the driver and smiled as they stopped strides in front of him, the big man setting the wheel-break. Solineus eyed the team, one donkey more grizzled. "And you must be Ears the Elder."

The man's girth betrayed his appetite, but his broad leather belt held two knives unsuited for the dinner table. Easy to take him as a soft man, considering his plump round face and extra chins, but the determined squint to his eye spoke of grit. "You know us?"

"No, but a friend suggested you might see me to Istinjoln."

"How the hells . . .?" The man spat on the road. "Who sent ya?"

"A woman, don't know her name. I might be handy if the din of your passing attracts the wrong sort."

"Thieves round about these parts are a cowardly lot. Still, they been thicker than normal of late." The man squinted, licked his lips as he eyed the sword over Solineus' shoulder. "Know how to use that damned thing, do ya?"

"I might."

"A hungry rat is less likely to steal from two dogs than one, if you take my meaning." Air trilled between his teeth. "See to not pokin' me with it, and I might see you to Istinjoln, by way of Choerkin Fost. Fast a route as any."

"A fair bargain." Solineus rubbed the donkeys between their ears before vaulting on the wagon with hand proffered. "Solineus Mikjehemlut."

"Ilpen Gurer, tinker by trade."

Solineus felt the glow of Kinesee's pearl in his veins as the wagon pulled away. It tugged his heart, calling him back, but he knew the emergency was a young girl wanting her new friend. He smiled, bemused at how a girl could gain hold of his feelings in such a short time. Despite not knowing if she could hear him, he closed his eyes and projected a single thought: *Don't worry, girl, I'll be back when you need me.*

"What by the gods sends you to Istinjoln?"

"I could ask the same."

The man laughed, a sign of joviality to come. "S'pose so. I met a young girl, not far from this road. An orphan. I couldn't leave her to the winter, so I brung her to Istinjoln, where an old priest I know prays. She's lived there since, and I visit each year." The man glanced at him. "You don't look so much the holy type. Despite your name."

"No. Not hardly." His gut squirmed as he searched for a lie, so he told something approaching the truth. "Someone told me to go, so I will. A voice in a dream, and I know, sounds crazy."

Ilpen snorted, leaning over his belly to release the wagon's break. "No more crazy than I've heard afore. The girl, well . . . never mind. Just rest assured I won't judge a man crazy over quick."

They shared a chuckle as the wagon rattled and bounced along the road.

Solineus learned much of the man over the next several candles. How Ilpen's wife sat at their home to the west with their only surviving son, his two other children dead from consumption, a boy and a girl.

Ears the Elder, as it turned out, was once Ears the Younger, until the eldest passed on. For more than thirty years the man only owned donkeys named Ears, way back to the original, now called Ears the Exceedingly Ancient and Deceased.

Solineus, Ilpen, and the donkeys met few travelers on the road until they reached a dirty village the locals named Red Rock, but Ilpen called Bloody Pebble. It was evening, and the tinker greeted several folks seeking his wares, so Solineus hopped to the dusty street and stretched his legs. Two dozen buildings hammered together from skinnier trees than ideal and roofed with bark lined a single dirt street, homes and businesses alike.

A large red boulder sat in what passed for the village square, an odd sight in this land of gray. Shackles and chains dangled from spikes driven into the stone, a namesake and a punishment. On the east side of town an inn and eatery sat across from each other, both doubling as taverns. These were the class establishments in town with clay-tile roofs and painted shingles hung over their doors. To the north a yellow bird's wing and across the road a dog chewing a meaty bone.

162

A breeze wafted his nose with the acrid odors of a tannery and human refuse. A dirty, stinky village with little to offer, in particular without a coin to his name.

There was a commotion and two men tumbled from the tavern and into the street, waving at each other with stumbling, drunken hay-makers. They needed a quality kick to their asses, but it was none of his business . . . until he recognized one as the slinger in the woods.

Solineus grinned and strolled back to Ilpen, who stood in the midst of selling several items and disappointing a couple folks still clamoring about needing their wares repaired.

"Quit your whining, Be. I ain't staying long enough for repairs. I'll get to it next time I'm through." Ilpen turned his back on the yammer-ing crone with a hole in her pan, and said to Solineus, "We can leave any time; won't earn me nothin' staying to repair a few pots and pans."

Solineus scratched his head, pointed to the inn. "Getting dark. Why not stay the night?"

The hefty man pulled his britches up, adjusted his knives. "The Bloody Pebble is dangerous after dark."

"Not so dangerous as me."

Ilpen gave him a troubled squint, and Solineus shot him an inno-cent smile.

"All right, you say so. Don't mind a hot meal m'self. Cook down yonder at the Dog and Bone ain't half bad, but the beds are full of bugs, so you won't mind sleeping in the stable to guard my wagon. I'll take the team to the stable, you get me a room. I'll meet you there and we'll eat." The man handed him several coins.

Solineus eyed the songs in his palm. "You trust a man mighty quick, don't you?"

"I'm already trusting you with my life, what's a few songs?" Man and donkeys sauntered to the stable.

Solineus liked him, hard not to. Honest and straightforward, jovial, the reception he received in even this ugly town spoke well of him. He clamped the coins tight in his fist and meandered along the street.

The fisticuffs left one man lying flopped over the boardwalk while the slinger leaned against a hitching post, rubbing his jaw and paying attention to no one.

Food, a half night's rest, and murder were on Solineus' mind. The sword wasn't his gift, the slinger was.

Solineus sat outside in a chair borrowed from the stable. He leaned back, chin tucked, and waited. *Patience is key for any predator*, he repeated in his head, but now and again it took deep breaths to keep calm.

In Bloody Pebble carrying a sword earned respect and glances. Solineus found plenty of liquored tongues willing to wag because of the heirloom. The slinger's reputation as a tough guy with a temper meant the locals gave wide birth while keeping an eye on his comings and goings. They weren't shy about cussing him, nor revealing his habits.

His woman worked at the Yellow Wing Tavern across from the Dog and Bone where Ilpen slept. Part serving wench, part whore, with a room on the second floor, the slinger spent every night in her bed when in town. The plan to remove a threat to Iku's girls relied on straightforward simplicity.

Not a soul wandered the black streets as he stood and walked to the Yellow Wing. A freezing night with straight-line gusts that forced him to lean to stay upright meant smart folks were in bed or fireside. He opened the door, met by a drunken, burly guard and the stench of stale beer and cheap tobacco.

The hulking man gave him a grin and glance.

"Any ladies available?" Solineus asked.

The man snorted, plopped back in his chair. "Nah, not this late. Whiskey, beer'll have to do ya." He leaned, his chair wobbling under his weight. "Stay away from the clear bottle, that piss might do ya blind," he said with a nod and wink.

A fire blazed at the back of the common room, but only ten patrons and a barkeep remained, and most rested their heads on tables or floor. Not one of the few conscious folks paid him any mind, and even if they noted his face they wouldn't be awake at dawn when Ilpen intended to ride out.

He tapped a drooling man's shoulder who didn't budge, nabbed the green bottle of liquor from his table and moseyed to the stairs. The woman's room sat smack in the middle of a row of doors and pressing close, he caught the rhythmic drone of snoring. The door gapped with a gentle push, jiggling a lock, and he slipped his finger inside, catching the hook and flipping it free.

The door creaked open, and the slinger stood naked, leaning against the wall, pissing in a bucket. Solineus stepped into the room and its weak lantern light, closing the door.

"Hey, no. This room's taken, hear? Son of a bitch! It's you!" Shards of green glass flashed in the firelight as the bottle felled the man into a lump.

A quick glance to the bed. The woman's sleeping breaths sawed from her gaping mouth. Blind drunk turned out to be handy. He had no idea what he'd do if she awoke, but Solineus figured she'd be happier not finding out.

He cracked the door and peered into the hall. If anyone heard, a breaking bottle didn't raise much suspicion. He grabbed the sling and coin pouch from the table, bound the man's wrists and ankles with twine from the stable, and stuffed the thug's mouth with the lady's smallclothes. He raised the window, gazed into the empty back street, and chucked the man headfirst into frozen dirt with a thump.

Solineus dropped to the alley in a crouch, checking if the man lived; the bastard's one chance for an easy death passed with his neck intact. Solineus grabbed his feet by their bindings and dragged him from the village, through rocks and prickly grasses and sedge until reaching a small stream. He hefted the man over his shoulder and hopped across, spotting a tree with an ideal branch. He dropped the man in the brook, shattering the veil of ice covering the slow waters.

The slinger awoke in a fit, sucking icy water up his nose as he flailed against his bindings. He sputtered, desperate and drowning. Solineus grabbed a foot and hauled him onto the bank, and by the time they reached the tree, the man quaked from cold.

Wrenching the thug to his feet, he said, "No worries, the ice won't be the thing to kill you."

Solineus looped the sling over a sturdy branch and tied it around the man's neck, ignoring his muffled cries before yanking him from the ground and tieing off the sling to the tree. He stepped back, making himself watch the flails and kicks, listen to the grunts and groans.

Death took the slinger and Solineus passed the brutal test set before him. If he got his hands on the lord priest, morality wouldn't stop him from protecting those he cared for, no matter how violent.

A gust spun the dangling carcass as Solineus strode for town, but he stopped, emptied the slinger's coin purse in his palm. Two dozen coins, a couple tiny and silver. He pocketed the silvers and returned to the corpse, tying the purse's drawstrings to the man's wrist. The songs should cover a box and a hole in the ground. It didn't feel right to make folks work for nothing, and a man should pay for his own funeral.

Eighteen

Smoke and Honey

From the Womb of Eternity was I expunged
With the cord still wrapped around my brain,
Filling me with the Rhythm of the Universe's Heart.
My vision so acute I am Blind,
My hearing so keen I am Deaf,
My feelings so sharp I am Dumb,
My wisdom so great I am a Fool.
My desire to die so strong I will live forever.
Perhaps if I wanted to live, then finally, I might die.
Come the Worms.

—*Tomes of the Touched*

Nine Days to the Eve of Snows

The party rode for the Omindi Pass in the morning and headed north, deeper into the mountains with Meliu by Rinold's side. Her eyes held a haunted glaze and she had the creepy habit of grinning at Ivin.

When young women smiled at him, he assumed it was to curry favor because of his family name, or they might be attracted to him, but Meliu's grin felt like she sized him for a hole in the ground. The Choerkin were no more popular in Istinjoln than the lord priest among Ivin's kin.

But as a guide she proved true. From the Omindi she led them up a scree littered climb onto a trail with a harrowing drop on their left. They led their horses one by one until reaching a box gap where they tethered horses and split the Wardens, with Modan striking camp to guard the rear.

Meliu rounded a massive outcropping several hundred strides later, and Ivin spotted a cave hidden by rocks and evergreen shrubs. A great, black, cat's pupil in an eye of snow and granite stared back at them, but when they arrived at the entrance, they found it wasn't so huge. The vertical crack in the mountain was skinny, its false height the result of blackening by fire.

"Don't know what the Twelve Hells happened here." Pikarn ran a finger across the blackened stone, streaking his glove, and sniffed. "Whale oil." He slipped an axe from his belt.

Meliu peered into the entrance. "Oil's used to enhance prayers of fire . . . possible they tried to seal the cave behind them."

Ivin stared at the girl's matted hair with an ugly thought. "These caves connected to the Ihomjo mines?"

Meliu hesitated and her eyes flashed to the ground for a flicker. "No, I don't think so."

She lied. The holies weren't just trying to keep a shrine hidden, they'd brought the tunnels down on those miners. Maybe sealing an evil from the world justified collapsing a mine shaft, and the lives lost written off as noble sacrifice in Istinjoln, but his father's voice cussing in the back of his head kept him from swallowing the justification bait. Nothing was so simple and innocent as it seemed on this journey: Istinjoln had plenty to answer for

The Wolverine thumped his shoulder. "You stay close. I don't want your clan blood on the ground first ride out, got it?" He turned his gaze to the priestess. "These Shadows, anything in 'ticular attracts them?"

She stared, then rubbed her eyes. "Prayers, maybe. They'll come to sound, light, movement, but prayer, it's like they feel the energy. I wasn't safe until I climbed into the Tears of the Gods, sitting silent, no prayers."

Ivin asked, "Tears of the Gods?"

"It's a stalactite formation, veins of some mineral run through them, glowing soft with power. I saw Shadows and Taken pass; they should've been able to see me. Their eyesight is maybe weak, I can't say for sure."

The Wolverine nodded. "No way we travel silent or in the dark."

"I didn't see a single one sneaking out, even with a little prayer to light my way."

Suvarn said, "I hope your luck holds, girl."

Several men stepped to the sides so sound wouldn't travel so loud into the cave's mouth and struck flint to steel to ignite torches. The orange flames cast wavering shadows on the ceiling and walls as they stepped into the caverns, their fluttering forms mirroring the sensation of the butterflies in Ivin's belly.

A reek which reminded him of burning, sacrificial lamb, struck Ivin's nose the moment they entered. A sickly sweet and nauseating odor, but beyond that, a deep breath revealed a peculiar hint of honey. Most covered their faces as the company pressed forward through the dark hall, their feet leaving prints on the soot-slicked floor.

A hundred paces in they passed an alcove housing a couple stall doors, but they were empty of everything but straw. A bridle and reins still hung from a spike driven into a wall. They moved on after a quick inspection, with Meliu leading them without hesitation past tunnels splitting to the north and south.

Even such a short distance in, unease crept into his soul. His brain told him the way out was simple and straight, but the dark outside the torch's globe of light rankled his nerves, oppressing his senses with the weight of the unseen.

Rinold stepped to Ivin's side. "Relax and keep your eyes on the heads in front of you, elsewise you'll be pissin' yourself the first bat we meet."

Ivin rolled his eyes, but the notion of a nickname blending turd and piss didn't settle his nerves. He took deep breaths, resting a hand on the hilt of his sword, and instead of focusing on the dark beyond the torches he turned his attention to what the light revealed. The tunnel was natural, with rough stalagmites and stalactites prodding into the bobbing and uneven light, casting dancing shadows where a being of flesh and blood could never tread. But Ivin found it hard to imagine a Shadow couldn't hide anywhere it damned well pleased.

The tunnel they followed made a steady descent, and after passing another tunnel which turned south. The slope felt as if it fell out from under his feet, taking a steep drop. Flesh shifted beneath his right foot and squealed: Ivin lost his footing and his ankle rolled. He hugged a stalagmite to keep himself from taking a tumble.

Rinold waved his torch and scorched a wounded rat, a blind, white-eyed creature squirming and flailing with a broken back.

Rinold smirked. "Lucky, if that'd been a fever snake you'd be bit and on a painful journey to dead."

"Fever snakes don't live in caves." Ivin raised a boot, putting the critter out of its suffering with a crunching stomp before kicking it to the side so no one slipped on the carcass.

Rinold's torch lit a smug grin. "Ratsmasher, I'm a thinkin' that's a name could be set to song."

"Squirrels and rats, they aren't so different really, don't you think?" Ivin mocked the man's nickname, curling his lip and protruding his teeth to imitate a squirrel gnawing a nut.

Puxele said, "I'll be working on the words, Rinold, you figure out the tune."

Pikarn's voice echoed from ahead, "Shut yer mouths, children, leave a man to his hobbies."

Stifled chuckles echoed through Ivin's pride as he continued the descent, but the jovial mutterings stiffened and froze as a man-shaped Shadow surged onto the ceiling in front of them. Ivin's sword wasn't alone in leaving its sheath as mail rattled and blades sang around him. Ivin froze in a defensive stance, but the shadow quivered and didn't move to attack.

Meliu said, "Belt 'em, boys." She strode forward and patted the hip of stalagmite carved into the likeness of what Ivin assumed to be a god. "This old man ain't moved in a right long time and guards the Hall of Faces."

The passage took a sharp turn right but leveled and faces carved into the walls' stone stared at them with terrifying visages. A three-eyed woman with horns, a howling man with a wolf's muzzle, a screaming woman without eyes, a face upside down with a snake for a tongue, a single head with two faces, one masculine the other feminine. There was a hundred or more, and every one of them strange and unworldly.

Ivin asked, "What are these?"

Meliu shrugged. "Images of the Vanquished Gods, some say."

"Blasphemy to depict the Vanquished."

"Which is why some argue they aren't the Vanquished, while others insist on their destruction."

Suvarn said, "I'd take a pick to 'em 'cause they're ugly."

Ivin grunted his agreement and kept his eyes on the back of the Wolverine's head instead of the haunting faces until they came to a crossing of four passages.

Meliu stopped, pointing to their left. "That there leads to the Tears of the Gods. . . ." She stared forward, then took a right turn. "This way."

Pikarn said, "I was assuming you knew the damned way, girl."

"Better than you do, old man."

Twenty strides later the tunnel split again, and this time the priestess didn't pause, turning left, and leaving Ivin with the belief he'd be lost if forced to find his way out.

The passage grew too tight for more than two side-by-side, but they'd passed numerous trails which looked so tight they might snag a man's gear and never let go, so he chose to be thankful rather than complain. His gratitude ended when they stopped to stare at a massive pillar standing in their way, stretching to the roof and shrinking the tunnel on either side into something that might give a fat badger pause. They made their way shimmying sideways, and Ivin stopped a dozen times to unhook his cloak from protruding rocks until the cave stretched wide again.

A hundred strides or so later, Meliu stopped to stare up. She gripped a notch in the wall and put foot to a slender ledge, and the light and shadows presented a precarious climb. The wall's walk was less wide than Ivin's booted foot and steep, unclimbable if not for the protrusions and cuts in the rock the priestess used for handholds as she moved like a spider up the wall.

Ivin's mouth gaped as the girl disappeared into a shadow seven poles above their heads, a fall high enough to kill a man straight out.

Meliu's voice came soft from above. "You brave men a-comin'?"

Suvarn said, "That's a climb for skinny little girls, not my big boots and fat fingers."

Ivin licked his lips, glanced at Suvarn. "Scared of a little climb?" He wriggled several fingers into a notch in the wall and tested the

ledge with his boot. It wasn't so bad as he expected, whoever had
carved the holds spaced them well, and the craggy nature of the wall
gave extra purchase. In little time he stood beside the priestess in the
dark watching others climb their way. As the first torch arrived, the
light revealed the girl's creepy grin, made worse by the shadows, and
he wondered if maybe she'd thought of pushing him.

I'm being silly. He smiled at her, but she turned into the dark, and
he followed her gaze. The blackness ahead wasn't so much dark, as
dim. "What the hells?"

"The troughs must be lit." She offered no further explanation as
they waited for everyone before moving forward. The passage curved
sharp and grew brighter as they walked. A rushing noise with intermittent pops grew in the hollow distance, some sort of fire he guessed,
and the smell of honey which had been so faint and common as to be
forgotten swelled in his nostrils. Cautious steps carried them around
the bend, their weapons at the ready, but the view defied expectations.

Their passage shifted into a hall and bulged to forty strides wide
and was lit by what must be channels carved into the walls of the cave
and filled with oil. The fires rushed as they burned oil, and either Ivin's
eyes had grown used to the dark, or the flames burned brighter than
any he'd ever seen. The channels ran the length of the walls, leading
deeper into the yawning cavern.

Ivin said, "No way for a Shadow to hide in this place."

Pikarn spat. "That's sure to've been the point, but we ain't sneaking across, neither."

Meliu's voice was soft, awed. "I've never seen it lit before, it's beautiful." She wandered into the hall, her head thrown back to stare at the
ceiling.

Ivin followed her gaze. The light of the brilliant flames reached
the heights of the cavern and ignited stars of shimmering gold. The

farther they walked, the more stars appeared, then streaks and swirls, patterns he couldn't pinpoint as natural or manmade . . . or by the hands of gods.

"Such wealth. Where are we?" Pikarn asked.

"The cavern's roof is called The Fool's Haul," the girl said with a grin. "It earned its name for all those who believed the sparkles were gold."

Pikarn squinted. "Count me a fool, then. How far to the Crack?"

Her grin disappeared, and she moved on. "It's here."

The hall took a mild curve to their left and opened into an even greater cavern. Three channels were carved into the heights of these walls, each row of flame staggered a pole higher as they rose toward the peak of the dome, lighting a ceiling fifty poles above their heads. Golden patterns swirled into a canvas no mortal could paint. Shimmering silver joined the gold, painting images at once too abstract to name, and too perfect to deny they meant something, if only Ivin could understand the language. The brilliant whorls drew the eye inward, focusing on a majestic circle of gold at the highest point of the roof, and in the center glowed a silver snowflake, the only image undeniable in its shape.

Ivin lowered his eyes from this shimmering piece of storm to find it fell eternal into a gaping maw in the world, a crack of darkness impervious to the light of this cave that stretched an easy fifty strides in length, and at its widest was fifteen strides across.

He muttered, "The Crack of Burdenis."

Meliu said, "As I've never seen it before. I've only heard rumors, it hasn't been lit in decades."

The girl was awestruck, but Pikarn kept priorities on his mind. "Now where we headed?"

Meliu nodded to the crack and led them to a point at its edge where a post with a bell on its top was splintered and leaning over the abyss. "Messages went up and down here."

Ivin caught her gaze slipping far to their left, but the space was empty except for several braziers long dark. "What's over there?"

She flashed him her first smile that didn't promise blood. "Nothing, just remembering a game of Hawk and Snake."

Ivin figured she'd won a handsome purse, and glanced into the Crack, where shallow steps carved into the wall descended into the abyss. "Did the priests carve these stairs?"

Puxele leaned over the precipice. "Looks to me like some damned goat picked up a hammer and chisel."

Meliu shrugged. "They were here when they discovered the cave after the Great Forgetting."

Pikarn scoffed. "Fairy tales'n legends."

Meliu returned the scoff. "I'll call you a fool twice, now. When these caves were first explored, they found a group of priests in the Chamber of the Forgotten, followers of the Pantheon of Sol. They guarded a stack of books. These people awoke without memories, lost in these caves. But they found each other, even if they never found their way out, and they died in that chamber. The Great Forgetting was very real. Some say it'll happen again."

Puxele said, "That's encouraging."

"Gotta survive gettin' to the bottom before worryin' about gettin' back," Rinold said.

Suvarn slapped Rinold's back. "Squirrels are some o' the best damned climbers, you go first."

"What, so you can knock me off when you fall?"

Ivin reeled at the stair's prospects. Even repaired, the post and pulley wouldn't handle a man's weight, and either way, scaling into that bleak hole scared him more than a walk.

They lit fresh torches and descended with Rinold in the lead, a trail of glowing ants. Ivin hugged the wall as he made his way to the first platform, where the stairs zigged back under the wardens who followed. He stopped to breathe and slow his heart, glanced back. His torch highlighted shadowy dimples in the walls, similar to those they'd seen in the Omindi.

Unlike in the Omindi, there were several sets of pocks, and the eye could follow them as far as torch-light traveled. He hoped they were natural; if they weren't, he didn't want to know what caused them. He focused on the steps from there and eleven zigzags later his feet found the bottom of the Crack of Burdenis.

Puxele came last and with a soft whistle of relief. Meliu grabbed her by the hand and tugged her onward. "Keep moving, less we're here the better," Meliu said.

Ivin approached Pikarn as they walked, whispered. "Did you see the pocks in the walls?"

The Wolverine nodded and handed him a chunk of jerked beef. Ivin took the hint, dropped back, and gnawed on the meat as they entered a passage tight enough that rough-hewn stone snagged their shoulders in places.

Rinold muttered, "If'n enemy sit on either side of this neck, we won't be walking out alive.".

Chittering noises echoed from ahead and they slowed. Ivin's grip on his sword tightened, and he slipped his shield from his shoulder

Foes didn't wait for them, but the rat feast the enemy left behind might make a butcher retch. The chamber was an irregular shape thirty strides across at its widest, and blood spattered the walls and pooled on the floor where arms and legs lay ripped from bodies, and a hundred blind rats scurried with sanguine faces and feet. The savagery of the mutilation made it hard to guess how many holies had met their end here. A broken table in the corner wore an eyeless head on one of its splintered oak legs.

Pikarn asked, "What was this place?"

Meliu's eyes were wide as she stumbled to a spot clear of gore. "A guardroom. My master had to check in here before heading to the Chamber of the Lost."

The wardens kicked rats from the remains, covering the bodies with robe remnants. Ivin's stomach turned but he managed to keep his jerky where it belonged. Meliu crouched against the wall, hands covering her eyes, rocking back and forth.

Pikarn wandered the room, glancing at the faces of the dead. "Do the best we can for 'em, but do it fast." He walked to Meliu, crouched beside her. "All right, girl. Where we headed next?"

There were five exits from the chamber aside from their entry.

The girl rocked and stuttered. "Give me a flicker, my mind's cloudy. I always had a guide. That tunnel there . . . no. The center tunnel?"

"Godsdamn it." Pikarn stood and called to Rinold. "See what you think of that middle pass, but don't be gone long, got me?"

The tracker nodded and disappeared down the dark hole and returned so fast Ivin half expected him chased, but nothing followed. "Its walls are caked with soot, and the smell of honey is strong. Last hole in the world I wanna go down so this is probably it." He emphasized his distaste with a hack and spit.

Pikarn grabbed Meliu by the hood of her robe and pulled her to her feet. "Let's go, girl."

A fire-blackened tunnel greeted them as promised, the floor coated with a thick layer of greasy soot slick beneath their feet. The tunnel was wide for a short jaunt but it turned into a stretch so tight Ivin's lungs tightened and he felt as if he were being buried alive. He ducked and squirmed, mail links catching on stone, and his helm banged twice on the ceiling, but this claustrophobic hell gave way to a wider tunnel thirty or so paces after entering.

Ivin stepped from the passage and knocked his helmet back on his head, his lungs filling in a relieved rush. "Tell me there's no more of that."

Meliu grinned. "Should be the worst spot we meet. It pays to be short and skinny, not sure your man is going to make it."

Ivin glanced back. Suvarn's broad shoulders were hung-up in a tight crease of stone, with Puxele scaling the rocks to unhook the man's gear. She sliced the caught piece, then hammered a jagged stone with the hilt of her dagger to free him. Once Suvarn came muttering from the hole, it took another quarter-candle before everyone made it through this tight space.

Soon as the last man stepped through, Meliu took them deeper, with the journey snaking past several branching tunnels until she led them on a steep switchback climb.

Meliu whispered, "Chamber of the Lost is straight ahead."

When they arrived their nerves were on edge. Although debris proved a fight took place, it wasn't the massacre of the previous cavern.

Pikarn lit a trough of oil with his torch, and in moments the flame traveled to circle the cave. The cavern was a rough, twenty-pace pentagon in the center of which sat a table carved from stone. Five stone blocks lay at each side, serving as benches. Meliu dashed to empty shelves carved into the walls. "Here, the books should be here. This is the chamber. Their books should be here." She scurried through the rubble, turning over debris in her search.

"Lost books of the Lost, no great loss you ask me," Rinold said, which earned a cuff to the head from Puxele.

Meliu struggled to lift a fallen cabinet and Ivin helped her, but there was nothing underneath. Ivin asked, "What kind of books?"

"The important kind." And that was all she seemed prepared to say until he helped her dig deeper into the mess. "The *Codex of Sol*, for one. I shouldn't even know it's here, but I heard tell."

It sure sounded important, Sol's name didn't get scribbled on a book for no reason.

"Never heard of such a tome," Pikarn said.

Meliu snorted in contempt. "Nor should you have heard of it now, but it was here; Ovin said he'd seen it himself . . . and was threatened a flaying if he so much as told a soul. *Sheve's Journal*, the *Tome of the Lost*, *Derdrin's Map*, *Istileus' Histories* . . . they all should be here."

"Well, they ain't." Pikarn kicked at some rubble. "Would these creatures, these Shadows . . . you think they'd be wanting such books?"

The girl cocked her head. "No, suppose not."

"Your priests prolly took 'em. Ain't no use to looking for 'em here."

She thought for a moment before nodding. "We should be moving on. The Shrine isn't far."

With three passages exiting the room they again took the central tunnel from their entrance. The passage climbed straight, with only a few side passages they ignored. Torches revealed dried blood in spots, but their only company was bats, rats, and the sound of their own feet. They slowed as their passage widened and sent Rinold ahead.

He returned in a few flickers, swiping his forehead of sweat. "Ain't like nothing I ever seen afore, but we're here, godsdamned guaranteed."

Nineteen

Diamond and Shadow

An eternal Eclipse in a static universe,
a ring of Fire and pupil of Black,
blazing petals of a cosmic black-eyed Susan.
Stasis, the lack of crackle between ears,
the dead sound of a universe Dead.

—*Tomes of the Touched*

Nine Days to the Eve of Snows

They entered the Hall of Burdenis to stand on a crenelated balcony with curving stairs leading to the floor on either side. A beam of sunlight entered through a fissure in the hollow above and reflected off a massive mirror before striking a shrine with a burst of brilliant white light, illuminating the hall.

Black masses dotted the floor of the cavern, some human, but twisted into unnatural shapes, while others were oil pots overturned and burnt out. Ivin had grown up with brazen tales of the glories and horrors of war, but what they found here wasn't the result of fighting alone. The bodies suffered teeth marks to the bone, many shattered to suck the marrow. Broken and empty skulls still with faces stared at

180

him without eyes. One corpse lay open and where a heap of intestines should have lain, the cavity was empty.

"Somethin' had a godsdamned feast down here," Rinold said.

Meliu hid on the balcony, her back turned to the horror, and Ivin wanted to join her. He shook the chill from his spine and dipped the tip of his sword, tossing empty, bloody robes to the side. A shimmer caught his eye. A sparkling crescent symbol marked the floor, drawn with a silvery powder. He assumed the sparkle was a reflection of light from the shrine, but as he circled, his shadow didn't diminish its shimmering beauty.

He took a few steps and kicked an overturned oil pot, revealing a symbol in the shape of an eye. "Look for more symbols hidden under things." Ivin's voice echoed louder than expected, and he grimaced.

Pikarn sucked his teeth as he studied the symbols, and the wardens announced more finds: Horse and leaf, several stars, and a spear. The old man looked to the balcony above. "Girl, what're these symbols?" He spoke in his normal voice, but in this cavern it traveled.

"I work with books, not arcana."

"Get down here and take a look."

"No."

The Wolverine rubbed his forehead. "Godsdamned girl. What do you think, Choerkin?"

"There are symbols—runes—at Skywatch, and the bones. They've hundreds of symbols but I couldn't put a name to one. And this? Glowing?" He shrugged.

"Wards," Meliu said, "to keep something out or in."

Pikarn glanced to the stairs. "What was that? Come down here and tell me."

"No."

This time the Wolverine chuckled. "Crescent moon?"

"Don't know, shape probably doesn't matter. Drawn with what?"

"Hells if I know. Powdered crystal?" Pikarn kneeled and rubbed the rune.

"Crushed diamond, probably enchanted with Life prayers, or Spirit," Meliu said.

"If this is life magic, remind me to stay away from death magic." Pikarn kicked at the rune, but the diamond stuck to the floor. He snorted.

Puxele kneeled twenty paces from them, her fingers dragging the ground and coming up shining. "There's loose diamond over here, and a small bag of the stuff." She shook her fingers, watched the mystic trail of glow as it fell from her fingers. She snatched the bag, sweeping up as much loose powder as she could.

The Wolverine grinned. "That's our Little Sister, always trying to get rich."

She smirked. "Little Sister always trying to stay alive."

Pikarn nodded toward the shrine and they meandered that way, moving scraps of cloth and overturned braziers that covered the ground so long as it didn't disrespect the dead. Several pieces of debris concealed symbols, or blobs and streaks of glowing diamond.

Pikarn said, "Creatures are smart enough to cover these sigils; Awakened Dead wouldn't much bother."

Ivin figured he'd beat Puxele to the corrective punch. "As the priestess said: Taken."

The oblong shrine dedicated to Burdenis bore mountains carved in relief along its edge with eagle heads at the corners, and its brilliance resulted from powdered diamond struck by the sun. The floor surrounding the shrine shimmered with dust, but it wasn't uniform.

"They hurried here, or ran out of diamond," Ivin said. He circled the dais and spotted something resting at its base, hidden in the blinding aura of enchanted diamond and sunlight. He reached in to find it was soft.

The world wavered, and a flicker later the air above the shrine rippled and pulsed, a wave of sound pushing everyone a few steps back. Ivin tumbled from the shrine with a leather-bound volume in his hand. The pulse lacked an echo; its *woomph* died once beyond their ears. The wardens congregated at Pikarn's position with weapons drawn.

Ivin dusted himself off and held out his prize for Pikarn to see. "One of the holy books, I'd wager. Locked." He feared to force the latch, such things carried curses.

"Liar," came the girl's voice. She popped her head over the wall. "What's it look like?"

"Brass latch, boiled-leather-bound. No words."

Her booted feet flapped down the stairs and sprinted straight to him. She stripped the book from his hands and clutched it to her chest. "That's not for you. We agreed."

Pikarn looked liable to kick the girl in the ass, but he planted his foot with a nod. "Aye, we agreed."

The world wavered again and this time the pulse collapsed to a point several feet above the shrine. They staggered as the force passed, staring. The air rippled in glossy waves, and from the center slithered a tendril of darkness impenetrable by the light.

Meliu's feet pattered for the stairs before Ivin understood the birth he witnessed. The thing fought and wriggled as if escaping the air itself. It launched in an arc, past the diamond dust, and landed with the silence nothingness would make.

Puxele stood as close as anyone. "What the hells is that?"

The thing writhed on the ground like a mute and blind newborn pup. Buds formed and tendrils sprouted, lifting itself from the ground with hazy arms.

Ivin drew his sword and swung, the blade disappearing in its darkness, but the thing didn't so much as twitch. He snagged a torch from

Rinold and plunged it into the creature's chest. The being's darkness swallowed and snuffed the flickers of fire. The dead torch rattled on the floor as the demon grew more distinct, more like a shadow a man would cast, except this Shadow turned to look Ivin in the eye with a featureless face. A shiver shook his spine with the malevolence of its gaze.

Pikarn shouted what Ivin's muscles itched to do. "Run! Get the hells out of here!" The rush to the stairs was a mad scramble with Pikarn and Ivin guarding their backs. The thing wasn't coming for them, not yet. Rinold reached the balcony first with Puxele on his heels, and they spun and nocked arrows to give cover if needed.

Right then Meliu shrieked from the tunnel. "Priest! Taken priest!"

The remaining wardens stopped but Pikarn was having none of it. "Go, damn you! There's only one way out, priests be damned!"

They trotted into the tunnel, weapons, shields, and torches to the fore. A priest waited for them, his arms and legs crooked, and his lower jaw missing. His eyes were wide and white as blizzard, and a spear went through its head before Ivin got close. It collapsed to the ground, but he could tell the thing wasn't dead as he passed. The priest's twisted body twitched and oozed thick black blood that sank into the ground as if it were sand instead of stone.

The party ran, driven by fear, their breathing labored.

"Slow 'er down! We've got a long jaunt ahead," Pikarn yelled.

The rush of fear and combat tried to convince Ivin he could run forever if need, but the Wolverine had the right of it, and as the tunnel weaved and undulated death could lurk around any bend. They needed a disciplined pace to make it from these caves alive.

The girl was in the middle of the group, still clutching the book tight to her chest, and three men formed the lead with shield and spear, while Puxele and Rinold watched their backs. Ivin and Pikarn walked on either side of Meliu.

Pikarn's eyes kept glancing to the girl's prize. "So, li'l priestess, which book you got?"

She stared straight ahead. "I don't know."

"A hundred pages that might well be chicken scratch and you hug it to your bosom like your long lost mama? Tells me you know something."

Meliu shrugged and when Ivin put a hand on her shoulder, she might've run if there'd been anywhere to go. Ivin said, "It's okay, Meliu. We don't want the book, we just want to know if it'll help explain what's going on here. Funny coincidence, that book sitting at the foot of the shrine."

She shrugged his hand away and pursed her lips.

Pikarn huffed. "Look here, girl, we wanted that godsdamned book we'd take it, nothing you could do to stop us."

"I don't know, I said. But you wouldn't be able to read it, anyhow."

Pikarn chuckled. "You think I'm so unlearned I can't read?"

She shot him a scathing glance. "Not so learned as to read this one."

"Then you do know what it is." Ivin tried not to sound cocksure, but the girl had talked herself into a trap.

"No, or rather maybe. But whether it is or it isn't, it ain't for the likes of you."

Pikarn glared. "Uppity little bitch considering we sewed her scalp back on, don't you think?"

Her knuckles whitened with her grip on the tome and she fell back a couple steps to keep an eye on them.

Ivin said, "Ease up on the girl."

"I'm not a girl, I'm a priestess. And a woman older than you."

The Wolverine snorted at the both of them as they stepped into the Chamber of the Lost. "Don't go worrying that scarred head of yours, girl. We make it out of here alive we'll make sure the book makes it to all our betters at Istinjoln. And Puxele, Rinold . . . put an arrow in her back if she runs." Pikarn stepped to Ivin's side and drew him from the girl. "Istinjoln, straight away. And if we can get a peek in that book before we get there, all the better."

When they reached the climb down not a soul complained or hesitated to take the treacherous path to the floor, but the pillar and its shoulder-knocking chasm made them stop to stare, not a soul was eager to go first. Suvarn said, "I'll go last, in case I get stuck again."

Pikarn ended the procrastination. "Squirrel first, then smallest to largest, except we put the priestess in the middle."

Rinold slipped into the crevice and his torch disappeared in a bend. "Clear."

Ivin exhaled along with others who'd held their breaths. Waiting his turn gave him time to think: A slithering Shadow birthed from empty air, and either these creatures or the twisted priests fed on the dead. If indeed the Shadows possessed the men, it made more sense the Taken fed on flesh. Revelation struck, obvious, a piece he hadn't considered.

Ivin glanced to the Wolverine, noting the priestess was already gone. "The first party killed and eaten was almost a year ago. These things didn't just arrive."

"Aye. You've a head on them shoulders, Ratsmasher."

"They contained the Shadows with symbols for a year. Didn't warn a soul. They lost control, brought the mine down to keep the creatures at bay. After so long, how'd they fail?"

"Better question is, how many are there? 'Cause more seem to be a comin'. Get your ass in there, Choerkin."

Ivin slipped between the tight walls sideways, bobbing and weaving, and snagging his gear only twice. Pikarn followed right behind, and a few flickers later Suvarn, missing his pack.

The big man grinned. "I left it for decoration, nothin' I can't replace."

Ivin's smile was flat, the humor lost with knowing what waited for them in the next room. The blood and rancid odors were unchanged, but they marched through the carnage unmolested. Ivin breathed easier in the fresher air beyond, happy to be away from the stench. Everyone's pace picked up through the wider passages and Ivin was eager as anyone to set foot on those treacherous stairs, but as they reached the bottom of the Crack, Rinold hissed and threw his hand up, crouching.

Ivin ducked and stared into darkness.

Pikarn asked, "What'd you see?"

"Thought I heard somethin', but the fear's more in my gut than my head."

The Wolverine spat. "I trust your gut more than most folks' wits, but we ain't got a shittin' choice here, we gotta get across."

It was fifty strides from here to the stair, but anything could hide in the dark torches wouldn't reach.

Rinold said, "They were Wakened Dead we'd draw 'em out easy enough for a straight fight."

"No guarantee we could even win a straight fight with these damned things." Pikarn shook his shoulders and huffed. "You take it slow as a snail uphill, and you see a godsdamned thing . . . ."

The Squirrel grinned, adjusted his steel skullcap, and nabbed a second torch from Puxele. "I know how to run better than I know slow. May the gods bless the shit in my britches."

And with that the little man eased into the darkness with a torch in either hand waving to his sides. It was a painful sight, watching him diminish into the cave's dark, uncertain he would survive the next step, but within a wick's time the Squirrel turned and waved both torches above his head.

Pikarn came to his feet and several wardens rushed ahead with spear and shield in formation until they reached the stairs. As the stragglers caught up, the Wolverine nodded to Rinold. "You keep the lead, rest of you I don't care about the order except the girl stays in the middle—I want her and that book kept cozy."

Rinold returned Puxele's torch and scooted up the first couple steps. The light from torches all around cast a wild array of shadows as men shuffled and jostled, waiting for their turn, and for a flicker as the Squirrel bound up a stair, Ivin's heart froze. It'd been a trick of his eye, whatever he thought he'd seen was gone.

Suvarn followed, catching his toe, throwing out a hand against the wall to catch himself and his torch fluttered in his hand. From the creases of the rock a shadow moved with instead of against the flame's flare. Suvarn smiled, embarrassed by his clumsy move, but his smile gaped into a silent scream and his eyes flew wide.

Ivin screamed, "No!" A hand of black stretched from the stone of the wall, plunging into Suvarn's chest, lifting the man who weighed at least seventy stones as if he were nothing more than a puppet.

The warrior didn't make a sound as his torch and sword clattered to the stone floor. The Shadow launched Suvarn from the second stair and hammered him into the ground, the black form plunging into the dying man's chest, and all Ivin could do was stare. Suvarn's hands and feet flailed as the creature invaded his flesh, but Ivin knew it wasn't because he put up a fight.

Puxele screamed and pulled her scimitar, slashing the disappearing Shadow, but the steel was as ineffective as attacking smoke.

There was a rush of feet across the hall and the wardens turned with shouts. Robed figures rushed from the dark, screeching in the warbling howls of men choking on their own tongues. Even as he planted his feet and brought his sword around two more wardens were dying, one with a broken neck, the other with a hand sticking from his gut. The cave, moments before silent and at peace, raged with the echoes of combat and dying.

Ivin buckled under the weight of a priest as it crashed into his shield, and he slid in someone's blood before setting his feet to throw the thing back. It came again, punched his shield with shoulder-jarring force, but he slipped the blow and plunged the sword through the back of its head as he spun.

Gore splashed up his forearm as he drove the blade so deep the skull clunked on the sword's guard. The weight of the falling priest pulled his sword down, straining to strip the weapon from his grip, but instead of letting go he went to a knee, and wrenched the blade from the priest's head.

Ivin stood in time for Meliu to dive behind him with a priest in chase. His broadsword cleaved the top of the priest's skull and it collapsed, shaking on the ground in joint-breaking fits. Ivin grabbed the girl, pulling her to her feet. Torches lit the area, but most lay on the ground, sputtering as they soaked in blood.

Five dead priests, and seven surviving wardens, plus Meliu. Worms of Shadow protruded from Suvarn, wriggling their way into his body. Ivin stood in shock, he didn't want to believe his eyes.

He backed from Rinold until running into Puxele.

Meliu said, "We need to leave. He'll be coming for us soon enough."

Pikarn said, "Gods help us, can we kill him now?"

The priestess shook her head. "Not so easy as you might think, it sets them in a fury and the Shadow's freed."

"How long've we got?"

"A candle at most, half maybe. Long enough we can make it to the Fool's Haul, I hope. And these priests . . . the Shadows will come from the stone not long after."

189

In the light of a torch lying next to a priest's body, the thick black blood soaked into the stone as he saw earlier, but now he could see a tiny maggot of Shadow wriggling from the pool. "What the hells?"

"I told you, the Shadows will come. We aren't running for our lives, we're running for our souls."

The group snatched torches and made their way up the stairs. Three strides and hop, three strides and hop, the rhythm burned his thighs and wracked his lungs, and still he fell behind. He slowed, but not by choice, his legs didn't want to go another step. He leaned against the wall, and a couple wardens eased past as he stared to where he wished a sky was, but all he could see was an icy white snowflake glowing in a golden fresco.

Ivin's exhausted mind saw the Shadow too late to shout as it scrambled up the stone wall like a spider and with the speed of a bat in flight, attacked. Entangled with the Shadow, the warrior and Shadow plunged from the stairs. Ivin watched in horror as the man's torch disappeared into the dark, realizing how Shadows left pockmarks in the stone.

Pikarn said, "Move it! Move on!"

Ivin's legs ached and shook from exertion by the time they reached the top, but stopping for a few flickers to drink seemed suicidal, let alone take time for rest. Still, they waited a couple wicks for everyone to reach the top. Ivin fumbled with shaky hands for his waterskin and squeezed water into his mouth, choking the fluid down before kneeling. When the last wardens dragged themselves over the top, they rested for several wicks, but not a soul wanted to linger longer than needed.

Pikarn gave the order. "Keep the pace steady, and stick together. No one gets lost, you hear?"

They forced their legs to move, running, stumbling, walking, anything that propelled them forward. Ivin was beyond exhausted by the time they burst from the cave and into bright afternoon sun. The frozen air assaulted his lungs so hard he collapsed to his knees, and Meliu cried amid fits of catching her breath. Unlo and Fularn both collapsed strides outside the mouth of the cave and Puxele leaned on Pikarn. Chest heaving, and his balance staggered, the Wolverine kept his feet while helping one of his own. Rinold strolled from the cave, the only one who didn't look like he was about to die.

Puxele sprinkled diamond dust across the entrance, sporting a pained grin. "It can't hurt."

They pressed on quick as they were able, and when they rounded the corner to the camp the Wolverine bellowed, "Modan!" But all that remained were their fifteen horses. Shoulders wilted, and they stared.

Rinold checked the fire pit. "Cold."

Pikarn cursed as he strode to the middle of camp. "Something spooked 'em, or they gave chase. But we can't be sitting on our asses and waiting for 'em. Gather the gear, load up the horses."

Pikarn dragged his heel through the campfire, forming a black "X" on the ground with a mark pointing southeast, while others gathered food and supplies. They rode from camp with a string of riderless horses after throwing on saddles and reins.

They reached the edge of the Omindi Pass, and the sliding trails down the slope of scree, marked by blood and horse hair, made it obvious Modan's wardens rode in a hurry. The party dismounted and led their horses down the slope, and Rinold wandered the area looking for signs.

The Squirrel scratched his head as he walked north several strides. "Looks like they turned south toward Ervinhin but spun and rode north faster than a whore's kiss. And here's the kicker, Colok gave chase."

The Wolverine kicked a rock and glared north. "Son of a gods-damned whoreson, gotta be shittin' me."

The Wolverine stomped over to a flat face of rock and scrawled an X with a longer line pointing south with a charred branch. They swung into their saddles and rode south with their string of horses in tow as a fresh flurry fluttered on the winds.

If the Wolverine had a plan, he kept it to himself, and attempts at conversation met discouraging grumbles. Ivin rode beside Meliu, so sore and tired his thoughts scrambled back and forth from priests and Shadows to being happy to be alive under an open sky.

Puxele rode on the opposite side of the girl. "Suvarn is one of them?"

The girl nodded. "Every time I seen a Shadow kill, it took the body."

"And those not killed by Shadows?"

"Plenty of bodies never rose again. I think the Shadows need the living host."

"They were waiting for us at the stair, weren't they?" Ivin asked. This notion bugged him. He wanted to believe the creatures were mindless killers.

"Can't say for sure, could I?" Meliu sighed, shrugged, adjusted the book in her arms. "I seen things, though. They have a cunning."

The Wolverine said, "Quit your yappin' and eyes up. I'd like to make it to the foothills alive."

Ivin fell quiet without the customary jerked beef offering and pinned his eyes to the walls of the pass. Neither Shadows, priests, nor Colok threatened and a candle after sunset they arrived at Ervinhin.

Pikarn yelled to a guard as the log gate creaked open. "Modan here?"

"No, sir. We ain't seen anyone for candles."

"Son of a godsdamned whoreson. . . . Secure the gates, but I want four men on the watch all night, you hear me? Unlo, Fularn, get the horses to the stable. Rinold, you head for the inn and make sure we got the best food, beers, and beds waiting for us. Puxele, Choerkin, and Miss Meliu, let's take a walk to the house of the dead."

The priestess didn't budge, her jaw set.

The Wolverine stood mute, but Ivin put a hand on her shoulder. "One of your people may still be alive; wouldn't it be good to know who?"

She shrugged his hand from her shoulder and glared, but didn't argue as she took the Wolverine's lead. She strode into the dark portal and exhaled a deep breath before lanterns lit. Her face twisted as she glanced at the corpses. "Lein." She muttered a prayer and touched two fingers to her forehead. "The, uh . . . the head is Loepus'." She craned her neck over a body for a better view of the faces and stood straight. "Tokodin. He's not here."

Ivin glanced at her. "Anything special about him?"

"A monk, with especially bad luck at dice, that's about it. I've known him since we were children."

Pikarn said, "One monk doesn't outrun Colok nor stand a chance in a fight. Might be he fell from a cliff earlier, or got lucky, left for dead. We'll have folks keep an eye out for him. Puxele, show this young lady to the inn for food and room for the night."

When the room emptied the Wolverine turned to Ivin. "They took a prisoner, I'm betting on it. Twice now."

Changes often came like storms in the mountains, surprising a man, but snow and gale winds were a force of nature; the Colok would need a specific reason to change their ways. "What the hells would Colok want with a holy?"

Pikarn's throat rumbled. "I can think of a dozen things I'd do with a holy, maybe the Colok hold grudges, too. Colok're up to somethin' and so are the damned holies."

"We got war brewing between Colok and Istinjoln?" The words felt tainted by optimism the moment he muttered them, and he expected another comment about his being his mother's boy.

"Might be, but it sniffs of a skunk in the henhouse to me: Just because you smell it don't mean it's there. Find a meal and bed and we'll see what breakfast brings."

Ivin skipped the food and went straight for the down-ticked cot without a care for what dreams might come. Whatever they brought wouldn't compare to his day.

TWENTY

Blood in the Briar

The Griffon's severed wings flailing the grass,
Feathered fish floundering,
Leaving Lion to hunt savannah instead of eyrie.
Are you the Griffon, the lion, the wings?
The claws clutching grass instead of clouds?
Who are you to complain with words without wings?

—*Tomes of the Touched*

Eight Days to the Eve of Snows

Eliles awoke and attended morning prayers as she ever did, but with a secret sewn into the hem of her robes. It wasn't the greatest hiding place, but other options nibbled at her paranoia. The message scared her, not only it could get her killed, but the monastery had been quiet, no one leaving. What did it mean if the lord priest sent no one to help?

Every word of the scroll was a matter for her betters, not her. *I'm unholy, defiled, what do I care what troubles they bring on themselves?* Done with the whole thing, that's what she was. Onward to the Divining of Bones and the priesthood, out of Istinjoln forever.

But first, the kitchen to listen.

She plopped next to a blazing hearth, opened her book, and bit a roll slathered in honey. Raucous kitchen chatter kept to culinary business this morning. Talk of eggs and chickens, pork and kegs, as well as potatoes and onions. But as she thought of leaving a young maid scurried down the stairs with the hem of her dress in her hand, sweating and breathless.

"A priest . . . a priest, dead. Thrown to the thorns."

Kitchen tongues wagged in a cacophony of exclamations and questions, but Eliles knew who lay in the thorns and why. With everyone's eyes on the maid, Eliles popped the loose seam in her sleeve and slipped the parchment into the hearth's fire, watching it burn to ashes from the corner of her eye. She wanted to run, to make certain the body was Rovol's, but instead she took the stairs leading to the bailey.

Guilt bristled in her innards, but it was a single quill on the porcupine of her fears. If they knew he copied the message, they might've forced her name from his lost memory. If they didn't have her name, did they wait to see who rushed to witness the scene, or did they wait to see who didn't turn out? If they knew, she should flee. If they didn't know, was there a correct answer?

The wind howled and whipped as she stepped into the bailey, but her emotions numbed her face to the cold. She glanced to the main gate, then to the southern wall outside which grew the thorns. She jumped as a young postulant darted from nowhere, grabbing her hand, yanking on her.

Twelve years old and bursting with more energy than normal, Sandele's flint-gray eyes gazed at her with gravity. "Eliles! Someone was thrown to the thorns! Come on!"

She feigned surprise. She couldn't deny the urgent tugs from the one girl of hundreds who treated her like a friend rather than freak or idol.

They climbed a stair and joined a burgeoning crowd. Beyond the parapets lay brown robes entangled in a thick mass of vines. The deadly plants curling the length of the wall bore spikes four inches long, and those convicted of crimes against the Pantheon were cast from the wall alive. Covered in blood, she couldn't discern the man's face, but the blood from his mouth likely meant his tongue cut out, fitting the crime she'd made him commit.

The body could be hers, with robes shredded from struggling with the vines before bleeding out. It should be her. It still could be her. She planted her hands on the wall to keep steady.

"I wonder what he did to deserve this?" she asked no one in particular.

Jumel, a priestess in her first year of vows, cast Eliles an uncaring glance, her voice callous. "Looks like that randy librarian. My bet is he took leave with a forbidden tome. Or perhaps hiked his robes on the wrong gal."

The girls covered nervous giggles with their hands.

Eliles went along with the banter. "Maybe, but we don't know. Leastwise, we won't have to sit through another funeral for this one."

Because they left the bodies to feed the soil around the vines. She loathed being so cold to a man she'd killed, but cold equaled survival. She turned for the stairs as the girls discussed their good fortune.

Free from the wall, Eliles decided on Dareun's chambers. A reasonable enough choice for an innocent postulant to seek her master. She slipped into the tunnels and tossed her hood back, trying to look inconspicuous and calm despite wanting to jump every time she met someone round a corner. Dareun's door stood open, so she strode straight in.

She should have knocked.

Woxlin sat with a scroll spread on the table. "Good morning, Eliles."

"Ah, my girl!" She took solace in Dareun's pleasant tone, but still felt she might throw up.

She bowed to both. "I was stopping by to return this book."

Dareun smiled and took the tome, plopped it on the table.

Her thoughts danced wild with the rhythm of her heart. She couldn't be covering her anxiety, they stared, she had to speak. "Someone was Thrown to the Thorns. A priest. It's horrible."

Woxlin stood so fast his chair rattled on the floor. "What? There've been no trials."

Dareun said, "A suicide of penitence isn't unheard of."

Eliles felt an embarrassing tear and stiffened. "A crowd gathered on the wall. The face, covered in blood from the mouth like that monk had his tongue ripped out when I was a child." The memory haunted her dreams for years.

"Murder isn't unheard of either." Woxlin sighed, rolled his parchment. "You'll excuse me, of course; we'll have to discuss your possible replacement another time." He put his hand on her shoulder before he left. "Don't worry, we will find the killer, if there is one, and they will be punished. Gods have ways to reveal the guilty."

Revealing, torturing, and killing. She felt as if the man toyed with her, but this was her guilt talking. She hated how much fun she'd had the night before, teasing the fool for her own gains. She sat and gazed at the door as it swung shut.

"You knew the man?"

"Maybe, someone said it might be Rovol, the librarian."

Dareun sat beside her. "A man worth your tears?"

Girl be damned, he noticed. "It isn't him, it's that boy. Long ago." She knew this would make sense to him, a valuable key to a lie.

"You quivered and shook for two days because it proved what might become of you if they found out your feral magic. I told you then it was horrific, but to use it as a lesson."

"We should take lessons from the dead as we do the living."

The old man smiled. "That's my girl. We may yet learn a lesson from this man's death. Then we can thank him to ease his passage along the Road of Living Stars."

Eliles managed a meager smile to soothe her master's worrying after her. She rested her head on his shoulder. "I'm being silly. Everything will be fine." What lesson would he learn if she were the next to rest in the brambles?

TWENTY-ONE

Chasing Choerkin

A heart's quiver in the rose of weakness,
Two Dozen arrows full,
Ebony shaft and peacock eye in flight,
Raging turquoise piercing the mouths of Angels.

—*Tomes of the Touched*

Eight Days to the Eve of Snows

Mecum lay bundled in a heap of furs next to the fire pit, wheezing with the puckering noise of mucus in his nose and lungs. The man's mortal shell was failing him despite prayers. The old priest drank a swallow or two but hadn't eaten in days; Tokodin would be the only human in the caves before long.

The sleep of his dying was plagued by nightmares. Mecum muttered and screamed, his hands flailing against invisible foes as his legs thrashed. Every time the man's sleep quieted Tokodin prayed for him to die, to escape this torture.

Mecum's body shuddered but his eyes never opened. "Nothing is something, like nothing that is something . . . they come. Shadows."

He focused on the man's breathing and didn't notice Zjin walk in behind him.

"Come. Choerkin."

Tokodin shuddered as a tense breath escaped. He turned and brown, fur-lined robes finer than his own hit him in the face, dust sucking up his nostrils until he sneezed. As he swapped clothes, he realized they'd belonged to a priest. He failed to earn the robes once, and he figured he deserved it less now than ever, but he wasn't going to argue with their warmth.

"Got a pint of Istinjoln ale to go with this, have you?" It'd been too long since tasting anything but putrid tea and ice water.

Zjin stared at him, blank-faced. Whether they brewed beer or not, a sense of humor would make these beasts far more likable. "All right, then, let's go." Sitting in a cozy hole in the mountain when he could be braving frozen Shadow-infested mountains grew boring anyhow.

Zjin led him down a winding tunnel and when they emerged he covered his eyes. The sun was never so bright as after days in a cave. It reflected off the fresh white snow; there was no escaping its blinding brilliance. He sneezed twice. "Gods curse it."

When his eyes adjusted, monstrous wolves stared at him. Even the smallest was capable of making a quick breakfast of him, but they weren't wild nor hungry. Their shoulders were high as his sternum, and when they raised their heads, they could look him in the eye. Tokodin had heard tales of the Colok running with Tundra Wolves from the Treaty Lands, but he'd never considered the Colok domesticating them. He'd never entertained the idea of Colok talking, either.

Three teams of ten wolves stood harnessed to sleds, and Zjin beckoned him to climb aboard. He stepped on the contraption and knelt behind one Colok while Zjin stood on the back of the sled. Tokodin held tight, but when Zjin roared and the sled lurched, he tumbled into Zjin's furry legs. His shoulder throbbed and one leg flailed in the air while the other pinned itself beneath a wool sack.

It didn't take long to discover the sound Colok made when laughing as he struggled to find his seat. The guttural rumpus thrummed through the air, sounding like what Tokodin imagined drums would sound like if filled with water.

Their speed amazed him. The scenery whirred past over hills, swerving between trees, even across rocky ground that banged the sled and threatened to flip him into the air. The snow-capped mountains and their sparse green forests were an alluring vision when you weren't slogging through waist-deep snow. It sounded funny, but it was the first time he'd ever been in the mountains without fear of a Colok attack.

Better prisoner than prey.

They traveled for several candles and all he knew is they headed westerly with a northern bend. Zjin didn't bother to tell him a destination, but he knew it when they arrived: The sleds slowed to a stop at the edge of jagged cliffs thirty paces high, overlooking the Omindi, and straight across from the trail leading to the Crack of Burdenis. Tokodin's journey was a painful circle returning him to the start of the mystery.

A Colok scaled over the edge of the bluff. The creature was beautiful, with white fur streaked with rusty brown, and sky blue eyes. He thought it might be female but couldn't be certain.

Zjin left him to speak with this newcomer and returned in a loping gait. He growled, "Men. Horse."

A Choerkin patrol investigating after the attack made sense, and maybe they'd even found the entrance to Burdenis' shrine. They should be warned of the sinister hole in the cavern, but he didn't have a clue how.

A quiver reverberated through his bones like an echo of something terrible. He recognized it from the caves: The pulse. So deep in the ground and yet he felt it here. He didn't know what it was or what it meant, but it set his nerves on edge. He wasn't the only one.

The Colok scrunched their eyes, surveying the region, sniffing the air. Zjin snarled and he and the new Colok jumped on the sled with Tokodin, turning and driving the wolves south. They stopped at a copse of trees, unloading from the sleds and leaving the wolves.

"Come," Zjin commanded.

Tokodin climbed from his comfortable seat with a grimace, none too pleased. "What are—"

Every Colok crouched, their weapons at the ready. Tokodin went to a knee.

Zjin pointed across the gaping Omindi, but Tokodin saw nothing. He shrugged, and the beast grabbed his head, cranking his neck to set his eyes straight. He squinted, something moved. A shadow of a man, but no one was there. It dashed from rock to rock, swift, sometimes invisible, and disappeared over a cluster of boulders in the direction of the Crack.

The Colok didn't give him time for questions. Zjin and his people descended into the Omindi every which way with great claws and massive hands, but there was also a trail his pathetic human feet could manage. He scrambled after them, sliding much of the way on his ass, but reaching bottom in one piece.

The scream of horses echoed. Zjin growled and the Colok loped north, leaving poor Tokodin by his lonesome. Alone in the Omindi? Hells, no. He ran after them, forgetting his pain and stiffness.

His throat ached from the icy air by the time he huffed around a corner to find his new allies skulking forward, and he wondered if he might not have been better off walking. What was he in for? A fight with wardens or Shadows?

Hooves echoed and twenty or so horses skidded down a

scree-covered slope. The patrol turned their way, then yanked hard on their reins on seeing the Colok. Fresh powdery snow billowed with skidding hooves.

Tokodin shouted, "We're here to help!" But he knew there was no way they heard him over the din of echoing hooves and shouting men.

A bearded man in black shouted orders, and the horses wheeled and rode north at a full run.

"No! We're here. . . . Ah, hells."

Everything happened in such a hurry he forgot to consider what those armed and armored men ran from. A silent and terrifying horde of Shadows swung around the cliff. They floated above the ground, disturbing nothing as they passed, not even raising a trail of powdery snow. They ignored him and the band of Colok, turning north to follow the fleeing men.

Well, no way they would chase down horsemen and Shadows . . . or maybe they would. The Colok took off in pursuit. "Ah, hells! Zjin! I can't run down horses!"

The Colok skidded to a stop and loped back to him.

"I appreciate your—"

Zjin grabbed him around the waist and tucked him to his giant furry armpit like a man might carry a log and took off after the others. Nope, Tokodin couldn't say he appreciated this at all. Bad enough to be chasing non-corporeal Shadow demons bent on killing folks, but stuck under an arm and bouncing until his ribs ached as much as his shoulder while choking on wet dog smell? This must've been what his dice warned him about the times they suggested he choose death.

Zjin's pursuit slowed with Tokodin dangling in his arm, and the rest of the tribe disappeared around a curve in the Omindi, but he didn't tire.

Tokodin tried to go stiff as a board, limp as an overcooked noodle, and everywhere in between to make his ride more comfortable, but after a quarter candle noodle was all he could manage. After another half candle, he considered that he might've made Church history by discovering the Thirteenth Hell.

He lost track of time and distance in the jarring discomfort, struggling to keep his head up until Zjin slowed. The patrol stood in the middle of the road, Shadows clinging to the walls of the Omindi, surrounding them. Colok stood between Shadows and men, protecting them. He'd be fascinated by this turn of events as soon as he could breathe.

Zjin trotted up to the wardens and plopped Tokodin on the rump of a horse behind the hairy man before turning to eye the Shadows. Tokodin knew him as the Wolverine's second, Modan, both from their visits to Istinjoln over the years and the fact the man had rammed a spear through a priest accused of rape several years back, without trial. Another day he'd hate this warden, but today he was damned pleased to be perched on his horse.

Modan squirmed in his saddle to glance at him. "Who the gods-damned hells are you?"

A fair question albeit a tad blasphemous. He held up a finger, still catching his breath. "Tokodin." He coughed. "I, we, need to speak to a Choerkin."

"There are more priests?"

He didn't bother to explain the cloak; it didn't hurt his feelings to be mistaken for a priest; just another sin to complicate his crossing the Road of Living Stars. "Let me rephrase. The Colok wish to speak to a Choerkin."

"Ain't no clan-blood here; he's in that damned cave."

Tokodin slumped. A Choerkin dead in a cave, perfect. For the longest time he figured only his luck with women was worse than his dice, but after this past week he considered there might be a new leader. He mustered the nerve to ask, "Let me guess, the Wolverine is in there, too?"

"Aye, that he is."

"By all that's holy. Could something go right?"

Modan laughed, but it was stiff and out of place as he surveilled looming Shadows. "Sure as hells hope so, Priest, or we're all gods-damned dead."

The man smelled funky, or perhaps the horse, but he had a point. No use worrying about whether other folks were dead or alive when your own fate was in doubt.

Twenty-Two

Gift of Words

Feline pride taken in stride eyeing golden eyes,
Pillow paws stalking soft the lives of man,
Slashing claws render mortality moot in bleeding immortal lies.

—*Tomes of the Touched*

Eight Days to the Eve of Snows

Solineus watched Ilpen count his wares after a predawn breakfast, confident not a single piece had walked in the night. They hooked up the team and rode side-by-side on the wagon toward the orange of a rising sun. A covered bridge spanned a gurgling ice-edged brook and on reaching its shade they saw a man hanged from a leaf-bare tree across the way.

Ilpen whistled, drew the team to a stop and looked around, suspicious. He nudged the donkeys with his reins and they clopped forward, the bridge's planks thunking as the wheels passed.

"Told you this were a dangerous village. Beaten, and bet'n they hanged him by his own sling."

Solineus feigned a hard look as they passed the dangling corpse. "I'd wager you're right."

"A bad man, brought it on himself, likely as not. Strung a man up once myself, back when I were younger."

Solineus shot him a sideways glance. Murder seemed out of character, but a tall tale didn't. "You don't say."

Ilpen chuckled. "Well, it weren't just me. This stranger came looking for work in town. A no-good character, could tell from the first. He killed young Tirnur, knifed him in a lung when the boy caught him stealing chickens. Me and some others didn't wait none, we dragged him outside town and lynched him, just like that." He spat. "I didn't slip the rope on him, nor heave him to the branch, but I was there. Watched the man's neck stretch. A horrible thing, but the right thing. Stabbing poor Tirnur like that, we couldn't let it be."

Solineus thumped him on his shoulder. "I'd do the same. Some folks ask for it."

Solineus didn't know how much the tinker suspected or knew, and he didn't care to find out. If Ilpen did know, and was trying to ease Solineus' guilt, the words were appreciated but pointless. Killing the slinger had come as natural and remorseless as putting down a rabid possum. What this said about his forgotten past, well, bouncing on the wagon's seat put him in no mood for those musings.

"How long 'til we reach the Fost?"

"Oh, midday, if we don't throw no wheel. Head out tomorrow, or the next morn, depending on business. Three days, four at the most, and we'll rumble on into Istinjoln."

True to the tinker's word the donkeys rolled them into Choerkin Fost in the afternoon with the sun well above the horizon. The western gate leading to the docks bared the teeth of two portcullises, and murder holes stared at them as they passed beneath. With walls thirty feet high, twenty feet thick, and round towers, the defenses were stalwart. His impression of an impenetrable fortress hardened once inside with a clear view of the castle proper, its white walls sitting on a sheer cliff overlooking town and bay.

He glanced to the docks as they rode into town, the skyward masts of the harbored ships listing to and fro with the waves. Several bore flags fluttering in the breeze, one catching his eye: a golden crown on a field of blue, surrounded by the eight phases of the moon in white. A Luxun banner. A frustrated smile stretched his lips. How in the hells did he know anything about Luxuns? They were blue-skinned folk with feathery plumage for hair and bore a reputation as great sailors and tradesman.

"Whoa." Ilpen reined in the team.

"Time to stretch my legs?"

"Aye. I'll set up shop for a while, got some business with the woman here. Don't be gone long, I'll be finding food and drink soon."

Solineus jumped from the seat and wandered. Several accents caught his ear along the crowded streets; the Fost supported a healthy foreign trade, both northern clans and mainlanders from the south. These diverse peoples went about their work with polite nods and patience, jostles and bumps met kind words instead of insults. Unlike the Bloody Pebble, a sense of calm prevailed despite the raucous calls of vendors and boisterous barter. Conspicuously armed guards lent to this sensation, no doubt.

The fluttering blue pennant drew him, but as he reached the docks, a woman's voice stopped him.

"I'm looking for passage to Istinjoln."

The voice reminded him of the lady in his dreams.

A raspy voice answered her. "In two days, if'n you can pay."

The voice wasn't in his head unless someone else was there, too. Solineus turned and weaved through street traffic to find a tall woman with golden-blond hair draping to her slender waist, where her silk-lined cloak was cinched by a braided cotton-and-velvet sash. "I'd prefer to leave tomorrow, if possible. I can pay extra."

A greasy merchant missing several teeth eyeballed her. "Yeah? How much?"

"A silver fifty-song?"

The familiarity was uncanny, but the accent hinted to a northern clan, as a guess. Solineus needed to see her face, and his words slipped out as the merchant laughed at her offer, "We're headed Istinjoln way."

The woman turned with an engaging smile and eyes the ruddy brown of dark sardonyx. They captivated him but her round face bore little resemblance to the lady from the blue sea. He regretted saying anything until she spoke again, hauntingly familiar.

"Ah! That would be wonderful. When can we depart?"

His thinking hadn't stretched beyond getting her to turn around. He stammered. "I-I'm not sure. . . . I'm just saying, I'm working for a tinker headed that way. Might be we head out tomorrow, but the ride wouldn't be comfortable."

Her voice changed, the words trilled and hammered an upbeat tempo. "Take me to this tinker."

She sounded nothing like the lady from his dreams. His ears deceived him, or her excitement altered her tone. He turned without a word, wondering what he'd gotten himself into, and she followed on his heels.

Her words came with the speed of galloping hooves. "My name's Lelishen, I'm making a pilgrimage to Istinjoln and wanted to visit several shrines in the mountains before the Eve of Snows. Years and years my mama told me about them, a dream of mine since I was but a wee girl. I do hope your employer is kind enough to take me on; the journey would be so much more pleasant with good company, don't you think? Hmm?"

He shrugged. "S'pose so."

"Ah, one of those serious, quiet types, a man of few words. I can be that way sometimes too, you know. Mmmhmm. Sure can." She giggled.

"Now that'd make a more pleasant journey."

"Funny and quiet, we'll get along just grand. Where is this tinker? Hmm?"

They rounded the corner and Solineus pointed. The woman raced like a hound that'd caught a scent and wedged her way through potential customers until stealing Ilpen's attention with fingers wiggling in his face. Solineus hung back out of earshot, watched as her hands talked as much as her mouth did.

A pilgrim might be useful. She could get places a merchant's guard wouldn't reach. If Ilpen succumbed to her gyrations and banter there wasn't much room for an extra passenger. Where would she ride? Any hope of Ilpen turning the woman down ended when coins changed hands. It must've been a hefty sum. Ilpen waved off customers and slapped the shutters closed on his wagon and locked them.

"Solineus!"

He turned to see a scruffy, barefoot man in loose-fitting clothes. The sailor smiled big and clamped his arm in greeting. "Godsdamn, man, I thought for sure you's drowned."

Solineus hadn't a clue. "You were on the *Resten*?"

The man cocked his head. "You all right, friend? It's me, Hadin Elost. Yeah, we's on the *Resten* when we rammed that berg. Me and a few others made it to a dinghy. The *Imidki* damned near struck us in a fog next morn, but they done saved us. How the hells you make it?"

"I don't know, don't remember a thing 'til I woke up on a beach."

'No joshin'? Son of a . . . . That's a long float with kind currents, my friend."

The memory of his made-up story for Ielu flashed in his mind. "Was the captain's daughter on board?"

The sailor's eyes struck the street's cobbles. "Yeah, yeah. I know you were sweet on her. Detu were sailing with us. Less she had your luck, she didn't make it. Cap'n Biun, neither."

Solineus' false story for Ielu took on new life, maybe buried memories after all. "Sorry to hear it." His mind scattered with a hundred questions, and he found it hard to focus on one. "I— Do you know, was I working on the ship, or . . . what?"

"You? A sailor? Son of a bitch, no." He laughed. "I've no idea why, I assumed your father or one of the Emudar done sent you to the Choerkin fer somethin', but I weren't fool enough to ask."

"My father is?"

"Godsdamn, man, yer ain't kiddin', are you? You're Adinvan Mikjehemlut's eldest boy, second cousin of Lidin Emudar, lord of the clan."

"I'm clan blood?"

"Holy hells, man. I need to be gettin' you home." Solineus shook his head as the man continued. "Me and the boys gonna jump the *Swane* tomorrow, if'n you're wantin' to head back to Emudar Fost, I'm sure we can sign you on."

Solineus glanced to Ilpen and the strange woman. "No, I've got a few things to take care of before I head home. How well did you know me?"

Hadin chuckled. "Well enough to know not to try 'n drag you home when you got a sword."

Solineus' breath left him as his heart sank, and he looked into the man's eyes with a solemn gaze. "I'm a right dangerous man, I reckon."

Hadin's lips stretched taught, any lightheartedness gone. "Yeah, I reckon that's no lie." He shifted his weight and crossed his arms.

"Look, I don't know what you're thinkin' or what you's done, maybe, but you ain't no bad man. A hard man, true, but not bad."

Solineus stared at the scrawny man, more grateful for those words than he would've expected. "I thank you for that."

"Sure, sure. Still thinkin' home might be a better remedy than this Choerkin dirt."

"I've no doubt, but I got myself into something. I've got a hundred questions—"

Hadin threw his hands in the air and laughed. "Whoa, I probably couldn't answer a dozen, if'n that. But me and a couple of the other boys'll be throwin' a few pints and sleepin' at the Bronze Beggar tonight, buy us a drink and we'll see what we might know for ya."

"Aye, that'd be handy. If I don't see you tonight, ride the waves safe to home."

"Sure. Hey, I'll be sure your family and the Emudar know you made it."

Solineus smiled. "Appreciate it." He offered the sailor a silver coin, but the man turned his hands palms down.

"Nah, my family owes yer pa more than you can pay. You better make sure to make it home safe, hear?"

"I'll see you back home."

Solineus gazed after the sailor as he merged and disappeared in the crowd. His name *was* Solineus Mikjehemlut of the Clan Emudar, any uncertainty lay quashed. The man knew him, his family, the ship, and the captain's daughter whom Solineus had thought to be nothing more than a figment of a hypothetical lie. He couldn't deny his own name and whatever lost history was his; it'd be irrational in the face of everything the world was telling him. But, somehow it still felt wrong.

"Solineus!" Ilpen waved him over, his crooked teeth on full display between heavy jowls, as the woman climbed onto the wagon seat.

"You'll be happy to hear we're heading for Istinjoln straightaway. But, uh, this one pays better than you. Hop on back."

So much for a hundred questions and pints of beer. The woman handed Ilpen a coin from her purse and Ilpen bit it as if it were a savory sweet. Its gleam explained Solineus' demotion and the speedy departure: Gold. Whoever this woman was, she knew the straightest route to Ilpen's heart was through his pocket. She also knew his favorite color.

Solineus climbed onto the back of the wagon's box, the boards creaking under his weight, and copperware rattling. He sat with his arms wrapped around his knees, lay on his back, his side, then resigned himself to sitting with his arms splayed for balance. The donkeys jerked the wagon and a wheel slammed a pothole, jarring his spine; teeth bared, he cursed under his breath. As much as he'd groaned about his sore ass while bouncing along rocky roads, he knew after a few rattles and shakes how good he'd once had it.

Twenty-Three

Digging Deeper

Craven Raven, black of feather and black of beak,
of what today shall we speak?
The universe. The Universe?
Dark and Glow, the Balance.
Yes, I hear you, I heard you, I will hear you again.
The Raven's caw, caw, kraa I hear you
But do you, noisy bird, understand what you say?

-*Tomes of the Touched*

Seven Days to the Eve of Snows

Eliles awoke exhausted, unable to sleep through blood-filled dreams. She pulled on her robes and stumbled with groggy steps to the First Hall for morning prayers. She bowed her head dutifully but let others chant their sonorous devotions. By the gods, how could she not sleep at night, but feel she should curl up for a nap in the middle of this mass of people? It was perverse.

She yawned and stretched, her mouth wide open when she spotted Woxlin standing at the fore with the Speaker's Staff in hand. She snapped her jaw shut and dipped her head to its proper prayerful repose. She couldn't escape this priest for the last week. When the final hymnal ended, Woxlin struck the floor with the iron-shod butt of the staff three times.

Heads raised, and the room went silent.

"As most have heard, Rovol of Teverle was Thrown to the Thorns. This was not, as so many expected, a repentant suicide nor murder. It was a duly sanctioned execution."

A murmur passed through the congregation.

"The night before last, while delivering materials to the Sealed Rooms, the lord priest's Keeper of Histories herself witnessed Rovol falsifying documents in such manner that might bring embarrassment to Lord Priest Ulrikt of Bain, and the Pantheon itself."

The chamber echoed with gasps and whispers. Woxlin banged the Speaker's Staff three times, commanding silence.

"With a witness undeniable, Rovol received the sentence of Thorns by the lord priest's decree, and the execution was carried out at dawn's first rays. If any should find a bearer's message purporting to be written by or sent to His Eminence, let it be known that it is false. Written in Rovol's hand, likely to impress an unknown woman. In Sol's name, we brand his name forgotten to the Slave Fields."

Woxlin's eyes scanned the kneeling adherents, and when they landed on her, she met his gaze without a flinch. Her heart told her he knew, but the voice in her head rationalized it as impossible. No, improbable. Impossible no longer existed. If they knew and did not come after her, they played a game, but to what end? She didn't know, and no longer wanted to know. She'd learned her new lessons: Stay small, stay humble, and stay out of the business of lord priests.

Woxlin handed off the Speaker's Staff and slipped behind heavy velvet curtains. She rose and departed with the flock, another obedient duck waddling her way to weekly devotions. She prayed the Sequence of Fire, kneeling before each God in turn. She arrived at the Alcove of

Sol last, the opposite of most to avoid a crowd, but the lack of even a single monk startled her.

She took a deep breath and kneeled, gazing into the blazing oil at the Fire Shrine of Sol. The traditional chant of observance struggled to pass her lips, then died.

"Do not turn around. Do not speak. Do not think. Do listen." The voice was a force, one impossible to resist. Her every muscle stalled in time with her voice choked, and her thoughts, even fear, scattered, but her ears remained keen. She knew the voice but couldn't attach a name. The prayer enthralling her was more powerful than she'd ever experienced.

"It was you at the library. Others say I should punish your curiosity, have you lashed until your ribs show, or bled to feed the hogs. I demanded mercy before the gods upon this Eve of Snows. Tampering with scrolls sealed for Sol is sacrilege, one I could not forgive. But curiosity is a fault, not a crime, even when soliciting sacrilege. If you asked, and he did not comply, would that be a crime?"

A hand enveloped her shoulder, gentle, but sending chills down her back as strong fingers kneaded her taut muscles. "No, my child. Is asking a crime because he chose to be a fool? Still no. So you shall live while he falls through the Road of Living Stars to a hell of his earning. It would, however, be a crime to discuss the contents of the scroll. Oh, I could force you to forget, as you did the Forgotten Sinner, but I need you to forget of your own will. This proves devotion. For my part, I, too, will forget. Until you make me remember. Causing me to remember would be disappointing and make the Thorns a gentle exit." His grip freed her shoulders, but a hand rested on her head, a gesture of imparting blessings on the devout. "You and I are the favored children of the gods, Sol grants our prayers on a whim. Yet there is a difference: I took three licks from the Maimer's Lash to prove to myself and my elders I had the mettle to lead. You still lack this strength."

His hand lifted and a boot ground on the floor's pebbles as he spun on a heel. But he stopped. "You have an idea something is coming, but you do not know its extent. Show your wisdom and demonstrate your strength at last, prove you are the cut diamond among soft cabochons, and someday you may succeed my rule. You have great potential; don't see it wasted by dying this young."

The paralysis of her fingers and toes faded, her throat able to swallow, her mind capable of reasoned thought, as the sound of footsteps trailed away. The obvious coalesced into her doom: Lord Priest Ulrikt. She'd heard his voice a hundred times delivering sermons meant to inspire profound reflection and a deeper faith in the gods, or to paint evocative pictures of the torments of the Twelve Hells. It was the second time he'd saved her, first from the Maimer, now from a fate more wicked.

She didn't bother to ask why, instead she fell to her face and wept, the only reasonable response to an emotional flood. When others came to pray she crawled into shadow, covering her face and tears and shame.

The oracle of bones would reveal her future tomorrow but even if Dareun were correct about the Traveling Wisdom, Ulrikt wouldn't allow her to leave Istinjoln. How did he know of Rovol's crime? If the lord priest's spies were so effective, was her feral magic "forgotten," too? It had never occurred to her before. If he believed her chosen, with a higher purpose, could he look past her feral magic? No impossibilities remained. None.

She stood, straightening her spine and setting her jaw. *I have possibilities too.* If they denied the Traveling Wisdom, she'd leave on her own. She wiped her tears as her strides carried her toward upper Istinjoln.

Priests be damned. Their gods didn't speak to her, anyhow. She didn't need them any more than they needed her. Curse them to the Slave Fields. She could've left any time, but she didn't want to fail Dareun. If the tinker and his donkeys arrived for the Eve of Snows, she'd meet up with him in a nearby town.

Still, a girl needed to stay alive to leave. She stepped into an alcove, closed her eyes, pushed her senses into the halls. A split-flicker to see if anybody followed her. She felt nobody and drew her senses in. Would the lord priest bother to have her followed? Was her knowledge so dangerous? Just scribbles on a scroll discredited by a lord priest's decree.

She climbed a ladder to upper Istinjoln, ignoring the monk and stepping straight into brisk afternoon breezes. Refreshed and goose-bumped, she strode to the northern wall's allure with her eyes locked on the gatehouse. The portcullis stood open, so easy to step outside the walls, so difficult to disappear.

The temptation to flee taunted her over the years, but by the time she grew old enough to survive on her own, Dareun had become her family. She blamed neither the walls nor Dareun for the hell the priests made here and tried not to blame the gods.

As a child, she'd believed escape a matter of time: Time was running out. All she needed to do was show the courage to turn her back on one life for a new one. She survived banishment from her village, she'd survive flight from Istinjoln.

The gatehouse chime signaled riders and her heart lurched. It could be Ilpen and Ears. No. If she gambled, she'd put her coins on guests arriving for the Eve of Snows. She leaned against the cold parapet, waiting to see if a friendly face entered the monastery.

This is why I never gamble. Seven palfreys came through the gates, a single priestess and the rest Choerkin Wardens. The Wolverine lead the group which meant no ordinary visit. The old man wouldn't remem-

219

ber her from a hill of manure, but he'd saved her from the inquisition days after she'd fled from her father. Ilpen's cart had been stopped by an inquisitor and his hunters, and Pikarn and his Wardens had stood between them daring the inquisitor to arrest her. Gruff and blustery, but she held a soft spot for him in her heart from that brief meeting. Meliu, a studious young priestess known for her knowledge of languages, her looks, and sharp tongue, rode with them. Of the remaining five she recognized four, but the only one she had a name for was a tracker known in Istinjoln as Rat. The final man she'd never seen.

They waited in the bailey, and she needed to know why. Eliles' legs carried her to the stables before she knew what they were doing. If gods gave her wisdom, she'd stop her feet right now, but she bore a curse, not wisdom. She hid in the stables and none other than Woxlin greeted the wardens. The second time in half a day she noted how wrapped in the mysteries of Istinjoln he was.

Woxlin haled Meliu and dismissed her after taking a book from her hands. Eliles castigated herself before she even thought it. *No way in the Twelve Hells! I am not going after that book.* Suicide, or worse. A brief conversation between Woxlin and the Wolverine ensued. Did she know his real name? In Istinjoln Wolverine was the only name he bore.

With the conversation finished, the priest strode toward the Long Hall. To her delight the wardens headed for the stable. The Wolverine's hatred for Istinjoln made him a tacit ally.

She hustled to the loft and hid in the stacks of loose hay. The men dismounted, and the one she didn't recognize was different: tall and blond. He handed the reins to a stable boy, as did the Wolverine, rather than unbuckling tack as the other four. He carried himself with self-importance, a confidence rivaling the Wolverine's, but more formal. He wasn't Modan Heklar, the Wolverine's second, famous as a priest killer, she'd recognize him by his smell if not his face.

The Wolverine's stern voice carried, and she ducked for no good reason. "More horses than I've ever seen in Istinjoln; it's lookin' like a right grand party for the Eve."

She'd been so busy sneaking she hadn't noticed. The number of riding and draft horses swelled every year for the Eve of Snows, but the Wolverine had the right of it.

"See to the horses, make certain they've oats, then meet Choerkin and me at Long Hall. We'll stay the night and see what morning brings, so take all the food and ale they'll give us."

Men laughed, and even stable hands dared grins.

Her eyes widened, and she ducked deeper. The Wolverine and a Choerkin? Whether coincidence, fate, or luck, new allies were in Istinjoln. If the Wolverine hated priests, it was because the Choerkin hated priests. In Istinjoln, Choerkin were famous for three things: bear-skin cloaks, a disdain for the gods, and executing Lord Priest Imrok of Girn for treason. Or as the priests of Istinjoln said: a Holy War.

Istinjoln's whispers spoke of five Choerkin boys, two at the Fost and three on the Watch. Two were blond, and one stood second-in-line to the Clan Head; they wouldn't send kin so close to the head of the clan. This Choerkin belonged to Kotin, his youngest.

It'll be nice to meet you, Ivin Choerkin. Oh, even echoing in her head it sounded insane after the lord priest's threats, but she needed to talk to someone. As the men brushed their horses, she constructed her plan. If she made herself at home in the stables, didn't return to the tunnels, they couldn't watch for her to leave. It'd be easy to find the building the wardens slept in, and there'd be a guard to deal with. A simple dweomer sending them to the latrine, and she would have time for her talk.

All she had to do was wait for nightfall, and for upper Istinjoln to sleep.

Twenty-Four

Failing Visions

Doom-Makers and Doom-Breakers
Fighting the same War from opposite ends.
A war, the War, for this time and all time,
battles destined to meet in the middle
where the Doom-Speaker sits and the Doom-Taker
takes.

—*Tomes of the Touched*

Seven Days to the Eve of Snows

The halls of Istinjoln were colder than Meris remembered, or her aging flesh and bones took their chill deeper. She'd arrived in the middle of the night like a thief, or more accurately, a treasure the thief carried. Her ninety-fifth birthday had passed unmentioned while jostling for days to and fro in a frigid, covered wagon. They stopped only to relieve themselves and change horses, and she wondered more than once if the journey wasn't meant to kill her. Alas, she made it alive for whatever fearful duty the Lord's Face put before her.

Nerves made her pace dark chambers beneath the monastery in her youth, unable to sleep. Aged hips, knees, and ankles kept her from walking the halls now, but she hated this dark without stars. She'd lived in black the past fifty years, but her darkness bore the pinholes of the heavens. She smiled as she closed her eyes, envisioning Skywatch, her heaven in the mortal realm.

A knock on her chamber door and a handsome, smiling priest interrupted her meditations. For a moment she imagined him as a young man from her past, a priest who had long since Walked the Stars. Remembrance of this age-old tryst brought a grin.

"Lord Priest Ulrikt will see you now."

Meris held her groan in check with a tight-lipped smile as she stood, the ache from days in a wagon making her feel older by a decade, if that were possible. She followed the young priest quick as she could, feet scuffing the ground with tiny steps until muscles limbered. She stopped to stare as the young man climbed a set of spiraling stairs. A deep breath and a prayer for strength later she managed the first dozen steps before her escort regained a modicum of wisdom and returned to help her. She leaned heavy on the poor boy by the time they reached the top, and to her relief the lord priest's chambers were twenty paces around the corner.

She let go of her escort's robes and shuffled through the door with a smile she hoped hid her agony. The room was lit like noon, bright and warm, and it took several flickers for her eyes to adjust.

"It's been too many years since last we spoke."

Ulrikt came into focus seated in a plush, high-backed chair beside a small table with a carafe of red wine. She remembered the lord priest as a young man fresh to the priesthood, not the distinguished older gentleman he'd become. Vibrant blue eyes sat beneath fine silver brows, and although the handsome man's hair had crept backward on his head and gone gray, the remainder still grew thick and groomed. The smile he gave her shone with kindness.

"Yes, it has." She'd never conversed with the man outside her role as an oracle, and as High Oracle of Skywatch scrolls and messenger had been their only communications. This was her first invitation to the chambers of the lord priest, and its ostentatious decor surprised her. Velvet and gold, silk and silver, and gem-inlaid exotic woods; she couldn't imagine where such bountiful treasures of craftsmanship came from.

Ulrikt stood, having caught her wandering eye, and lifted a vase from its stand. The glazed colors in auburn and violet hues swirled into patterns which resembled a stylized writing system, letters of a sort, only she didn't recognize them. He flipped the vase, showing her the base, and she leaned in, muttered a quick prayer so her old eyes might read the faint squiggles. She pursed her lips; eyesight wasn't the only problem, the scrawls were foreign.

"What does it say?"

The lord priest chuckled. "I don't know. Best our people can figure, it's in a language related to Obereut, the maker's name I suppose, a date perhaps."

She nodded, as if she knew what he was talking about as he returned the vase to its perch, but it must've been obvious she didn't understand.

"We've several books deep in our libraries in this same language; the tongue has defied our scholars for centuries. And yet, when our forebears restored Istinjoln, priests found it hidden among other treasures."

"It is beautiful."

He slide-stepped and pointed to the chair he'd been sitting in. The wood was exquisite, with tight grains, and burls of red and white in its pale yellow flesh. The cushion in its seat was emerald green with brass tacks. "This exquisite piece sat in this very room; foreign hands carved it from an exotic wood we don't even have a name for. Most everything in this room, right down to the glass holding my wine, is from somewhere else; we don't know when they came here, how, why, or even who crafted them. Of all the things in this room, only you, me, and Timus, your guide to these chambers, are native to this place. Please, sit. I've little doubt your journey was swift and wearying."

Meris sank into a chair's velvet cushions and feared the plush was so deep she might never get out on her own. "It's an impressive collection."

"So tell me, and feel free to be honest. Any regrets, having chosen Skywatch?"

She wasn't sure what he was digging for, so she hid her face in a swallow of wine until he continued. The wine rested on her tongue with an edge of sweetness she liked, so taking her time was a pleasant burden.

"By that I mean, you would have been in consideration for lord priest, if you'd stayed. Ever consider what might have been?"

She lowered her goblet, trying to stymie the shake in her hand. All people who lived long enough bore the weight of regrets; this man needn't know any of hers. "I am precisely what I was destined to be. The stars of Skywatch are my home and refuge, there's no more beautiful a place in the world, to me."

He raised his glass in salute. "I've held the mantle of lord priest for thirty-seven years now, and there've been times I wished someone else had taken my destiny."

Meris already sat in the stars by then, but she remembered well when Herald's Watch announced Lord Priestess Sadevu's passing and the name of her youthful replacement. At thirty-two, Ulrikt had become the youngest to attain lord priest, and he climbed the ladder of influence among the seven lords with astounding alacrity and lack of blood. But these things were history; she wanted to know about the now.

"Your destiny seems beautifully aligned to your talents. The bones were right about you."

A wistful gaze passed across his face, surprising her. "Were they? I suppose so. The foresight seemed more pleasant than my hindsight."

His words baffled her. The Lord Face sent her here for a purpose, and she doubted it was to discuss the merits of their lives, chosen or destined. She took a mouthful of wine to bolster her nerves. "I loathe blunt words, lord priest, but with so many years behind me . . . Why am I here?"

The man concocted a gaze brimming with dimwitted innocence, and she wondered how long he stared into a mirror to perfect it. "To break bones on the Eve of Snows, of course."

Meris shifted in her seat, so cozy and yet uncomfortable faced with his smile. "Your Lord F—"

"My emissary."

"Your emissary implied something of importance, but wouldn't give me details." Implied, and threatened her body and soul if she should fail. Missions without descriptions, but full of consequences made her nervous. "He said I would know."

"You haven't forgotten how to break bones, have you? Then you will know what to do. Bones, lives, storms, even waves, none are truly equal no matter how they appear. You know the differences in bones better than anyone, and you will not flinch when fate requires you to speak of doom. That is why you are here, plain if not simple." He refilled her wine and settled back in his seat. "I can't impart some great wisdom upon you nor tell you what futures you will see."

She smiled, knowing full well he could learn of any smoothed bone if he wished. Wine swirled in her mouth as she studied his cold blue eyes. He didn't say all he could, but she sensed no lies. "Fine."

He smiled, and she thought she detected both sadness and mirth buried beneath his words. "You were a cranky old bird even back then, but of course I couldn't say such a thing with threat of the whip."

Her head bobbed, she couldn't deny these things, even though there seemed no point to them. "You brought me here to air an age-old grievance?"

Ulrikt chortled. "No, dear no. I always admired you and regretted never getting to know you outside our occasional correspondence. Quill and ink are no way to get to know another, I dare say. So I used this, the most grand Eve of Snows in generations, with the alignment of the Road of Living Stars, to invite you here, to meet with you, to get to know you a little. Simple as that."

Those final words might well be the biggest lie she'd heard since she herself had told Pineluple Choerkin she and her daughter would live. But everything before that rang true, and were the most befuddling words she'd ever heard a lord priest utter. She couldn't think of a single reason for this powerful man to take an interest in her.

"Don't you remember? The divination of my high priesthood, the last you oversaw before traveling to Skywatch. I'm sure it's been a thousand bones since for you, but for me, only a few."

So many bones, so many cracks, so many years. "I don't. I'm sorry. Most of those bones were smoothed, anyhow—"

"Not mine, not that night. Lord Priestess Sadevu saw to it. I needed the truth, and you gave it to me. Your words, 'You will get to know she who writes your destiny and glory, which lights your path to the First Star of Heaven.'" His fingers drummed the rim of his goblet. "Don't you see? You are she who will write my destiny, but we've never had a chance to get to know each other."

"You've brought me here to fulfill the promises of a prophecy I uttered over forty years ago? How would this old woman write your destiny?"

"Humor me." His smile turned impish, like a child too proud of his game. "Please, drink, tell me about yourself."

She relaxed into the cushions with a sip, the wine going straight to her senses after long years not partaking in drink. She'd gone decades without considering who she was outside the context of Skywatch; she didn't know where to start. After decades, maybe there was nothing else. "I'm not the master of Skywatch. I am Skywatch." *The murderer in the stars.* No, some truths the lord priest needn't hear, even if he already knew.

"The murderer in the stars. More poetic than I'd expect from you. Do go on."

She cursed herself for muttering her guilt out loud. Or had she? She must have, not that he cared, permission to kill had come straight from Istinjoln. Ulrikt and a dozen high priests shared in her murderous guilt over Pineluple and her daughter.

After she'd communicated her fears of the unborn child, the next communication from Istinjoln told her to do what she deemed best. Best, but not what she deemed right. "The stars have been my guide and my life, no matter where they took me." Wine loosened her tongue, and she needed to be more careful, keep her words and thoughts more mundane and innocent.

So she spoke of her family, and her youth, in and outside Istinjoln. The lord priest listened with an intent gaze, nodding and prodding for explanations of simple things from playing with dolls to breaking her first prophetic bone in Istinjoln. All the while, he gave her no clues at all as to why he cared.

TWENTY-FIVE

Holy Mole

*The blind man follows a mole relying on whiskers not his own,
To what end does he shave? To rend at the end, the spring trap
Steel Flowering red-gold, vultures instead of bees,
Withering vines, limbs, fingers for thorns and toe roots
Unable to feast as the mole passes him by with a snicker.*

—*Tomes of the Touched*

Eight Days to the Eve of Snows

Ivin awoke more sore than mornings after being beaten with a waster in training, which at least made him forget his saddle sore ass as he slipped into wool pants and padded jack. He wobbled down the stairs to find the dining hall, a room colder than the fire in the hearth suggested.

The Wolverine sat with feet propped before the fire, staring into the flames and looking like he'd been awake for candles. Meliu sat on his left, elbows propped on the book over her knees and irritable, and Puxele paced his right, head swiveling with a glare that never left the Wolverine's brow.

Ivin nabbed a bowl of porridge and a mug of ale from a serving boy and settled on a bench to catch up on what he'd missed.

"I could have twenty men in the mountains by midday. What the hells we waiting for?" Puxele asked.

Meliu's face was pale, and her infected wounds flared red, but whatever her condition, her eyes fumed. "You promised to get me to Istinjoln."

Rinold bounced down the stairs, spry as any other day, and Ivin hated him for it. "I'll lead the tracking party. After food." The serving boy scuttled to him with a bowl and mug, and the Squirrel didn't bother with a spoon, slurping.

Pikarn turned to the priestess first. "We'll get you to Istinjoln soon as that there infection's gone——"

"I'm good to ride."

"You're good to ride when I say, and my whiskers say we've snow blowing in. As for Modan, if any son of a bitch can drag his ass out of the mountains with his head intact, it's that one."

Rinold poured ale into his porridge. "True nuf, but that don't mean we don't go lookin'."

Puxele puffed her chest and stared at Pikarn.

Pikarn said, "We ain't throwing more lives into them mountains until we give the man a chance. If he ain't through the gates by dawn tomorrow, you get your men, Little Sister."

"Rinold and me, we'll bring the man home."

Pikarn blurted, "No."

Puxule's face tightened. "You ain't keeping me from them mountains."

"No, I'm not, Squirrel's with me. You'll lead the party."

Ivin squinted at the back of Pikarn's head. "She'll need a tracker."

Pikarn didn't bother looking at him. "A few candles in the mountains and Ratsmasher thinks he knows it all. Orvil's in town, he can track. When this girl ain't burnin' red no more, we'll head for Istinjoln, whether you're back or not, hear me?"

"I'm healthy now," Meliu insisted.

"You're pale as snow and yer eyes're glazed as ice, so shut your yap and enjoy the fire and food and beer a couple days, peruse that godsda— that book of yours, whatever it takes to keep yourself quiet. I'll get you to Istinjoln."

"The herbs're messing with my eyes." The priestess snorted, not even selling herself on that story. "Yeah, right, you better."

Pikarn groaned and clasped his forehead, dragging both hands down his face. "Healing's the easy part, girl. But Modan will prove my faith and ride through them gates."

The next morning, Puxele rode for the Omindi with Orvil as her second and fifteen more wardens at her command, leaving the Wolverine standing in town gnawing beef. He stared to the mountains, cursing the gods. When neither party of wardens returned by the Eighteenth of Yistole, Ivin feared the Wolverine might gnash his own teeth to splinters with worry while running out of expletives. Ivin learned the Wolverine had iron nails for teeth and an extensive vocabulary of the profane for every god.

The weather in Ervinhin remained gray and dry while snows blanketed the higher mountains, and as Meliu's red wounds turned to pink, Pikarn lost his excuse for putting off his promise to the priestess.

Ivin met Fronk, Lidin, and Wilhart for the first time that morning. Of the men the Wolverine still had in town, these were the wardens he deemed least likely to spout off and get them in trouble with the holies.

They departed a few candles past dawn, and after six quiet candles in the saddle they arrived at the base of the legendary monastery's road. When Ivin was a child, his mother spoke of the monastic fortress in reverential terms. A pious woman born and raised in Erxlikt, a short day's ride south of Istinjoln, she'd attended numerous festivals during her youth and received the Seven Blessings at the hand of the lord priestess herself. The fortress was nestled in the Jonin foothills, and she spoke of how the towers paid homage to the snow-covered mountain peaks with towers capped in white marble, and how the gods themselves carved the central tower in an Age past.

As they approached Istinjoln in the light of fading day, Ivin had to admit his mother didn't exaggerate its magnificence and beauty. The location was idyllic, with mountains in the background, and a long, rising road curling its way like a serpent's tail to the front gate. Although young when she died, Ivin remembered how she always saw the candle in the dark, and the good in all things.

Perhaps once he'd been his mother's child, but for the past eleven years he'd been his father's. The effect of the view upon arrival was intentional: impress and awe. It reminded everyone of its purpose, a fortress thousands could throw themselves against and fail. He was small and powerless against its majesty, for here lived the gods incarnate as stone walls, here defiance and assault became suicide.

But his father had also forged into his brain that the gods lied.

The harrowing, cliff-sided road narrowed as it approached the gate towers until no more than four horseman would feel secure side-by-side. A drawbridge of oaken planks stretched across a twenty-foot chasm, leading into a gatehouse with three iron portcullises and murder holes above. These were peaceful times, and before dark the yawning entrance was open, protected only by two mail-clad guardsmen who granted entry with bored nods.

If Istinjoln hid dangerous secrets, they lacked concern over them being found. Or at least, anyone carrying them past these walls alive. Despite his mother's praise, the monastery carried a trident's reputation: Quiet, unforgiving, and brutal. Three bloodstained points to keep the curious from prying, and those with knowledge, from talking.

More than likely coming here would prove fruitless or suicidal, but the Wolverine was not a creature to be dissuaded.

They waited in the bailey, the only souls in sight guards who walked the allure. The outbuildings were dark as the sun set, and he grew cold while sitting still on his horse as mountain winds whipped across the barren bailey.

"Do they know we're here?"

For a moment, Ivin was sure he'd receive his third hunk of jerked beef today, but the old man surprised him. "It takes time for a worm of the proper rank to crawl from its hole, but they know we're here, sure as hells."

Meliu paced several yards in front, and Ivin wondered if her manic steps were nerves or she was staying warm. Ivin's toes were growing numb by the time two priests arrived, making him grateful to dismount and invigorate his blood. The high priest walked straight to Meliu, touched her head, clucked, and whispered words that brought a smile. He took the book, glanced at it, then handed it to the lantern-bearing priest with a nonchalant grace. The high priest took the girl's cheeks in his hands and kissed her on the forehead.

"Get yourself to the healers, my girl. Off now."

Meliu disappeared into a dark building and behind them a portcullis ground to a close. Ivin glanced back, hoping he wasn't a witless rat caught in a trap, but the priest's smile as he turned eased Ivin's rodent worries.

"Pikarn, truly, it has been too long."

The two men shared cordial nods.

"High Priest Woxlin, this is Ivin Choerkin, my new hand."

"Modan is well, I pray?" The priest's concern seemed genuine.

The Wolverine grumbled. "The boy's not a replacement, leastwise not yet."

Woxlin turned to him and offered his ringed fingers. Ivin bowed his head until his forehead touched the man's ring, and thanked the gods Kotin wasn't here to witness this obeisance, even if it was an act to gain trust.

"We don't see many Choerkin in Istinjoln these days."

Ivin managed a smile. "I wish it were under more pleasant terms. My mother spoke well of Istinjoln."

"She is remembered as a devout and gentle soul, surely settled well in the Seven Heavens." To Ivin's relief the priest maneuvered to a topic which promised to thaw his toes. "Tend your horses, then meet me at the Long Hall for food and drink."

Pikarn led them to an impressive stable pressed against the northwest wall. The building was long and two-storied, capable of holding maybe two hundred horses, but at least half the stalls stood open and empty. Still, it was an impressive number of horses to see in one place. Considering what a decent horse fetched at market, a fortune in horseflesh. He handed his reins to a stableboy and waited as the Wolverine eyeballed the stalls.

"More horses than I ever seen in Istinjoln, lookin' like a right grand party for the Eve." Pikarn spoke to himself as much as anyone else, then turned to Rinold. "See to our horses, make certain they've oats, then meet Choerkin and me at Long Hall. We'll stay the night and see what morning brings, so take all the food and ale they'll give us."

Ivin chuckled along with the other men and caught a stable boy grinning.

Pikarn nodded to Ivin and strolled to the door, leading him across the bailey and into dark, winding streets. The buildings were dark and windowless until they came to what must be the Long Hall. Stone with tiled roof, it sported glowing windows every couple strides down its length and two chimneys puffing smoke.

Scattered inside were several long tables seating a host of monks and postulants, who ate porridge and bread, drinking beer. Woxlin cleared a table in the corner with a glance. Monks brought them food and drink.

"The fare is unspectacular, but there is plenty. How did you come across our young priestess?"

Pikarn related the tale from the Ihomjo mines, while Ivin spooned his porridge and watched among the hooded holies for anyone who might pay too much attention. He caught one glancing more often, but his only glimpse beneath the cowl was a flash of pale skin and blond hair. He kept his eye on this one, but likewise, they seemed to have an eye on him, and that first glimpse was the only one he caught.

Pikarn kept his voice quiet as he reached the meat of their story, but didn't hide an angry growl. "There were Shadows that took the bodies of men, and those men eat the dead, best we can tell. Trouble is, this has been happening for damned near a year and not so much as a courteous whisper from Istinjoln."

"I only heard about troubles at the Shrine recently myself—"

"Horseshit."

Pikarn's voice carried too far for Woxlin's taste. The priest stood. "My apologies, please everyone, excuse yourselves."

Benches ground on the stone floor as everyone rose and exited without finishing their meals. Ivin caught sight of the watcher: Beneath the cowl a lock of blond hair and a comely face. A young woman, and unless she had a twin, she'd be easy to pick out in a crowd.

Woxlin sat after the room cleared. "It is not the duty of Istinjoln to inform you of all goings on."

"It damned well should be when people are being killed and eaten! For Sol's sake, Priest—" The Wolverine took a couple deep breaths. "And what about that cursed book?"

"Book? Oh, nothing more than a treatise on the history of the Shrine."

"Horseshit and donkey piss."

Ivin stuffed his mouth with bread to keep from smiling.

"That tome may as well've been written on her own skin as much as she wanted to part with it."

Woxlin kept calm, his demeanor unflinching. "Histories carry important information."

"What kind of information we speaking of?"

The priest sighed and shrugged. "So then . . . these things appeared at the shrine last year, out of nowhere. They took our people by surprise, and some escaped."

"Some? How many?"

"Impossible to say. A dozen? A hundred? Only two priests made it here with the news. The book spoke of something similar, during the Age of Warlords, and suggested the prayers to seal our world from those of the Shadows. We managed to close the door, not lock it. So to speak. We studied the tome and gathered priests from across the island, and we sent them to lock the door. Apparently—"

"They failed."

"Yes. And the book is our hope, so you can understand her commitment to it."

The Wolverine leaned back in his seat, staring down his nose at the priest. "Those . . . things, are still coming out. We saw one."

"We'll contain the shrine, as we did before, and we will figure out how to close it, I assure you. Our people will hunt the Shadows and destroy them."

"I'd like a bed for the night to think on things."

"Of course, I will have quarters prepared for you and your men. We'll speak again on the morrow, after you rest."

Woxlin departed with the other priest and Rinold led the remaining members of the wardens into the hall for a meal. The Wolverine gnawed on jerked beef, spitting splinters of rock-hard meat into the cook fire while conveying Woxlin's words to the others.

Rinold picked his teeth and downed beer before saying a word. "So, what ya thinkin', then?"

"I'm thinkin' we're covered in horseshit and half truths. What's in your head, Ratsmasher?"

Ivin grunted at his new name. "I don't think he spoke enough truth to know what kind of shit we're covered in."

Rinold cracked a grin. "I might take a liking to you yet, boy."

The Wolverine guffawed and thumped Ivin's shoulder. "You might be right, Choerkin. Too damned right. We'll see what we can dig from his compost tomorrow, beggar another night. Either way, we want eyes on this place come Eve of Snows, but we don't wanna be inside."

Ivin smiled, proud to feel like a member of the wardens for the first time. "In, out, what's it matter?"

To a man they laughed, but it was Rinold who answered. "Istinjoln on the Eve . . . . Hard to keep eyes on the holies when yer blind drunk, and ain't no way in the hells they'd let us stay sober."

Pikarn said, "Aye, it'll be a shame to miss, but missin' it's the wiser."

They finished their meals, and a monk guided them to a windowless building with cots to bunk them for the night, and a fireplace with plenty of kindling. The sagging bedstead didn't help Ivin's aching muscles a lick, and amid the snores of the other men, sleep was fitful and filled with disquieting dreams. After midnight he awoke to the flutter-rush of fire in his ear, first passing it off as an awakening dream, but as he closed his eyes again, a crackling voice spoke: "Choerkin?"

He sat straight and glanced around the room. Everyone slept but him. His ear was warm.

"Choerkin?" asked the voice.

He turned and clung to his cot to keep from falling out. A tiny flame hovered a moment then dipped through the air to slip under the door. Uncertain whether he was dreaming or awake, he stood and stared, and in a moment, it peeked under the door, and zipped out again. It wanted him to follow.

If the notion of a tiny ball of fire wanting him to follow its trail wasn't disturbing enough, traipsing after it into the dark of Istinjoln should've terrified him. With his heavy cloak already wrapped around his shoulders, he realized how foolish he'd become.

Ivin slipped into darkness with tentative steps. Lanterns burned by guards atop the towers, but the bailey was blacks and grays. Had it been a dream? No. His eyes adjusted and he spotted wind-blown robes in the shadows. A dark arm gestured to him. Killing Lokar's nephew in the middle of a monastery seemed a dangerous ploy, but he couldn't discount it enough to keep his heart from pounding as he approached.

"You are Choerkin?" The voice was soft and female.

"Ivin, yes."

She took his hand with a touch that made his heart race and pulled him into a dark building, windowless like so many here. A ball of fire appeared, larger but otherwise identical to the one he'd followed, lighting the room enough to ease his mind. There were no furnishings of any sort and they were alone. Except he didn't feel alone. He had the inexplicable sense that the hovering fire watched him. Judging him?

The postulant lowered her white cowl, revealing the young lady who'd watched them earlier. Her golden hair framed the gentle curves of her face, and her eyes caught the light of the fire in such a way that even from a distance, he noted they were blue. If they were on the docks of the Watch, Rikis would be showing off his strength and Roplin impressing her with his glib tongue and parlor tricks, while Ivin sat in the corner wishing she'd notice him. She'd noticed him, but he didn't know if she wanted to kill him.

With no idea what to say, his first words blurted out. "Is that . . . alive?"

She smiled. Damn, she had to smile. She must think him an idiot. "My name is Eliles."

"Ivin." He coughed, clearing his throat. "Ivin Choerkin."

"Yes, you said that before. Kotin's third son. Why are you here?"

His head cocked, a trick question? "Ah, well, I don't know how much to say. I—"

"We've both things maybe we shouldn't say, and either we do or we don't. I found you, so you first." She smiled, disarming him with a few words and a twitch of her lips.

He wanted to put his lips to hers. Ivin stammered before getting a grip on his voice. "Okay. Fine." Where to start? Where to stop? "Creatures, Shadows, killed a group of priests in the Omindi Pass and we tracked them back to a place called the Crack of Burdenis. A shrine. We found one survivor."

"Meliu, yes. She carried a book. What was it?"

This holy had been watching them longer than he knew. What was her game? "The high priest told us it was a history of the shrine."

She stared at him so hard he wondered if she wasn't trying to work some sort of prayer on him. "Guntar bore a sealed message from the Crack, and he died to deliver it. He was a friend of mine. Was it these . . . Shadows or Colok that killed him?"

She sought answers in a friend's death. A lover, maybe. Strange, experiencing a pang of jealousy for a dead man. He took her hand without thinking, feeling her warmth and pulse, shocked and euphoric she didn't pull away. "Colok, but Shadow-Taken priests fed on the others later. The body count was short one priest."

Her brow wrinkled. "Who?"

He wouldn't surrender every secret. "I'd ask you the same thing."

"It's not an answer I can find. What did Woxlin say about the Shadows?"

"He didn't say a word." Her lips curled, teasing him; she knew he lied. "Fine, they appeared at the shrine a year ago, they tried to use that book to keep them from our world. Damned if I understand any of it."

"We're taught the universe is full of worlds, near but unseen . . . like the heavens and the hells. And the Road of Living Stars is a path for the soul to these worlds."

Ivin didn't like the direction the conversation took. "These Shadows come from the Twelve Hells?"

She pulled her hand from his, the look on her face suggesting surprise at having her hand held. "No, no. In Ages past, priests could connect to these worlds with powerful prayer. But this was during the God Wars."

Ivin scratched his cheek. "Why, for what purpose?"

She looked at him cockeyed as if he were a child asking a silly question. If she were the Wolverine, he'd be biting jerky about now.

"They summoned the servants of the gods to battle, and sometimes the gods themselves. Opening Celestial Gates."

He'd heard of such things, in fireside tales, stories woven from myth for children. Only now he'd seen one of these gates, and the Shadows coming through. "Did these gates, did they ever appear from nowhere?"

She smiled, and he realized she'd led him to this point. "No."

"Woxlin lied to us."

"Yes." She leaned in, her blue eyes intense. "I managed a glance at the message Guntar died for." The words hung in the air as she appeared to weigh her next words. "As I understand, they meant to speak with Sol, but instead the Shadows came. The scroll read that the lord priest would be pleased, the ritual went well until the end. The final words called for destruction of the shrine."

Ivin mulled these tidbits. "Speak with Sol? Why?" There might be a million reasons to speak to the King of Gods, but he doubted their cause was idle banter.

"I don't know. Not exactly. But why does anyone ever speak to the gods?"

His father's words came back to him: *People praying to their gods are as children beseeching their parents, the kindest words come when they want something.* "Power. To rule the clans."

"Istinjoln has a guest, the Lord Priest of Fermiden Abbey. Here for the Eve of Snows."

Fermiden Abbey sat at the foot of Broldun Fost, blood enemy of the Choerkin for a hundred years. Triwan Broldun's mother was a high priestess, and rumors abounded of his son Dunkol ascending to lord priest in a secret ceremony.

"You're sure the Shadows weren't intentional?"

"Yes. But not much else."

"You should speak with Pikarn—"

"No. No one else."

He cringed. Who outside the wardens would believe this? Pikarn might even balk. "Can you get a look at that book? Find proof?"

"Too dangerous."

Gazing into her eyes, there was no way he'd want her to risk herself. "I understand. Can keep your eyes and ears open?"

She nodded and pulled her cowl over her face, then said, "Yes, it is alive." The ball of fire disappeared in a blink and she walked into the night, leaving Ivin to contemplate how to share her message.

He skulked back to bed, surprised to find everyone still asleep, and tried to close his eyes. Slumber eluded him with visions of the girl, but not a girl, a holy of Istinjoln he reminded himself. But her smile and blue eyes haunted his waking and dozing mind no matter how he tried to forget her. The oracle had spoken of love and false love, and possibilities. As his mind slipped into slumber, visions of Eliles as his bride danced through his dreams.

TWENTY-SIX

Nearing the Son

The Worlds sit in a sea of outshining stars.
Pale we wail, shrinking and shrieking, in the naked eye,
the taken eye,
Of the one-eyed Eternity, She! She knows the truth
But even when she speaks it we can not understand
We the incapable of comprehension,
We who lack the context
To know what is real and why

—*Tomes of the Touched*

Six Days to the Eve of Snows

Eliles awoke at dawn covered in itchy hay. A night in the stables was an imperfect plan, but it kept her from having to explain her comings and goings if someone bothered to notice her. Speaking with the Choerkin was worth the risk only if she didn't end up feeding the thorns or meeting some other horrible fate.

She scurried from the mounds of hay in the loft to find Feres, marshal of the stables, gnawing on a loaf of bread. She slipped past the old woman, but scuttled back to nab a saddle brush to clean hay from her robes. With a mane pick and fingers she made herself presentable

enough to slip from the back of the stable. She skulked through shadows before sauntering into the morning sun with a straight face.

She climbed to the allure where guards would pay her no mind.
A stroll at dawn fit her routine, and when the faint drone of morning
prayer rose from vents in the bailey, the timing was perfect.

She trotted, bumping into a guard and flashing a smile, kissing her
fingers and touching her forehead. "Sorry, I'm late." With this seed
planted in the guard's memory she found the nearest entry into lower
Istinjoln and slunk into the back of the morning's hymnal chant.

Head bowed, she managed to relax. A smidgen. The Choerkin—

Why did she think this way? Because that's how she always heard
clan-blood named. The Choerkin were a faceless mass without first
names, a hornet under the Church's saddle.

She didn't have to think this way.

His name is Ivin. A right fine young man, some might say. Tall,
good looking, even if he did smell a bit like a horse—

She snuck a sniff of her robes. Hay, fine, but not horse. Hay would
be easier to explain as it lined garden beds; horse manure would be
trickier.

And Ivin's blond hair. Unusual for the Choerkin men if rumor
held truth. He seemed sweet, not at all as the Church elders painted
the clan. She recalled his touch, the sweat of his palms, and stealing
a kiss crept into her mind. She blanched. No. Whatever kindness she
saw resulted from her dweomer.

Whatever girl he saw who softened his eyes, made him feel for her,
didn't exist. Did he dream of her? She chided herself for a silly girl.
There were far more important matters to attend than some boy's lips.
Stop! No more lips.

She should focus on Shadows and Celestial Gates, but what she
knew wouldn't fill a single parchment. Meddling with this arcane art

resulted in excommunication from the Church, or worse. Celestial scholarship wasn't banned, but those partaking in its study spoke of such things only among themselves and in hushed tones. The library concealed knowledge, but even if she had the time, she'd see the hells before stepping in there again.

The morning hymnals closed with a bass drone.

Eliles remained kneeling as the front rows exited. Lord Priest Ulrikt made his threats clear, nibbling around the edges of the mystery would prove poison if caught. Get through the Divination of Bones tonight, then run, run as soon as the opening came. The entire monastery would be drunk on the Eve of Snows, giving her what might be her first and best chance.

A hand touched her shoulder, and Eliles froze despite wanting to lurch to her feet. Gods, let it be Dareun.

"You must be excited." Woxlin stood above her.

She rose slow and controlled, heart pounding, gathering her thoughts. "Excited?"

He laughed. "Yes, of course. Your vows are days away! With your holy gifts you might sit beside me in no time at all."

She blushed. Her a high priestess, it would be a mockery of all things holy. "I could only dream of the high priesthood."

"Modesty, or you sell yourself short. The gods and the lord priest himself favor you."

He rubbed her shoulder and she cringed at his familiarity. "As you say. You are far more worthy to judge the gods and his Holiness than I."

He smiled, crooked lips and crooked yellow teeth, and she knew he judged her.

"I believe your master now. Dareun has long said your modesty was true, but no one believes him." He took her hand and kissed it, a disturbing gesture that brought bile to her throat. "Count me as a believer."

Woxlin departed to visit with a young priestess and her heart slowed, eyes drifting to the stone floor. Woxlin had spoken maybe ten words to her in twelve years. To turn up singing her praises, and his kiss, no way by the Twelve Hells were they coincidences. Keep your eyes down and your prayers vocal, two rules to stay alive by.

"I stopped by your cell this morn, you rose early."

Her heart lurched at the sound of Dareun's voice. By the Slave Fields! Did the world set out to sneak up on her today?

"Yes. I admit, I'm anxious for the Night of Bones."

"I can't blame you, my dear. The breaking of bones will go smoothly, my girl. Ah! A glorious day. The priesthood for so many."

She struggled to smile. No way he'd forgive her for botching everything, but she could never even apologize, because he could never know. The Night of Bones should be their crowning achievement in twelve years of hiding her curse, maybe it could still, but the trajectory was a disaster.

"Glorious, yes. Let us pray it's so."

"Go. Go my girl, enjoy the day. The Night of Bones will be here soon enough."

A smile and a hug, he deserved them. She gripped her old master tight. "I'm sorry for the troubles I've brought you."

Dareun patted her on the back. "No troubles at all, dear girl."

Eliles stepped back, fought the tears in her eyes with a smile. What a tremendous lie he'd just blessed her with. But that's why she loved him.

TWENTY-SEVEN

Rider's return

Horses afield, no pride in duck and hide, pennants flutter
bright for the houses of men,
Dyes paint hues on cotton and silk and leather.
Brushes paint shields in depictions of fanciful life.
Steel paints only in red dries black, the favorite colors of the gods.

—*Tomes of the Touched*

Six Days to the Eve of Snows

The world shook and threatened to collapse, and Fronk stood over Ivin kicking his bedstead. "Time to wake, the old man's getting food."

Visions of wedding the girl faded, and he wished he still slept. The bed creaked, one odd twist from breaking a leg, as he swung his feet over the edge. When the Wolverine returned, Ivin told him about the pretty postulant over hard bread and beef stew, but he left out the flame. A living ball of fire would make him question his own credibility.

Pikarn stared with unquenched skepticism. "You sure you weren't dreaming, Choerkin?"

Fronk chortled. "He'd been dreaming he woulda taken the pretty priestess right there."

Ivin blushed, if it'd been a dream he would've married her. "It wasn't a dream. Which means there's a Broldun dog in Istinjoln."

247

Lidin said, "Way I hear, Fermiden's lord priest is a Broldun."

"Lead dog or shit end of the team, they're Broldun." Pikarn cracked the door, the sun creeping over the horizon to light the bailey. A monk stood across the way, faceless in a cowl, but watching. Pikarn called out, "Hungry for a roll?" When the monk looked but didn't answer, Pikarn closed the door. "That holy was out there the whole night, leastwise each time I checked."

"You don't believe me?"

"It ain't I don't believe. But we can test the truth of the dog easy enough."

And test it the Wolverine did. Woxlin had no more opened the door when Pikarn said, "We were heading up this way anyhow, 'cause scouts saw Broldun making their way to Istinjoln."

The high priest stood straight-faced, weighing his response. "Does our Lord Choerkin now forbid Broldun dignitaries?"

The Wolverine frowned. "Of course not. But a twittering bird in Fermiden Abbey suggested it be the lord priest himself lugging his fat, powdered ass all the way here."

Woxlin smiled through his rancor. "Now, old friend. We all know the Lord of the Abbey does not travel. Particularly nowhere in reach of the Choerkin."

"You saying the brothers would murder a lord priest?"

Woxlin dismissed his words with a wave. "I will have your horses saddled and ready, as clearly you seek to wear your welcome thin."

Pikarn ripped a piece of jerky. "On the contrary, old friend, I think our welcome is fattening up. We'll be staying another day, see if we spot a fat dog taking a walk."

The priest nodded. "As you will. We've gruel enough to keep you fed." He exited, the door closing behind him with a rattle.

Pikarn turned to Ivin. "The bastard's here all right, and the whispers are true, the new lord priest is Dunkol Broldun. Which means his entourage of little boys and girls are with him."

Ivin cocked an eyebrow. "What now?"

"We wander the yard, eyes open . . . but no poking the bees in their hive. I'm the only one to open his yap, got me? That goes double for you, Choerkin. That name of yours could get you killed as easily it saves you."

Ivin took up whittling during the morning. His goal was to turn a hunk of wood into a smaller hunk of wood with a less natural shape. By setting his goals low he achieved in spectacular fashion, even smoothing out notches to make a better fit for his hand.

Why, it might make a nice toothpick if he kept on.

He tossed whatever it'd become to the ground and kicked it. He took aim and threw his knife, the tip striking the hard ground and somersaulting to a skidding stop across the yard.

Bells chimed from the main gatehouse as he bent to grab his knife. A wick later riders entered the monastery, saving him from finding another hobby. Modan led the wardens, including Puxele, and they rode straight to Ivin. "Where's the old man?"

Ivin pointed to their housing and Modan dismounted in a hurry, his steps threatening to break into a trot. Ivin's feet fidgeted with curiosity to follow, but he wasn't sure if it was his place.

"Come on, Choerkin. You need to hear this."

Ivin broke into a jog, enthusiastic for damned near anything after standing around all morning. After reaching the door he waited as Fronk and the other wardens exited. Whatever Modan had to say, it wasn't for everyone's ears.

Jerked beef lofted through air, a flicker from hitting Ivin's face before he snagged it.

"We were outside the cave when there was, I don't know, this feeling, like a breeze down your spine." Modan rubbed the back of his neck as if he still felt it.

The pulse that birthed the Shadow, I'd wager. Ivin worked strands of meat between his teeth instead of his vocal cords.

"The horses spooked, but they calmed. Didn't see nothin' right off. Herin was standing by the cliff and called out. Damned if there weren't Shadows climbing, coming for us. I put an arrow right through one's head, and it didn't flinch. We tacked up and spurred out of there hard as we could, but the damned things were fast. We lost Herin and Dere before we made the Omindi and godsdamn us if there weren't Colok on the road south, so we rode north. Even hoped the Shadows might go after the Colok but the cursed things came on after us. Once in the Pass, the horses outpaced the things."

Modan wrestled a canteen from his hip and took a drink as the Wolverine got in a question. "The Colok?"

"I'm a-gettin' to them. We slowed and stopped round about Baer's Rock, thinking maybe we were safer there than moving into the Treaty Lands. Seemed that way, too. The sonsabitches came on the sides of the ravine like spiders, crawling in the shadows until they surrounded us. Larsin dismounted for a fight and one landed on him, drug him off. I told everyone to hold their positions and ride hard when attacked. They didn't come for us."

"Why?" Ivin couldn't help himself, despite the mouth full of jerky.

"Best I can figure is they knew we weren't alone. The Colok surrounded us, squaring themselves against the Shadows. Never seen nothin' like it."

"And the Shadows?" Pikarn asked.

"They did nothin'. We stood there for candles, surrounded by two enemies until the Shadows went away. Not a damned thing we could've done against either except fight and die."

"The Colok saved you." Ivin said.

"Aye, because of you. But it's your last name they were after, not so much you."

Rinold's eye twitched and he rubbed his scar. "Whoa, how the hells you know that?"

"My tale gets nothing but nuttier, Squirrel. The lead Colok is Zjin—"

"Colok have names?" Ivin blurted, and he apologized to both men with bowed head and silence.

"Yeah, turns out they do. They had a priest with 'em, name of Tokodin. Said the Colok took him, to use him to speak with the clan. We weathered three days of storm in one of their caves before riding out and stumbling on Puxele north o' the Crack." He grinned. "Anything stronger than water here?"

"When your story's done," Pikarn said. "What do they want with the Choerkin?"

"The priest said it was to do with the Shadows. A common enemy if I'm put to a guess."

Pikarn grunted. "Colok never minded our dying to Snow Daevu."

It occurred to Ivin they were neglecting a potential foe. The thought brought a spasm that choked his breath. Every cherished memory of his mother and him at prayer stood tarnished if his fear were true. "What if our shared enemy is Istinjoln?" The moment the words left his mouth he wanted to take them back, but the spoken word wasn't a hook to be pulled back to shore empty.

Pikarn's voice was soft, but edged. "Don't speak them words again."

"The boy's right. What if Istinjoln is headed for open rebellion?"

"I ain't saying he's wrong, I'm saying don't speak them here, the stones might have ears."

Modan grimaced. "Anyhow. The Colok want to meet at a tower the priest called Snow's Eye."

"I know it," Pikarn said. "Two, maybe three days ride. Not another word of this here. Modan, gather the men and get the horses ready; Choerkin, you stay with me."

"Godsdamned good to see you alive." Pikarn filled a mug of ale for Modan from their small cask, putting a foamy smile on Modan's face as he strode outside. The Wolverine stared at Ivin, a smirking crinkle on his face. "Sick of that name of yours yet?"

Ivin stifled a laugh with a snort. It wasn't the first time the name had given him grief. That honor belonged to the evening he'd met a lovely lass who knew his brothers' reputations. So much for stealing that kiss. At least this time his name afforded him a mixed reward. Sure, he might die, but it'd be interesting. A man must be born with powerful luck to have a name imbued with such power.

"Might be one of the few times I liked it, actually." He poured a pint of ale. No hot meal anytime soon, he may as well drink. "Why the hurry?"

"If this turns out to be more than Istinjoln's typical poke in the Choerkin eye I don't wanna be behind these walls when they find out we know."

No point in arguing such wisdom. But if Istinjoln and the Choerkin were about to collide that'd make it right difficult to court the pretty postulant. His brow scrunched. It was for the best; she'd likely laugh at him behind his back, anyhow.

Ivin asked, "So, we're headed to Snow's Eye? If we get hung up out there, we'd miss whatever's happening here."

"Aye, we should make it back, but ain't no guarantees. You think we should stay closer?"

Ivin grimaced, it sure felt like the better option. "We can't pass up this chance, whatever the hells it turns out to be."

He sighed, poured ale, but the Wolverine yanked it from his grip and drank it himself. "Let's get a-movin'."

They mounted in the bailey, joining Modan, Puxele, Rinold, and the other wardens. Woxlin made his way to see them off, but he didn't approach, and Pikarn wanted nothing to do with the priest, either. Ivin looked for Eliles' familiar face among the holies, but they hid under their cowls and he couldn't tell if the girl was there or not. He wanted to believe she watched them. Him.

The Wolverine spun his horse to give Woxlin a wave. "We'll be back by Eve of Snows."

The high priest raised a hand, but didn't say a word.

When the portcullis remained open at their approach Ivin breathed easier, and as hooves clattered across the drawbridge, he let himself smile. An attack would've been more a surprise than being allowed to ride free, but these days surprises were lining up.

Once on the narrow road they passed a small wagon that rattled and clanged, pulled by a two-donkey team. The driver was a rotund man Ivin recognized as a tinker with a quality reputation. Unlike the last time he saw the man at the Fost, he wasn't alone. An attractive woman, tall, with her hair wrapped in a fancy braid rode beside him, while relegated to the back of the cart lay a man tall enough to be a Choerkin. An old sword lay beside that one. He didn't recognize the two, but he wished them well on their journey into the hornet's nest.

TWENTY-EIGHT

Fortress Over Maze

Rain falls from the clouds of her stormy wings,
Riding bands of lightning through turbulent winds,
Soaking boiling stone.
Hiss and Pop, a calamitous roar of combative Elements
Preparing the skein of a thousand Worlds
To receive the Eggs of her children to be.
She never asks why the universe created a nest so perfect.

—Tomes of the Touched

Six Days to the Eve of Snows

Turned out Lelishen told the truth: She could be quiet. Whether she sat staring into the distance marveling over the scenery, or pondering whatever her pilgrim's mind bothered to think on, she remained a pleasant traveling companion. But gods forbid you ask what she was looking at or thinking, because once her lips flapped open it damned near took the next meal to shut them. If it weren't for the fact his body distracted him with aches and pains in places he never knew could hurt, he might've let himself fall off the wagon to follow from a quieter distance.

Still, she was an attractive gal. Solineus assumed it was her looks which kept her alive when folks wanted her to shut up.

254

The day had been peaceful, nary a word over breakfast and only a few stray thoughts flung from her lips until Ilpen broke the pleasant knocking and creaking rhythms of the wagon.

"Only a couple candles out from Istinjoln, now."

"Do you fine gentlemen know much about the monastery?"

Was she looking to impart a candle's worth of knowledge or did she fish for information? The answer that kept her quiet was what he shot for. "Nothing much."

"My mama's cousin's great-aunt Firde studied in Istinjoln years ago, pride of the family. Well, until Daddy made his fortune on the silver mine, anyhow. Still, pride of that side of the family."

Solineus groaned; another wrong choice in a fifty-fifty game. Of course, the game could be fixed and unwinnable.

"A fortress like none other, she always said. . . . Etinbin, guard her soul from the Vainglorious Hell, which she probably deserves mind you, yet, all people deserve peace eventually, don't they? Anyhow, she was always saying how the fortress sat above ground, but the tunnels are the true redoubt of the holy."

Maybe this woman's mouth wasn't worthless. Solineus rolled over, propped on his elbows. "Tunnels?"

"Oh, yes! A maze like you ain't never seen, so she always said. Filled with shrines to all the gods. Priests walk miles on their devotionals, but I'll be lucky to see one or two, I suspect. And of course the great halls."

A maze, perfect. "So the Eve of Snows, what should we expect?"

Ilpen chimed in. "Food, booze, and hangovers a-plenty. Older I get, more I try to stick with the food. Not you can't tell." He patted his belly.

"Prayer services?"

"Oh, I hear those are just lovely," Lelishen said. "Inspirational."

Ilpen glanced to Solineus. "You don't seem the praying kind."

Solineus grinned. Pray for a shot at a lord priest's life. "A man can have a bout of religion if he likes."

"Praise Sol, yes, of course he can! Any man, even the most heathen."

Ilpen grunted at both of them. "Food is my devotional, as it were. But a high priest holds a ceremony outside the bailey for the lay folk."

Damnation, there went one hope. "Mightn't the lord priest bless the flock?"

"Not I ever seen, and I were in Istinjoln for the Eve the past decade."

"Well, ain't unheard of, neither. Lord Priest Hevlin, who I might add had his eye on my mama's cousin's great aunt for something a little extra devotional, you know what I mean . . . Firde said he'd oversee some prayers on the Eve for the small folk. Which reminds me of a great story."

Solineus rolled onto his back, tucked his hands behind his head and hugged his ears with his arms. It didn't deafen him to every word, but muffled them. He closed his eyes, hoping maybe the Lady would reveal a way to get to the lord priest.

If this pilgrim got permission to visit the shrines, it gave him a chance. A chance at getting lost in a labyrinth with a bunch of holies. The Lady in his dreams sent him here, and so far she'd proved she knew pieces of the future; maybe she knew a way through the fortress, too. He opened his eyes and watched the clouds and sun pass through the sky.

The wagon creaked and groaned, and gravity tugged him toward the back of the wagon. They made a steep climb. He sat up and laid eyes on Istinjoln.

"Son of a godsdamned . . . . Sorry." Good thing he had a way past those gates, else he'd have to be a spider to get in. The monastery didn't compare to the size of the Fost, but its crenelated walls were as impressive.

Horsemen bundled in thick furs rode from the gate as they approached, the wagon's width forcing them to ride single file past them as the road narrowed. They didn't have the look of priests, with their swords, bows, spears, and determined faces set in stone.

Ilpen extended a friendly wave and sucked his teeth. "That were the Wolverine and his boys."

His memory drew its expected blank. "Wolverine?"

"Aye, heads the Estertok Wardens. Choerkin loyalists to a man and none too friendly with Istinjoln. Musta been a Colok attack nearby or something of the sort."

Solineus nodded as if he knew what the man talked about and the woman kept mum. They passed through the shadows of the looming gate and into the bailey, flagstones rattling the wagon and his bones until they came to a stop in front of the stables. He groaned and rolled from his perch, his joints popping as his aching muscles propped him upright. He grabbed hold of a wheel, its iron skein chilling his fingers as he brought one knee to his chest, then the other. Stretching hurt, but in a relieving sort of way.

Istinjoln's central tower drew the eye first, with its height and crenelated white marble crown sitting atop its head. Squat buildings surrounded the tower in what appeared random placement, but they were that way to force an enemy's approach to the keep confusing and more dangerous. Every bit of this fortress loomed as a trap to ensnare and defeat an invading army, but where an army would fail, a lone man might prove deadly.

He turned to Lelishen as she slid from the wagon without so much as a hitch in her stride, smiling at him. He'd feel better if she groaned as if something ached. He smirked at her, but her head snapped to gaze across the courtyard. Lelishen stared at a pretty young girl with long blond hair, a postulant if he understood the meaning of her white robes. Something passed between the two, and the girl bolted into the shadows of nearby buildings.

What'd I miss? "You know the girl?"

Her words came slow and measured, not her usual cadence. "Hmm? No, no." Lelishen's lips were tight around those perfect white teeth. She recovered. "The darling did remind me so of my second cousin, also named Firde, I might add, that it gave me a start."

It wasn't the first time he wanted to call the woman on a lie, but it was the most obvious. "Pretty lass." He didn't need to poison the waters, he needed answers. Lelishen portrayed the simple pilgrim, but there was a puzzle beneath the pretty. If he solved it, it might help him get close to the lord priest.

Ilpen startled Solineus with a hand on his shoulder. "Let's find ourselves a meal and a pint."

Food sounded good, and oddly enough, so did chatty feminine company. "Aye. You joining us, Lelishen?"

"Why absolutely, I'd be delighted to join you good men."

Lelishen's facade resurfaced strong as marble, but Solineus knew now to watch for cracks. Good thing the woman was pleasant to look on since he wasn't going to take an eye off her.

TWENTY-NINE

Breaking Bones

Glory speaks a language all its own,
a tongue dripping sweet saliva sugar on your soul,
A grander Grandeur of greatness over
the little man with his knife in your belly, the demon's kiss
and the Dragon's lick, fire, flier, Liar,
So tired.
Sleep and slumber eyes wide
to die, I've failed the hundred ways I've tried.

—*Tomes of the Touched*

Six Days to the Eve of Snows

The Night of Bones began in the evening, and Eliles had few duties during the day. Sure, she should be meditating in prayer to thank the gods for their generosity, but by late morning she succumbed to temptation to spy on the gates. And the handsome Choerkin. It was fine to think of him as a Choerkin in this way, but she reminded herself his name was Ivin.

She followed the Shrines of Fire after morning prayers, faithful to propriety on such an important day, but afterwards she made her way to the northern wall. She smiled, watching him work far too long on a piece of wood with his knife only to throw it in the dirt. A handsome boy, but she could throw a knife better.

The gate bells rang and more wardens arrived, and after a brief meeting in their barracks, they rode out, with the Wolverine hailing Woxlin on the way. The wardens would return by Eve of Snows.

Her enthusiasm deflated. She couldn't stomach the notion of being weak for a boy, so she determined her reaction was from losing her new allies. Their return still might provide a chance for escape.

She climbed from the wall, figuring she'd finish her devotionals, but the gate bells rang along with a clatter in the air, which stopped her in stride. Her eyes widened. *Ilpen!* The tinker had found her wandering the wilds as a child, and it had been his idea to hide a defiled girl in a place where the miracle of Fire was commonplace. The man and his donkeys were better family than her own blood.

Two sets of donkey ears came through the gates, Ilpen sitting on the wagon with a gracious smile for every guard. Same as he ever was, only more gray hairs, and maybe an extra hole in his belt.

Her feet wanted to run to him, but she stopped. Ilpen brought passengers she'd never seen before. Who were they? What were they doing with her Ilpen?

The man rolled from the cart to land on his feet with a stiff stretch. In his twenties, maybe thirty, he was tall and rangy with sandy hair, and a sword slung over his shoulder. It'd make sense for Ilpen to hire a guard if bandits were thick this year.

The woman, on the other hand, defied explanation. An inch, maybe two, from being as tall as the man, braided golden hair rested on her head as might a crown, and she carried herself with a noble's grace.

Eliles couldn't resist. She stared and nudged her senses to the woman to see if she could gain a feel for her. A round face with deep brown eyes and a pleasant smile for the swordsman, she was attractive in a docile, sweet manner.

But something was wrong, the woman's eyes flickered, shifted. Eliles' vision of the woman warped, a mirage waving into a new reality. The woman turned and caught Eliles' stare with midnight blue eyes flecked with silver. Soft round features turned chiseled with high cheekbones. Gorgeous, the word rang hollow, and insufficient. Inhuman was fitting.

Eliles panicked and strode away, drawing her senses into herself. Fool girl be damned! The woman came from Eleris Edan, a Trelelunin, if the books she read were right. Pagans with a foreign god, but they lived for centuries and drew on skills developed over an immense time. This foreigner had caught her in an instant where human priests hadn't noticed her spying trick for twelve years. If she told anyone of Eliles' little game? Death.

She hurried for lower Istinjoln, making sure not to break into a trot, and only breathed again when safe in the tunnels. Her thoughts slapped back and forth in her brain. The woman didn't hide who she was; she hid what she was. Hiding meant she wouldn't reveal Eliles' trick—or so she tried to convince herself. The woman would have to give herself away to reveal Eliles, wouldn't she? For the love of Januel! Why couldn't she keep her nose out of trouble?

She huffed and as she rounded a corner, she collided with another postulant.

"Sorry, so sorry," came the squeak from the youngster.

She didn't bother to look at his face, just continued along the tunnel cursing herself. She needed to stay out of trouble. Do as her elders commanded and be early.

By the time she reached the Hall of Bontore to await the breaking of bones, she'd calmed and refocused her mind. If the foreign woman proved a problem, she'd handle it then, allowing her heart to race over a possibility was foolish.

The Hall of Bontore was a semi-circular cavern with the dais and the Shrine of Bontore standing at the straight edge of the chambers, across from her entrance. Lanterns burned along the walls, ringing the Hall beneath a railed balcony, and two chandeliers hung high in the domed ceiling, ambiance more than effective lighting, as they lit veins of silver minerals to twinkle in the carved stone.

Four steps led to the top of the dais, at the center of which stood the altar. Solid silver polished to a sheen and set with carved amethyst, the favored gem of Bontore, every year this shrine hosted the breaking of bones. To the side hung curtains, which concealed ranking priests.

Postulants preparing for their vows of priesthood on the Eve of Snows, high priests, and the lord priest himself received their divinations tonight, a special honor for those successful in their trials. Everyone was welcome to attend and the balconies and room filled with the holy.

She remembered the years of squeezing between people to get a better view, the stink of sweating men and women, of incense. But she held the best seat in the house this evening.

Eliles knelt in the front row of ascendant postulants and waited. She relaxed every muscle in her face as she sought to become a vision of patience and confidence, but her calm was resignation. She accepted her fate however written by the bones and Bontore. Dareun's success or failure didn't matter, her future belonged to her.

A grizzled old woman with pasty-white, wrinkled skin sauntered into the chambers and the observing postulants and priests hushed. Her toes scraped the ground with truncated strides, carrying her across the Hall to the marble Dais of Bontore. Her hips twisted and knees buckled as she climbed the steps, but she kept her pain silent.

Meris of Esedon. Whispers of her arrival had traveled fast. Revered and renowned as the master of Skywatch for the past forty years, and master of bones for seven decades, her reputation bordered on legendary. An divination by her hand honored the recipient.

Meris' home caught her ear also, another coincidence? What possible connection did she have to Ivin Choerkin's arrival? She shook her head. Not a single wild-haired conspiracy came to mind.

"Sodole, twelfth year postulant, come before me and listen to Bontore's words."

Meris' voice betrayed what her body hid: power. Shriveled by time, her voice still held the impact of a hale and gifted oracle. She must've been a sight in her day. Eliles imagined the crone was at least cute in her youth.

Sodole bounced to the dais, eager to hear his fortune. The boy had taken the brunt of many jabs over the years being scrawny and freckled, with a crooked nose broken and left unset in his youth. Eliles always thought him odd, with an unnerving cast to his beady eyes.

Kneeling before the oracle, the crack of the bone resounded throughout the room, and only flickers later the High Oracle broke into her spiel. Eliles gave the old woman credit, at least she didn't waste time on theatrics.

"The gods have spoken well to you, Sodole. Here we see a line passing through the Heart of Januel and splitting. You will know two potential loves, but I can not tell you which is prettiest and which will bear you the most sons."

Sodole bounced on his knees, nodding at the woman's humorous play.

Eliles rolled her eyes, no doubt such a creepy fellow would buy into this future. She'd heard thousands of readings over the years, set up or kindness?

"And here, the line passes near the Sun's Spear, brave deeds are in your future, and how that line connects to the loves of Januel? This tells me that your deeds earn your chances at love. With this crack, too, by the Anvil? Have you considered serving as a bearer? You should." The postulant nodded, eager for his future.

Eliles wanted to giggle. She ignored the remainder of the prattle, the divination directed him with subtlety, and a hammer. The rest of the woman's words meant nothing until the finish.

"Rise, Sodole, and take your name. What name did you bear to Istinjoln?"

"Sodole Henstikir." The boy's excitement made her want to puke.

"What name do you bear at Istinjoln?"

"Sodole."

"When your vows are spoke on the Eve of Snows, you will forever be known as Sodole of Inkris so you may be the pride of your village."

"Thank you, venerated master."

Eliles stifled a yawn, bowed her head, and meditated to quiet the annoying prophecies. The lies. The manipulation.

The crack of bone wiggled into her consciousness, and a small piece of awareness listened to the ancient priestess muttering to postulants, senseless murmurs on the fringe of her consciousness. Postulants came and went without interest; her divination was last, the only marker of time she needed. A benefit of her lone scar.

With her name called she rose without hesitation, as if she'd paid attention to every fortune read. Dignified strides climbed the dais, and she took the old woman's hands, knelt before her. Meris' eyes were kind, more gentle than expected. With hands entwined instinct pushed her senses into the ancient woman, she felt darkness, and retreated. Regret lived within her soul, but the dark was pervasive, murderous. Her eyes told lies her soul didn't conceal.

The oracle's hands slid from hers and Meris smiled, another lie, as she brought Bontore's needle to a glow between rubbing hands. She jammed the needle into the bone with a flourish, the crack sending shivers down Eliles' spine.

"Bontore has spoken with us, young Eliles, look as I read to you his words."

The bone cradled in the woman's frail hands fractured in peculiar ways. The engraved Wanderer's Star bore no crack: an ill portent.

"My child, Bontore smiles on you." A chill struck her spine as the oracle pointed. "Here we see a line crossing Januel's Heart, a love in your future. But here! Oh here, here, such a strong crack across the Fires of Sol, linked both to Rock of Besi and Eye of the Winds, your destiny is cast in fire and stone, raised by the ten winds to greatness."

Her brown, wrinkled finger traced another strong crack. "And here the Crown of Sol, your favor will rise in the eyes of the King of Gods and His lord priests'. My girl, stand and take your name." Short, imprecise, and unexpected. What did it mean?

She rose and turned, her eyes landing on Dareun. Her master stared wide-eyed. Who rewrote her future and why?

Meris' voice reverberated through the chamber. "What name did you bear to Istinjoln?"

"Eliles Hunvad."

"What name do you bear at Istinjoln?"

"Eliles."

"From this day forward, you are known as Eliles of Istinjoln, Priestess of Sol's Fire."

Her knees buckled. Of Istinjoln. Most took names from the village or region of their birth, to take Istinjoln to name meant direct service to the lord priest. No doubt now who smoothed her fortune. And the oracle named her priestess before she took her vows. Unheard of.

Escape became damned near impossible; she'd be living in the heart of Istinjoln.

She stepped from the dais and stumbled with wobbly knees. She should've said words, thanked Sol or Meris, maybe even Lord Priest Ulrikt, but her tongue was tied in the same knots as her thoughts.

They had anticipated and severed her path. She'd been a fool to think she could escape.

She returned to kneel among the postulants, but without taking a vow, Meris had decreed her a priestess. She sat as an outcast among her peers again. Hundreds of eyes bore into her. She felt the jealousy and hatred rising in the room. Eliles wanted to disappear more than ever, but she couldn't leave this Hall any more than she could fly from Istinjoln. The divinations of the high priests and the lord priest himself were yet to see bones.

Her swirling thoughts and panic defied meditation, but still, she found herself lost in a trance of sorts. The dark robes of high priest after high priest knelt on the dais and bowed their heads to their fortunes, but the words drowned in the frantic screams of her mind. She cared not a twig for any of them. As a girl enthralled with hearing people's futures, even knowing the truth of smoothing, she listened intent for candles. But now, only one interested her.

"Lord Priest Ulrikt, come before Bontore, kneel and know the glory of Istinjoln."

Ulrikt stepped through a wall of tapestries depicting the hallowed history of Istinjoln and the Gods of the Pantheon of Sol. Clad in pristine white robes threaded with strands of gold and silver, he shone as a beacon of light in these dark chambers. Tall and thin, with a nose and ears grown long by age, he carried himself with an aura of confidence personified by intense blue eyes capped with silver-white brows. Dignified, handsome even in his advanced years, and powerful in both the ways of prayer and men, he was her master now.

Dareun always said the lord priest's bones were honest, and she hoped the divination spoke of ill winds for this vile man. His vile monastery. May a single crack lead to Etinbin and the Road of Living Stars. Too much to pray he fell into the hells?

Meris rose for the lord priest, then knelt before him. Ulrikt did not take a knee.

A young postulant brought Meris a large clavicle for the last divination of the night, and the ancient bone-reader took it with reverence, resting it on a cushion gentle as an infant being put to bed. She rubbed the needle between her hands and raised it for the crowd, revealing the intense star-white glow with a theater reserved for the final show.

"Mighty Bontore! Reveal for us the future and glory of Ulrikt and Istinjoln!" The needle plunged and struck.

A blinding flash. An explosion rocked the chamber.

Screams split the ringing in her ears as she cowered, and Lord Priest Ulrikt crashed into the stone floor a pace in front her. Shards of bone pierced his snow-white robes, bleeding bright crimson. He didn't move. His eyes stared heavenward. Piercing blue, unblinking.

Dead. The lord priest was dead.

Eliles stared in horror before a rush of high priests knocked her to hands and knees, swarming over their fallen leader with shouts and commands. In the back rows, panic. Adherents fled the Hall in mass. Chaos, terror, confusion. Assassin? Wrath of Bontore? The first salvo in an attack? She heard every accusation in the screams.

Dareun? Where was Dareun? She crawled between oncoming priests, bouncing off knees and her vision spun from a shin to her forehead before powerful hands yanked her to her feet. Her old master hugged her tight, then held her at arms' length, adrenaline shaking his body.

"You? Was it you? Somehow?" Furtive questions and desperate. Never before had she seen Dareun beside himself. He knew something, despite questioning her. Almost as if he preferred her to be guilty.

She shook her head. She wanted to say more, but how?

He hugged her again, whispering in her ear this time. "Find a safe place. This bodes well for neither of us. Go!" He shoved her, and she ran.

But where could she find safety in Istinjoln? Ivin and the wardens had departed. Ilpen and the strangers . . . should she risk dragging them into her troubles? The depths of the caves offered dark and distance, but they were a trap. Upper Istinjoln offered open air and a gate to wilderness, but the temptation to run to Ilpen haunted her.

The safest place was the eye of the storm. Hundreds would gather to pray for the lord priest's soul. An innocent should behave as an innocent. She turned and slowed to a walk. The Chamber of Etinbin, Patron God of the Dead and Overseer of the Living Stars. Courage or foolishness, she sought safety in plain sight.

Dareun's ears rang from the explosion of the lord priest's bone, and surrounding the body screams and shouts thundered amid shoves and elbows. The press of bodies frightened him, his joints and bones had spent too many years kneeling to wade into the jostle. He scanned the crowd for Eliles but it proved impossible, too many hooded faces. With luck she'd escaped the stampede.

His thoughts returned to his night in the Hall of Bones; he'd witnessed the assassin's meddling, but knew nothing worthwhile. Feeling ancient, useless, and afraid in the maelstrom, he considered leaving, but the chaos had left a woman forgotten.

Dareun hustled to Meris. Slack-jawed and unmoving, her breaths gurgled. Dareun turned the woman's head, and blood trickled from her mouth. Three shards of bone were lodged in her chest and abdomen, while the lord priest looked as if he'd fallen on a porcupine. Crass thoughts even for these times. He mumbled a prayer in apology.

Crass or not, the observation bore meaning. Whoever sabotaged the bone possessed skills and knowledge beyond his own. The Bones of Divination reserved for the lord priest were guarded by deadly prayers so they remained unsmoothed. Clever and devious to alter those prayers to explode the bone with the precision of an attack.

"I need a healer over here!" His prayers might suffice, but gods knew there were plenty more gifted in those arts.

A young woman slid to his side, he couldn't remember her name.

Her hands went first to Meris' chest, then neck and head. The intensity of her prayers made the threat explicit: Despite the lack of blood, Meris neared death.

Dareun took deep breaths, ran his fingers through his hair. Meris wasn't the target and yet was severely injured, which meant Lord Priest Ulrikt walked the Road of Living Stars the moment the bone fragmented. Could even Meris, Master of Bones for decades accomplish such a feat?

He cast the ancient woman a suspicious glance. Meris lay sprawled on the floor, rasping and bleeding. The healer smiled and nodded, and Meris' breaths came easier, clear of fluids.

A Master of Bones for longer than any before, she was one of a handful. He couldn't wrap his head around a motivation for the oracle to risk her life in murder, and it was hard to imagine her making the climb in and out of the Hall of Bones. *Hells, she hadn't even been in Istinjoln yet!*

She could've passed on the knowledge. Political underpinnings might fuel a plot, it wouldn't be the first time a lord priest was assassinated, but best he knew, Meris sat in her stars and avoided controversies in the canon. She had written an interpretation of the stars in support of the Prayer of Edofus and its position on poverty for missionaries, but that had been over a decade ago. No, he doubted her involvement in such a horrific act.

A commotion erupted as priests lifted Ulrikt and rushed his body from the Hall. The entourage disappeared through the west wing and a lull passed over the chambers. The silence was a blessing on his ears, but still felt wrong, considering the violence moments before.

His thoughts cleared in the tranquility. He needed to check on Eliles. His girl needed him about now, after a dead lord priest landed within a stride of her lap.

"Thank you for healing this woman." The young priestess smiled. He'd be sure to remember her name tomorrow and show her proper gratitude.

A commotion behind him, and before he turned to look, powerful arms grappled Dareun and crashed him to the ground, a knee driven into his back, blasting the air from his lungs. He gasped and choked, unable to breathe a prayer and too old and frail to fight back. His wrists were twisted and burned by rope and his joints wrenched. He screamed as priests he knew by name flipped him to his back. Anger and hate twisted their faces.

He tried to speak, but his lungs heaved. The blur of a leather sap from the corner of his eye.

THIRTY

Written in Glory

Wandering wooded mountains in dark and cold,
without lodestone, or stars, or fungus, or moon.
No sense of direction except faith in the teachings of man
on the words of Gods. Cracks in bone, chasms in the world,
Leading Somewhere, Anywhere, Nowhere, Red Hare?
Red hair once white, silver meets steel meats crimson,
Cracks, cracks, in palms, faces, mountains, and bones,
cracks bleed blood, lava, or lies.

—*Tomes of the Touched*

Five Days to the Eve of Snows

The Hall of Bontore crushed Meris' spirit with claustrophobia when she compared it to the expanse of stars she called home. Small, cramped, and its only light supplied by mortal fires. Chandeliers flickered high above, highlighting speckles of silver that a healthy imagination once conjured into stars. She'd sat in the Hall as a young woman, pointing out constellations of her own making to a lover, but they were pathetic imitations now.

Swollen rows of kneeling priests and postulants knelt before the dais on which she rested, adding to her claustrophobia. She'd never sought the priesthood for its crowds. In fact, a distaste of preaching to

271

the masses drove her to Skywatch as much as her gift for reading the bones. She enjoyed the relative solitude, communion on behalf of the gods one-on-one with the faithful.

Meris saw her calling as serving the gods first, the flock second. For many this might be counterintuitive, she brought prophecy and the word of Bontore to the people so they could use this knowledge to better their lives. While a service to the mortal, she saw her mission as providing the gods with a way to communicate with their obedient and devout servants, and even the occasional heretic, in order to manifest in the mortal realm the will of the Pantheon.

On this the day before the Eve of Snows, while breaking bones for those moving on to the priesthood, as well as for the high and lord priests, she felt disconnected. She focused on each bone brought before her, searching so hard for what she needed to find, that the connection she felt with Bontore became a dull warmth in her spine, instead of a soothing heat enveloping her body like a steaming bath. Even the faces of those coming before her to hear their futures blurred into a fog. She read the portents from every bone with practiced precision. The bones were smoothed, their cracks predictable before she struck.

There were no surprises.

Until the girl. Even as far away as Skywatch Meris knew the name "Eliles," a girl gifted with prayers of fire unmatched in the history of the monastery. Rumors swirled of her as a chosen one, but nobody offered a clue of what for. She was attractive in the manner of teenage girls: Tall, with slender hips not yet mature, long blond hair, straight teeth, and an oval face unblemished by time or scar. Meris took the girl's hands as she knelt. When looking into her eyes, the girl was nothing special, except maybe a hint of violet in her irises.

Meris smiled. Her favorite aunt had violet eyes, such a rarity, she didn't recall seeing another since her relative had Walked the Stars.

She glanced at the bone resting on its cushion. Smoothed, and more than once if she wasn't mistaken. She'd never seen this before. Two factions within Istinjoln might battle for this girl's future, and she couldn't tell which way the bone would break. She rubbed the oracle's sliver until it glowed white, turning frigid in her warm palms, and struck. The echoing pop of the bone breaking resounded as a thousand times before, but the cracks stretching across the surface were few and strong. In eighty years of breaking bones she'd never seen a pattern this strong.

A tiny fissure stretched from the crack passing the Fires of Sol and spiraling around a tiny carving of a star known as the Light of Istinjoln.

Meris interpreted the bone in typical words, "My child, Bontore smiles on you. Here we see a line crossing Januel's Heart . . ." She continued but her mind focused on the spiral and what it meant. *She would know*, the Face had assured her, and before uncertainty forced a bead of sweat, she decided: To her knowledge, never had the bones declared someone's priestesshood, let alone connected them to the King of Gods in this manner. Lord Priest Ulrikt didn't just want this girl connected to Istinjoln, that could be achieved with subtlety, but this? The strength of the cracks, their precision, this meant Ulrikt wanted her shackled to Istinjoln and close to him.

But why? A man so powerful couldn't fear this child, but he wanted her close, no doubt. Eliles' divining would be a first, and Meris didn't fear to make the proclamation.

"What name did you bear to Istinjoln?"

"Eliles Hunvad."

"What name do you bear at Istinjoln?"

"Eliles."

"From this day forward, you are known as Eliles of Istinjoln, Priestess of Sol's Fire." The girl faded to white before her eyes, and for a flicker she thought Eliles might faint as she stumbled from the dais steps. Meris suspected that Ulrikt would take this new priestess under his wing, hone her prayers, honing her prayers to be the next lord priestess? If that was the case, this poor child wasn't the only one in these chambers feeling ill.

No matter how bizarre, for Meris the prophecy came as a relief, the girl's prophecy must have been her mission. A subtle play of smoothing, to get a girl proclaimed to the priesthood and tied to Istinjoln by an oracle's words. She exhaled and relaxed, the high priests' bones coming next.

These bones cracked true and unsmoothed, challenging her art, instead of making her read bones which may as well be books. Meris enjoyed interpreting these bones more than she had in twenty-five years, and with Lord Priest Ulrikt's prophecy still to come, there remained something to look forward to.

Meris found Ulrikt a kinder and more gentle soul than she'd imagined. When Ulrikt ascended the dais from behind the golden curtain his bearing was regal, the stiff in his spine, the tilt of his jaw, the cool gaze of a man comfortable with his power. Meris rose to take his hands, and if a younger woman she would've blushed and perhaps deigned to flirt.

She kneeled before him and he smiled at her. A young boy brought her the clavicle of a bear, and she rested the prophetic bone on a cushion. When her eyes parted with his she gazed at the bone and its carvings. At first nothing struck her as unusual. The bone held a deadly enchantment, assuring that any attempt to smooth its cracks ended in death. Except, the fine grains and growth patterns bore signs of smoothing. An impossibility. And striking this bone for prophecy meant doom.

Meris looked to the lord priest and Ulrikt whispered, "It was good getting to know you."

She hesitated. Her first thought was to throw the bone from the dais, as far away as possible, but then she realized why she was here. She knew. She wouldn't fear to speak of doom. The lord priest had invited her to his chambers in order to get to know the woman who would kill him.

Meris wrote Ulrikt's destiny when the glowing shiv of steel plunged into the bone.

A flash. An explosion. Blind and deaf and lying on her back, she knew she bled with needles of bone deep in her flesh. As conscious-ness waned, she knew what she had done, she couldn't grasp why. She hoped to live, so one day she might understand.

THIRTY-ONE

Scat and Blood

Darkness sees light, but light is Blind to Darkness.
Truths are ugly and beauty lies in lies.
Fear me not, oh worthy!
Surly, curly, whirly, oh Worthy.
Fear not my Beauty and see not my Darkness!
Come come and succumb, smiling blind and dumb.

—*Tomes of the Touched*

Five Days to the Eve Snows

Icy water splashed his face and the reek of salt of hartshorn burnt his nostrils, making him gasp for air. Dareun's face throbbed. He struggled to open his eyes, his right tearing through matted blood, but his left didn't open. He blinked into torchlight.

A dark shadow loomed.

Woxlin leaned in with a depraved smile. "A sad . . . . No, tragic day, when a lord priest is assassinated, don't you agree?"

"Yes—" The slap ground the fractured bones in his face, and consciousness wavered before salts pressed beneath his nose again.

"I will tell you when to speak."

Dareun closed his eyes and prayed for healing, but couldn't focus.

Cloud Water, of course; they'd forced the poison down his throat to make sure his prayers would go unanswered.

Woxlin studied him, but what did he seek? The man's grin twisted. "You may speak."

"What's this about?"

"The question is what did you do? Or why?"

Fog cleared. They thought he'd murdered Ulrikt. His head sank. "Meris." Dareun didn't believe the accusation himself, but he'd sacrifice the oracle for himself without a thought. "If anyone could—"

"Meris! Oh, my. That's desperate. That decrepit woman mustered the gumption to walk to the Hall of Oracles, smoothing the bone of her lord priest so she could destroy it in her own hands? Think long before that's your claim."

The absurdity struck a deeper blow than the man's palm. "I didn't kill Ulrikt."

"A witness saw you at the gate to the Hall of Bones several nights past, but we thought nothing of it. 'Faithful Dareun, what harm could that old man do?'"

"I did nothing." With his mind clouded by the blows, an excuse escaped him.

"I will be your confessor." Woxlin pulled a scroll from his sleeve, a quill and ink from his pocket, and set them on a wobbly table. "When you're ready, call for me."

Dareun squirmed, letting the man walk from the cell felt like doom. "I admit I was there. I visited the bones, an odd habit of mine, I saw someone down there—"

Woxlin spun, "Who?"

"A priest's robes, but I didn't see a face. I swear."

"This priest, short, hunched, with a limp? First you try to blame a hobbled woman, now some faceless priest. I suggest the truth if you wish to avoid a Sundering." Woxlin exited, the heavy door grinding closed. He didn't bother to turn the lock.

Dareun curled into the corner and wept. The torment of the Slave Forges would find him if they didn't discover the real killer.

Rusty hinges squealed, and the door groaned open. Woxlin returned. "Hello, old friend."

The face, the voice, they were Woxlin's, but something was wrong. It could be sarcasm, and Dareun had met the man only a few times before today, but the tone rang different.

"I'm not going to confess to a damnable deed I had no hand in." *Least not until you torture me.*

"I know you went to the Bones to smooth the defiled girl's oracle bones. I've known since the first time."

Dareun's heart stopped. Woxlin couldn't know this. Twelve Hells, what was happening? His blurred vision sank to the floor.

"You think you are so clever as to bring a defiled into my monastery and I wouldn't notice? To smooth her bones year after year against my will?" The voice changed. "Without my noticing?"

Dareun raised his head and with his one good eye stared at a ghost: Lord Priest Ulrikt. Dumbstruck. He couldn't even protest. He'd seen the man die, hadn't he?

"I need your help, old friend."

They were never friends. But how to argue with a ghost? "You're a ghost. Or I'm hallucinating."

"Ghosts need salvation and hallucinations need to be forgotten. I need your help." The man tapped the blank scroll. "I need you to confess."

Dareun stared at his boots, the toes scuffed from his being dragged here. "You want me to confess to killing you? How about I scream you're alive, instead?"

"So much wisdom and foolishness in one man." The lord priest squatted, his finger touching Dareun's face.

He flinched at the touch, expecting pain, instead, bones shifted and the agony subsided.

"All your pain may be taken away, or it may be amplified until your screams are joined by your pretty pupil's."

Why threaten Eliles? "What do I care of any of my students' pains. Why? Why kill me?"

"Convenience? Oh, I would've been fine blaming the whole thing on Meris and some cabal she'd fallen in with, but why, when I have you? Someone tried to kill me. I don't know who, but I need to know. They will stay tucked away so long as they believe we're looking for them. But with me dead, and the killer tortured into confession and executed? They will stick their head up from whatever hole they've crawled into, we will find them, and sever it. This comes down to two unpleasant choices."

The lord priest stood and his face shifted, the skin slithering over shifting bones until Eliles gazed at him with innocent eyes and a smile for her master. The voice remained deep and calm, Ulrikt's. "You will either confess and face summary execution, or you will confess after torture and face the Sundering of the Ten Winds, along with your pet defiled." The voice changed to mimic Eliles, the precision of tone and cadence disturbing. "You risked death for me all these years, accept this fate to save me."

Rumors of the so-called Lord Priest's Face had persisted over Dareun's decades in Istinjoln, but never once had he heard of Ulrikt himself being capable of the feat. It was difficult to believe that Ulrikt, a man studied in Fire, could also master prayers of Life to conquer this trick.

"How do I even know it's you? You might be Ulrikt's Face. His double come to trick me."

The vision of Eliles rubbed its eyes with a wrinkled man's hand, and the girl dissipated into the lord priest again. "Dear, dear Dareun. How do you even know if the man you knew as Ulrikt was ever me at all?" He rubbed his temple as if fighting a headache. "None of this matters. What matters is how you choose to die, and whether you die alone. I am trying to save your soul, not your life. Choose nobly."

The lord priest patted him on the head like a pitied hound, pulled his hood over his face—whichever one he might choose to wear—and exited, the door creaking closed.

Dareun had never imagined his life coming to this. He sat on damp straw in the midst of rat scat and the reek of urine, choosing between executions. To Sunder a person meant breaking the invisible tie between the immortal soul and the gods. Wicked for anyone, but anathema for a priest, damning the soul to never reach the Road of Living Stars. No heavens, no hells, not even the Slave Fields for redemption, he'd find himself a severed spirit, a ghost, until fading into nothingness.

He could deny his hand in the death of a man still alive, but only until the torture grew too great. By then, he'd have dragged Eliles into his pitiable fate. He struggled to his feet, his body aching, and stumbled into the door. "Guard."

A face appeared in the barred window. A thick mustache, and day-old beard, dark brown eyes, and a scarred nose, but for all Dareun knew, it was the lord priest himself. "Send word to Woxlin, I've decided to confess. And, who left my cell a wick ago?"

The guard laughed. "You've gone soft in the head. You've had no visitors since Woxlin."

Saliva blinded Dareun's good eye before the guard turned and walked away. A rare opportunity for a prison guard to spit on a priest; Dareun hoped he'd enjoyed the moment.

He moved to the back of his cell and slid down the wall to take a seat. He'd lived a good life, spent decades doing a thing he loved, touched the lives of a great many people. An inglorious end, but he knew the truth. It couldn't save him, nor dull the pain, but the truth would serve him well on the Road of Living Stars.

✻ ✻ ✻

A white human skull with black stars for eyes stared at Eliles. Carved from white marble, and four times larger than her own skull, it was a work of art with its eyes filled with sparkling, crushed black diamond. Never having born flesh or skin, nor any other burden of being alive, was perhaps why its vision of death appeared so peaceful.

Eliles kneeled before Etinbin's altar and its ominous stone head, praying for the lord priest's soul. As Patron of the Dead and Overseer of the Road of Living Stars, Etinbin sat at the fore of everyone's prayers when ranking priests passed from the mortal world. A priest who served the Pantheon of Sol could rely upon Etinbin's judgement to assist in walking the Road without falling into one of the Twelve Hells, and prayers of the devout encouraged the kindness of the Overseer.

True, she didn't care for the man's soul, but appearances kept dissenters alive.

Scant few priests were here when she arrived to mouth her prayers. Most didn't have the lord priest strike the ground right in front of them. She knew what others didn't: Ulrikt died before hitting the ground. Only a miracle from the Age of God Wars could return the man to the living, and then only if you believed the stories of resurrections. Most spoke their prayers at the shrine of Erginle, daughter of Sol and Elinwe, the Patron of Healers.

The smell of lilacs and the rustle of kneeling robes beside her caught her attention, but she didn't dare interrupt her prayer by opening her eyes. A man's voice entered into prayer, soft and sincere. So quiet she couldn't say for certain whose voice, but she feared she did.

Her prayer finished, she prostrated herself on the ground, pressing lips to the cold stone. The adherent was polite enough not to interrupt her grieving, but determined enough to stay; she curled back to her kneeling stance and turned to blink into Woxlin's solemn face.

She'd become accustomed to his showing up everywhere these days, so she managed a straight face. "High Priest Woxlin, this is a surprise . . . Does this, I mean, Lord Priest Ulrikt?"

Woxlin nodded, whispering. "You were right to seek Etinbin's hall; His Eminence has passed on to the Road of Living Stars."

"When I saw him . . . I knew, I hoped I was wrong, but . . . ." She'd wanted the lord priest dead, but it was like wishing a pox on your master, if it happens, you still feel bad. Yet, if she'd had the power to the save the man, would she have?

"His death came with mercy, quick and painless. I have a question to ask of you."

Years of hiding secrets paid off. Her thoughts buzzed, but her heart and face stayed relaxed. "Of course. I was close, but I saw nothing more than anyone else." It also helped not to have to lie.

"No, I suspect not." He rubbed his chin, which strengthened the smell of flowers in the air. She realized the odor came from mortuary perfumes, meaning Woxlin had visited the lord priest's remains. "Still, there's a puzzle that needs solved here. I always liked Dareun, thought he was a good man, a great instructor, and faithful."

"He is all those things." The conversation's direction scared her. Dareun's words, the lord priest's death not boding well for him or her, resounded in her mind.

"Yes, which is why I find it hard to ask this. Do you know of any reason he would visit the Hall of Bones in the dead of night?"

"He never mentioned such to me. I know he studied the Oracle's ways in his youth, and spoke in reverence of those days, easing my fears of seeing my future as a child."

The high priest's face remained solemn, respectful. "Yes, the future can be terrifying, but it's the past as concerns me now. Several nights ago someone saw him leaving the Gate of Bones. We discarded it as nothing. Rubbish, some quirk, or a romanticism of his youth to visit the Hall."

She stared, her thoughts a barrage of screams and denials, of hopeless excuses. The only reason she could give was the truth, and honesty killed him quicker than a lie. It might also kill her. She gnawed truth from her tongue, took a deep breath, but words didn't come. She looked away, pretending to think, taking another breath so she could speak in normal tones. "I wish I had an answer, but nostalgia, as you suggest, is the only reason I can think of."

"I want you to know I don't believe he is guilty of vaticide, but if he is, I regret to say I will be his confessor."

"He is not!" Her words echoed through the chambers, and she regretted her outburst. She mellowed her tone. "No, it's not possible."

"Someone turned the lord priest's divination into murder, and he was the only one seen entering the Hall without cause to be there. You tell me, what else should we think? I can't find the real killer if they torture an innocent man into confession."

The beating of her heart shredded her ability to think straight. Nothing, she could give the man nothing without killing Dareun. Hope lay in finding the real killer, as Woxlin mentioned, so no matter what wanted to blurt from her lips, she needed to swallow her confessions without choking. Exasperated, cheeks quivering to fight tears, she muttered, "I have no idea. I wish I did."

His hand came to rest on her shoulder. "I understand. If you think of anything, please, come and tell me. I fear we have a guest who would serve as Inquisitor, and I'd rather not see the Broldun get his hands on your master. I—"

"High Priest Woxlin!" A young priest, breathless, jogged into the hall, his shoes flapping on the stone. He rushed to Woxlin to whisper in his ear, but Eliles could hear. "The Master of Fire wishes to confess."

A wave of tingles washed her body, her heart choking her senses. *Confess?* She stared in horror at the high priest. The stunned gaze Woxlin's face left no doubt to his surprise.

Woxlin bent over, scratched his face, eyes darting back and forth. "Hmm, uh. Yes, tell him I will be there shortly." The young man trotted away. Woxlin couldn't meet her gaze. "I know this may be difficult to believe, but I am extraordinarily sorry. If it's any consolation, this will save him pain, and his soul."

Eliles couldn't manage a word when he stood to leave. After all these years, she'd gotten her master killed.

"Again, I am most sorry."

He turned and took several steps, but hesitated, then spun on his heel to face her. "A peculiar thing, isn't it? If he'd chosen not to confess, as a postulant you would've come before the inquisitor yourself, but as a priestess they would've needed proof of collusion before calling you to an inquisition. It seems the gods are looking out for you."

She watched as he walked away, her throat aching as she fought tears. There was no joy in his steps, nothing eager to his strides, but still she hated him. Hated him all the more for his parting words; the gods didn't watch out for her, and the vile man who did so twice lay dead. She fought the urge to visualize Woxlin's eyes burned from his head for fear her friends might comply, but she swore, she'd burn everyone of them straight into the hells if it saved her master.

Her life had fallen apart around her brick by brick, and the blame rested with her. She was the mortar of her own life, and she'd always been weak, flawed.

She stood before she realized where she intended to go. Ilpen, she had to see him. A simple man with the simple gift of easing her worries and pains. She needed to talk to someone, but she couldn't get the old tinker killed, too. Even if she only spoke to Ears, at least someone would hear.

A youthful hand snagged her arm as she exited the hall. Sandele held a finger to her lips, glancing around, nervous. "Your master wants words with you."

She wanted to believe the girl. "What? How would you—"

"My cousin is a guard, but there's no time to explain. He's hurt bad."

There wasn't time to think, her feet moved on hope alone. Eliles followed the girl's mousy brown hair until they descended a set of stairs leading into the prison vaults. She'd passed these halls a hundred times but never found cause to venture where they led. They stopped, the girl pursing her lips.

"What now?" Eliles asked.

"Jant said, let's see. . . . Down until you see a boulder painted red, a right turn, then the second right after. He's in the fourth cell on your right."

"You're certain?" Too good to be true.

"No, I'm not. But that's what he said. I'm sorry, I gotta go." She smiled. "You wouldn't get me down there, anyway."

"Thank you."

"Good luck."

Eliles watched her ponytail sway until she disappeared into a turn. Instinct told her she was a starving bear stumbling into honey bait. Too simple. Too convenient.

She pushed her senses into the stairwell: Nothing from the ordinary. If a trap, it was the undeniable honey.

Trepidation slowed her first steps, but a sense of rhythm grew and sped her down the spiraling climb. An old saying came to mind: *Death finds the coward as surely as the brave.* Philosophers argued whether the scripture spoke of destiny, or if it were inspiration for battle.

Sparse lanterns lit the stairwell, but their light was sufficient to note the color of the rocks marking passages. When she reached the red, her count reached five levels, and still the hole twisted into the depths. She poked her head through the arching stone portal on her right, not a soul in sight, just rows of doors carved into stone with barred windows. Her senses reached out; the hollows in the stone were tiny and empty, but she felt breathing, two individuals maybe twenty paces around the second corner on her right, one behind a door, precisely where the girl had said they would be.

Eliles took the first turn and skulked through the darkness, stopping before the second passage on her right to glance down the corridor. A guard stood in leather and mail across from a door on the right side of the hall. The man rocked on his heels, fidgety. Nervous because he set a trap, or because he allowed a visitor? She called to her fiery friend, sensed the reassuring warmth before she risked anything. "Jant?"

The guard spun to look her way. "Aye. Hurry girl, we don't have long. Don't like risk'n my head for a few songs."

"Eliles? You there?" She recognized the voice and dashed down the hall, peered into the dark cell. Her master dragged himself from the straw-piled floor. "I promised this man silver, in my chest at the foot of my bed, get the girl Sandele the coins for him."

Tears washed her cheeks as she nodded. She reached fingers through the bars to touch his bloodied and broken face.

"I'm fine, my girl."

"I can get you out."

"And what, carry me into the mountains and hide? No. You must promise me, whatever they do to me, don't try to help. I no longer matter."

"I will find a way—"

"You won't! Promise me. I need to know you will live."

She stared into his eyes. The old man recognized her lies, and the deception struggled to her lips. "I swear by Januel, I will not risk my life for yours." Despite her inner battle, she knew the words true once uttered. She owed dedication to his final wish, she wouldn't break the vow.

Intense eyes held her gaze. "Good. Even with Ulrikt dead, many will seek to use you. They see divinity in your skills."

"A Choerkin was in Istinjoln the other day—"

"No! Trust them less than anyone. They would see the Church in ruins."

She nodded, but these words struck an ill note with her. Her master had spoken of Clan Choerkin once or twice over the years, but when he did, the words were more gracious. Plus, she refused to believe this of Ivin. "I will do as you say," she lied.

The old man showed a smile made crooked by his broken face. "That's a good girl. Now, go. Honor and remember me as I was, not as I've become."

She sniffled, breast quaking as she staved off sobs. She touched his face once with a kiss on her fingers and departed.

Eliles rubbed her eyes and steeled her will with clenched teeth. She promised to not risk her life to save him, but he mentioned nothing of revenge. If she found who framed her master, no power would protect them from her wrath. The only person in Istinjoln she could trust was Ilpen. Folks trusted the tinker with more than their kettles and pans, they blathered to him for candles on end, more gossip than the kitchens, she wagered. A rumor wouldn't give an answer, but it might point in the right direction.

Find Ilpen, let him know what happened, and make sure he listened for loose words. He'd be more than happy to help. She passed the Hall of Etinbin, filling with mourners as word of Ulrikt's death spread, and made a beeline for Upper Istinjoln.

Two guards with crossed spears and a monk barred the door. The monk said, "No one is allowed into Upper Istinjoln for a time."

She grimaced and turned, heading for her cell. It made sense to lock the exits, but with so many trapped underground, they couldn't keep them penned for long before mice became badgers. In the meantime, she needed to fight her every instinct and keep quiet.

Hinges creaked and groaned and Woxlin entered Dareun's cell for the second or third time, depending how you kept count. Dareun studied his mouth, thinking maybe he'd find a clue in his crooked teeth to determine who he spoke with. No luck. Hells, he'd swear they both smelled of mortuary flowers, one from visiting, the other from being dead.

"You look peaked, are you yourself?" Dareun never considered himself a funny man, but he chuckled at his joke.

"You summoned me to confess or to make japes?"

Dareun rolled his one good eye. "I will sign whatever you want me to sign. I've no reason to dawdle."

"Ah, well, good then." Woxlin stretched the scroll on the table, dipped the pen in ink and offered it to him.

Dareun scoffed. "Write whatever you will; it no longer matters to me."

"I'd prefer it were in your hand. Sin is a malady, and confession a salve for the soul."

"I'm admitting guilt. I don't know how I did it, nor why. But by the gods I murdered him, write it down."

The pen dangled idle in Woxlin's fingers. "Bearing false witness might find you in the Liar's Hell, among the others you're bound to suffer."

"And if I don't I will never see a hell, nor be able to earn redemption in the Slave Fields. You see the truth."

"You killed the lord priest, this is the truth I'm here to witness. I will write it."

The pen scratched its mark.

A lanky man clad in black stood in the door. No priest, but he served one.

"Mmm, I will handle the writ, if it pleases."

The Broldun inquisitor. Torturer might be more accurate.

Woxlin stood, relinquishing his seat, and the ugly man put pen to vellum in a hurry.

Dareun mumbled, "My apologies for confessing, disappointing you."

"You ain't disappointed no one yet, no."

The man's smile sent a quiver through Dareun's bladder. He decided to keep his mouth shut.

The inquisitor tapped the pen in its well and wrote until putting a period on the end with tip-bending emphasis. "Should do nicely, yessir."

Dareun crept to his knees, signed, though it was difficult to recognize his own scrawl. The other men signed as witnesses. Woxlin rolled the scroll and was about to say something before the inquisitor interrupted.

"You will leave now." The inquisitor pointed to the door and gave the high priest a shove.

"I promised this man generosity."

"For killing your lord priest? Generosity? And why did he not write in his own hand? Why did he not utter his confession of guilt for you to transcribe? We must have a reason." His hands reached behind his back and produced tongs and pliers suited for a forge, and a hooked knife, slammed them on the table. "Now, get out."

"Woxlin, don't leave me with this man. I confessed of my own free will."

The high priest turned, closing the door behind him as he exited.

The inquisitor bore a pursed-lip smile. "Disappointed? Nah, I thank you. Normally, I'd need listen through your screams, pause and ask questions, wait for your confession. This way, we skip them pleasantries, mmm."

A fist clubbed Dareun, re-breaking his cheek. He cried out as he collapsed into moldy, reeking straw, squirmed as the man's heel drove his face into the floor, dislocating his jaw. Pliers seized his right thumb and wrenched it from its socket, and for the first time since a child, piss warmed the priest's leg.

Thirty-Two

Snow's Eye

The Snow Owl sits White in the green of ice-covered pine,
Invisible day or night. It sees you, a mouse, a sparrow, a bunny.
Your eyes see only the Shadow of that which feeds on your flesh
and vomits your bones.
You rest forever rotting at the base of some tree, the forest floor,
having given sustenance to that which consumed you.

—*Tomes of the Touched*

Six Days to the Eve of Snows

When the Wolverine said two or three days, it wasn't due to distance; it was because of the grueling terrain and snow. The drifts in several stretches reached the bellies of their horses and more than once they dismounted to ease the labor of their mounts. They found shelter in a cave the first night and braved a fire. Ivin damned near caught his feet on fire trying to keep them warm. The next day he might have preferred flaming boots. They climbed to higher trails where winds lashed the mountains with a ferocity which cleared much of their trail. They made better time, but at the price of putting ice in their veins.

Trees were a blessing among the rocks, ice, and snow, both shelter from the wind and a supply of kindling as they moved deeper into the mountains. Near midday, Pikarn's voice managed to carry over the winds.

"Snow's Eye!"

Ivin raised his eyes, excited, but when he realized the Wolverine pointed up, his stomach sank to his aching toes. An ancient tower jutted from the mountain's stone, overlooking a crumbled wall stretching the width of the pass. The towers would control passage through this region of the Estertok Mountains, if there were trade or enemies, but weather and climate made the work and expense of erecting these defenses appear foolish nowadays.

Dark figures wavered in and out of existence in the snow-clouded winds ahead. Pikarn halted the party, and they spread out the best they could, weapons in hand. It was a perverse relief when they realized the creatures were Colok rather than Shadows. Whether friendly Colok or not, they were flesh and blood if a fight were at hand.

Modan rode to the front, haled the group and when answered by a roar he called them together. Ivin's first sight of the Colok made him grateful these were friendly. Most were nine feet tall and covered in piecemeal gear that ranged from padded leather to mail, and if their teeth and claws weren't intimidating enough, their steel weapons were more than capable.

Modan said, "Zjin leads them. Steady hands, don't do nothin' stupid."

A Colok came forward, his black and white fur tipped by ice. "Choerkin?"

Ivin had never heard his name take so long to say, but it was there amid the guttural growl. "I'm Ivin Choerkin, third son of Kotin Choerkin."

The man-bear smiled with teeth that could shred flesh from bone. "Come. Shadows." Zjin turned, swinging his glaive in an arc over his head, and the Colok warriors formed a loose circle around the men.

Ivin rode beside Puxele. "Did he say Shadows?"

She shrugged. "Believe so. I haven't seen a thing."

They'd heard right. They weren't more than a thousand strides before Shadows slithered from trees to rocks, rushing ahead, crisscrossing the trail, but they didn't attack. What power did the Colok possess which kept the Shadows at bay? Ivin knew they had magics, but no more than the priests at the Crack of Burdenis. Physical strength didn't make sense, he'd seen a man shaken in the air like a child's toy by a Shadow.

Zjin didn't let them slow down, but he wasn't frightened of the Shadows. His confidence bled into the men, and hence the horses. His mount didn't care a whit about the stalking Shadows, but shied at the Colok. Why? The question had time to bounce ear to ear before the horses tensed and Zjin brought them to a halt.

Colok eyes focused on a ridge descending from on high ahead so he stood in his saddle, squinting to make out figures in the snow. Their awkward loping gaits left no doubt, Shadow-Taken. "Looks like we've got a fight, after all." He lifted his shield from its saddle hook and drew his sword.

Modan said, "Worry first about the Taken. Keep your asses in the saddle at all cost and stay close to the Colok!"

Zjin and his people didn't pull weapons, they set their feet and crouched, the bare skin beneath their eyes flushing red with the blood rage. The horses stomped as the Taken approached. Shadows gathered, hovering above the ground, instead of hiding in the dark spaces of nature. Ivin counted fifteen.

The Taken wore the tattered clothes of priests, miners, and trappers and they swerved in and out of each other as they ran. It'd be easier to count milling chickens in a coop. If not for the Colok, this would be the day Ivin died, but because of them he had hope.

Rinold eased his mount beside Puxele, an axe and shield in his hands instead of his usual bow. "Breathe deep, Little Sister."

Puxele's eyes betrayed the nerves her voice hid. "Breathe any way you can, just make sure you stay that way. Goes for you, too, Ratsmasher."

Ivin's throat was too dry for words. He exhaled a cloud before his eyes and gazed upon the enemy. They came at a dead sprint without sign of fatigue. A Taken larger than the rest led the group, his face twisted and garish, his eyes blind white.

Rinold spoke before Ivin could think it. "Ah, shits. Suvarn."

There wasn't time for sadness, the creatures didn't lose a single stride as they leaped, soaring through the air higher than mortals should. Zjin and his people snagged them by arms, feet, necks, whatever they got their hands on, their claws tearing flesh and dragging them to the ground with devastating force. But the Colok didn't have enough hands to kill them all. Suvarn and others careened into the wardens, scratching, biting, clawing, clubbing anything alive.

Horses and men screamed amid the thunderous howls of the Colok and the flailing Taken. Ivin's mount wheeled, and he struggled to bring her under control. In a blur he saw the Wolverine cleave a woman from shoulder to pelvis, Suvarn grappling with Modan, and a couple horses collapsing as the Taken slipped beneath the reach of blades to assault the horses' legs. He spurred his mount toward Modan but Fronk's horse reared in front of him, the man clinging to saddle and reins as the horse bucked to rid itself of a Taken. Ivin's sword lashed out, severing a Taken's arm before a leaping miner struck his shield. Ivin twisted his arm, as if deflecting a weapon, but the creature clung to the targe's steel rim, clawing and kicking.

He toppled and his horse staggered under the awkward weight, struggling to keep its feet in the ice and snow. The saddle twisted under the wrenching weight of the Taken fighting to pull Ivin to the ground, and he leaned hard to his right, yanking the Taken with him to make certain the saddle didn't spin beneath the horse's belly.

Fingers scratched at his face over his shield and he struck pommel and fist to the thing's skull. Dark blood spattered up his arm over and over until Puxele removed the Taken's head for him. His horse spun, and he saw Modan trapped beneath his thrashing mount, disarmed, screaming in a rage as he held Suvarn from throttling him. Suvarn's teeth gnashed close to Modan's face but before Ivin could get close, a Colok grabbed Suvarn's head in its massive hand and crushed his skull. In a flicker of time, the face of a man he'd ridden beside was pulverized into unrecognizable gore.

A screeching woman without eyes landed on the Colok's back, biting and punching, and the Colok stumbled and flailed from the wounded warden, dropping onto its back to crush the Taken.

A Taken launched from beneath Puxele's horse from the corner of his eye and he spun in the saddle without a flicker to spare. Luck and instinct drove his sword straight through the creature's chest, and it slid dead from his blade. In the chaos of the melée he lost sight of the Wolverine, and the next glance he had of Modan, the man had struggled to his feet with a severe limp, and his bloodied horse had bolted, already thirty strides from the battle.

Ivin spurred his horse but not quick enough. The Shadow came in a blur of darkness, striking its fist straight into the man's chest. Modan's head rocked backward, his mouth agape as Ivin's sword passed through the Shadow's neck. A mortal creature would have dropped in a splash of blood but the Shadow didn't so much as acknowledge the blade passing through its substance.

Ivin was powerless as Modan's mouth hung open in silent horror like a fish speared and lifted from the water. Zjin came from behind the Shadow and swiped his massive paw at the thing's head, and for an instant the Shadow's darkness distorted. Strike after strike separated bits of Shadow, and a horrifying scream split the air, a shriek that left

Ivin's ears ringing. The Shadow released Modan from its grip and fled to the rocks and trees.

Zjin saved Modan from a fall, lifting him by the back of his cloak and lay him across Ivin's saddlehorn. With a grunt, the Colok dashed into the dwindling remains of combat. Three of the wardens and their horses were dead, and injuries could hide anywhere under the blood-soaked gear of survivors. Bodies of the Taken lay strewn in pieces across the battlefield, and the Colok dismembered them further, even after they were dead. The Shadows waited still and silent, emotionless.

Puxele said, "What I understand, takes longer for the Shadows to return if they're scattered."

Ivin could only nod, horrified. He turned to see Pikarn on his horse, the Old Man sat straight, unharmed, his axe and targe still in hand.

"Modan?"

Ivin sheathed his sword to better keep Modan from sliding off the horse's withers. "He's breathing, can't say much else."

Rinold slumped in his saddle over the scattered remnants of Suvarn, tiny tendrils of Shadow already wriggling from the Taken's flesh. "Goodbye, brother."

Puxele said, "We've got more brothers out there, I'm a-bettin'."

Ivin stared at the mountains beyond Shadows and carnage, savoring every breath. When he brought his eyes back down, Pikarn's horse straddled a dead Taken.

As Ivin kneed his horse to walk closer, he heard Pikarn. "Ungar."

"Your friend, from the Ihomjo mines?"

The Wolverine wiped blood from his ax on his saddle blanket. "No friend, he was your Uncle Lovar's man in them mines. We had an idea the holies were up to somethin', but we always thought they were hiding a gold strike. Leaves no doubt in my mind them unholy whore-sons dropped them mines to seal the entrance."

"Can you blame them?"

"Yes, I can. And so do you."

The time for justifications was over. "I suppose I do."

"Mhhm." Pikarn spit a mouth full of blood and rubbed his jaw. "Best we ride, no time for niceties with the dead."

With Shadows watching their every move, and tendrils already wriggling from the blood-drenched stone, Ivin couldn't argue. But logic be damned, it hurt to leave them lying in this frozen waste.

The wardens and their Colok escort arrived at the wall with Ivin lost in dark thoughts. He stared at the snow-splotched stones, the rusted gate that once must have been magnificent, but his thoughts struggled with Modan and the blood on his gloves. They'd caught the man's horse, and he managed to sit his saddle, but without Puxele and Rinold on either side, his wobbles would send him to the ground.

Puxele said, "The dead are gone, but Modan is a tough, stubborn bastard, we'll see him through this."

Ivin smiled the best he could. "Yeah. We will." *Worry about the living, not the dead. Why the hells is that so hard?*

He shook off a blood-soaked glove and rubbed his face, trying to bring some warmth back to his skin. The Shadows were farther away but still watching, defeated and victorious at the same time, and unconcerned either way. They watched, they waited, their time to kill would come again.

Three Colok moved a boulder from a crumbling tower, revealing a door. Inside, the ground floor, basement, and second floor were still intact, and here they spent the night. Their kindling rushed into flame and the men huddled around the fire while the Colok sat clustered, leaning against each other in a circle, their thick fur and shared heat making them impervious to the cold.

Modan had a place of honor by a fire while heaped with extra furs. He moaned throughout the night, a purple-black bruise marking his chest and back. They applied salves, but best they could tell it eased his pain not at all.

The next morning their Shadow stalkers were nowhere to be seen. They rode up the side of the mountain until the frozen snow rose high enough they could walk their horses to the top of the wall. They dismounted for the uneven, oft-icy steps leading to Snow's Eye. As the day wore on, dark thoughts of death and dying turned to fatigue. Burning muscles and sweat on an icy wall returned focus to staying alive.

A wide platform of parapeted stone greeted them at the doors to Snow's Eye Tower, along with a half dozen Colok guards. Bellows, roars, and hand gestures passed between their guides and these guards. The doors opened and they entered with horses in tow.

Fires lit the great hall of the tower. Tapestries still hung from the walls, depicting scenes of glorious victories and gods, long forgotten.

Fronk and Rislin carried Modan inside and lay him beside a fire. A priest came from a spiral stair and marched to the wounded man the moment he noticed Modan. "Where's his wound?"

Ivin answered. "His chest. A Shadow attack."

The priest squinted. "He survived a Shadow?" He parted the folds of Modan's cloak and extra layers, revealing a swollen welt of black and purple. He sucked his breath. "Mmm, oh dear."

"Can you do anything?" Pikarn asked.

"I don't know." The priest looked to Pikarn as he lay hands on the man's wound. "You must be the Wolverine."

Ivin heard the nickname spoken aloud so rarely it surprised him, and more surprising perhaps, the old man didn't correct him.

"Do your best." Pikarn went to tend to his horse.

Ivin stared, hoping to see a miracle bring the swelling down, for the colors to fade to flesh tones. Nothing of the sort happened.

"Healing is not my strength, and honestly, it's difficult to tell what's wrong with him. Are you the Choerkin?"

"Yes. Ivin Choerkin."

"I'm Tokodin of Vohan. We're fortunate they didn't demand a particular man of the blood. We'll talk more soon enough." The priest closed his eyes, muttering a prayer, but nothing happened far as Ivin could tell, until…

Modan's body spasmed and went stiff as a board, his eyes flying wide, and a scream rattled the walls of the hall. Tokodin's whispers turned into fervent commands and Modan calmed.

"Well, I can ease his pain, at least, and make certain he moves on to the Road of Living Stars with our blessings. Saving him, I don't know."

Ivin towered over the shorter man as Tokodin stood, wanting nothing more than to slap his scarred face, slam him back to his knees, to demand more prayers and healing. Instead he nodded in acquiescence. "You're the priest who speaks with the Colok?"

"Yes, sort of. You can speak to them as well as I, the few who understand our tongue, but I've had more time with them to better understand their message. We should settle beside a fire with your commander and talk."

Ivin led them to an open fire, and called for Pikarn, before whispering, "And don't call him Wolverine again."

Tokodin's eyebrows shot up. "Ah! Yes! Right."

Pikarn arrived with a small cask under his arm and cracked the spigot on the ale.

Tokodin smiled with a predator's glint in his eye. "Istinjoln brew?"

The Wolverine sat with a huff. "Woxlin said they had plenty of gruel, so I assumed they wouldn't miss a sniff of ale, either."

"They may hate you in Istinjoln, but I love the both of you." They saluted each other and drank. "Gods have mercy, that's the best ale I've ever had."

Ivin agreed, although it might be the hellish situation making it taste so good. "Why are we here, Tokodin?"

He wiped foam from his lip. "Grolkan is our host. This tribe is known as Broken Snow, or at least, best we got for a translation."

Pikarn let the words slide, but Ivin couldn't. "We? Who's we?"

"Mecum and me. We can thank Mecum for the Colok being able to speak to us. They took him about a year ago and forced him to teach several of them our tongue."

Pikarn thudded the man's mug with his own. "Straight to it, Priest."

"Yes, of course. Now I'm put to it, I'm not sure how to say this, rightly like. Without, well… anyhow. Grolkan is not happy with Istinjoln. He believes—going against all I told him!—that Istinjoln is to blame for the Shadows."

Pikarn laughed. "We already knew that. I hope you got more for us."

The man's eyes shot back and forth between Ivin and Pikarn.

"All right, yes. They were doing something at the Shrine. Sol's hand on my heart, I swear I don't know what. But Grolkan thinks it started beyond the Omindi, at the Steaming Lakes."

The Steaming Lakes were in the Treaty Lands, a place cursed by the Wakened Dead if rumor was straight. The beat of his heart quickened. "Last I knew nobody, not even Istinjoln, dares approach the region."

"I saw it from a distance once," Pikarn said. "Many years ago. Things not living walk there. Seen them myself, walking the fogs."

"The Colok avoid those ruins, too. Mecum told me Istinjoln staked a permanent camp there about four years ago and then Grolkan's warriors spotted a messenger, killed the group, and by taking Mecum, they also found this." He pulled a wooden tube from within his cloak and tapped until a scroll slid out. "I'll let you read it, to interpret the words yourself. It's a bit cryptic." Tokodin unfurled the scroll on the ground and weighted its corners with stones. The monk's fingers jittered.

Addressed to Ulrikt himself, the letter spoke of the Steaming Lakes and exploring cairns of the dead. Ximfwa, Cimdine, Komdwom, and Extek, family names which didn't sound Silone. It also mentioned something called the Sliver of Star and Golden Conch, in addition to a long list of names, noting who'd died in their search.

Ivin said, "They're nosing into crypts? Sliver of Star, what power does it possess to make it worth all these lives?"

"And what the hells is a Golden Conch?" Pikarn asked.

Tokodin's tone denoted exasperation. "The Conch was one of the first artifacts pulled from the Treaty Lands before there was a treaty. A faction of Clan Emudar stole it around the hundred-fifteenth Year of Remembrance, and half the clans went to war to retrieve it. After the war, the Church took it to Fermiden Abbey for study and storage. Slivered Star? Now that I've never heard of."

Ivin doubted this Conch and a visiting lord priest from Fermiden were a coincidence. "What good would the conch be?"

"I'm only reciting history, and I'm not a scholar of artifacts. It reputedly held the power to enhance a priest's prayers, a weapon of sorts, as I recall. Bugger if I know for sure. As to why crypts, the peoples who built the cities and other places of power secreted away fortunes in treasures with their dead, and it's said the crypts date to the Age of Warlords, if not to the Age of God Wars. Wealthier the family, the greater the bounty."

Pikarn squinted at the text. "They weren't after no golden coins."

Ivin too glanced at the message, and the connection struck him. "Meliu spoke of a Codex, the Codex of Sol. And that book she carried?"

Tokodin's attention shifted to them from the brew in his mug. "Meliu is alive! Thank the gods."

"Thank us and a lot of luck," quipped the Wolverine. "And the skin of her head." The old man chuckled, but Tokodin's knit brow said he didn't find it amusing.

Ivin said, "About that Codex?"

Tokodin answered only after their stares refused to go away. "The Codex of Sol, prophecies. It's whispered about, dangerous tome to speak of. There are other notable codexes, too."

"Meliu told us this one was hidden in a library near the Crack."

Tokodin shrugged. "Meliu would know better than me, I'm just a lowly monk... Yes, ignore the robes the Colok gave me. But we can't know of which this scroll speaks."

Pikarn said, "We don't want to be blinded by coincidence, but we can't ignore it, either."

Ivin considered letting Tokodin's words get away, but couldn't. "And what? What would she know?"

"Nothing, really. I mean, Meliu was known to study Old Silone and the Holy Tongues. But they'd never let her near the Codex of Sol, if it even exists."

"She said we wouldn't be able to read it," Ivin said.

"And we just delivered her and that godsdamned book straight to Istinjoln."

Even right choices sometimes had wrong-headed consequences, a truth his father had beat into his memory. Priests lie, another he'd come to believe. Tokodin's being a mere monk didn't change that. "So, Monk... Why wouldn't she be let near it? More and more you sound like a man not wanting to say what he knows."

"Bones and barnacles. You're Choerkin, you should know better than me."

"What the hells are you talking about?"

"Ailing Stars Prophecy?"

"The Ailing Stars?" Ivin and the Wolverine shared a pensive glance. "That prophecy was destroyed hundreds of years ago. If ever it was real."

"Lord Priest Imrok was killed by your great-great… distant grand-father, set him ablaze and paraded his blackened skull across the island in the Fifth Year of Remembrance. But the text wasn't destroyed."

"What the hells would the Ailing Stars have to do with this Codex and Shadows?"

The priest shrugged. "The Codex, they say, is full of prophecies of the gods from the Age of God Wars."

When the clan brought up the Ailing Stars Prophecy, it was to shame the holy. The text had read of an age when the gods walked the lands and priests ruled the Silone people, not the clans. If a new generation of priests adhered to these beliefs and wanted to make it so again, Ivin imagined only one result: Holy War.

Zjin sauntered to them, his eyes drilling into Tokodin. "Tell."

The monk in priest's robes sighed. "I'm getting to that."

Zjin gestured in a manner that brought to mind popping the man's head from his shoulders. Judging by Tokodin's scrunched shoulders he wasn't far off.

"Here's the thing." Agitation in the monk's tone grew. "Colok scouts came back the other morning, they're breaking camp at the Steaming Lakes and a party is by now well on its way back to Istinjoln."

"Meaning they found this sliver-star thing?" Pikarn asked.

The monk said, "We can't know that."

Zjin growled, poked the monk with the butt of his halberd.

"All right! The Colok believe the priests summoned the Shadows on purpose, and they believe they intend to summon more with whatever this artifact is."

Zjin growled, "Zwinfolkum."

Ivin shook his head, not recognizing the word, unsure if he'd even heard it right. "Zwinfolkum?"

Zjin grunted and bore what might've been a toothy smile. "Zwinfolkum rule Shadow."

Ivin glanced at Zjin, back to the monk, puzzling the words together. "The Shadows have some sort of king?" Zjin growled with a nod. "And if they're bringing these things here on purpose, Ulrikt could be trying to use this king to some end."

Tokodin scoffed, his face flushing. "They're wrong. The Shadows were an accident; I know it in my soul."

"I said *if* they're right."

The butt of Zjin's glaive jabbed the monk again. "They want you, the Choerkin, to join their fight. To ambush these priests and take the artifact, to stop the Shadows by killing all those people. An ambush in the Omindi Pass, tomorrow. Gods forgive me for speaking." Tokodin chugged his ale, grabbed the travel keg from Pikarn's limp grip and marched away.

Zjin growled, "Fight." The Colok nodded, his stare intense, frightening.

What would the Colok do if Pikarn refused? Ivin glanced to the Wolverine, but the old man was no help as they stared at each other. "Godsdamnit, boy. I'm not making that call, this is killing our own people we're talking here, holy folk. Pieces of shit they are, but still. Let's say we get this Sliver of Star, what the hells then? Sit on it like some damned hen on an egg?"

"Destroy it, throw it in the strait, gods be damned if I know, but it'd be war, succeed or fail. And if this is true," Ivin said, "most of these holies can't know the evil they're plotting. I won't believe that. We'd be slaughtering innocents, holy innocents, pious men and women." He rubbed his forehead.

"Aye, but if true, no way in the hells we can touch the bastards responsible, best we can do is stop this Sliver. You're the Choerkin, the clan blood, this is your decision in the name of your father and uncle. The wardens will follow you, no questions asked."

"And if you were clan blood?"

The Wolverine stared at him without a flinch or a hint before smiling. "We could surround them and ask for it nice like."

Ivin chuckled, grateful for the levity. "Just what we want, a band of priests who know we're coming. Whether the Colok are right or wrong on the lord priest's intent with these Shadows, we're talking Holy War."

The Divination of Bones spoke of bloodshed, of war in his destiny. Rise within the clan to make a decision. What would Meris think if that decision was to butcher a bunch of priests? What would the gods do to his soul? But if they were right, the gods would recognize the sacrifice to save so many, but if wrong he'd have to march through every last hell before sniffing redemption. If he made it beyond the Slave Forges.

Zjin growled again. "Fight."

He glanced to Modan, the man's rasping breaths, his agony even with the prayers of the monk easing his pain. Ivin had traveled north with the hope of bringing clan and Church together, but more and more it felt like the only chance for peace was to end Ulrikt and his plans. If taking the Sliver of Star prevented the prophesied destruction of the clans, it was a war which needed fought.

No matter how he flipped scenarios in his head one choice stood out. Ivin nodded to Zjin, then the Wolverine. "We fight."

The Wolverine jumped to his feet as if he had a spring beneath his ass. "Puxele! Take three and ride to Ervinhin—no stopping! Every man who can ride needs to gather at the mouth of the Omindi, and let there be no doubt: By command of clan blood, no holy leaves the Omindi alive."

Tokodin sat on the keg of ale beside Modan, passing a hand over his wounds in prayer, but stopped at the Wolverine's call to battle. He stared at the dying warden's trembling muscles and took a drink. He closed his eyes and prayed to ease Modan's suffering, but no longer called for his body to mend.

Tokodin drank from his cup, but his mind was on the silver vial of poison in his pocket.

He should have swallowed the elixir when Mecum gave it to him. War was coming to Istinjoln, home. Ulrikt was to blame, the Choerkins were to blame, while people like Modan and himself suffered for it. *The way of the world is pain and we're caught wounded in its middle.* His fingers fidgeted with the dice and poison. Both were a coward's way out, dice to make a decision, poison to end decisions. He wondered at what pain the poison would bring, and smirked at his own weakness, too afraid to take the coward's way out. If Ulrikt betrayed the gods, there was hope, Tokodin wouldn't need the poison.

Another prayer for Modan and the Warden's shaking calmed.

"Do you think you can save him?"

Tokodin glanced at Ivin, a man born with everything handed to him. Tokodin envied him, loathed him, and pitied him, for being born into a name which would see him fall into the hells. "It's a decision for the gods, all I can do is try." Tokodin cringed as Ivin put a hand on his shoulder.

"You're a good man; you'll do all you can. I'll pray for him with you."

He doubted the prayer of a Choerkin meant anything to the gods. Tokodin smiled with a nod and eased his own pain in drink.

THIRTY-THREE

Ambush Choke

Living in Lyrical Melancholy,
heart beat, Beat, drumming—a dirge in celebration of eternity.

—*Tomes of the Touched*

Two Days to the Eve of Snows

The plumes of Ivin's fogged breath whirled and dispersed in mountain winds. A damned cold day for a ride, and too damned cold for a fight. Ivin stood beside the Wolverine and Tokodin, imagining the disparate worries of the two men. Pikarn fretting for the lives of his men, and the monk praying for everyone's immortal souls.

The stretch of the Omindi Pass they chose was such an obvious place for an attack it bore a nickname: the Ambush Chokes. The Chokes looked like a snake that'd swallowed a rabbit: fat in the middle, and skinny on both ends. Ordinary folks traveling the Omindi hurried through this canyon on their guard for any attack, but the group coming wasn't normal.

Scouts reported fifty-two afoot, with four horsemen. Most were priests and monks, the rest guardsmen. Swords and arrows didn't worry Ivin so much as the priests' prayers of fire and lightning. If high priests rode in the mix, the fight would prove savage, but Ivin refused to consider defeat.

Twenty wardens and thirty Colok stood scattered in strategic positions overlooking the Omindi. Every advantage he conceived was theirs, except the power of prayer. Colok never attacked parties this large, the holies wouldn't be ready. When amassed for travel they figured themselves invincible. Scouts confirmed this when they reported the priests traveled without a single scout.

Ivin glanced to Pikarn, still as stone except for his jaws working beef. The man was a study in confidence, but most wardens couldn't say the same. They missed Modan. Not a one he'd overheard or spoke to forgot to mention his name. And despite being loyal to a man, they weren't happy with the Colok as allies.

The call to battle better be right; if not, even victory was disaster. Impossible to imagine telling his father or uncle he'd killed a bunch of holies over a mistake. Still, a wrongheaded victory was better than a headless defeat.

A Colok loped in from the north with Puxele on its back. She slid from the beast's shoulders, a crooked smile on her face. She'd been the only warden to volunteer to take a ride, and by the looks of it she enjoyed herself.

"They'll enter the Chokes in a few wicks." Her brow scrunched, and she looked to Tokodin. "What hell is it you go to for killing a holy?"

Tokodin turned a pastier shade of ill than normal. "The Malignant. Unless of course the kill is deemed righteous."

She nodded. "Well, boys, let's hope the gods appreciate our bloody dance. I always imagined making it at least as far the Lustful Hell."

The Wolverine chortled, and Ivin couldn't deny a grin.

They lay behind boulders and drifts of snow, most fidgeting as combat approached. Rinold rested with his head propped on his pack, his eyes closed, for all the world looking like he napped.

Kotin complained about sitting outside the blood of war, wielding commands instead of steel, when he recounted battles. He said, "Watching men die to win a fight I started turns my stomach in ways no sickness ever could." Only now did Ivin understand the sentiment. He loathed the notion of his head being more important than another's, but win or lose they needed his skull intact, if for no other reason than to take the blame if they were wrong about everything.

The priests sang as they approached, and it wasn't a holy chant dedicated to the gods. A bawdy lyric based around a blind-drunk husband, a cheating wife, and wolves stealing a keg of ale rose from the Pass. More a song for a dock tavern than holies. Their laughter guaranteed surprise, a boon for his confidence while burning shame into his gut. Screams would echo between canyon walls as blood painted the ground, people dying without a chance to defend themselves.

Ivin's fingers dug into the snow. The gods would never forgive him; he wondered if he'd ever forgive himself.

He peeked through a crack in rock and snow. Guards and priests filed through the first choke point, followed by riders. There was no turning back, they'd come too far with too much on the line.

Puxele crept to Rinold's side and jabbed him in the ribs with a toe before she lay on her back, taking deep breaths, resting her bow on her chest with an arrow nocked. Rinold feigned a yawn and blew Little Sister a kiss before nocking his own arrow. Tokodin stared at the clouds.

Ivin slipped his targe from his back, covering his head and shoulders with it, as he stared into the Chokes. His heart pounded in his ears as the party reached the center of the snake's belly. He glanced to Puxele and her pensive eyes, nodded.

The woman rose to a knee and launched the arrow blind over the rocks; the whistle-head squealed over the chasm. The priests didn't have time to react to the signal before a hail of stones and arrows rained from the sky.

Men and women fell, writhing and screaming or stone dead. Bows thrummed a second time, then a third, before retaliation. Lightning flashed from the sky and fire rushed from the ground, striking the heights of the cliff. A blast thundered nearby and a warden flipped into the air, plummeting to his death at the base of the cliff.

Two riders collapsed to the rocky ground in the first waves of arrows, and with magic in the air Colok roared through the northern choke, sprinting at inhuman speeds to collide with unsuspecting priests. Fifteen-foot spears thrust through light armors and glaives gashed the flesh of guardsmen and holies as the rain of projectiles focused on the front of the group. The execution went as well as Ivin had hoped. There were losses and injured, but far fewer than in his nightmares.

Hooves pounded the stone floor, wardens riding through the southern choke; their addition would end this battle. Confidence surged. The Colok killed their way through the footmen, drawing close to the remaining riders. One of the priests must carry the artifact they were after, with Colok bearing down, and riders coming, Ivin rose to a knee for a better view of victory.

A priest on horseback struck their hand in the air and an aura of light erupted in the valley. The Sliver of Star? A huge mistake, everyone targeted this holy now.

Bowstrings sang. The aura sparkled and blurred red.

It took several moments for his eyes to understand what they saw. The perimeter of the aura had shredded holy and Colok alike into a fine, sanguine mist. Eviscerated bodies fell to the ground while the living scrambled with severed limbs from the horror.

Ivin's mind froze, his mouth gaped, silent, as his heart sank.

The aura died in a splash of gore and the priest with the Sliver spurred their mount, charging headlong for the oncoming wardens riding in from the southern choke. The priest's hood flew back, long black hair flowing, a woman. Her hand raged in the white aura as she bore down on the wardens.

Ivin screamed, "No!" And the gods seemed to listen, even if nobody in the Omindi could hear him.

The priestess vanished.

The wardens reined hard, confused, their mounts spinning in chaotic circles.

Ivin and Pikarn screamed in unison. "Loose!"

Only ten or so holies remained alive, standing as awed as everyone else. But they weren't going down without a fight. Arrows and rocks ricocheted off prayer magic, but more Colok scaled the cliff walls, and the mounted wardens recovered to charge forward.

Ivin looked to Pikarn. "Gods be damned, we've got to find that priestess." He sprinted south, cutting across open ground until stopping where the Omindi twisted in front of him. He slid to a stop, lungs heaving billows of fog. The priestess rode down the trail with an open road to the foothills.

Puxele and Pikarn slid to his side.

Ivin said, "To the horses."

Pikarn nodded. "Wardens in the foothills've got no idea what's comin'."

The foursome ran to a copse of trees and untethered their horses and mounted, joined by Tokodin, Zjin, and a handful of Colok, along with the wardens who tended the steeds.

Ivin leaped into the saddle, reined his horse, shouting, "Stay with me, if we catch her we'll need every hand."

They rode hard until they reached a manageable trail leading into the Omindi. They lost precious time getting down the slope in one piece and pacing their horses was another consideration. The wardens' horses possessed a speed advantage over the short-legged pony, but mountain ponies possessed uncanny endurance.

Ivin imagined a massacre in the foothills if the wardens confronted the priestess. The whirlwind of blood, the disappearing act—the artifact gave the priestess powers Ivin hadn't imagined. Unless they put an arrow through her, dropped her mount maybe, they'd be chasing her fifteen leagues to Istinjoln. And what the hells would they do if they caught her? Fight and die, he supposed.

They'd need fresh horses from the foothills or Ervinhin for a race to the monastery. Their horses were lathered, even in the cold mountain air, and they slowed to a trot.

❄ ❄ ❄

Sagebrush, jagged stone, and boulders dominated the entrance into the foothills. Heads popped from hiding as they thundered into the gap. The wardens were alive, their arrows pointing at the Colok warriors running beside Ivin.

They reined their horses to a stop and Pikarn bellowed, "Quiver them shafts!"

Ivin called, "Seen a priestess?"

The group of wardens pinned their eyes on the Colok, and no one spoke.

"A priestess, godsdamn it! Did a holy ride through!" the Wolverine fumed.

"No sir, we seen nothing."

Ivin swung from his horse. "Bring us fresh animals." He looked to Zjin. "How are you and your people holding up?"

The great bear's chest labored from the run, but he gave a curt nod.

Pikarn moved to Ivin's side. "What're you thinking?"

Truth? Ivin figured they'd failed. "We send the Colok straightaway toward Istinjoln, save them some distance. We'll take fresh horses to Ervinhin, send word to the Fost... remount and ride for Istinjoln."

"Aye, sounds good."

Puxele asked, "What's the point? No way we catch her now."

"Her pony could pull up lame, she might get cocky, a Shadow might kill her... We don't give up now."

Tokodin said, "I'm thinking the woman is High Priestess Sedut, you put arrows in her pony and she wouldn't let it go down. Odds of catching her?" He spat, shaking his head.

Ivin glared at the monk, judging the man. He figured the holy was as trustworthy as using a viper for a sling. "There's hope. If we can't catch her, we need to be there, try to get an idea of what the hells is going on. With me?"

They all nodded, except the damned monk.

"Couldn't I stay in Ervinhin?"

Ivin would love to leave him behind. "No, we might need your help."

Fresh horses arrived and they mounted. "Zjin, head for Istinjoln, rest in the foothills and we'll be along fast as we can. If you catch her, do what you can, but don't get killed for nothing." Zjin nodded and he and his people leaped over rocks, disappearing east. "Those who are staying here, keep your eyes open for any priest for several candles yet. Should be more wardens coming, too, I hope. A lone woman, a priestess, kill her, no questions, no delay. Detain or kill any others." He spurred his fresh roan and they trotted southeast.

The sun fell toward the peaks of mountains in the west as they entered the gates of Ervinhin. The sky was cloudless and promised a frigid, windless ride through the night.

Puxele paced as she waited for fresh horses and full canteens; the remaining wardens stood stiff and tired. Ivin overheard a couple grousing about fighting beside Colok, but didn't address their worries. He couldn't blame them. To a man they'd fought Colok since joining the wardens, lost comrades to the creatures. Now they relied on them as allies against the Church.

Fate shoves food in your mouth— "Your choice whether to swallow or spit it out."

Pikarn cocked an eyebrow in his direction. "What's that?"

Ivin chuckled. "Something Kotin told me."

"Thought it rang familiar. Your old man has a way with words."

"Who're your best three riders in town? We need to get word to Lovar at the Fost."

"And tell him what? We started a war with Istinjoln and probably every holy on the island? Better to ask which three riders I like least, sending them into that hellstorm."

Ivin grinned, point taken. "Either way, track them down and get them horseback soon. No written word, don't want a letter falling into the wrong hands. Have them warn every waypoint on the road as they swap horses, too."

The Wolverine nodded. "Aye. I'll see to it."

Puxele grinned at him, but it wasn't pleasant. "Look at you, pulling Choerkin rank and giving the old man orders."

Ivin flushed and scowled. "I'd rather be taking orders."

The woman winked. "I'm just shittin'. But mind how your words sound to those who don't know what's going on."

Damned if Puxele didn't have the right of it. Last thing they needed was strife within the wardens. "Thank you."

She scrunched her nose and blew him a kiss he interpreted as "You're welcome." He smirked and turned his back to the wind as they waited, wondering how in the hells they got to this point in such a short time. In a matter of days he'd gone from bickering with his dad and brothers on the Watch to the bloom of a holy war with him stuck in the middle. When Meris and the cracked bone spoke of war it struck him as hyperbole, but all those cracks, had they spoken of this?

The clop of hooves on pavers rattled him from his musings. Several wardens led a dozen horses covered in extra blankets for the night's ride.

Twelve riders and five Colok against a single priestess, if they managed to catch her, and still he didn't like the odds on winning that combat. If she made it through the gates, well, they'd have to deal with failure then.

Packed with gear and food, including grain for their steeds, the wardens rode out the eastern gate as the last orange rays of sun faded on the horizon. The ride in daylight with fair weather took six candles at an ambling gait, but at night with temperatures plummeting, and needing to keep an eye out for signs of the high priestess, Ivin figured they'd be lucky to see Istinjoln by daybreak.

The winds picked up a candle from town, blinding them with drifting snow despite clear skies lit by moon and stars. Men and horses ducked their heads, hiding their eyes from the onslaught. Two candles out the weather defeated them, and Pikarn asked the Squirrel to lead them to a cave to wait out the winds. The tunnel was tight but opened with space enough to sleep thirty and their horses. In a dry alcove in back they found kindling for a fire to thaw their bones.

Rinold sat staring into the flames. "Coldest godsdamned year in my memory. Shouldn't be like this outside the mountains."

Ivin glanced from the Squirrel to the melancholy monk as Tokodin rubbed his hands over a fire. "Would even a high priestess travel in this cold?"

"I'd say no, were these normal times. But…" He shrugged, shaking his head. He reached into the folds of his robes and produced dice carved from bone, three white and one black, and a small silver flask.

Ivin asked, "Whiskey?"

The monk blew on the dice in his hand and rolled them on the floor, but Ivin couldn't see the results by the light of the fire. "Sadly empty."

Ivin nodded. "I never was much for games of chance."

Tokodin chuckled. "You're a wiser man than me." He stuck the dice and flask back in his robes.

Ivin flopped his bedroll on the hard floor and rested his head, watching smoke billow as it hit the ceiling. "We lost our one chance in the Chokes."

No one disagreed.

Thirty-Four

Beaten to the Kill

Yap and flap, noisy bird,
wallowing in the snake's shadow
of pointless pity,
corn-worm in apple,
dragon in snail's shell,
haunting spirit in living man's body.

—*Tomes of the Touched*

Two Days to the Eve of Snows

Solineus understood the monastery's reputation as a foreboding place of power. What he didn't understand was the tense silence. When they arrived on the nineteenth, the gates were open and welcoming. Priests and monks were jovial, looking forward to the celebration. The guards were loose and rested.

Everything changed on the twentieth. Guards were doubled on the walls, tripled by the gates, and eyes drooped from the extra work overnight. Wagons came into Istinjoln, but not a soul left, not even the peasants who lived in the village a candle's walk south.

Something had happened, but not even a rumor managed a whisper from those tunnels. He doubted the guards knew a thing and pressing one for chatter might be his undoing. Ilpen's young friend hadn't reached out to the tinker yet with most of the holy folk locked in their badger hole. Any chance to learn of this place lay in ruins. He'd be forced to rely on luck instead of guile to reach the lord priest.

He'd hoped Lelishen and her pilgrimage would unlock some doors. She prattled to any holy who'd listen, but even when priests were plentiful, they didn't care a lick about this woman, Firde, or her journey to see the shrines of Istinjoln. They didn't allow her a stride inside a sacred building. It was as if people didn't make pilgrimages to this holy place.

Random musings may have struck the truth—he needed to converse with the woman. Time spent with Ears the Elder grew tiring anyhow; after all, the old donkey made no claims at being a great conversationalist. He rubbed the critter between his namesakes and stepped outside.

Solineus rounded the stable's corner and a young woman in priestly robes came from nowhere, plowing into him. She gasped and ricocheted to her rump, staring up at him with striking green eyes Solineus would never forget, despite the change in robe colors. The same girl who'd broken Lelishen's charade.

Solineus smiled and offered his hand. The connection clicked so hard he wanted to slap himself for not seeing it earlier. "Are you Eliles, by chance?"

Her hand took his, a puzzled look crossing her brow as she stood, rubbing her shoulder. Her eyes were blue now, making him blink before dismissing the oddity.

"Ilpen spoke of you as we made our way to Istinjoln. A good man, full of chat."

She dusted herself. "Yes, yes, I am. And he is. Is Ilpen nearby?"

The girl's tension came from more than bumping into a stranger. "I don't know, but I'm sure he isn't far. Anything I can do?"

She fidgeted, glancing around the yard.

If she uttered a word everything she wanted to say would come pouring out, if he could just pump the well. Solineus put a hand beneath her chin, raised her eyes to his. "Whatever it is, you can trust me. As we're friends of Ilpen's I'll keep your words as my own."

Her cheeks quivered before a flurry of whispers. "My master, my master confessed to murder. Murder of Lord Priest Ulrikt. I was there, I saw it, the bone exploded. He couldn't have done it."

Solineus stared at the girl's flapping lips, but heard nothing else. Well, how was that for a son-of-a-bitch? He traveled for days to come and kill a man he figured nigh on impossible to reach and somebody beat him to it.

She continued. "They're going to kill him, I know it. I've got to save... avenge him."

Solineus shook his head. "Whoa, girl." The frantic look in her eyes as she rambled tore at him. He grabbed her shoulders. "Eliles." She looked to him, tears welling. "Slow down and think." Think of what, by the gods? "What can we do to save him?"

Her blank stare turned to tears, and he pulled her into a hug. A desperate girl to return the embrace of a stranger, she needed more than he could give. He looked around, aware hugging a priestess might raise eyebrows, and spotted his savior. "Ilpen!"

The big man raced to Eliles faster than Solineus would've imagined and swept her into his arms. "What is it, sweetheart?"

Solineus kissed the girl on the head, patted her shoulder, and walked fast as he could from the stables. His heart raced and his teeth gnashed; crying girls robbed him of reason. Thank the gods Ilpen came along.

Deep breaths retrained his focus, and instead of wandering he turned for the storehouses. The maze of crates and sacks brought in for the Eve of Snows would give him a quiet place to think. Ulrikt dead. Could the Lady from his dreams be so wrong? Even if the lord priest survived, he wouldn't so much as piss without a guard.

The rhythm and tenor of Lelishen's voice, like someone trying to shake the chirp out of a sparrow, ended his pursuit of silence. "I so much want to see the shrine of Elinwe; it would mean so so much to me and my family to light a candle for Firde."

Solineus followed the noise until he found the woman trying to coerce some poor monk into letting her into lower Istinjoln. The poor man's eyes were wide, she grabbed his shoulder every time he tried to flee.

"Could you at least light a candle for me?"

Solineus came to the man's aid. "Light a candle for which Firde?" The monk bolted, shoes flapping on the pave-stones.

Lelishen turned a frown on him. "I do so adore you, but you shouldn't be interrupting a lady's conversations such."

"Mmmhmm, maybe so. But you aren't getting into those caves any time soon, not by invitation anyhow."

"What font of wisdom did you drink from?"

"You recall the girl, the one who looked like one of your Firdes? Turns out she's Ilpen's friend." Bringing up the girl focused the woman's attention, now to knock her off balance. "Someone assassinated Lord Priest Ulrikt."

Her eyes scrunched. "Well, that does paint a grim picture of my visiting the shrines, doesn't it?"

The twittering bird faded from her voice, but how to take advantage. "How do you say your name again?"

"Lelishen." The accent changed, she caught her inflections and her frown morphed into a wry smile. "Is he truly dead?" There was no hint of the woman he'd listened to for candles on the wagon ride.

"I'm not half so clever and truth is better than a lie. Pilgrims don't make it into Istinjoln's shrines, do they? What are you doing here?"

"You first."

He tried for a straight face but surrendered to a laugh. He glanced around to make sure no one watched. "Oh, I don't think so, lady."

"You mustn't want to know."

She turned to walk away, but he spun her by the shoulder. The withering glare and balled fist suggested she wasn't used to being man-handled. He dug his fingers into her and leaned to whisper his last weaponized truth. "I came here to kill a man who's dead." He let go of her shoulder and strode down the aisle. He expected her to say something to stop him. She didn't. He would've paid the few songs he held to know the look on her face, but he held resolute and didn't turn around.

He stepped into the courtyard, stopped for a deep breath. To hear himself say those words, uttering the truth, removed a weight from his soul and he hoped, put it on hers.

Her voice came right next to his ear. "We should talk." The woman was quiet as a cat when she wanted, that's for sure.

She led him into a box canyon built from crates and eyeballed him. "By whom?"

The ugly question he hated to answer struck him again, he grew tired of sounding like a lunatic. "A woman who visits in my dreams. I washed ashore with no memories, except… she visited the first time while I was unconscious, floating in the bay, and told me my name."

She didn't laugh at him, he figured that was a positive, but she studied him. He gazed into her brown eyes until they turned a dark blue with flecks of silver, no longer human. He blinked and she returned to normal. "You experienced a Forgetting."

"The Forgetting was five hundred years ago, if it was even real."

"Very real." She pulled a chain around her neck to reveal a charm. "Inside is my name, and other personal notes like family and friends. It isn't unheard of for localized events to strike, erasing memories. Do you think this woman lied? After a Forgetting, the mind is impressionable, it'll seize any name given it."

"At first, but I met a man who knew me." He spoke of Kinesee and Alu, the family who succored him, as well as the sailer from Emudar, and after she listened intent, he asked his question. "Now who the hells are you?"

She smiled as she weighed her words. "I am sent here by the Edan to observe the Eve of Snows, nothing more. I had hoped to learn more, but alas…"

The immortal Edan who never left the Eleris, their Mother Woods. A phrase came to mind. "*Uvolum, lorebol kellis.*" Not only did he know the words, he knew their meaning: Greetings, forest sister.

Her smile fell. "You… Not one in ten thousand Silone could speak to me in the *eler imosta*. Who are you?"

The mother language, he knew more than how to say hello. "Solineus Mikjehemlut of the Clan Emudar, just as she told me." Voices grew close. "Can you help me?"

She stared, and her eyes dropped. "I can't help you kill a dead man."

Priests checking inventory rounded the corner, prattling about lost whiskey. "We're done here, then." He strode past the robed men, his mind ablaze. He knew so little, but knew too much. When he'd become convinced he at least knew who he was, fate gave his reality a spin.

THIRTY-FIVE

Barred from the Stars

Reality the rigid master with a million eyes,
where no two pair may ever agree.
Memory the feckless lover,
often telling us only what we want to hear
and forgetting the rest.

—*Tomes of the Touched*

One Day to the Eve of Snows

Eliles stood among a throng of priests along Istinjoln's northern wall
with the sun igniting a cloudy red horizon, waiting for Ulrikt's funeral
procession to begin. The Eve of Snows was tomorrow, but the mood
was bleak. It was a mood she shared with the monastery's whole, even
if they mourned different men.

She kept her promise to Dareun by burying her nose in pious
books or bowing in prayer for her master's life and soul. She made one
embarrassing trip outside to talk with Ilpen, running into the stranger
called Solineus. She turned into a blubbering fool and would never
forgive herself. A kind man, but he'd scurried like a chicken seeing a
hawk's shadow the first chance he got.

323

A gong resounded from the Tower of Sol, a bass reverberation only heard during funerals, and the mourners marched in unison, ordered by rank. They passed the stables in a gradual arch before swinging into the main courtyard. Ilpen and the stranger, Solineus, leaned against the stable wall. She managed a smile Ilpen's way, but neither of them saw her, and when Eliles realized the Trelelunin woman stood beside them she averted her eyes.

The procession slowed as it reached the Dais of Etinbin. Priests climbed the stone in single file. Most days the granite slab was plain, but today it sat covered in brilliant silks and bore the weight of a golden sarcophagus. The Broldun lord priest, sixth in line behind the body—

Eliles froze in stride and a priest bumped into her. She stumbled forward and cast a sheepish smile to those around her.

The six wore the gold threaded robes of lord priests. Ulrikt made number seven. Every lord priest on the island of Kaludor was in Istinjoln. They couldn't have traveled so fast.

They were already here. Why?

When she stepped onto the dais, not a single lord looked at her, a relief. She kept her eyes on the ornate sarcophagus. Every lord priest of Istinjoln rode to the crypts in this masterwork of art and death, the gold plating highlighting in relief imagery the gods and the Road of Living Stars.

She took her turn to step to Ulrikt, she should say a prayer, instead she stared. Round, black cobaltite cabochons held Ulrikt's blue eyes shut, the lustrous opaque stone treasured for fending off the forces of the Wakened Dead. Corpses never rose from the holy crypts, but tradition demanded the honor of these gems.

She pitied him, despite being happy he was dead. Regal and handsome in death, the restoration of the color in his cheeks and lips from the pallor of death impressed her. A peculiar art, making the deceased look alive. She bit back disgust and mumbled a prayer to guide his soul to the heavens.

She gazed across the courtyard as she descended; rows of high priests knelt with heads bowed, silent. Priests filed behind them, kneeling in rows precise as corn, and she followed suit, blessed to be done with her role, but she knew her knees would be sore before this ordeal finished. A couple hundred priests followed her, then monks and postulants; she didn't bother to count, but the numbers surprised her. At least a thousand monks and half again postulants. Many had to be guests for the Eve.

The gate chimes shattered the respectful silence, and every eye turned to the grind and clank of the portcullis rising.

A guard shouted from the tower. "Rider!"

It couldn't just be an ordinary rider. They would've held the gates until after the ceremony. Even a bearer would be outside the gate waiting. Hooves echoed from the bridge and a lathered mountain pony, lungs surging and breaths billowing in the frosty air, slid to a stop. A priest— a high priestess—slid from the saddle, her long black hair tangled over her shoulders. Eliles didn't recognize her from this distance, and she feared to reach out with her senses with lord priests and the Trelelunin woman so close.

An animated discussion with a guard ensued, and the masses broke their polite silence, mumbling one to another. The woman shoved the guard from her path and stomped toward the dais with angry strides. As she passed, Eliles recognized her as Sedut, a high priestess sent to serve in Gebelis Monastery years ago.

No one dared step in her path until she reached the base of the dais, where the Broldun lord priest and his black dog barred her way. When they stopped her, Eliles risked pushing her hearing, but with the mumbles of the crowd turning to a roar around her, she couldn't make out a single word until Sedut did the unthinkable and screamed at a lord priest.

"I swore on my life to bring him the star, and no man will stop me!" Sedut reached into a pouch at her side and withdrew a ball of white light, and Eliles' senses recoiled, slamming into her skull.

Her ears rang, pounding with every beat of her heart, and her consciousness wavered. She planted her hands to the ground and sucked a deep breath to stay conscious. Panting, she straightened, forcing herself to keep alert through tear-blurred eyes.

Whatever the hells the star was, the Broldun and his inquisitor stood down and Sedut charged onto the catafalque without further hindrance. She went to Ulrikt and bent, it seemed she gave the dead man a kiss while placing the light within the sarcophagus. Sedut kneeled in prayer, hands planted on gold stars.

Eliles' head thrummed. Sedut called it a star, but it held power she'd never felt before, slamming her senses against her like a mace. People stood throughout the throngs, craning their necks to see, but when the six lord priests dropped prostrate to the ground, Eliles shut her eyes, whatever was about to happen she didn't care to see.

Murmurs turned to gasps, and her eyes crept open with unstoppable curiosity. She wiped tears and watched the star rise into the air. Her muscles knotted, fists clenched. The star's power killed any notion of stretching her senses. She felt an evil.

A shoulder appeared from within the golden casket as Ulrikt rose to hands and knees, arching his back, screaming in agony. No one else made a sound above their own breaths. The lord priest stood and faced the crowd with the white star floating above his head.

His voice shook the ground. "For four days I stood at the foot of the Road of Living Stars, the hand of Etinbin himself preventing me from traveling further. I watched! I listened! I learned!" His gaze shifted to the high priests. "Bring me he who is accused of my murder."

Woxlin leaped to his feet and ran to the tower behind the dais, the Broldun dog on his heels.

Hope crept into her pain. Ulrikt would know her master's innocence. Dareun should be pardoned to meet his natural end. She prayed, but prayer left her with an empty sensation.

Ulrikt raised his arms toward the heavens. "Sol, our Eternal Lord, has delivered upon an ancient promise, gifting us with the Sliver of Star foretold in prophecy." His raised hands cupped the glow of the star above his head. "Sol's hand reaches for us from the Conqueror Heaven, all we must do is grasp his immortal palm and welcome a new era of peace and power for the Pantheon in the mortal world."

Dareun stumbled from the tower, shoved by the Broldun inquisitor, and all of Eliles' hope dissipated.

Her skin chilled at the sight of her master painted in feces and blood, his wrists gnarled, fingers twisted, and dragging a limp, useless leg. The face was her master's, but broken worse than last she saw. She chewed her lip, fingers digging into her thighs.

Woxlin brought the confession to Ulrikt, who perused the words as the dog dragged Dareun to the dais.

There wasn't surprise in Dareun's eyes when he saw Ulrikt. Maybe the torture distorted his features, but for a man seeing his reputed victim alive, his reaction left her flat. He should scream his innocence, proclaim his own virtue. Instead, he lowered his head and accepted defeat.

Ulrikt raised the confession above his head. "This priest… this man I called friend killed me. He killed me in collusion with the Clan Choerkin! By their direct orders."

Eliles' mind went numb with the accusation and the puzzle slid together.

"This is why the gods would not let me die. This is why they made me turn my back on eternal peace in the heavens. The gods demand

327

retribution! We will sunder this priest from the gods, and on the Eve of Snows, summon the Sword of Sol. By His hand will we rend every last Choerkin soul from their bodies and from the gods. Their spirits will fade and die in the lands of the mortal, never seeing the Living Stars."

Ulrikt snatched the star from above his head, its light casting a horrific pallor over elegant features. Beautiful, powerful, and malicious. He stepped from the sarcophagus and pointed the star at Dareun.

Gusts swirled through the bailey blowing dust, hair, and robes in a disarray of direction until the wild air collected in streams, sparkling as if each carried flecks of gems. Diamond, sapphire, ruby, amethyst, emerald, citrine, peridot, topaz, aquamarine, and tourmaline. The Sundering of the Ten Winds.

The horror set in and she screamed, but she couldn't hear herself over the Sundering's roar in her ears. Her throat burned raw.

The winds coalesced and struck her master, lifting him into the air. His mouth gaped, body shaking in violent spasms as the colors thrashed his body.

Instinct told her to run to him. Suicide. No, she'd made a promise. She wouldn't try to save him. She tried to close her eyes, but the warbling cries demanded her eyes stay open.

Reality quaked and shimmered where the man hung in suspension, the miraculous rainbow altering the universe until ten versions of her master stretched inches one from the other, each bearing the hue of a wind. No longer did one man scream, ten voices echoed across the bailey, each disjointed from the other in time.

The bile in Eliles' stomach rose, but she forced it back into her burning throat with anger and hatred. No more. She could take no more. She locked her stare on Ulrikt and tied every lord priest into a vision of a noose of fire and called her friends.

Flickering heat engulfed her senses, like holding your finger close enough to a candle for tongues of hot air to lick the skin, only it was everywhere. The energy surrounding her swelled; she couldn't see her friends, but they came from everywhere. Burning to her call, raging with her fury, soon there would be enough to burn them straight into the hells.

She meant to stand, but gentle, chilled fingers held her shoulder down. She wanted to wail, she needed to see them burn, but a peace passed through her. She remained on her knees, her friends departing as silent as they arrived. A shiver coursed through her body, and tears slid down her cheeks. Anger faded into deep sorrow.

She watched through blurred eyes, limbs and core shaking with sobs as her master dropped lifeless to the dais. The hand massaged her shoulder, but nobody stood beside her. She fought for control and wiped her tears. Smiled.

He'd signed the confession, and against sworn promises, he'd still suffered the Sundering of the Ten Winds. Ulrikt lied, why? He was more than a scapegoat.

The Sundering of Ten Winds was a breath-taking display of power. He'd seen it before, a decade ago, it took Ulrikt and a dozen senior high priests half a day to perform the ceremony. Rising from the dead was not enough—Ulrikt had needed to prove his might and consolidate control over the Church if he was going to ascend to King Priest.

Dareun stared at his hands, flexing his fingers. They were straight again, healed. There was a discomfort, a pressure in the joints, maybe the memory of pain. He heard himself scream. His body floated above the ground, wrenched to and fro by flowing auras of white light sprinkled and streaked with violets and turquoise. Northern lights, only focused, intense even beneath the sun. Beautiful, yet he knew the beauty killed him.

He sighed from frustration, not sadness. At least the end came. Ulrikt, or whatever passed for the lord priest now, stood in a raging shower of sparkling energies, a range of colors he'd never imagined. His life made a spectacular end at least, and he found himself grateful for bearing witness.

Eliles. He glanced to the crowd, over two thousand souls. She stood out as a fire in the dark. Hale and strong, surrounded by overwhelming energy. A ring of fire enveloped her. No. Flames, hundreds of tiny flames and more came, darts of energy streaking from the sky, the mountains, the stone beneath everybody's feet, collecting around her. Eliles stared at his screaming body. *No, no, no.* She couldn't—

Dareun stood behind her.

Startled by his travel, he followed her gaze. His body stopped screaming, but still shook and quaked with forces driving through flesh and bone. Power crackled around his girl. Her anger focused and the tiny flames flitting around her grew. She was going to do something horrible. Many would die, but the lord priest and the artifact he wielded were too powerful. He couldn't allow her to confront him.

She raised to a knee, and Dareun placed a hand on her shoulder. "Shhhh. All is well, my girl." She relaxed under his touch; whether she heard him or not, she sensed his soul. She must have. Her anger faded beneath his fingers and shoulders sagged, he felt her tears pool and drip down her cheeks as if they were his own. Flames flickered and withdrew in streaking wisps. Her release was his, and he smiled.

She was powerful, more powerful than he ever imagined. He didn't understand her gift of feral magic anymore than when he lived, nor even its extent, but if he were still alive, he might have feared her for the first time.

She bowed her head as Ulrikt let Dareun's body collapse lifeless to the dais. With the Sundering of the Ten Winds completed the force drawing him to the Bridge of Living Stars disappeared. Ulrikt doomed Dareun to never lay eyes on the heavens, and it wasn't as terrifying as he expected.

He rubbed her shoulder and a peculiar tingle or twitch sizzled through his being. If he were alive, he'd swear somebody watched him. The sensation persisted. He looked to Ulrikt, but the lord priest stood with the star held above his head, praying.

A chant rose in the courtyard, and filaments of energy connected the prayerful to Ulrikt, feeding his power. The tingle persisted.

Dareun turned. A man with a sword watched him, near the stables. He and a woman stood out from the crowd, but in different ways. Dareun waded through the droning faithful, his eyes locked on the pair.

The woman's features became crisp as he grew close. She wasn't human. By the gods! He'd lived his life dreaming of meeting a Trelelunin, and only after he died did he see one. Her sharp features, the high cheek bones, and an aura of sky blues fading into white. She didn't see him, didn't sense him.

But this man? An indistinct face distinguished the swordsman, a charcoal drawing with a thumb dragged across his features. Wherever the man's flesh showed from beneath clothing was a smudge on the world, unknowable, unreal. What sort of demon was he? A Trelelunin wouldn't associate with a demon, at least if she was aware of the evil.

"Hello, Dareun." The demon spoke perfect Silone, but carried Emudar inflections to his words.

The dead priest smiled. If still alive, he imagined his heart would be in his throat, but fear of this nature no longer concerned him. "Who are you?"

The man sighed, shook his head. "I can't hear you."

The Trelelunin woman stared at the man. "Who're you speaking to?" She followed the demon's gaze and stared through Dareun.

"I'm a friend of Ilpen's. I will protect Eliles if I'm able. But I need to know something. I need to kill Ulrikt, can you help me?"

Dareun stood stone still, he'd never done more than flirt with the notion of killing before. But now?

Ulrikt's voice thundered in the background. "We begin tomorrow with the sun at its zenith. Holy War! Together we shall avenge this affront to the gods. Together we will return the Pantheonate to power and eradicate the enemies of Sol."

It turned out being executed left a bitter taint to his soul. Dead and cursed from the heavens, nothing remained to deter him from protecting the girl he'd come to love as a daughter.

Dareun mouthed the words and nodded to the demon-man. "I will try.

Thirty-Six

Eve of Snows

The Tower's eye blind, fly, fly, my eye
Flake Blind White into the Night.

—*Tomes of the Touched*

Dareun's world radiated light. The rays of the sun weren't so bright as when he was alive, but more colorful, and pitch-black tunnels for the living were lit like twilight. Even walking through doors and walls only turned his vision to muted grays and browns. He could travel the grounds of Istinjoln in an instant by focusing on a location, an enjoyable trick, but in the end these things meant nothing.

He watched Eliles in her cell, but he couldn't utter a reassuring word, nor tell her to run. He reached for a quill to dip in ink, but no matter how hard he focused, his fingers remained insubstantial.

If Dareun were still alive, he'd walk up to Ulrikt and stab him in the throat, but being dead didn't allow for suicidal heroics. His only hope was the demon-man, and a small hope it seemed unless the demon wielded miracles. Still, he had promised to try.

He found the lord priest in his chambers with High Priestess Sedut and Lord Priest Dunkol. Dareun was happy to see the Broldun didn't bring the bastard who cut his tongue out and broke his fingers for fun—some scars passed from living into death.

Dunkol held a goblet of wine in both hands, but his eyes strayed to the glowing artifact in the middle of the table, an uncut fist-sized diamond pulsing with white energy. The star gave Dareun the jitters.

"When first I read the Prophecy of the Twelfth Star, mmm, I thought it might be mine." Dunkol's fat jowls jiggled as he cast Ulrikt a grin and chuckle.

"An amusing if misguided thought, m'lord," Sedut said. Her eyes squinted, the tense muscles of her face betraying a mistrust or dislike for the Broldun. The use of his clan title rather than his holy name also supplied insight into her disposition.

"The Sliver is only for he who is destined to wield its power." Ulrikt settled into a chair. "But this is not it."

Sedut blanched, her fingers shaking, loosening their grip on her wine. "My king, I—"

King Priest, is it? Ulrikt's ambitions weren't surprising, but Dareun would've thought him more subtle than to take the title so soon.

"You failed me, Sedut, but even so, the gods have their reasons." He picked up the shining gem, stared into its aura. "Our attempts beneath the mountain failed and brought death. If we are to succeed, we must perform the ritual beneath the stars, where the gods may see and feel our devotion the clearest. Go to the lord priests and wake them; they are to meet us in the Commons of the Pantheonate, at the Altar of Sol. We will reach the heavens and bring forth Sol's hand to guide us."

The woman hesitated. "My king? So late?"

"Did you hear my words and do the stars not shine? Then heed me, do not fail again."

Sedut tipped her goblet for a final drink and bowed, departing the room with hasty steps.

The Broldun laughed, and chill shivers quivered through Dareun's soul. Temperature was a thing he hadn't given a thought since dying, not until now.

"This's a thing I always liked about you, mmm, not one to waste time."

Ulrikt cast the man an irritated grin. "On the contrary, I've wasted decades to reach this night. But the will of the gods cannot be rushed."

Dunkol flicked his fingers in the air. "Mmm, so, what would you have me do?"

Ulrikt smiled and refilled Dunkol's wine. "You and me have plans to make, old friend."

Ulrikt had lots of old friends, it seemed, but just as when the lord priest had visited him in his cell, Dareun sensed an edge in his tone.

"Sometimes old friends, allies even, must speak more directly than they might like."

A chill swam through his being, a thousand frozen worms wriggling within his soul. Dareun backed to the wall, tense. He looked around, raising his spectral hands, his palms tingling: The cold radiated from behind Dunkol's lavish chair. Dareun edged along the wall until a darkness came into view. It bled from the floor's stone, shadowy tendrils growing into the air.

The Broldun guffawed. "Mmm! Seems to me you're doing the opposite. Let us speak plain, shall we?"

"You know I always envisioned you as my second. Sometimes things change even as they stay the same. Sadly, it isn't to you whom I need speak." Ulrikt's smile met his wine glass, his intense blue-eyed stare trained on the Broldun.

Two arms of Shadow plunged into Dunkol and Dareun stepped back until halfway through the wall behind him. The Broldun's body stiffened into a flabby board and his mouth wilted open, but no sound escaped his lips as the Shadow slipped into the quivering body. Possession, an evil art long forbidden by the Church, but this was worse still, more a sacrifice to something wicked.

Dareun stared, unable to move until Ulrikt's demented gaze turned to him. "Now you realize the mercy I gave your body and soul, and the true torture I reserved for this dog."

He knows I'm here!

The lord priest and his chambers, the Broldun, everything disappeared. Dareun stood staring at another demon, a smudged face asleep in a stable. Whatever this demon was, its terror paled when compared to the Shadow. He needed to figure out how a ghost could wake the living.

He jumped in and out of the man's body and screamed, and with little else to do paced up and down through the man's torso. Flustered, he stood staring until the demon groaned and his eyes fluttered open. He waved his arms in front of his eyes in a frantic fit.

Solineus snorted, rolled over, and awoke staring at stable rafters through the translucent eyes of a ghost waving his hands. His heart lurched for a beat and he reached for his sword. Beautiful women visiting him in his dreams, and dead priests waking him in the middle of the night. He didn't want to know what form of spook he might be haunted by next. He sat up, the blade of his sword disappearing into its sheath.

Dareun's ghost looked as if he'd seen a ghost, his eyes wide, brows pinched, and his lips straight as a nail. "Did you find something?"

Dareun glanced about, his mouth moving without words, before he slumped, exasperated.

Solineus pulled his cloak over his shoulders. "Can you show me?"

The specter led him into the bailey, past the Dais of Etinbin, then down lantern-lit streets until they stood in the deepest shadow of an outbuilding. The wind howled, knifing through any gap in his cloak, chilling his cheeks. The area was empty. Dareun pointed to the Tower of Sol, its heights glowing halos in the frigid night.

"The tower?"

Dareun nodded as he held up six fingers, and pointed to the ground or the building's shadow, and lowered a finger. "Seven, a shadow, and six, what the hells you mean? Take me. Show me."

The ghost shook his head, pointed toward the gates, and waved his arm while running in place. Now that Solineus understood. "We're standing outside, me whispering to a dead guy no one else sees, someone's going to notice me. We couldn't run until sunrise when the gates open, anyhow."

The ghost stared until his lip twitched, but didn't budge.

"If Ulrikt is at the Tower, take me to him."

Dareun slashed his finger across his throat several times with a fierce frown. He pointed to the tower, then a small rock on the ground and traced a semi-circle in front of it, and stared at him.

"The Tower of Sol and it's courtyard?"

Dareun pointed to the sky.

"The heavens?" Lelishen mentioned a celestial alignment, an eye of the Fire Lion. He gazed at the speckled veil of darkness above and a pattern formed in the stars. There were hundreds of fanciful formations his eyes might draw in the night sky, but the Lion struck his memory. "The Fire Lion. They're performing the ritual tonight?"

Dareun led him from shadow to shadow with caution, stopping at every corner to make sure the roads were empty before reaching their destination. The Tower of Sol rose into the sky before them, a gray pillar wearing a crown of white marble lit by a ring of lanterns and torches. The plaza was empty except for a few figures, but even to his heathen's eye at night, he recognized the robes as those of lord priests.

There was no way to cross several hundred yards of open ground to kill a man when any one of them might torch him with a prayer.

Solineus nestled into the shadows beside the ghost's legs, waiting for the show to begin. The arched doors of the tower opened with a surge of light and two men descended the stairs, making the number of lord priests seven. Ulrikt stood out with the glowing gem called the Sliver of Star in his hand, and the one beside him he'd heard called the Broldun; his girth left no doubt as to who he was.

"What are they doing?"

Dareun pointed, then cupped his hands as if holding an invisible ball.

"The thing Ulrikt called a Sliver of Star?"

Dareun smiled with a nod, crossing his hands back and forth.

"It's not the Sliver of Star?" Again the ghost nodded, then pointed, but Solineus couldn't tell at what.

"The building? The tower, the priests?" Dareun raised seven then six fingers, pointed again. "Shadow?" The ghost nodded. "I've no idea what you're trying to tell me."

Dareun frowned, waved his arms, but all Solineus could do was shrug, clueless. With what appeared a frustrated sigh, the ghost disappeared.

"I reckon I should've expected that." Dreams and ghosts were fickle partners.

The lord priests milled outside the tower, forming a circle around Ulrikt. A masculine voice droned, its reverberations dancing off the stone floors and walls of the outbuildings with an unnatural warbling echo.

The Lady's voice echoed between his ears and a chill spread through his body. "Remember."

Solineus' heart chugged in his chest, an ache pulsed in his temples, and a vision appeared: A forest of ancient trees higher than towers surrounded an open vale, amid which stood a group of people, blurred by the glow of a stone. A pillar of light streaking black, a presence, an evil. The pain in his forehead pulsed and faded, freeing him from the vision but filling him with dread. He'd seen this ritual before, but he couldn't say when or how, or what it meant. Something terrible was about to happen.

He backed away, pressing tight to the wall, and Dareun appeared inches from his face. The dead priest pointed to a door, then mimed getting knocked in the head before stepping through the oak. Solineus hadn't a clue what the apparition meant, but followed, startling a monk on guard duty. Solineus landed a punch to his jaw before the man could raise a hand, dropping him like a potato wearing a sack. Dareun grinned and descended a ladder.

They ran and ducked into an alcove as a pair of monks passed at a crossroad. Dareun disappeared. After a couple hundred beats of Solineus' heart it felt too long. The longer he hid, haunted by direction-less echoes of conversations and footfalls, the more he wanted to flee.

Dareun reappeared and nodded to a side corridor, taking the lead. They wound through a maze, left, right, right, left, right, until Solineus lost track, and they came to a set of stairs. The priest blinked from exist-ence and returned a moment later, taking him deeper into the bowels of Istinjoln, where the dark was lit by lanterns burning with unnerving burgundy flames. Fewer voices echoed, and not a soul crossed their path, but he still appreciated the dead man's cautious pace.

Dareun led him onward until the only directions he knew were up and down. They descended stairs, ducked into alcoves, until stopping at a door.

"Why're we here?"

The ghost folded his arms and walked through the door. Solineus' heart raced as a tingling thread of energy passed down the corridor, massaging through his body. Maybe his imagination, but he doubted it.

He cracked the door and slipped across the threshold into utter dark. Soft breathing, at rest, and the mystery's answer came to him.

"Eliles? It's me, Solineus."

A tiny flame lit the dark, the girl sitting up, ready for a fight. Dareun rested a hand on her shoulder and her tension eased.

"What're you doing here?"

"Dareun brought me here, but we haven't time to waste. We need to go."

"Go? Why, where?"

He glanced at the ghost, but Dareun shrugged and mimed running.

"I don't know where, but Ulrikt and the lord priests are performing the ritual now. We need to leave."

"How do I know to trust you?"

"Dareun's touching your left shoulder as we speak, and you know it."

Tears welled in her eyes and she spun, and Dareun's hands cupped her cheeks. He leaned to kiss her forehead. "He is here, isn't he?"

"Yes, please, let's go."

She stood and dashed across the room, grabbing a priests' robes and threw him one. He slipped into the wool, an imperfect fit, but it helped hide his sword.

A shiver of energy passed through him, leaving tendrils of prickle between the goose pimples covering his body. He glanced to the girl. "Did you feel that?" The terror stretching her face answered his question. She darted out the door, and he followed, with Dareun trailing close.

She led them quick and straight, passing numerous priests who didn't look at them twice. They stopped at a ladder stretching into dark heights lit by a single lantern at the top. "Keep close, the guard will bow, you nod and walk."

They climbed into a torchlit room where a monk bowed and opened the door for them. They passed without a word into the frigid night air as another pulse sent shivers racing across his skin. "Do you know where Ilpen and the lady are? Wake them, get the team and some horses ready. And tell the woman Ulrikt doesn't have the Sliver of Star. I'll see to the portcullis."

The girl took a step and turned. "What's that supposed to mean?"

"I don't know, but she might." Solineus stuffed his hands in the sleeves of his holy robes, sauntering to a guard tower by the gate. He glanced at the dead priest. "No, I've no idea what I'm doing."

The guards were lax since the assassin had met his trial and death, and the once-murdered dead lord priest walked again, so Solineus figured he might get lucky. He pulled on the door: Locked.

He knocked, the rap of his knuckles warbling into a quivering unreal noise, a deep-throated bird call heard from underwater. The ground shuddered. He turned to see the monastery ripple in a wave of reality, and his lungs seized before an invisible force heaved his body against the door. He rose from the ground and staggered, his ears ringing.

A blinding streak of light rose into the sky from near the Tower of Sol, rising to the Eye of the Fire Lion, a Twelfth Star in a constellation of eleven. He'd seen this before. Whether in a nightmare or a life forgotten, its familiarity engendered an agony in not remembering. He choked and gasped, fighting fear, forcing himself to swallow and breathe.

The light reached the star, and he imagined the beam of light being consumed by blackness, but only a single bar of dark streaked its middle. He watched, terrified, mesmerized, as the black passed in front of the heights of the Tower of Sol.

A guard stood in the gatehouse door, staring at the same vision. A heavy, unnatural silence swept into Solineus' ears until deafening even his thoughts, and then it came, a wave rippling the world before his eyes, slow as poured molasses, but still he didn't move fast enough.

Dareun disappeared before the energy launched Solineus and the guard into the gatehouse like leaves riding the surf.

Solineus gasped for breath as he struggled to his feet, ears ringing, the distortion fading in a return to clarity. "Raise the portcullis." He coughed, struggling to find his voice. Three guards leaned heavy against the walls, one with an arm hanging limp, his shoulder dislocated. "As a priest of Istinjoln, I command you, raise the godsdamned portcullis! Raise it or we're godsdamned dead!"

Those last words got their attention. The men rushed to the levers and gears, setting the counterbalance in motion, the bells of the tower chiming.

He stripped his priest's robes, grabbed an arming jack, a mail hauberk, and nasal helm hanging on the guardroom wall, and slipped into the comforting weight of their protection. A tight fit and short in the sleeves, but better than nothing. Still woozy he stepped outside to see the beam still stretching into the sky, familiar yet different from what his teasing memory told him. Eliles sprinted across the bailey with Lelishen by her side and Ilpen trailing, lumbering as fast as his old legs could carry him. They were alive, a good start. His balance returned as he stretched his legs into a run, but he slid to a stop.

A fiery flash lit the streets, and a shriek rose from the heart of the monastery, its pitch rising to tear at his eardrums. He scrunched his eyes and cocked his head, enduring the wail to its end.

His legs lurched toward the Tower of Sol, carried by a hope he might still kill Ulrikt, but he forced himself to the stables. Ilpen's team was in reins and yoke, the typically stubborn Ears' compliant as if they too wanted to flee from this place.

Eliles and Lelishen were throwing bridles on horses.

Solineus grabbed a saddle from a rack and tossed it on an animal, then another. "Hurry, but don't be hasty. Cinch 'em tight, we don't wanna be bouncing on our heads down the road."

Ilpen asked, "Would you tell me what the hells is going on?"

"The beginnings of a Holy War, as the lord priest promised."

Eliles yanked a cinch tight, grunting. "Did they reach Sol or fail? Were there Shadows?"

"Shadows?" The girl and her master were both worried about shadows, and it clicked in his head: *Living shadows*. "I didn't see nothin' of the sort. How about we jibber-jabber once we're outside these walls?"

Ilpen lumbered into his seat, tightening his belt and situating his knives, and Solineus hefted Eliles into the saddle, her eyes wide and lips tight. "Ride much? Grip with your knees, hold tight on the mane; the horse is rein-trained most likely; use them to guide its head. Worst case, it'll probably follow us." It was an optimistic worst case, but it'd do. She nodded, but the giddy-terrified smile never left her face.

They exited the stables on nervous beasts as a crackle of lightning lit and thundered over Istinjoln. Eliles' mount spun with her even as Solineus' gelding hop-bucked. He squeezed his legs tight and pulled the horse's nose to its chest, staring at the open gates as a dozen riders stormed through.

Ivin rode with mane and rein clutched tight, leading the wardens with Pikarn, Rinold, and Puxele clustered beside him. They'd reached Istinjoln to find its gates barred earlier in the day and setup camp in a copse of woods to spy. When a beam of light split the midnight sky they'd mounted and spurred toward the monastery.

A concussive boom surged from Istinjoln and an energy drifted across his skin from over half a mile away, raising the hairs on his neck and arms. He pushed on with the wardens strung behind along the road, and moments later the chimes of the gates sounded. They spurred from an amble into a canter, and charged until passing through the gates, reining in their animals on the stones of Istinjoln's bailey. Not a single guard moved to stop them; in fact, the only guards they saw bolted right past them.

As the wardens dismounted and tethered their horses to a hitching post, he noticed the tinker's wagon and three riders. The same people he'd seen when leaving the monastery days ago, only this time Eliles was with them, clad in the robes of a priestess. He ran to them, his eyes engaged with the girl.

He grabbed her horse's bridle to slow the beast's prancing. "We almost had the Sliver of Star, but we failed. They fulfilled the prophecy?"

"They tried. But they didn't have the Sliver."

Ivin cocked his head. "We saw a high priestess with a deadly magic."

The lanky man he'd seen riding the cart dismounted and strode to him. "Master Dareun told us it's not the Sliver. With you and your men we might still stop what they're doing, but I want these ladies out of the monastery."

Eliles glared at the man. "I'm not some baby bird you need carry cupped in your hands."

"I promised Dareun I'd help you, sweet girl, and that doesn't include taking you back to that tower. Stay with Ilpen, please."

Ivin loved her courage, but wanted to protect her more than his own life. Thunder bellowed from the heart of Istinjoln, and his eyes darted to the tower. "Let's go."

Ivin trotted into the dark streets with Solineus taking the lead.

The wardens followed with the tall woman he didn't know. He cast his eyes back several times, thankful he didn't see Eliles among them. A whiff of smoke and honey caught his nose and grew stronger as they approached, a smell familiar after the Crack of Burdenis, an odor he'd never forget, and one that brought a chill to his soul.

When they reached the edge of the courtyard, they weren't alone. Guards from the walls, monks, priests, and folks more common stood and stared, dumbfounded. A couple hundred paces away a priest hovered in the air, his robes billowing in eddies of translucent light twined with Shadow that streamed between him and the six robed priests around him. One stood out.

Ivin looked to the Wolverine. "Dunkol?"

Pikarn nodded and spat. "Puxele, think you can put an arrow in the fat bastard's back?"

"I'll do one better and put it in the flying man."

Ivin said, "Bad idea."

Puxele smirked. "You don't give all the orders 'round here." She trotted through the scattered gathering, nocked an arrow, and let fly without a single holy bothering to stop her.

The arrow arched into the light before disappearing and Ivin sprinted forward as she nocked and loosed another. The arrows suspended in the sky above the floating priest who must be Ulrikt. He grabbed her shoulder. "It's no use."

She stared at him and snarled as she nocked a third arrow. "This one's for Suvarn."

Ivin let go her shoulder and nodded. The taut string sang in his ear and he watched the arrow soar, a lower trajectory which split the middle of the Broldun's head. But the man didn't fall, slump, or run, Lord Priest Dunkol raised his arms with the grace of a priest beseeching his flock to rise, and looked to the eye of the Fire Lion. Tendrils of Shadow slithered from the wound around the fletching jutting from his skull, and his voice thundered with inhuman volume that made Ivin's ears ache. A chant of rhythmic, guttural roars Ivin didn't understand, but their intent he felt: They called for power and spoke of doom.

A crackle of energy vined up the light in the sky and formed an oblong halo higher than the tower's peak and four times as broad. Ivin grabbed Puxele's shoulder and pulled her toward the wardens, churning their feet but unable to take their eyes off the sparkling spectacle.

A ribbon of black within the aura of light expanded, contorting and wriggling. The patch of black tumbled to land at the Broldun's feet, a living Shadow splayed on all fours like a crouching wolf.

The wardens and the stranger stared in horror as Ivin and Puxele returned.

Ivin said, "Get to the horses, we're too late."

Pikarn bellowed, "Fall back!"

Everyone fled but the two strangers. Ivin put his hand to the man's shoulder. "We can't fight these; our swords are nothing to them."

The man thrashed his shoulder free of his grip and looked at him, without fear, but eyes full of desperation. "We must kill Ulrikt."

A wailing shriek pierced the commons, driving them to cover their ears. When he glanced behind them, eight clawed fingers with nails the size of grown men stretched a gap in the fabric of the universe, and Shadows spewed through the opening, plummeting to the pavers as dark splotches of rain. A great green eye appeared in the opening, a malignancy of evil hoping to find its way into their world. The first Shadow rose and attacked, striking a nearby monk, and a cacophony of chaos rang in their ears as prayers smote the creatures, appearing to kill several as they dissipated, but the surviving Shadows slithered and spread, ducking into buildings and attacking priests and monks in their paths.

"Not here, and not now. We need to regroup and pray the priests can handle this."

The tall woman grabbed the man by his shoulders and spun him to look in her eyes. "You have not failed, not yet. There is hope, but he's right, we need to leave this place."

The stranger's determination faded and with a sullen nod he turned, trotting to the bailey with Ivin and the lady on his heels. The Wolverine, Rinold, and Puxele waited for them, mounted, but the rest of the wardens were through the gates. Ivin leaped into the saddle, eager to leave this fight to the holies.

Pikarn asked, "What's going on back there?"

An explosion rocked the monastery, and Ivin's horse reared. He reined his mount's head into its chest, regaining control. "A hell, maybe all the hells, I don't know."

Ivin spurred his horse into a canter and rode through the gates, passing a number of common people, cooks, stable hands, and sundry others who labored for the holy, until reaching the tinker's wagon with its donkeys clopping double time.

Ivin twisted in his saddle, watching as people flooded from the gatehouse, many opting to slide down the steep bluffs along the road to faster reach the distant town below. He hated leaving them, but this was a fight steel and sweat couldn't win.

The stranger rode beside him, offered his hand. "Solineus Mikjehemlut of Clan Emudar."

The man's last name rang familiar, clan-blood. Ivin clasped forearms. "Ivin Choerkin."

"A Choerkin, perfect." The man's smile felt sincere, a pleasant surprise these days. "It's a dark day, but you and me, we'll persevere and kill every last one of those sonsabitches."

The man wore plain gear, and carried a sword several decades old judging by its hilt design, but Ivin loved his attitude, and it was infectious. "We'll meet up with the Colok and see what we can do about that."

"Colok? Who's Colok?"

Ivin glanced to the man, puzzled. "Not a person… You've never heard of the Colok?"

The man's eyes turned to his saddle horn with a nod. "Oh, Colok. Understood."

The man was off in the head maybe, but his courage couldn't be questioned. Priest magic and Colok claws were the only thing he'd seen so far able to hurt the Shadows. He prayed there was at least one more thing.

THIRTY-SEVEN

Running Wolves

Whiskey washes raining Fire and Fish,
turbid waters turning, learning
The sermon's shadow, turning back Shadow.
What have I? I have nothing but what you do not.
The nothing no one needs or wants but still will die for,
Distilled in the universal still, pure alcohol, pure life, pure death,
I have nothing but the end and beginning of all things
That should never have been.

—*Tomes of the Touched*

Ivin and the wardens led the group from Istinjoln before leaving the road to find their camp, where Tokodin sat idly by the fire waiting for them. Ivin had forgotten the monk in the race to Istinjoln.

Ivin said, "Good to see you in one piece."

Tokodin's face bore a haunted grin in the fire's light. "Staying alive is staying smart."

Thunder echoed from the monastery, and Ivin couldn't argue the man's logic, only his courage. Men and women were dying, others taken by Shadow to kill their friends and colleagues. The horrors in Istinjoln were just beginning if the priests didn't destroy the threat.

Ivin dismounted and popped his canteen, the dribble of bracing water that remained chilling his tongue and cutting the dry in his throat. He pulled a hooded lantern from his pack, held it facing Eliles and it lit without saying a word. The Colok would see the light and arrive soon. He eyed Lelishen, the tall woman with a strange name. "You said something about hope back there, what hope?"

The woman smiled and took a deep breath, he soon learned why. "Well, back when I was a wee tiny girl my aunt taught me things, she was a priestess in Istinjoln as some here know, well, she taught me bits and pieces of High Silone." The man he knew as Solineus looked near busting a gut as he listened to the woman's prattle. "That's the tongue some few priests still speak during rituals if you don't know, and well, so… long story short that big thing with the green eye that looked like it was trying to get through that there gate? Would you call that a gate? Well, it needs the Sliver of Star to get through. Which apparently they don't have."

Eliles said, "Then Dareun was right."

Ivin asked, "Who's Dareun?"

"My master. He was executed for assassinating Ulrikt, but he was innocent."

"Ulrikt is dead?"

"No, the gem they believe is the Sliver raised Ulrikt from the grave."

The Wolverine grunted. "How many piles of horseshit do I have to wade through to find out what the hells is going on here?"

Solineus said, "I spoke to Dareun's ghost after Ulrikt sundered his soul. He managed to tell me they had the wrong artifact. I've no idea how he knew."

The Wolverine's face froze in a smirk before he replied. "Are you shittin' on me? Shittin' on me, really?"

Solineus fumed. "Look, old man, all you need to know is Ulrikt declared Holy War on the clans when he rose from the dead."

Pikarn stalked to the man, staring up at him. "Old man, is it?"

"An old man dumber than a shit-covered horseshoe if you think you want to pick a fight with me."

Ivin coughed. He'd never imagined anyone giving Pikarn lip, and despite the man's ill-fitting armor and old sword, he thought Solineus might be able to back his words. Pikarn's chest puffed, fingers trembling by his side.

Ivin shoved between them. "You're both pissing blood to kill something, but neither of you are the enemy."

Both men glared but backed off.

"Aye, my apologies," Solineus said.

Pikarn paced. "So this dead guy, this ghost, what else did he say?"

Solineus shook his head and leaned against his horse. "Mostly, he wanted this girl safe and made sure I knew to get the hells out of Istinjoln."

"If they don't have the Sliver, they'll be after it, then." Ivin tried to remember the names listed in the lord priest's scroll. "What were there? Six names listed for tombs they needed to search?"

Tokodin said, "Five: Ximfwa, Cimdine, Komdwom, and Extek, plus one unnamed."

Eliles said, "I burnt a scroll with a couple of those names, only the nameless mausoleum remained unexplored. Something about 'Wakened Dead' inside."

Pikarn gazed at Eliles as if noticing her for the first time. "Do I know you, girl?"

Eliles smiled, her eyes turning to her feet. "We met once before."

"Sure as hells we have. Good to see you survived Istinjoln." He relaxed, his tone more sober. "So, some godsdamned crypt in the Steaming Lakes holds this Sliver. Maybe. Guarded by the Wakened, what the hells? What godsdamned good does that do?"

Lelishen said, "The Shadows and Taken will go there to bring back the Sliver. Just me, maybe, and I'm crazy and all, but I don't think that'd be much of a good thing."

Ivin asked, "There a chance this Sliver could destroy what the priests wrought?"

Eliles said, "I don't think a soul here can answer that, but we can't let them get it either way. That thing loosed on the island? There'd be no hope."

The Wolverine said, "Then we head for the Steaming Lakes to kill or die."

"No," Ivin said, and he endured the Wolverine's scowl. "I need you at the Fost. My uncle needs to know what's going on and you're the man he'll believe."

Pikarn snarled but nodded. "Makes sense. Ain't gonna be no easy trip north, and you'll be racing Shadows and Taken. Don't envy you, boy."

Tokodin said, "Zjin's got three wolf sleds, they'd haul one or two men each."

"Well, Monk, you just volunteered. Who else is goin'?" Too many hands rose, but only one surprised him: Eliles. Ivin's heart was in his throat, and he ignored the girl. "Puxele, I want you and most of the wardens getting back to the Fost, and make sure this fine tinker gets there safe, too." He glanced to Puxele and cut off her protest. "I'd appreciate it if you paid special attention to this man's safety with that bow of yours."

Puxele twisted her head and smirked. "Seeing as you asked so nicely."

"Much obliged, friend," Ilpen said. "Gods know Ears and I need to get back to the family."

Solineus said, "No way in the hells I'm not going, and don't discount this woman, she's been useful."

Ivin nodded, glanced to Lelishen. He didn't like it, but her knowledge of languages might be useful. Eliles stepped forward, her eyes boring into him, but he stared right back. "No, we'll need more steel in a fight." And he wanted her safe.

"If a storm hits the tundra who'll keep everyone warm, a sword or me?"

"Tokodin has prayers, too; he'll suffice."

The monk laughed. "My vote is for One-Lash over every one of you. Rest of you are fodder." The monk spun on Solineus. "Except you, you scare me."

Solineus asked, "Do we need this one? I'd prefer two more swords."

Tokodin retreated from the man. "That wouldn't hurt my feelings, not at all. I'm volunteering to ride to the Fost."

Pikarn said, "Much as I'd prefer him with me, take the Squirrel with you."

Rinold grinned. "I'm in, if'n you say the word. I'm for anything keeps me from town."

Ivin nodded to the tracker, as the donkeys and horses brayed, pawing the frozen ground, and everyone's eyes looked into the darkness. "Colok are getting close," Ivin said. Or at least that's what he hoped. "We'll have Colok and wolves with us, you might need more bodies than we do to make it south. Rest of you get moving, we don't want the animals spooking when the Colok arrive."

They shared handshakes and hugs and said their goodbyes until the party of six stood alone on a dark hill with their horses. Ivin clutched his shoulders, shivering and impatient for the Colok to arrive. He looked around, everyone seemed comfortable despite the howling winds, and he wondered if he were the only one who got cold. He wandered to Eliles' side. "Anything to keep us warm?" A fire appeared, hovering in the air, and everyone huddled around it.

Tokodin stared. "The rumors of you were true, you've mastered prayers of Fire. Prayers without words at such a young age."

Eliles looked to the turf. "I am blessed by Sol."

"So you are, my dear, so you are." Lelishen's voice caught Ivin's attention, and he detected a hint of humor, but he didn't have time to consider these nuances.

Zjin trotted into the far reaches of their light and stopped before Tokodin waved him closer.

Ivin smiled at the giant. "Zjin, this is Eliles and Lelishen, and over here Solineus and Rinold."

Solineus looked the creature up and down. "No wonder we don't need more swords."

Zjin growled, "Eliles, Lelishen, Solineus, Rinold."

Lelishen stood with her mouth open and her eyes wide with excitement. "Oh, how I'd love to spend time with you and study your language."

Tokodin pursed his lips. "They aren't all warm, furry hugs like you might imagine."

Ivin said, "Zjin, we need to go to the Steaming Lakes, to the priest camp. Fast. Could you take us by sled?"

The Colok licked his teeth. "Danger."

"You might've been right, these Shadows might have a lord, but it hasn't made it to our world. We need something from the lakes to keep it out forever."

Zjin stared, his fur flowing with the winds whistling over the hill. "Lost many."

"You'll lose more if we don't stop this lord."

The Colok's clawed feet dug the ground, and he sighed. "Come."

They followed the Colok, a company ten strong, until they reached a crumbled tower half buried in snow. Ivin figured it was an outpost for the wardens in summer months from the bales of hay stacked in a corner, and makeshift stable worthy of an overnight stay. They led their horses inside.

Zjin stood in the doorway. "Rest. Sleds. Morning." The Colok left them.

They fed the horses and made beds of hay and blankets for themselves and the sun rose so soon Ivin felt he hadn't slept. Zjin rousted them from their makeshift beds and led them outside. Ivin had seen Tundra Wolves pulling sleds when heading for the Ambush Chokes, but he'd never been within a couple strides.

The lead wolves were twelve hands at the shoulder, he'd swear, and their tongues lolled between yellowed fangs the length of his finger. The largest dogs he'd known in his life were half the size of these beasts, and even the angriest mongrel lacked the intensity of stare these wolves gave him with every step he took closer.

Tokodin climbed over the edge of a sled and leaned into the handle bar with hands clutching the top rail and looked downright comfortable, so Ivin fought his nerves and climbed onboard with a team of seven man-eating wolves casting glances over their shoulders at him.

He took Eliles' hand, and she eased onto the cushioned seat, leaning into his chest. He kept his hands on the rails and took a deep breath, not sure whether the wolves or the girl made him more nervous. "I prefer a horse."

She giggled. "I don't know, I think this is exciting. But then I've lived in tunnels for the better part of my life."

The sled rocked and creaked as Zjin climbed on back and roared. The sled lurched as the wolves dug snow and ice and he wrapped his arms around Eliles' waist. She didn't argue, so he left his hands there, fingers knotted as she relaxed into him. He smiled and glanced back at the sled on his right, where Solineus and Lelishen talked, though he couldn't hear them over the wind and grind of runners over the snow and ice. They looked cozy bundled together. Tokodin and Rinold rode off to his left, far less at ease in each other's company, sitting tight and trying not to touch each other, while making sure the keg of Istinjoln ale rode nestled beside them. Ivin supposed they should all be thankful for that keg, but he couldn't help wishing it were bigger, or at least full.

Thirty-Eight

Ageless Catacombs of a Past Age

Snow dancer, ice Walker,
Dragons without Wings still find clouds.
Clouds rain high above tears,
Clouds draw sweat to fall from skin,
Clouds muddle your thoughts with dreams
hiding the Depth beyond the surface of Reality.

—Tomes of the Touched

Priests spoke of the Treaty Lands as a place forsaken by the gods, a place where the heat of Sol's love had left the world, leaving the lands and its peoples frozen in permanent ice. Ever the skeptic, Eliles expected everything she'd heard to be an exaggeration, but as the Tundra Wolves pulled their sleds from the heights of the mountains, the air grew colder. The winds carried flakes and pebbles of ice that dug their way through any opening in her bundle of clothes. If it was this cold on the twenty-fifth of Yistole, she didn't want to know what it was like to face winter in this land.

The wolves left trails of steam rising from their bodies, snow and ice melting as soon as it touched their fur. The amount of heat these animals produced as they ran confounded her, but she was grateful for their speed, power, and endurance across the bleak, featureless wastes of the Treaty Lands. They took occasional stops for food and to melt ice to refill canteens.

The Choerkin... Ivin, was as sweet as he first appeared, hugging her close when the sled rattled across hard ground, and even apologized red-faced for his arms brushing her breasts. It took her several flickers to figure out what he said sorry for; she hadn't felt his touch through her layers of wool, but she still appreciated the sentiment and smiled. He was shy and courteous, a pleasant change from the men in Istinjoln, who either came at her with brash propositions or couldn't meet her eye if they dared speak to her.

The bones had spoken of love in her future, but she didn't dare imagine they might contain some truth.

They stopped only to rest the wolves and to melt ice and snow for their canteens. What sleep she got was nestled in Ivin's arms as the sleds glided over the terrain, and in short stints. Grinding runners passing bumps and cold winds slipping to frost her face kept her dozing light, but saved her from any dark dreams.

Night came and went, and her eyes grew heavy after a meal of potato bread. By midday Eliles didn't even know she slept until Ivin's gentle touch nudged her awake. "We're here."

Her back arched, shoulders pressing into his chest. Her arm stretched back into Ivin's hood, her hand brushing the warmth of his face. She smiled to touch him, and her eyes opened to a wonder. A roiling, world-bound cloud stood before them, a dome as high as a mountain's peak trapped in a glistening basin of ice. Tendrils of steam escaped into the sky in weak streams, but it seemed some force held the cloud's escape in check. She'd glanced at books in the library with illustrations of volcanoes, their craters smoking and full of fire, and she wondered if this place was somehow similar. The notion didn't settle her nerves one bit.

The wolves eased to a trot, then walk, bringing the sleds to a stop yards from the drop that sloped into the Steaming Lakes. A damp heat washed over her face. Eliles' father had told her stories of armies from the seven clans engaged in battle here, only to disappear in a winter's storm, and of men seeking treasure in the fog to return as the Wakened Dead. She hated those stories even when she adored her father, now it was another reason to loathe him. Fate possessed a cruel sense of humor to send her to a place which spawned childhood nightmares.

Eliles climbed from the sled, glancing at stakes left driven into the ground where tents would've been pitched and blackened circles of stone that must've been campfires. A few tools and pieces of other gear lay scattered and abandoned as the priests broke camp, but it was the huge bowl fashioned from the world and filled with steam which held her attention.

The haze of fog curved away from them in an arch, stretching toward the horizon. If stories were true, a lake lay beneath the cloud, riddled by geysers to sink the courageous and their flat-bottomed boats. Hidden in the depths of the lake lay an ancient city and its citizens, hundreds or thousands, who'd wakened to torment the living who dared disturb them.

She spotted a trail descending into the Steaming Lakes a few paces to the north. The iced slope was chipped and broken, probably from spike-shod boots she'd seen priests carry for journeys into the mountains. Following this trail might be their best way to find the unnamed tomb.

The fog on the edge was thin, and she could see the bottom of the slope where snow turned to dirt and rock, but the cloud grew thick soon after. There were no Wakened Dead she could see, a small comfort.

Rinold looked at the same trail, peeling back layers of gear in the newfound heat. "We've enough rope to make our way down, slow but safe. Stories I've heard, the dead only come for ya if disturbed, no skipping rocks or other childish fare, and sure as shit, if you fall into the water, plant your feet, or paddle calm like, no thrashing about."

Tokodin asked, "How the hells do we find our way in such murk?"

Ivin stepped to Eliles' side. "Priests could do it, so can we."

Tokodin chortled. "By that logic, we won't find the Sliver, seeing as they didn't."

Eliles ignored the irritating monk. "Best we know, they narrowed the search to two cairns, and thought they found the Sliver in one. That leaves one."

Tokodin asked, "The Colok won't go into the mists. Something about steam and their fur freezing when they come out, and… dead people. Don't forget those."

"A pity, I must say," Lelishen said, "though I don't blame them."

Eliles glanced at the woman, wondering for the hundredth time why a Trelelunin was on Kaludor, and why she joined them. Her mysterious nature, not to mention the cadence and pitch of her voice, were annoying as hay in your smallclothes. "So, six of us." The notion of walking into the Steaming Lakes loomed as a more horrifying prospect than it had a couple days ago when faced with Shadows in Istinjoln.

Ivin spoke to the monk. "No plea to stay behind?"

"I'd be more than happy to throw bones with the Colok."

Rinold spit and grinned. "Don't need me to find the way down, I say send this monk first." He held out a roll of thick rope.

Eliles took a step forward and traced her toe across the sheen of the bowl's lip. Thick and slick, the fog and cold combined to make a treacherous slope for even a skilled mountain goat, but its angle toward the bottom suggested a different approach. She exhaled a determined breath and smiled at the tiny group and the Colok behind them. "We don't need rope. Well, folks! I give you the last fun we'll probably have in the short remainder of our lives."

Eliles sat on the edge of the ice and pushed off before the others could say a word, gliding down the hill, leaning back, gloved hands struck to either side for support and to control her descent. She bit back the urge to unleash a resounding whoop as she reached breakneck speeds. She slowed as the grade leveled, but not enough for her taste.

She planted her feet, knees bent, and dropped to her back to slow herself, and went into a wild spin before coming to a stop scant feet from bare dirt and haze. Wide-eyed, she scooted to the thawed ground and leaped to her feet with a thrilled smile. By the gods, she wanted to do that again.

Ivin followed a moment after, trying to slow himself by driving his sword into the ice a bit like a steering oar, but that managed to send him into a spin worse than her own, albeit slower. She offered her hand when he reached bottom and pulled him to his feet. They laughed, forgetting for a moment where they were, and glanced into the fog looking for dark shapes.

Solineus and Lelishen arrived with such comfortable ease you'd swear they did this sort of thing daily, but Tokodin was another story. Ivin tried to grab his robes as he slid past, but the man spun out of control until hitting lichen-covered ground and tumbled into the cloud.

The monk scrambled back to them, robes soiled, a hand wiping his brow to find a scrape and blood. Rinold slid into the monk, feet raised to shove the man into the fog several steps.

Tokodin blurted out, "Unholy hells, man!"

"That's for your boney godsdamned elbows on the ride here." The Squirrel launched to his feet and offered the man a hand, but Tokodin refused with a silent, mocking laugh.

Ivin grinned. "Now we survived the easy part remember these names: Ximfwa, Cimdine, Komdwom, and Extek. They might point to the unnamed mausoleum."

Visibility wasn't as poor as she expected once at ground level. Dense towers of steam rose in the mist, scattered to and fro, but in most spots the cloud hovered no worse than a light fog. Orange and green lichen covered the ground leading east into the fog, and thirty paces in she caught sight of murky water, the marsh the stories promised.

Ivin said, "Stick together, and stay quiet, no need to wake the dead."

A tiny elemental flame appeared on Eliles' finger. "Fire?"

Her friends might attract unwanted attention, but if Wakened attacked or Shadows came for them, she figured the Fires should be ready. He nodded, and she bowed her head with eyes closed. A flame appeared above everybody's head. Lelishen poked her finger at the tiny creature, and it rested on her knuckle, mesmerizing the woman.

Tokodin, too, stood in awe. "I'd read in books where some priests could call living fire, but I'd never thought to see it."

Eliles did her best to smile as she lied. "Sol has blessed me and our cause."

They entered the marsh on a piece of ground wide enough to stand abreast, but the boot-marred path narrowed after leading thirty strides into the marsh. While much of the water was brackish green or gray, they passed broad pools with crystal clear waters in wide stone basins which glowed of their own accord with vibrant yellows and greens and blues. They were surreal, unnatural, and breathtaking in their hues, and in the middle, broad tunnels spiraled into the world.

The heat and humidity stifled their lungs and sapped their energy. They found themselves stripping layers of winter gear and stuffing them in their packs. It wasn't long before they wished for more layers to remove without going naked.

The muddy turf lay pocked by the feet of passing priests in every which way, lending them no aid in picking a direction. Rinold stopped to stare at tracks a dozen times, and trotted ahead now and again, but she was sure his choices were as much a guess as anyone else's would be.

Short, crooked trees with branches draped in mosses and thorny vines grew scattered through the marsh. Rinold broke branches and carved trees to mark their trail. The trees, bushes, and vines were foreign to Eliles, she couldn't put a name to a single one, but she recalled drawings in books that resembled them, with giant, broad leaves, but how plants from distant lands would find their way to Kaludor perplexed her. Twitters and tweets of birds from the branches were scarce and outnumbered by the croak of frogs and the whistle of insects.

There were fewer critters than there might otherwise be, Eliles surmised, because of the multitude of snakes, ranging from the length of a finger to longer than three men. The slithering creatures swam in the green water and dangled from branches, but they only cared enough about the travelers to stop and stare, or flee from their path. Snakes were an oddity on Kaludor; most on the island were Fever Snakes, which didn't need the sun for heat, so she found their variety of shapes and colors fascinating and creepy. For the most part, she tried not to think of them at all.

The narrow strip of ground they traversed split into three paths. Rinold glanced to the ground for tracks and chose a rising trail leading to a hillock surrounded by swirling towers of vapor. A few hundred yards into the fog they found the entrance to their first crypt. The massive stone door lay cockeyed—moved and replaced without care. Violet and green moss grew thick on the rock's face, but priests had scraped clean the symbols carved deep in its face. Eliles didn't recognize the runes. It never occurred to her the names wouldn't be written in Silone. "Anyone able to read it?"

Everyone looked to each other, until Lelishen sighed, her speech different, slow and melodious. *"Lomkonu everhit be volu sede Erœ Vuntu Ma.* 'Here lies Erœ, Lord of the house Vuntu.' More or less."

Tokodin stammered. "Horseshit. Mecum said it took weeks for scholars to translate… to even find the names on these tombs, and not a one speaks the tongue. This woman's full of horseshit."

Lelishen shrugged. "I've picked up a few things in my travels. The language is Old Hostorun, pretty much a dead tongue since the Age of Warlords. We best keep moving."

The woman strode into the marsh, her voice and bearing changed, and smooching the flicker of fire riding on her shoulder.

Ivin sidled up to Solineus. "Who the hells is she?"

"Can't say. But she knows things."

Eliles wanted to tell Ivin, but figured it wasn't her place. And besides, she appreciated how the woman rankled the monk, no need to spoil that fun.

Rinold skirted ahead of Lelishen with the group falling in line again, and they twisted and wound through the marsh, leaping skinny stagnant streams to make better time, and examined every mausoleum entrance they came across. They headed deeper into the marsh where the pools became broader and deeper, and the trails more narrow and treacherous.

Eliles and others slipped several times, scarring the muddy sides of embankments, but no one fell as far as the lake itself. She couldn't say when night fell. With the steam cloud and the fires floating above their heads, not to mention her eyes focused on every skittering thing that moved, time felt irrelevant. She beckoned more light from the Fires, and sent them ahead here and there so Rinold could better see where he was going, but the dark around their flames unnerved her. Her Fires lit a moss-slicked stair, leading the way to yet another crypt door.

"Tsst!" Ivin raised a hand, crouching, and Eliles stopped on his heels, heart beating in her throat.

A blur of motion caught her eye. Ivin drew his sword and crept the last few stairs. A gigantic mannish skeleton ambled past a cairn's door, the Wakened Dead damned near invisible in the dark and steam.

Rinold's bow flicked from his shoulder, nocking an arrow, but Solineus nabbed the rest and arrow, making sure the man didn't let loose. "That might get us all killed, and what's an arrow gonna do to them bones? Come with me." Solineus eased forward, sword in hand, but passive in posture.

Eliles followed, but her sweat came faster the closer they got. Having Ivin right in front of her and Rinold behind with his bow didn't hurt her feelings a bit, despite Solineus' point. She'd seen Wakened several times, brought into Istinjoln to purge the evil, but they paled beside this thing. A skeleton clean of flesh, and if it straightened, it would stand eight feet tall. If it attacked, its bones would strike as cudgels.

Solineus stepped in its path. The creature paused before sidestepping the living man and passed into the fog.

Ivin asked, "How'd you know it wouldn't attack?"

"A hunch. Check the door."

They walked to the crown of the hillock to find a slab of white marble a foot thick and open enough for men to squeeze through. The face was scraped clean of mosses and bore no inscription.

Tokodin said, "No name, but the scroll spoke of Wakened guarding the entry. Not a lone wanderer."

"It didn't mention whether they were inside or out," Ivin said.

A shriek in the distance set Eliles' nerves on edge. She spun, staring into the dark behind them. *Give me light.* The flame hovering above her head sped into the dark and grew, casting light for a hundred paces in every direction. The shadows of trees and vines and bushes danced with deceptive wavers, but after a few moments her eyes picked out the fearful reality.

"Shadows."

Ivin leaned beside her, his breath hot in her ear, giving her a chill. "You're sure? I don't see any."

The demons soared above the ground, appearing and disappearing in natural darkness. They weren't so far away, separated from the party only by stale puddles of water and slow streams. Why didn't they come straight for them?

Lelishen said, "I see them. They're avoiding the water. If we get inside, close the door, we might have a chance."

Ivin exhaled and led the way. "This is what we came for."

Eliles asked the Fire above Ivin's head for more light and it grew brighter the moment he entered the tunnel, what was once dark now shining bright. The hall's steps and walls were fashioned from polished white marble, the stone chiseled with intricate floral scenes interspersed with hummingbirds, sparrows, hawks, and eagles, and on the ceiling a wingless dragon soared above their heads, its gaping maw and tail stretching the corridor's length. The hall was a marvel, pristine, unmolested by water, moss, tree roots, or time.

"No peasant's tomb, for sure." A clatter echoed from the deeps as Eliles' whisper faded, reminding her of whitetail antlers clashing during rut. "It's so beautiful. It looks like the artisans could've finished this morning."

A Shadow's scream, followed by the warbling call of a Taken spun them to face the entrance. The damned things were coming faster than she'd hoped. The men put their hands to the massive stone door, but it didn't budge.

Ivin asked, "See anything for leverage?"

A Shadow rushed through the entrance and Solineus dove from its path to the hard floor. A flame darted into the shade of the demon's body and ignited in a burst before she'd bothered to ask for help. The substance of the Shadow showered dissipating tendrils in the air, and with a hollow howl the Shadow disappeared through the door.

Ivin lent a hand to launch Solineus to his feet and glanced to Eliles. "Can you keep those fires guarding our rear?"

With her nod five flames darted between them and the door, the sixth remaining above her head.

Ivin said, "The Taken will be here soon enough; let's move slow and steady."

The tunnel descended on a gradual slope until reaching broad stairs carved with flowering ivy vines. By the time they reached the bottom, Eliles figured they were below water level, but still the floors and ceiling were dry as desert bone. Four Shadows followed as far as the first steps, watching them, but after the corridor turned north, the Shadows stopped. Little comfort in not being able to see your enemy.

Thirty strides farther they came to a longer flight of stairs which led into a chamber five strides wide and long, empty but for a bowl carved from silver-veined marble which sat in the middle of the room. Its rim was three feet high and stretched a man's height across its middle. Eliles stood at its edge and looked into the bowl: At its bottom yawned a hole large enough a child could slip into its dark depths. Some sort of well, she suspected. Or a place to make offerings to unknown gods.

The corridor bent north, entering a room with four central pillars. Statues of men, some close to nine feet tall, lined the walls. Warriors armed with spears and shields, wearing breastplates and determined expressions. She recalled the giant skeleton outside and wondered if the statues were more life-sized than she'd otherwise assume.

Eliles requested five fires to remain at their rear as they climbed a short stair, entering an antechamber lined with maple benches carved with exquisite dragons and sunbursts, and covered in golden silk pillows. The sheen of the maple was flawless, as if oiled yesterday, the threads on the cushions immaculate, as if fresh placed and never sat in.

Stepping from the sweltering, muddy haze of the outside world into these halls was like walking into someone's perfect dream.

"This place is unreal," Ivin said.

Lelishen replied, "I've never seen anything like it. Not even—"

The rattle of antlers interrupted, louder this time, and from the direction of the door.

Ivin crept close, his targe to the fore and broadsword over his head. "Eliles, could you send a fire in there?" A rattle followed his words.

She snuck to his shoulder and sent her tiny flame dancing along the ceiling; it stopped twenty strides ahead. Something was there, but it was indistinct in this light and distance. The scene became clear after a few steps down the passage where another corridor crossed beneath the Fire's light. It might have been a city street crowded with people ranging from seven to nine feet tall, except the people were bones frozen in the act of walking. Pristine clothing and armor hung slack on their shoulders and limbs.

"Holy hells," Tokodin muttered, and the skeletons moved, several bumping each other, their bones clacking. In moments they stopped again.

Ivin said. "At least we know what the scroll meant by Wakened guards." The skeletons clicked and clacked into motion as he spoke, but they didn't acknowledge the presence of the living.

Solineus rubbed his forehead. "They seem as passive as the one outside, but that was one, not a horde."

Eliles strained her memory for anything that might be useful. "I've heard of secret passages in tombs?"

Ivin smiled. "Good notion."

Solineus took a drink from his canteen, frowned as he gave it a shake. "Aye, but the priests were here before us and would've thought it, too. And they had time."

Ivin looked to Lelishen, "Any ideas?"

"Oh, goodness no, and if your priests couldn't destroy them…?" For a moment she broke back into the prattling speech of her façade, before settling into her real voice. "No, I'm sorry to say. People, languages, are my expertise, not the Wakened Dead."

History books which survived the Age of Warlords didn't tell what had happened to the city beneath these waters. It didn't even have a proper name, far as Eliles knew. A place and people lost to water and time. "We need to find a way across. If we put these things between us and the Taken… Solineus, your hunch earlier?"

"You want to trust my memories?" The man chuckled, easing closer to the cluster of traipsing skeletons. "Way I seem to understand it, Wakened without flesh are less… sentient? Conscious? And less aggressive. The more flesh on their bones, the more apt to attack unprovoked."

Tokodin said, "A skeleton rose from the Umptor family mausoleum when I was a child; it killed three people in their sleep before being destroyed."

"We'd be dead by now if these were aggressive. So could we simply walk through?" Eliles asked.

Solineus said, "If there were a path between them, I think so. Bumping one, knocking it over, well, I don't think it takes much for the Wakened to get riled."

Eliles stood close to the walking bones, leaned out to glance down the hall they traversed. The walls were honeycombed with empty holes where these dead once slept. The corridor ran thirty strides in either direction, ending at sarcophagi carved with fantastic creatures, winged and horned, that she didn't recognize. Here the skeletons turned, swarming as graceful as might a flock of birds, in an endless oval.

She muttered, "The priests of Istinjoln would never have thought of the subtle."

Her companions bickered the merits of fire and steel, of searching for secret passages, or trying to fight their way back out of this trap, but Eliles stuck her arm into the path of an oncoming skeleton. It altered course without hesitation, brushing her fingers as it passed, and the next several skeletons followed.

She stepped into the gap and held her breath, ready to dive if the bones in the velvet dress headed for her, but graceful as a dancer the Wakened eased around her. Inch-by-inch, Eliles shuffled her way among the dead. Cold, empty-eyed skulls passed without a glance, but they knew she was there, she felt that in her own bones. She slipped her arm in a gap and the dead parted, but shuffled to a stop.

Eliles' heart lurched before she realized everyone had stopped talking to stare at her. "Keep talking, please."

The dead lurched into motion with a clatter as the group spoke, and her heart raced. She shuffled another step.

Ivin yelled, "Eliles!"

The sound of her name didn't catch her attention at first, over the clatter of bones and her focus on slipping into the next gap of Wakened. She looked back at Ivin, squinting, straining her ears.

"That one's looking at you!" But she couldn't see him well enough through the bones to see where he pointed.

She glanced frantically, spotting more than one who pinned empty eyes on her. Panic struck, her mouth drying out. A skeleton sat in each sarcophagus at the ends of the hall, staring with the emotionless visages of naked skulls. Wakened passed in their lines of sight but their gazes didn't flinch. But from Ivin's vantage, he wouldn't be able to see this pair. Eliles scanned the passing skeletons until she looked to what had been an empty corridor across from the party. She saw the one now, taller than the statues and draped in vibrant gold and green silks woven with silver. Two swords were stuck through its belt, horribly undersized for this giant.

Tales of the Wakened who wielded weapons other than fists and teeth never ended well.

Eliles' body tingled as the swarm of dead stopped in their tracks, then parted to make way for the armed Wakened. It kept its hands clasped behind its back in a dignified manner, leaning over her sweating brow until Eliles' eyes were inches from empty sockets.

"What do you see, little mortal, when you look into my eyes?" The voice was masculine, deep and sonorous, and spoke flawless Silone.

Eliles gazed into the depths of the creature's skull. "All I see is darkness."

It stood straight, skull nodding. "We shall speak further. Come."

The skeletons cleared a path and the rest of the party joined her, following the dead man into deep halls.

Ivin glared at her as they walked. "That was reckless. You could've gotten us all killed."

Eliles recognized the truth in his words, so didn't argue, despite wanting to. She grinned. "You're just happy I'm still alive."

His stern frown faded with a roll of his eyes and turned into a smile. "Yeah, that I am."

Eliles stole a glance back to see the ranks of skeletons close, sealing their fate or protecting their rear.

THIRTY-NINE

Tomb of the Touched

Dance beneath the eye of the Creator,
soar without wings and cast your seeds.
Your Children, your children, they will set wing to sky
blocking sun and star and moon, mighty.
But seeds grow weaker even as they grow greater.
Seeds in heavens, seeds on wind, seeds growing from dirt, until dirt is all they know.

—*Tomes of the Touched*

Lanterns illuminated a chamber lined with book-filled shelves. A white marble sarcophagus sat atop a black onyx dais in the middle of the room, both relief-carved with stars and moons and soaring dragons, several with wings, a couple without.

A large desk and chair stood to the side. A fat book sat open on the desk, and beside it a pen and inkwell. Ivin strolled close to the table, disappointed to see blank pages before turning his attention back to the dead man.

The skeleton sauntered around the tomb, took a seat in a high-backed chair resembling a throne, and crossed his legs. The room reminded Ivin more of bedchambers than a mausoleum, except the bed was for the dead.

They stood silent, the fleshless man staring at them as though they sought audience with a king.

Ivin broke the quiet. "There are creatures—"

The Wakened's eyes turned to the desk, and he spoke in a language Ivin couldn't understand. Ivin glanced to Lelishen, but she shook her head. The man's gaze returned to them.

"The Shadows, the Shadows, the Shadows of Man all men should dread, but so often they see their shadows not until too late, but the Shadows they do see they should not fear, not here. And the little men, the Taken, bones will take."

Ivin turned again to his companions. Eliles shrugged. "I think he means we're safe?"

But before they could clarify, the skeleton turned to empty air and spoke. "Dark feathers and dark wings, in the bloody maw of feline, of cat, of lion, no gryphon, without wings? Could a gryphon it be without feathers?" He looked to the chamber's ceiling, back to the party. "My apologies. It is so good to see you again, not yet. Do go on. I will try not to spoil your fun, fun, fun, this time round."

Ivin stared, lost for meaningful words. "Who are you?"

His laughter echoed and he thumped his sternum, pointed to the desk, babbling in a foreign tongue to nobody before addressing them again. "You seek me without knowing my name? No. Of course you did, you did again, you'll do again, until you learn. Names are not things, names are things earned. You earned your name wriggling from the belly of the now dead, how should you earn my name? Chewed back into the belly of the hungry dead? And you!" His eyes fell on Lelishen. "Trelelunin woman, you have been here before or perhaps not yet, have you not earned my name?"

Eyes landed on Lelishen as the Wakened spoke to her in a lilting language Ivin couldn't comprehend, and she answered, but in

Silone. "I've never seen you before, here or otherwise, and your name is unknown to me."

Trelelunin were a people of magic who lived in forests across the Parapet Straits. Tales spoke of their culture's wisdom, but if true, how did it make sense she was here with them on the island of Kaludor? He shook off these questions for another time; he needed to focus.

Ivin said, "We didn't come here for you or your name."

"Indeed, but perhaps you should have. You come seeking hope when all I can give you is truth in falsehoods. But you should be able to call me something, pick a name, choose a name, Craven Raven is taken already, he and his surly beak. But you may call me as I have been called by so many who knew my name but chose not to use it. My name you may choose is the moniker the Touched, whether simply erroneous or a lie or a misspoken misspeak, it will suffice all the same."

"The Touched," Solineus said. "Touched by what?"

"He who doesn't trust the name which is his own questions the source of mine title? Precious and precocious in wisdom and foolishness. How old are you, ancient soul, immortal child, favored of the slaves of man, two weeks or thirty years? Burping baby or hoary elder? When next you come to speak to me, we'll delve further. This little man, among others, this Silone"—his gaze fell on Ivin—"seeks me out this day, and finds me. For what?"

Ivin stammered for words under the scrutiny of the unnerving, faceless gaze.

The Touched stood, bony fingers grabbing the top of his skull, pulling, and he roared a wordless song in anguish as a layer of pale bone-white peeled from his face, revealing flesh beneath, and where once were empty sockets, an eye of blue and another brown. As hands stretched beyond his chin, lips formed, and a tongue quaking in his shrieking mouth. The Touched released the osseous layer, flesh and eyes fading into bone and black.

"Does it help to look into my eyes, young mortal? You speak not to the cursed dead, no, you speak to the cursed to be alive." He eased into his seat, dignified, rubbing the cheeks of his skull. "An immortal not meant to be."

The Touched's bony fingers rattled on the arm of his chair as Ivin took deep breaths before speaking. "We seek the Sliver of Star."

The skeleton stared, featureless and unreadable. "A white star or a black star, or just a star, star? Shall a spider cast its web to pull a piece to Kaludor for you? No! I jest. A Sliver of Star, you say. *The* Sliver of Star, perhaps its trail of dust. There is no Sliver of Star. I fear, you feared. The Sliver is a name unearned, the unhappy ending, the unhappy naming, of a false vision given to prophetic falsehoods bringing most major pain. Tom— Tom— Tomorrow. Today. Not yesterdays gone."

"It isn't real?"

"No, no, and no. Chasing unearned names in the holes of the worlds, I feel bad for you, most certain I do. Changes come, changes go, changes always staying the same. Your face is strange. Traditions they might be called with a name earned. Tradition suggests gifts, and gifts I give, because they never truly leave. What would you like, oh mortal man, what of my treasures?"

Ivin didn't know what the hells the man meant with his words most of the time, but he wasn't a grave-robber. "Silone do not plunder the tombs of the dead."

"Noble sentiment from a person of people willing to fill tombs with smelly things no one except desperate loved ones would wish to retrieve, but I repeat: I am not dead, so how a tomb to rob? But if these gifts are gifts unearned as they appear, I will choose for you."

The Touched leaped to his feet, waltzing with an invisible partner to the sarcophagus, and dipped her imaginary form above its opening with a kiss. He reached in and withdrew a shield, black as night and sparkling with stars. Only they weren't stars. Fifty arrowheads or more, several with pieces of broken shafts still in them. Steel and stone, three of glass.

The Touched flung it at him, and Ivin caught it in defense of his head. Larger than his targe, about three feet in diameter, it still weighed less than his steel-rimmed shield, as if constructed from thin wood rather than a quarter-inch of black metal.

"It suits you well, and makes for fitful slumber in the rare times of my rest, a most prickly pillow I assure you. I will not miss it until it comes back."

Ivin had no idea what kind of shield he held, but it sure wasn't what he came for. Time was a luxury a skeletal madman had plenty of, but in the south people were dying. "We need a way to stop the Shadows, the Celestial Gate—"

"Man child who fears the Shadows of Man, and no wonder, but I am not a man and therefore need fear not your Shadows. No Shadow nor little man Taken will penetrate the shield you now bear. You came looking for one gift unreal you will never hold, I give you a real gift, think me a horse to look into my mouth?"

Horse, Twelve Hells. How could one man speak so many words in Silone without Ivin being able to piece them together? There wasn't much else to say. "Thank you."

"And you, little mouse man of the gods, too shy to ask?"

Tokodin stepped behind Solineus to hide from the creature's gaze. "Me? I'm a simple man; gold is good."

"Silver and gold, only a man who values these things gifts such things, and I know what you value most."

"The lives of our people?"

"Clever man of gods, but no, what you value third then, after your people and skin your own." He walked to a shelf and grabbed a bottle, presented it to the monk. "Careful with that, what year it is in your now I am uncertain, but this is old no matter, and is liable to make even a dragon forget their own lies with but a whiff."

"And you!" The Touched turned to Rinold, who faced the skeleton with a smirk and a hand on his hip.

"I don't need a damned thing."

"Squ- Squ- Squirrel, where is your cute fluffy tail? Ha! I jest, I know your tail—excuse my lack of an eye for a mischievous and knowing wink—travels south with clopping critters long of ear. And, here! Yes, here, not there, is what you need for there next."

The skeleton reached into its robes and tossed a golden ring that flashed sapphire and diamond as it arched over the tomb. Rinold snagged it from the air before it thudded his nose. "I, uh... Huh."

"She'll swoon, I declare with a swear." The Touched turned to Solineus, bent and planted a kiss on his forehead, making the man blanch. "For you a gift, a kiss, from pellucid blue dreams. I jest! Ha ha ha!" He pointed to the desk and chair. "Note the laughter, be sure." He removed the swords from his belt along with a leather harness, knelt and handed them to Solineus. "These are for you, perhaps I borrowed them from you already, I don't recall. The Twins, the Twins, never long shall they part, but part they will the Shadows of Man. But beware the words of singing Latcu."

Before Solineus could thank him, the skeleton leaped to his feet and waltzed to stand before Lelishen. "You, inhuman, you I cannot gift with what you want, your gift you must select but one only one. To the tomes, off with you now."

Lelishen didn't hesitate, she walked to the shelves and perused their spines.

The Touched took a smooth dancing step to stand before Eliles. "And for you, my little girl with eyes of blue, cousin mine, with eyes more colors than mine own, who's end I cannot see. Will we see, speak, hear again? Will we dance before or after eternity's end? For you and you alone a gift with name unearned." The Touched cupped his hands, and when he opened them a blinding light emanated, forcing Ivin to avert his eyes. When the intensity faded he turned to look, and in the man's bony palm rested a crescent moon, like a ten inch blade of a curved knife.

Eliles touched it, tracing its shape. "What is it?"

"It is a truth among falsehoods, a thing of hope and hopelessness with name unearned. A shard of that which blinded mortal and immortal with all they wished to see. Better they'd seen darkness than hope, for darkness was the truth, the Creator in the black. For you it is summer the eternal glow, for you, sweet soul of innocence and Dame of Fire, it will earn a name not given by false eyes and tongues cast in pathetic, prophetic, and false visions."

"This is what the Shadows seek?"

"Did I not just say that? Once gone it will always be here but to never return. It is my most precious gift, the Craven Raven rues I give it to you now, because he yet did not know it exists. He watches us now, or rather then, when? No matter. So you see, girl, I give my greatest gift to you, and I receive the only gift ever given me: being rid its light and fright. Better to live in the dark with happy worms than in the light with angry dragons."

Ivin watched as she took the crescent from the Touched's bony hand, expecting something. They stood and watched, even Lelishen, with a book tucked under her arm.

Nothing happened.

Eliles gaped at the treasure in her hands, it glowed as a moon on the darkest night, warm to the touch, and vibrated with a cat's gentle purr she could feel, but not hear. When she blinked, a wild brocade of light flashed through her mind, and she opened her eyes to stare at the skeleton's emotionless face. Her mouth opened, but instead of speaking she closed her eyes and held them shut. The hues were brilliant, shifting and flowing in waves, a spectrum unimagined before now, and when she opened her eyes again, the light of the real world too had changed. Subtle, maybe ghosts from within her mind, but before she grasped its intricacies the vision faded.

She inhaled a shuddering breath. "Will this destroy the Celestial Gate?"

"Oh dear, oh fear, yes, and no, and maybe, depends on whether what you intend to destroy exists for first in the real place, and whether you find destruction an end, or prefer defeat in creation of the destroying fire defeating. It is capable of more and it is capable of less, aren't we all? What you really want is how, not just will, and that is an ages old truth only you can question into answers, not me, not lowly me, he who awaits the worms only to find the flaming breath of dragons in your tower's spire."

"Dame of Fire? What tower? I've no idea what you're talking about."

The Touched sighed and strode away, sullen. "I keep forgetting which time this is we speak. It's tricky not to confuse when yourself are confused. A tower, a tower, an autumn flower, read the oracle's bones and find your tower, the first, the second build in kind. Find. In kind. Tear-blind build. I love fish soup, do you?"

Eliles scrunched her eyes, trying to focus on any clues within the babble. Meris read her future beneath the Tower of Sol, she'd been named priestess of Istinjoln. If he spoke of another tower, she couldn't conceive of it.

Ivin's finger stretched toward the artifact, and she slapped his hand with a warning smile.

"The Dame of Fire is right, no other should touch that of unearned name. Fire the renowned destroyer."

Eliles brought the crescent to her breast, the warmth immediate through her clothes, before she slipped it into her bag.

"Always a joyous day when the eternal repetition comes to taunt the Craven Raven, but a sorrowful day, too. Parting with this treasure is like parting with one of my own ribs! Ha ha ha! Note the laughter, damn you! So sorry, I fear the Raven knows your faces, the squat good it will do him, he won't remember, like me, until many days after yesterday."

It sounded as if they had another enemy, and Eliles couldn't resist. "Who is this Craven Raven?"

"A name unearned, dame not yet, but fear no fear not, the Craven Raven too knows his name not yet, the ebony feathers and black blood and green eyes, the multicolored lies he will tell himself have just begun." The Touched settled into his chair. "Rest with me, yes rest, sleep as you haven't slept in days, safe and full, as you've never slept backward before. I will bid you awake when you should leave and impart a final gift on the morrow not. Good night."

His chin slumped to his chest, and his bones relaxed. If Eliles hadn't seen him moving, she'd swear the Touched had been dead in that pose for centuries.

Ivin asked, "Did anyone understand what the hells just happened?"

"Bits and pieces," Lelishen answered. "If the Touched can be believed, we hold the Sliver of Star, and we know our enemy."

Eliles glanced at the woman everyone now knew to be a foreigner and a liar, and her tone growled her suspicions. "And who the Twelve Hells are you?"

The woman glared, but her eyes softened. "Lelishen Emedwer. I sailed from Eleris Edan to observe the Eve of Snows."

"The Edan? How'd they know of the Eve?" The Edan lived in forests across the Parapet Straits, hundreds of leagues from where they stood, an immortal people who never left their homeland if rumor were true.

"I am not Edan, so I'm not privy to their means. But this was not the only ritual being performed for the alignment of the Eye of the Fire Lion. By my prayers, I hope the other fared better. The Edan feared the twelfth star, but if they had known… they would've sent someone to stop it, not observe."

"I was sent to stop it," Solineus said. "I failed."

Ivin said, "Enough with pity and mistrust. What did you mean 'we know the enemy'?"

Lelishen meandered to the writing desk, and Eliles followed on her heels. "The Shadows of Man."

The pages that were blank when they entered the mausoleum were covered in flowing script written with calligraphic precision. Eliles gawked. "Everything he said is written, but nothing we said." Impossible, and yet there the words sat. Eliles flipped a page, but something, someone, turned it back. She did this three times with the same result.

Rinold asked, "A ghost?"

Lelishen started to sit in the chair, but moved to a bench. "We're not in a place for mortals, so it's possible. As I was saying, I've heard of the Shadows of Man, but I don't know much about—"

"Son of a bitch!" Solineus jumped, but Eliles couldn't tell why. "Sorry. Nothing, don't mind me." His eyes glanced from the hilt of one of the Twins to the other.

"The Shadows of Man are mentioned in tomes dating to the God Wars. They were summoned to fight, to destroy humans. They were powerful then, but in that time, the gods and the elements were far more powerful. The Shadows were a small piece in many wars."

Ivin said, "Zwinfolkum, the Colok mentioned the Shadows having a master, or lord. That's what the Colok are most worried about."

The woman's eyes twitched back and forth before settling on the ceiling, and she sighed. "Another name for Winfoldin, Rifoldun, maybe, which means Great Mother or something close to it. It would make sense if it's true the gods bred these Shadows."

The God Wars were real. Eliles had always thought these fables were more lies of the priesthood. If even half the tales were true, the ramifications disturbed her. "If Ulrikt summoned the mother of these creatures, what do we do then?"

Tokodin burst in. "No! No, whatever this is, it's an accident. A mistake. The prophecy speaks of bringing the Word of Sol to the world, the power of the Pantheon, not some mother of Shadows. I don't know a lot of things, but I do know this."

Rinold took a step toward Tokodin but Ivin barred him with an arm. The tracker glared. "That son of bitch lord priest of yours got my brothers killed."

"And many more of mine, but it doesn't make it any less a mistake," Tokodin retorted.

Eliles turned to the monk, quoting the *Book of Leds*. "'Only the gods may judge by a man's intentions; mortals must judge by results.'"

Tokodin threw his hands in the air and wandered to a corner, pulling the stopper on his bottle.

Lelishen said, "If Winfoldin made it into the world? There's no way to say what would happen. The Edan imprisoned a Celestial Being in the Age of Warlords… enough to say this Zwinfolkum would be very bad."

Eliles turned back to Lelishen. "How do we destroy these Shadows? Stop this mother?"

"I don't know. The gods banished them once. The elements are able to kill them, but so long as the Celestial Gate is open… Our hope is the crescent in your hand."

Everyone looked to Eliles; her face burned and she wanted to hide. "Me? I'm no god. I'm not even a priestess!" She caught the strange look on Tokodin's face as he took a pull on his liquor, but she ignored him, tears welling in her eyes.

Ivin walked to her side, addressed the group. "Let's take the skeleton's advice. Relax, sleep if we can. Neither Shadows nor Taken have made it here, so I trust the Touched's promise of refuge."

He put his arm around her, and grateful for his support, she allowed him to escort her to a cushioned bench.

"Lie down, rest. We came here for hope, and we have it now. Let's enjoy the moment while we can."

She took a seat, smiled, but it was forced. "Thank you."

Lelishen and Tokodin meandered to the bookshelves while Solineus tinkered with the harness to his new swords. They rode on his back until with a click of a latch they dropped to either hip. She pushed her senses toward the man and listened. "Gods be damned if the belts don't fit without adjusting a notch." And Rinold chuckled nearby, but the more curious and disturbing feeling came from the swords themselves: They felt alive, aware of her watching.

Eliles wanted no more surprises today and was too tired to care about swords. She stretched along the bench, resting the bag with the crescent on her bosom, and smiled at Ivin again, more sincere this time. "Thank you for everything."

His smile was warm, gentle. "Anytime, always." He leaned in and kissed her on the forehead before sitting beside her.

She took his hand, a warmth and chill conflicting her spirit. The Dame of Fire was nothing more than a girl with fiery friends, without a clue of what to do. She eased into the cushions of the bench, propping her head on the hood of her cloak, and closed her eyes.

※　※　※

She awoke in the middle of the night and turned with sleep-blurred eyes to see a vision that a few days ago would've made her wonder whether she was dreaming. The Touched paced the room, the man the skeleton had once been, his mismatched eyes wide, impassioned, evocative, as they glanced to and fro. He was larger than life, a performer on a stage, not a mere giant, and beautiful in his own gaunt, sallow-faced way. His mouth and his hands gesticulated as if in the middle of a debate, but there wasn't a sound, not even the steps of his feet. The skeleton still sat in its throne, unmoved, and in the far corner sat Lelishen, a book in her lap as she watched the scene.

Eliles slipped away from Ivin as he slept, creeping to sit with the woman, and spoke under her breath. "What's going on?"

Lelishen grinned. "I don't know, but isn't it amazing?"

Bizarre and downright creepy. "How's it possible?"

"I don't know, not exactly, but… You are a child of Fire, this is a place of Time, maybe more. As the Element Fire is a part of your nature, so the Element Time is part of this tomb's nature."

She'd never heard Time called an element. In Istinjoln they spoke of the Ten Elements of the Universe, the Ten Winds. Fire, Water, Earth, Air, Heat, Cold, Life, Spirit, Light, and Dark. "I'm not sure what you mean."

"Time is an Element just as Fire, or Light, and Dark." She held out her hand and a tiny luminescent ball appeared without words of prayer. Unlike Eliles' little friends, this Light was not alive. "How do you know this is Elemental Light?"

Eliles smiled, feeling a sudden kinship. The woman sat in a shadowless halo. "It envelops, it doesn't cast shadows."

The ball turned to flames, and shadows danced on the wall. "Light or Elemental Light?"

"Fire gives off normal light."

"Until it doesn't." Her shadow disappeared, but the change in the Fire was so subtle it was hard to notice: A radiance of Light hid in the edge of the flame's flicker. "A blend of Elements, Fire and Light. Elemental Fire burns without fuel, even without air, it doesn't even necessarily produce heat. Dark cannot be penetrated by light and instills an unnatural fear. All Elements have something that sets them apart from their more common cousin. Time is no different. The time we live in travels in one direction, more or less constant. Elemental Time produces flashes, déjà vu, small twists in reality that may travel forward or backward. It may give us memories, our own or even those of others."

"My Fire is different."

The woman stared at her, making Eliles uncomfortable, forcing her to question herself even before the woman spoke. "How so?"

"The Fires aren't mine. Since I was a child, they come from my little friends. Or, sort of, it's part me."

The woman's nose wrinkled, then she smiled. "The little flames you summon? Ah, my dear, the flames aren't your gift, they come because of your gift."

"I'm defiled, cursed—"

"Hush, don't let the words of your priests slip from your lips. The Vanquished Gods are just that, gone. To connect to our world again would take something more special than even you. Maybe that thing in your bag?"

Eliles' chest constricted. "And Istinjoln's killing all those like me, another mistake?"

"The holy and common folk around the world don't understand,

and therefore fear those like you, and what people fear, they often try to destroy."

Eliles shook her head, memories of so many children marching to their doom flashing through her mind. She needed a change in conversation quick. "The fires, what you said about me and the fires?"

"The same cut on one man festers, on another it heals in a week, a third in a matter of days. Life is all around us, running through us, for the lucky Life pools, healing. The truly fortunate will find they can heal others even if they don't fully grasp their ability. You are one of these people, except yours is more rare, with Fire."

"And Spirit. I… influence people often times not knowing it."

"And Spirit? Spirit is more common. Mortal peoples are beings of Life and Spirit. Fire and Spirit may explain the fires that follow you. The Edan call them *te-xe*, 'Elementals.' They are everywhere, but passive, invisible—"

"Alive."

"Yes, alive. It is rare a child is born so attuned to an Element. The *te-xe* are attracted to them, but it's not unheard of. And when you harness the power of Fire, they're attracted to your energy, as they are with natural fires. If you look close, you might find one in a campfire at night." Lelishen stifled a giggle. "They can be playful and dangerous, too. The Kingdomers—you've never heard of them, I suppose—who live in the Dragonspan Mountains far south on the continent, have a powder which flames, and they fashion explosive sticks of the stuff they call stonebreakers. They handle these stonebreakers sparingly and store them away from each other, to make sure a *te-xe* doesn't set off the whole stock. A mine came down at least once because of your pesky friends."

It didn't sound funny, but still she grinned: She'd always figured the little things held a streak of naughty. "They help me. I don't necessarily ask, they seem to know what I want. I can't say for sure."

"If you influence people without knowing, it's likely you have an influence over them, too. It's remarkable, however it works."

A cork popped from across the room and Eliles jumped to her feet, startled to see Tokodin staring as he took a drink.

Lelishen continued, ignoring the monk. "The Edan would understand more; my knowledge is small in such matters."

Eliles tore her gaze from the monk, conceding the loss of her secret, but still, she figured a change of subject was due. "This Sliver, what is it?"

The woman's mouth crinkled and her shoulders shrugged. "What do you think it is?"

Eliles thought on it, her mind focusing on the warmth it brought, and on the words of the Touched. "A shard of which blinded mortal and immortal with what they wished to see? It isn't alive, not like the flames, but I feel a life, a presence, a connection to something... I don't know. And when I close my eyes while holding it, there're colors I can't describe."

"The colors I can't explain, but, well, it is no doubt a reservoir, then."

"A what?"

"Your priests teach diamond as the stone of Life; this isn't coincidence, it is the same around the world. The Elemental energies are everywhere, passing through everyone and everything, but diamonds are apt to trap Life. This crescent sounds like it catches Life and Spirit, giving it the sense of a living presence without being alive, and its harnessed energies can be unleashed, as with a diamond."

Eliles wasn't sure about the explanation for the presence, but it didn't matter. How the thing could be used was what counted. "What use would this Life and Spirit be?"

The woman closed her eyes, lips pursed in thought before rubbing her eyes open, looking Eliles straight in the eye. "This is an answer you will have to find. But I can say this: The Shadows of Man are corrupted creatures of Spirit. And all magic involving the Celestial, whether speaking to deities during the Age of God Wars or summoning a demon, involves Spirit. A reservoir of Spirit could empower a summoning, or end it."

"Even if… I've never… Fire, the Fire I know better."

They stared at each other until Lelishen shrugged and pointed: The living version of the Touched sat in the chair, his body merging with the skeleton. "The dead man has the right of it. Go, get some rest. Dream for the answers. We both will."

Eliles took a step but turned. "I think you should take the book with the Touched's conversation with us in it for your gift?"

Lelishen glanced to the book cradled on her lap, then glanced to the desk. "You're probably right. I will consider it."

"Thank you, for everything." Eliles turned and made a straight line to the monk. "How much did you hear?"

The man shrugged. "It all makes sense now. Your not being a priestess, the fiery demons." He took a drink and shoved the cork into his bottle before lying back down, turning his back on her. "What's it matter anymore? Nothing matters anymore."

Just her secret didn't matter anymore, the holy were taught to despise feral magic from the moment they entered Istinjoln. She stared at the back of his head a moment, then returned to Ivin's side, lying down to sleep as she slipped her hand back into his, and found freedom from dark dreams for a few candles.

FORTY

Freed from Darkness

Questions, yours bud and leaf on the branches of the tree,
No direction, no cause, no use, no care for where they grow.
Questions better are Roots in dirt,
Growing in direction with purpose to water, see.
Slip the knot and stretch the tree,
Dangle and dance with me.

—Tomes of the Touched

The world shook once or twice, and Meris awoke in abject blackness, neither a Heaven nor a Hell, nor without light could it be the Road of Living Stars. Her body ached and she couldn't move, so she drifted back to dreams before deciding whether she was alive or dead.

When she awakened to a room lit by Light, the man sitting in front of her was so impossible it convinced her she had died. Lord Priest Ulrikt smiled at her. Reality rallied in her mind, and she determined it must be his Face. Or maybe the dead Ulrikt was the Face.

"It's good to see you again, Meris. I apologize for yesterday, and the splinters that struck you instead of me, but you know how unpredictable bones can be." He raised her head and dribbled water into her mouth.

389

Her throat scratched out a few words, painful and awkward with a swollen tongue. "I saw you die."

"The Road of Living Stars is a wonder to behold, but I put my faith and my life in the hands of Sol. When the gods are unable to come to you, you must go to them for a conversation, and Sol saw fit to return my soul from the perfection of death to this flawed world."

Meris couldn't raise her head on her own, and she wondered if they'd denied her the healing arts. "How?"

"Not as I expected, I assure you. The Prophecy of the Twelfth Star—"

"The Eye of the Fire Lion." She admonished herself for not seeing it when the Face spoke to her at Skywatch. The whispers of the forbidden tomes she heard in her youth spoke of a prophet resurrected by a God Wars relic known as the Sliver of Star, and this prophet would lead the Silone people into a second era of the Panthenate, beginning the long journey to dominion over the world. "Resurrected by the Sliver of Star?"

"Surprisingly, no." He waggled his finger at her with a pleased grin on his face. "You are a bright woman, you should've served in Istinjoln instead of wasting your years in the stars. The gods saw fit to raise my flesh, but to deny me the Sliver, but it will come. Soon. And when it does, Sol's fury over the loss of this world will be unleashed upon the unfaithful. The battle has begun, and we will find victory in a fortnight."

"A war fought and lost once before."

The man's voice lost all semblance of calm, taking an edge she'd never heard from the lord priest before. "Imrok Girn was a fool who lingers still in the Hell of False Prophets." With a grin and a swipe of his hair the silk tongue returned. "My words are perhaps harsh. Imrok was impatient, filled with ambition upon seeing an opportunity.

He read the words of Sol, of the Prophecy of the Twelfth Star, of the Fire Lion, of the Dark Sword. He watched as the clans tore one another apart, how weak they'd become warring with each other even as they found peace. He saw an opening.

"The Tome of Sol promised the lord priests rule of the Silone people, but the promise stretched centuries into the future. Why wait, when the clans were ripe for holy conquest now? He learned too late to save his soul from the hells, I fear, and his mistake brewed mistrust between church and clan that cost a great many lives. How things are today are not how they are supposed to be, and much blame falls on the shoulders of the venerated Imrok Girn, I fear."

In a century of stories, preaching, and honest debates on theology and history, never had she heard Lord Priest Imrok's name bandied about with such disrespect from within the Church. It was shocking, and brought defensive bile burning to her gut. "And you, the new King Priest of the Panthenate?" The other night talking in his chambers, even now, it didn't fit. Power suited the man, but he didn't come across as obsessed with its trappings.

"May I be honest? I don't know the will of Sol, but no, I don't believe so, although some call me such. Maybe it is with flawed pride that I allow their tongues to wag with flowery titles." He bore a wistful smile. "I can't be too honest with you, but neither will I lie. The gods play games framed by time in ways we mortals find difficult to conceive. The question is, are you ready to continue playing, to serve Sol, or are you content to walk the Road of Living Stars? If the latter, I will make sure your end is swift and painless, and you are sent on your way with prayers for your journey, but if you believe you can dedicate yourself for a time yet to the will of the Pantheon, you will journey back to your stars, safe and well. Sol has one more duty for you if you are willing. You have earned this choice through your decades of faith and service."

The lord priest offered her life or death, and her heart pounded in her breast. A prominent shadow in the back of her mind clamored for the Road, but the most base of desires shared by all things living still dominated her consciousness. "I will serve Sol and his Pantheon until such time as Etinbin comes for my soul."

Ulrikt smiled and passed a hand over her eyes, and a warm shiver quivered through her flesh and bones. "When the time comes, a boy will tell you who you need to assist, and who you need to kill." Her aches faded and her fatigue disappeared, replaced by a vigor she hadn't felt for decades, if ever, but she swallowed hard on word of another murder. He held her shoulders to the bed when she tried to sit, her eyes wide.

"Your body is not as able as it feels. Rest still. Sleep."

Her next memory was of her eyes fluttering open in the light of day, muted by canvas arching over a wagon. She kept still for the first moments as wheels rattled on cobbles, then turned her head to either side. She was alone, so she propped herself on an elbow and pried open a flap, a half-inch crack to gain a glimpse of the outside world. Istinjoln's outbuildings, walls, and stable rolled past. A hunched priest lumbered across the yard, but he was too young to be arched so. A back injury? She closed the flap and lay flat, staring at the maple hoop holding the canvas above her head.

Something was wrong in Istinjoln, but decades of wisdom told her she didn't want to know the answers to what or why. Istinjoln was Ulrikt's problem, not hers. She didn't need answers, she would return to her stars and follow their guidance, serve the will of the gods as she always had. What was one more murder on an already stained soul?

Dareun sat beside Meris in her wagon as it clattered on worn pavestones toward Istinjoln's gates. He couldn't help but ponder how much this woman knew of the horrors and their cause, but the unsettled frown on her face when she rose to an elbow to look outside gave him hope that this aged soul wasn't privy to Ulrikt's plans.

With a thought, Dareun returned to the prison cell where he'd been tortured, a morbid habit he'd developed since dying. He sat in the corner, staring at the bloodstains he'd left behind. The physical pain no longer lingered in his mind, not even the terror; he was at peace with these things. The humiliation of soiling himself as the inquisitor began his torture still haunted him, and there was a mystery aching to be solved: What had they done with his body?

He'd sat in the solitude of this cell for candles considering possibilities, but they'd all proved wrong. They hadn't thrown him to the thorns, not a single funeral pyre burned, nor were there fresh graves. A multitude of dead lay in the streets and tunnels of Istinjoln, rotting without a care, and he'd checked every face he'd thought might be his own.

Where would they put him that he wouldn't think to look? His mind went around and around, but always came back to this question. Perhaps he'd phrased the question wrong all along, where did he not know to look? When the notion struck him he smiled at the irony: The oubliette, where feral children were reputedly thrown to their deaths.

Stories of this deep hole hidden in the bowels of Istinjoln persisted since the first day he'd walked through the monastery's gates. He needed to find this place, to discover his body's resting place, but he couldn't put a finger on why finding his mortal form mattered so much. Perhaps for the reason he returned to this cell at least three times every day.

The next moment he stood in the hall, his specter's eyes having no trouble seeing without light. He wandered, taking every turn he'd never taken before, and when he met a loop or dead end, he spirit-traveled and started a new trail into the unknown.

He lost track of time, a remarkably easy feat when dead. The monotony of the search would've grated on his living conscious-ness, but his soul he found to be patient beyond his expectations. He explored more than two hundred tunnels, fascinated by the nuances of their twists and turns and how they interconnected, as well as their rock formations and carvings. He became so absorbed in a statue carved high in a ceiling, a horned gargoyle swooping with bulbous eyes and razor talons, that he stood ten strides over open air before realizing he may have found his goal.

His soul hovered over a gaping hole in the cavern, perfectly round and so deep his vision faded before reaching bottom. He stared. Dareun couldn't say he was nervous, such an emotion didn't seem to exist, but he questioned his need for answers, whether knowing the answer would be worse than a mystery.

But he succumbed to curiosity and sank into the oubliette's gray featureless depths. Until there was white below. At first it was a blur, but as he grew closer the white in his ghostly eyes took on the shapes of bones, old and fleshless, and in the middle, two black and broken figures in robes.

Dareun descended to the twisted corpse lying on its back, but it was difficult to discern the face until within a few feet. The body stared at him, and he at it, until he drew close enough to recognize the eyes as his own.

Lord Priest Ulrikt had him thrown into the hole Eliles would've been cast if her feral magic had been revealed. By Ulrikt's own words, he knew the girl's powers the moment she'd arrived—Ulrikt could've been lying, of course; it could all be part of the same game. Except…

He gazed at the floor of bones, pristine white in his vision. They must've been dropped into this hole nude, as not a stitch of clothing remained, but it was the lack of flesh that triggered revelation: Three feral children had marched into Istinjoln a short time ago… where were their bodies? *Where are the bodies of the others brought to Istinjoln hooded and bound by rope this past year?* He wasn't an expert on decay, but bones shouldn't be so clean.

The skeletons were all of a size he'd expect for the young and doomed. This must be the resting place of feral children, but without recent bones… What if Eliles wasn't so unique? What if Ulrikt had spared every feral child since becoming lord priest?

The potential answer rocked his conceptions of the Church and the lord priest to the core. If such a basic teaching of the Church, the evil of feral magic and the Vanquished Gods, could be subverted without a Council of Lord Priests and its findings announced, what then was sacrosanct?

No, Ulrikt must have found another way to murder those children. There wasn't a modicum of kindness in the man's soul. But might it make sense if Ulrikt let Eliles live while knowing of her feral magic?

The questions thundered in his thoughts as he stared into his dead eyes, and it took several moments to remember the second body that lay on its side. He stepped around the feet of his body and kneeled for a view of the dead man, and if he'd still had a heart, it might've stopped.

Ulrikt.

Shards of bone still protruded from his bloodied cheeks and neck, and the words spoke in the torture cell came to him: *Dear, dear Dareun. How do you even know if the man you knew as Ulrikt was ever me at all?*

Dareun knew more now than when he was alive, but he understood nothing.

FORTY-ONE

Shadows in Istinjoln

A fleeting bird is the Dove, but a Crow, not so,
The Dove's burning wings do not bring her haste in pace,
While winds of calm lift feathers not, the Crow strives for speed not grace,
Two birds who never will meet in destiny's spiral,
these tornadic winds of pretense,
even when brought to this same venerable place.

—*Tomes of the Touched*

A skeleton garbed in red and black velvet awakened the party, but the Touched remained as he sat when they'd fallen asleep. The walking bones pointed and meandered to the exit to wait, dutiful as any servant in the halls of Istinjoln. Eliles stretched, finding Ivin's hand still in hers, and they shared a smile. Her fingers slipped free as she stood.

When he'd sat beside her last night and she'd felt the warmth of her hand in his, there was a niggling question resting pensive on her tongue. "Tell me something, and no games?"

His brows scrunched. "Of course."

"What color are my eyes? Have they changed?"

"Changed?" She'd flustered him. "Your eyes are blue, same as that night. Lighter than my own, with a dark ring."

He was right. "Nothing has changed? My hair, my nose… nothing?"

He grinned, taking her hand. "The only thing that's changed is you smile more since we met." Her face flushed and she must've donned a goofy grin, as his eyes widened, and he slouched. "I'm so sorry, I sounded like my cousin right then."

She smiled a second time, so what he said may have been true. "Your cousin must be very sweet."

She stood on her toes and kissed a man on the lips for the first time in her life, but if she'd noticed their audience she would've waited. Solineus coughed and Lelishen leaned on the man's shoulder, her lips pouting as if she'd gazed upon the world's cutest kitten.

Tokodin sauntered between them with a bloodshot glare, and she wondered if it was from opening his bottle last night. "About blessed time." He burst open a loaf of bread and handed chunks to everyone. "We've slept on it, so what's the plan?"

Eliles said, "We need to stop the mother."

"It's stopped, we have the Sliver," the monk said.

"Not good enough." Eliles hated Istinjoln, but she didn't want to leave it to the Shadows of Man.

Lelishen said, "He has a point. But if Shadows are still coming through the Celestial Gate, when do they stop?"

Eliles' stomach clenched. "We must destroy the Gate."

"Suicide," Tokodin said, "and worse, the Shadows get the Sliver."

Solineus said, "I'm with the girl."

The skeleton clattered his metacarpals, pointing, proving the dead could grow impatient.

Ivin said, "If we're able, we destroy it, if not… The plan is to destroy it. Let's go."

Eliles clutched the Sliver in her right hand, tucking it into her sleeve. It was warm to the touch, but was neither hard nor soft.

The surface flexed when she squeezed, like grasping a finger to find bone.

She followed Ivin into the hall, fearful, but there was no sign of Taken nor Shadows. She'd expected to find Taken mutilated by skeletons, but there were no signs of a fight. The skeletons parted, and they met nothing on their way out. They stepped into the haze of the Steaming Lakes, weapons bared and shields to the fore, but the demons from yesterday were nowhere in sight.

Eliles couldn't understand their good fortune and didn't want to squander it. "Keep moving, they'll be back any time."

Solineus asked, "Think they're lying in wait?"

Ivin kept his new shield in hand, eyes plying the fog for movement. "They waited for us at the Crack of Burdenis, so yeah, don't underestimate the bastards. Keep quick but quiet."

They'd traveled a few hundred strides before Rinold cursed, holding a branch in his hand. "I broke this branch marking our trail yesterday, I swear it."

Eliles asked, "What do you mean, it healed?"

"I mean it weren't ever broke." He grunted and lead them onward, snorting here and there before stopping to gawk at a patch of ground. "Priestess. Didn't you damned near take a bath here?"

She strode close; there was no mistaking the location. She'd slipped on the bank, catching the slimy root of a tree and scrambled to stay out of the lake until Ivin pulled her back, but the gashes in the mud had disappeared, the soil still covered in the green moss she'd worn on her legs. The older footprints, those of the priests who'd explored before them, were still there. "How's that possible? Are we lost, then?"

Rinold snorted and gave a stare. "I ain't never lost, it'll just take a candle longer than expected." The Squirrel wrinkled his nose in thought, appearing to savor the challenge. He stopped to stare at numerous crossroads, glancing at the sun through the haze. He'd cluck his tongue in a manner that reminded her of the chatter of his name-sake until he made a decision unerringly correct.

He stopped at a dead tree Eliles recognized as near their entrance, and turned to face them, eye twitching. "Wanna leave where we came, or a little off, in case that spot's guarded?"

They shared glances, and Ivin said, "Better safe than sorry."

Rinold nodded and swung them north along a skinny branch of soggy ground before finding a trail west, where the fog thinned and they found the bowl's icy wall. They shared smiles, even the whiny monk, and headed south with confident strides.

Voices broke the silence, and they ducked behind a fallen tree at the edge of light and fog. Eliles peeped through bare branches to see herself sliding from the heights of the bowl, Ivin joining her, and the laugh they'd shared. Solineus and Lelishen came next, then the monk tumbled into the steam before growling at Rinold for his antics. It didn't take long, and the other Eliles called her fiery friends, and yesterday's group slipped into the cover of the Steaming Lakes.

"What the Twelve Hells was that?" Tokodin asked.

Eliles' mind whirled. "It was the final gift from the Touched, the gift of a head start. We slept backward, just as he said." She grabbed Ivin's hand and ran to the slope where priests had used spikes to ascend. "Zjin!" A furry head glanced over the edge. "Throw us rope! Fast!"

"And again I ask, what was that?"

Eliles grinned. "It was our yesterday, which means the Taken aren't here yet. Don't you get it?"

"How in the hells is that possible?"

Lelishen said, "She's right, how doesn't matter." Rope slithered the ice's length, landing at their feet. "Everything we witnessed in the tomb tells us time is… unstable there. Climb."

It only took a few wicks to ascend the slope, with Colok pulling them, and they took seats on the sleds. She leaned into Ivin as they snuggled in for a long ride, but she looked to Zjin, unable to refrain her curiosity. "How long were we gone?"

The Colok's lips wrinkled above his fangs, resembling a shrug. "Moments."

She closed her eyes, the warmth of the man sitting behind her making her feel safe in a world gone angry and senseless, and the warmth of the Sliver reassuring her that at least there was hope to recover a semblance of what peace they'd lost.

She smiled, pulling Ivin's hands around her waist. It looked like they'd make it back to Istinjoln a day early.

In the two days it took to return to the mountain outpost and their stabled horses, Solineus didn't see a sign of Shadow or Taken. Every time he closed his eyes he prayed to sleep and for the woman to visit him, to help him, tell him something of importance, but she never graced his dreams with her beauty or words. He'd failed to kill Ulrikt, and as they reined to a stop in the foothills overlooking Istinjoln, he couldn't fathom how he'd be able to do so now.

The beam of light was visible even in the light of midday, and if a war still raged in the monastery, the blood flowed underground. Not a single guard walked the wall. During the journey to and from the lakes, he'd harbored a faint hope the priests had defeated the enemy and their travels would've been for naught. This fantasy dissipated, and he dismounted to stretch his legs.

Everyone stood silent, except Zjin, who growled orders to a score of his people who joined them for the final leg of their trip. Solineus rested his hands on the Twins' hilts and whispers invaded his consciousness. His eyes blinked, rapid and uncontrolled for several flickers, until the whispers slowed and weakened. He exhaled until his lungs emptied, taking control of the rhythm of his heart. *Beware the singing words of Latcu,* the Touched had warned him, but at the time he'd had no idea what the skeleton meant.

The Twins whispered songs in his head when he touched them, but he didn't understand the tales their lyrics told. He'd be as successful translating the conversation between two hissing snakes. When he pulled one from its sheath Lelishen had gasped, declaring them forged during the Age of God Wars, maybe by the hand of a god. The blades were translucent and smoky blue, like frosted topaz hammered into a perfect edge. Latcu, which Lelishen told him meant "unbreakable glass" in the Edan tongue. The eye suggested they were brittle, as if they might break with the lightest rap, but running the sword's edge along a sled's steel runner scarred the metal. What mattered now is if they'd part Shadows as the Touched claimed.

He uttered a quote that jumped into his memory, but he couldn't remember who'd first spoken the words. "'To what end have we come, to glory or damnation?'"

Lelishen grinned at him. "You're well read for a warrior and sailor, albeit a peculiar translation."

"I can't even remember reading it, let alone what it's from." He looked to Ivin and Eliles, the pair having become inseparable since first they touched one another on the sled. Not that he could say much, the Trelelunin woman made him not want to wander far, either. "We've come this far, what next?"

Eliles said, "We destroy the Shadows."

Tokodin laughed. "You've got verve, girl, but unless you can tell me how you'll defeat seven lord priests and Shadows"—he threw his bedroll to the ground and sat—"I'm right here."

The girl stepped toward the monk. "Tip your bottle like you've done every day and go on as a godsdamned coward."

"One Lash, you're brilliant." Tokodin grabbed the bottle the Touched had gifted him and popped the cork. "And a godsdamned defiled girl."

Solineus wanted to knock teeth from the monk's smug smile, even if he had no idea what defiled meant. Still, Tokodin had a point. "We traipse in there with nothing but our balls hanging out they'll cut 'em off and shove 'em down our throats." He grinned at the two women, hoping to break the tension. No luck. "Excuse the expression."

"It's true, courage alone won't win us a thing," Ivin said. "We've no idea how many Shadows or Taken are in there, but we've surprise and Colok on our side."

Tokodin wiped his mouth. "The bigger trouble is what the hells the defiled girl will do with her Sliver. What prayers you got for a piece of star?"

"I don't have any prayers."

"Right, right. And still you rush in. The gods didn't favor you with prayer nor wisdom—did a fine bit with your ass, I admit."

Solineus stepped between the trio. "Forget the godsdamned monk—"

"Yeah, forget me, I'll be drunk over here."

"Best seal your lips around that bottle before I gut you." Solineus glared as Tokodin tipped the bottle, nursing it like a babe at the teat.

The Touched wasn't kidding, the liquor in that bottle was potent and fast, bringing out the worst in the man. The monk was worthless sober or drunk. Solineus turned back to Eliles. "I don't mind dying so long as I have a chance to live, so the biggest question is do you think you can do it?"

The girl squirmed. "I can do something, I just don't know what."

Solineus eyed the priestess and the Choerkin then cast a glance to Zjin. The girl and her holy artifact were the wild cards, but the Colok were the down cards, and necessary for the win. "I'm in if you give the word. But we all need be in, except the bleating monk, and you, Lelishen."

The Trelelunin smiled. "I'm with you, the Shadows of Man can't hurt me; all I need worry about are Taken."

"Ivin, Eliles, Zjin. The decision lies with you three."

Zjin growled a single word. "Fight." The rumbles from his tribe reinforced their willingness to do battle.

Solineus clasped his hands, gazing to the young girl whose decision might determine the fate of a people, doom or salvation. He felt for her, no one should bear such a burden, let alone someone so young.

"We need to try," she said, "but if it proves impossible, we can't hesitate, we need to get out."

Ivin wrapped his arms around her. "You're certain?"

The girl's eyes were blued steel. "We won't want to fight Shadows in the dark, and we won't get any stronger waiting."

Ivin asked, "What about the monk?"

Tokodin's mouth gaped, his eyes cracked so Solineus wasn't sure if the man was awake or not. "He can watch the horses, or we can tie him to one, makes no difference to me."

❄ ❄ ❄

Ivin ordered the horses tied off in a copse of trees several hundred strides north of Istinjoln with Tokodin the stumbling herdsman. He took the job without a single complaint until they confiscated his bottle. Ivin stuck that in his pack, happy to take on the extra weight to make sure the monk stayed conscious while tending their animals. A young Colok stayed behind to watch the man.

There was no way to hide on their path to the monastery, no cover closer than a thousand strides. Every plant or stone capable of concealing a spy or an attacker had been removed over the centuries. On the other hand, there weren't any guards on the wall, either, and the gatehouse stood wide open. The new rulers of Istinjoln were cocksure or setting a trap, and Ivin prayed for the former.

With open ground in front of them they trotted as quick as they could without winding themselves until they pressed against the outer wall, resting. No alarms rang in the air, no screams of Shadows or Taken. Ivin peered over the rim of his black shield as they skulked around towers until reaching the gatehouse. They peeked around the edge of the wall, to see a Taken walk beneath the open rear portcullis, its dull gaze on the ground as it strolled their way.

Ivin waited, listening for the scrape of the woman's dragging toes on the ground. He spun, sword slicing flat through the air and the only sounds the Taken made were the thuds of head and body hitting the ground. Nothing raised an alarm as they made their way beneath murder holes.

What plan they had was flexible, depending on what they saw, and everything so far showed the bulk of the demons and possessed had spread into the countryside, or marched on the Fost in their Holy War. The courtyard tantalized with its emptiness.

He glanced back at the corpse, slender tendrils creeping from its flesh. A dash to the stables, or to any building, might run them straight into the enemy; at least on open ground they'd see the attack coming, and the longer they waited the more likely they'd be caught flat-footed. He waved his sword. "Straight on, all the way to the tower, if we're able."

The Colok fanned out around them as they ran until they cleared the bailey and turned through labyrinthine streets. The quiet broken only by the fall of their feet unnerved him, there should be enemies, something to fight. Ivin's heart pounded in his chest by the time they reached the inner courtyard.

The beam pulsed and a Shadow fell from the dark crease in the air, squirming and writhing on the pavestones, and the Colok bustled past the humans. The Shadow rose to quivering hands and knees, shrieking without a mouth as the Colok descended, shredding its gauzy darkness with their hands.

Ivin slid to a stop the moment he realized Eliles wasn't beside him and turned. She stood with the Sliver of Star in her hands and it pulsed with a silver radiance. He counted four Taken standing in the streets surrounding the courtyard, blocking their escape.

Humans and Colok gathered around the young girl, making a circle. Taken, once monks, priests, and common folk, arrived to stare at them.

A voice echoed across the courtyard, powerful and stern. "The bones told me you might one day hold the Star, but they didn't tell me you'd deliver it straight to me." The doors to the Tower of Sol creaked open, and the Broldun lord priest stepped outside, but the voice came from elsewhere. "Unfortunate you brought these souls with you to die."

Ivin looked into Eliles' wide, bloodshot eyes and felt her fear as she spoke. "Ulrikt, do you see him?"

Ivin's eyes scanned the tower and rooftops, but all he saw were a growing number of Taken. "No."

"I've killed you all."

"Not here, not today. Do what we came for, destroy it."

The Sliver pulsed blinding silver as she raised her arms, a mercury shower cast before their eyes and lit by a blazing sun, and when he could see again the Taken were charging them. Ivin stepped between Zjin and Solineus with his shield couched.

A Taken leaped through the air, a man in priest's robes with a broken face and an eye hanging from its socket, and crashed into his shield. He braced and slid with the force of its weight, then pushed back, spinning to cleave into the thing's sternum, and it crumpled to the ground.

Colok roars deafened him as they battered, crushed, and rent all comers. Solineus pressed into the melée, his swords cleaving flesh and bone. His footwork and the graceful arcs of his blades proved the man was a natural predator.

Ivin drove his shield into a Taken clawing at Zjin's side and slashed another. Bodies lay scattered around them, worms of Shadow squirming from their gore, but more came. Fingers scratched across his face but Zjin took the Taken's head in his massive hands and crushed its skull before Ivin could bring his sword to bear.

They might kill every Taken in Istinjoln to die at the hands of Shadows, except for a young girl with the weight of their lives on her shoulders.

Eliles stood as an island in the maelstrom, unmolested by the terror around her. The sounds of battle and dying washed over her, but her eyes focused on the Sliver of Star. Power rushed through her core, a vibrance that made her question whether she might indeed be a god. It overwhelmed every sense of her being until the sounds of battle disappeared, until her vision was pure silver, and every nerve of her being felt exultation, the essence of pure Spirit and Life. She wanted to run, to fly, to burn the world to cinder.

Hints of oranges and yellows and reds and blues tinted the silver of her universe and she exulted in the rise of fire, in its ability to turn things living to dust. The mercury in her eyes turned to magma, flowing and spouting energy, and her fiery friends gloried in its blaze, dancing in its surging waves. She could kill on a whim. Ravage the island, reduce the forests to ash and rid the world of Shadow and Taken, including her people and friends.

"We are children of Fire, you and me," Ulrikt's voice said from within her head, soft but drowning out the clamor of battle, as if her ears were going deaf but the senses of her mind growing stronger. "Children of Fire, but there is no need to burn the world. We may yet have peace, all these people yet may live, and you and I could speak to Sol through the Eye of the Fire Lion, unleash his wisdom to enlighten the world of unbelievers."

The gentle words caressed her emotions, and her vision of the world around her slowed. Her valiant allies slaughtered Taken, but Shadows would rise and evil never relent. This was the end for all those she cared for.

Ulrikt's voice purred. "Even those taken by Shadow are not beyond saving. Sol will return every last soul. You can save them by obeying his will."

She screamed, torn by raging desires. Succumb to the hope of surrender or embrace the rage of a child spurned, to destroy herself and everyone around her so she'd never feel pain again. Tears came to her swollen eyes and her throat ripped raw with flagging breath, and she knew she couldn't hold the power in stasis much longer, she either needed to unleash its fury or set it free.

Dareun appeared before her blurred by tears, a ghost lit by the fiery hues surrounding him. He looked into her eyes and shook his head, and she knew that neither was the way. The mercury and its Spirit was what she needed, not magma nor the nothing of surrender. If she destroyed the island in a wave of Fire, this light with its core of blackness would remain, the Shadows would return, and still she and her friends would be dead. The heat pulsing through her veins and the flames becoming her world were pure destruction.

Did she *find destruction an end, or prefer defeat in creation of the destroying fire defeating?* The words of the Touched came to her and she froze.

Here, now, the destroying fire was defeating, she'd win a battle while losing a war. What she needed wasn't victory or defeat, it was escape. She felt the Fire beckoning, and the creatures demanded destruction. She needed to give it to them.

What she wrought she must unleash, and pray she kept them under control.

She willed the flames and energies into an incendiary wall around her friends. Taken disintegrated in the blaze of her creation, but she couldn't hold the *te-xe* in place without risking her friends. She exhaled a single word, "Incinerate." The encircling wall of flame blazed into living sparks, with every crackling flicker bent on killing her enemy. The rapture of the Sliver's power faded, returning her to reality with a rush of loss that drove her to hands and knees. She gasped for breath, chest heaving and drool draining from her lips.

She raised her eyes to her Master, her vision of his soul fading with the release of the Sliver's power, but as he disappeared he smiled.

When Solineus drew the Twins together for the first time, a rush of whispers and power blurred his vision and a tingling thrill to battle prickled every nerve of his being. The mutter of foreign tongues and the blur of charging shapes shunted every thought from his mind while driving feverish instinct into his muscles and bones. It was the heat of the sun, the tranquility of a spring loaded, potential energy until his eyes cleared and the enemy was on them.

The timbre of his heart beat a rhythm to the songs of swords as he stepped into the dead-eyed Taken who drove and leaped at him. The blades met flesh and bone, severing the creature from shoulder to pelvis with the resistance of scything a stand of corn. Pitch blood painted him from chest to thighs, but the Latcu blades shook free of the splatter, pristine clean in a sweep to sever another's leg, then a head.

The Colok roared around him and he wanted to match their raging screams, but the focus the Twins forced on him kept his lungs breathing steady and eyes clear. The whispering song changed and he ducked, spinning, a Twin twisting to send its blade through a Taken flying from behind, thrown by a Colok. Gore washed over his clothes, seeping down the neck of his cloak, but there was no sense of decorum now, no pandering to gentility and kindness, his focus was survival and butchery.

A Colok bellowed in agony and Solineus spun, watching as an ally fell dead with spikes of ice driven through his body. The Broldun lord priest strode toward the fray, ice sweeping from the sky to kill another Colok. The songs in Solineus' head melded and swept into a different tune and he stalked toward the fat man whose eyes seeped snakes of Shadow. He slipped into a sprint, slashing three Taken from his path as he ran. If he couldn't kill one lord priest, another would suffice.

Frigid cold besieged him, his lips and face frosting, the air so cold his lungs seized, but another energy surged through him, thawing his breath. An unintelligible scream ripped from his throat as he charged the Broldun.

The Twins deflected spears of ice, the world took on a fiery orange hue, and sweat beaded on his forehead. The Twins rose and slashed at the priest with his hands raised in prayer, severing them at the elbows. Black blood, bone, and flesh hit the ground, but tendrils of Shadow slithered from blackened flesh, reaching for Solineus' neck.

The Twins followed through, sweeping the man's head from his shoulders, and the body collapsed, but unlike Taken before him, this Shadow stood unfazed, and bitter cold struck a second time. The Twins crossed in front of him, parting streaks in the Shadow that glowed orange with the light of the world on fire. The Shadow froze and moments later dissipated into nothingness, a death so quiet it angered Solineus further.

The whispers warned him and he twisted, blades striking through a Taken, but two more crashed into him, driving him to the ground. They clawed and bit, defeated by his mail, and he smashed one's head with a hilt, but another came for him. He thrust the tip of a Twin through an eye and rolled to the Broldun's headless corpse and spun the man's body onto him.

Taken feasted on the Broldun's flesh but missed his own, and he lashed out with the Twins, severing an ankle and an arm before blazing sparks raged into their bodies.

Eliles's voice penetrated the din of battle. "Run!"

Solineus rolled from beneath the lord priest's body and scrambled to his feet as the world returned to its natural color. Tiny fires streaked the air, striking the enemy, burrowing into flesh and Shadow. Smoke rolled from the mouths and ears of the Taken, some fighting, others collapsing into heaps of smoldering meat.

He trotted after the group as they ran. Ivin limped, but everyone but Eliles was so covered in blood he had no idea of injuries. They'd lost three Colok, but were otherwise intact. When the party entered the gatehouse, Solineus stopped at the edge of the bailey, darts of fire lighting the sky. The stables were on fire, everything that could burn smoldered and smoked, but his job remained incomplete.

He turned to the tower, arms outstretched with the Twins in his hands. "Ulrikt! Come to me, you coward! Face me!" He waited, chest heaving, the whispers in his head singing a furious tune. "Ulrikt!" A hand grabbed his shoulder, and he spun nose-to-nose with Ivin.

"Don't be a fool, let's get out of here."

Solineus seethed, licked his blood-caked lips, and nodded. He followed the other man through the gatehouse, knowing he'd failed and worrying after two young girls.

Fires still danced in the smoke over Istinjoln as they untethered their horses. Ivin looked to Solineus. Blood and filth covered the man, and his lips quivered, his legs and arms vibrating with nervous energy. "You're the craziest son of a bitch I ever met. Are you hurt?"

The man's eyes flashed to him, and Ivin thought maybe a madness took him, but his voice was calm. "Bites and scratches, nothing worse than your own face, I reckon."

Ivin wiped his cheek and gazed at the red of his own blood amid the black of the Taken. "Damned near forgot about that."

"And your leg."

A limp. His right calf bore a gash, but nothing a poultice couldn't handle. "I'm good enough."

Lelishen kneeled, taking a look at his leg. She poured water from her canteen on the wound and wrapped it in clean cloth. "Good enough to ride, I'd say."

Ivin took Eliles' hand. "We tried."

"And I failed. I should've known… but I didn't."

"The mother won't get through so long as we hold the Sliver, we haven't lost, not yet." His words felt flat even if true. "We should ride for the Fost, then get the Sliver to Herald's Watch, safest place I can think of."

Ivin swung into the saddle, but Tokodin stood with his back to them, staring at fires licking the heights of Istinjoln's towers. "Monk, you with us?"

The man turned, a solemn look of loss and tears in his eyes. He didn't answer, but walked to his horse and mounted. Ivin grabbed the man's bottle and handed it to him, receiving a nod and grin for thanks.

"We'll make for Ervinhin first, see if we can find fresh horses. Either way, we make straight for Purdonis Bay afterward. Zjin?"

The Colok stared, his face unreadable. "Home."

Ivin nodded. "We can never repay your people for their blood and kindness. One day I hope to fight by your side again. Thank your father for me."

"Choerkin. Live." Zjin roared to his people, and they trotted north, disappearing into an icy ravine.

They pressed their horses into an ambling gait as the sun drifted toward the western horizon and the glow of Istinjoln lit their back. The walls would remain and the towers rise high, but at least maybe the fire earned them a head start.

A glow rose in the heart of Istinjoln and Tokodin leaped onto a boulder for a better view. Fires sprang into the sky and raged a circle around the Tower of Sol, and he knew he would never see his precious bottle of liquor again. The fools would get the fools' end they asked for, he figured, but the bottle didn't deserve to be broke, the liquid jewel within seeping into the cobbled streets. Perhaps, boiled away by the defiled bitch's feral magic.

The flames circled, licking the sky, power beyond his imagination. Maybe they'd succeed, destroy the Shadows and Taken, shut the gate on the mother.

I'm a coward, I should be there for the victory.

He loathed himself, until the flames of victory faded, and the shaft in the sky remained. Istinjoln burned, but it wasn't enough.

Now they're all dead, and I'm the wise one… the living one, the coward. He turned to the Colok left to watch the horses with him. "We should go, they're dead."

But the beast ignored him, and against all odds, he was proven not just a coward, but a dumb one, as the party returned. Gore clung to their cloaks and armor and fur, remains of people he'd once known. But his bottle survived with them, so he forgave their living for a time.

They rode west for Ervinhin and he had little choice but to follow, but he didn't have to stay sober. He waited a candle into the ride, long enough for folks to forget him again, then eased the cork from his bottle and took a swig. Familiar notes of sweet cloves and raspberry kissed his palate, and he swirled it full around his tongue before swallowing. The alcohol burn warmed him all the way to his belly. It wasn't the warmth of prayer; it was better. No gods necessary, Pantheon of Sol, nor Vanquished. This warmth didn't tell him what to do, how to live, what to believe… but the Touched had been right, he needed to watch his tongue when drinking the stuff. Throwing down a finger of the liquor could loosen the tongue and make him say the damnedest things.

Not that the defiled girl didn't deserve a terse word or three. How the hells did a defiled girl hide in the monastery, right beneath the lord priest's nose? Make her way through the ranks, celebrated by the priesthood, taking only a single blow from the Maimer's Lash while Tokodin struggled, enduring scar after scar until admitting defeat. He remembered the day perfectly, fifteen and wailing like a child, like the day his father took a switch to his face instead of his ass.

At least he made sure I closed my eyes.

Tokodin shut his eyes tight, clinging to his saddle horn as he wobbled, trying to drive the memories of whip and willow from his mind, but they wouldn't leave until clove and raspberry washed his tongue and put a fever into his gut. He eased the bottle back into its place of honor in his saddle bag and stared at the girl's back.

It was unfair. One Lash. A defiled. He spit and rocked in the saddle, damned grateful it was cinched tight or he might've been taking a nap on cold stone. Or better, just be dead. That wouldn't be so bad, or it might be, who knew what hells he had coming? He grinned a stupid grin, but he couldn't help himself.

The girl. Yeah, her. The pretty one, she didn't deserve the accolades, and now there she was tight as a noose with a Choerkin, those sons of bitches. Probably taking his pokes every godsdamned night too, if not yet, godsdamned soon. *Unholy bitch and the son of a son-of-a-bitchin' Choerkin.* "Ha! It makes perfect sense!" And he laughed before he realized he spoke out loud. He decided he'd either drunk too much or not enough.

Every last one of the bastards turned to stare at him, but not the girl, she didn't deign to look at his scarred face. His laughter stopped and he reached for the bottle, another sip, a tiny sip. "What the hells you sonsabitches looking at? Eh? Damn your eyes."

He made certain the bottle was safe in its home, but he couldn't remember if he'd taken another drink as he leaned over the horse's mane, face resting in the coarse damp hairs, the musky smell of animal and hay and sweat filling his nose.

"For the love of Januel, monk! Wake up!" He tried to raise his head, to give whoever the hells spoke to him a piece of his mind, but instead he sagged, arms draping over the horse's neck.

FORTY-TWO

Reunions and Departures

I miss the smell of the fallen sky,
The rain, the vision of bows without arrows,
A world cleansed without sterility of fire.
Trapped in a hole worms can not conquer
The smell of marble and granite, fresh carved forever,
the only thunder the sealing of fate each day
Serving to weary my Bones.

—Tomes of the Touched

Ervinhin was a ghost town by the time they arrived, but the lack of blood gave them hope that everyone had fled before evil arrived. They washed and grabbed fresh gear not caked in blood before barricading themselves in a room to sleep for the night.

When morning came, they struck south cross-country instead of sticking to the roads, hoping to avoid the enemy and speed their trip. They warned one group of hunters they came upon to head for the sea. Later they found bodies and blood in a small village; prints leading south included children. Ivin swallowed hard, it was hard to drag his eyes from the horror, and he breathed easier when Rinold veered the party east.

The second night out from Istinjoln the shrill screams of Shadows echoed over the hills, and they eschewed fire. In the morning they rode hard, hoping they might make it to Merutven before the enemy, but smoke billowing from the small fort the next evening spoke of a last-ditch defense instead of fresh animals.

Ivin ran his fingers through his mount's mane, fighting tangles while rubbing its neck. "We're less than a day's ride from the Fost; we can be there by morning if the horses hold up."

Solineus said, "And we don't fall out of the saddle asleep."

"It might be our only chance to reach the Fost before them." Determination marked all their faces, except Tokodin, who sat in his usual state of melancholy, silent and staring at his hands. When he spoke, it was to piss and moan, but Ivin asked anyhow. "What say you, monk?"

"The high and mighty bothers with my opinion?" His chin slumped to his chest. "We'll be rotting in one hell or another come soon."

Ivin shook his head, disgusted. "We might make for a village along the coast, but there's no guarantee there'd be boats to take us to the Watch."

"A Luxun caravel is anchored at the Fost waiting for me," Lelishen said.

Ivin pursed his lips and squinted. "Luxuns or no, there'll be ships and boats in harbor. How wealthy are you?"

"The Luxuns say, a favor owed is a favor paid. The Captain owes me." Her smile was innocence

"We press on to the Fost, then." He looked to the monk. "You're welcome to stay here if you want to find which hell you're headed for sooner than later."

"You let us know which hell soon as you get there." Rinold slapped the monk on the shoulder as he rode by, taking the lead.

They nudged their horses into a walk and the disgruntled monk fell in behind, so far back that in the darkest point of the night Ivin knew the man was there only by the clop of hooves on turf.

The Squirrel's navigation turned out flawed after so many candles in the saddle without sleep. Sunrise found them on the shore of Purdonis Bay, but the Fost was candles to the west. Exhausted horses and riders found the road, and about the time Ivin thought he might learn to sleep in the saddle the castle walls appeared on the horizon. Too tired for fear, they approached the wharf-side gates to find them guarded by living men.

"Hail! I'm Ivin Choerkin, ridden here from Istinjoln."

A watchman cried out, the portcullis lifted, and the inner oaken gates swung open. Ivin pulled his sagging eyes open with a hand running through his hair as guards approached on their entry. "I need to see my uncle, Lord Lovar."

The men stared as the portcullis ground closed behind them, and the lead man with horsetail trailing from his helm cleared his throat. "Lord Lovar Choerkin was murdered, on the Eve of Snows, he and his kin. Knives in the night, taking the blood of his lordship and his children, except... Lord Eredin sits as head of the Clan now."

Ivin sat numb, awake but wishing this a nightmare. "What of Herald's Watch?"

"No ill word, not as I've heard. The Fost has been sailing to the Watch since Pikarn brought word from Ervinhin, so I'd guess we'd have word by now."

Ivin nodded, thankful for a kindness on a bitter day. "We'll need to speak to Eredin ."

"He's been in the main keep for days, best I know."

Lelishen dismounted. "I'll check on the Luxun captain, if you don't mind."

Ivin nodded to the woman, too tired to care. "Rinold, give this lady escort; we'll meet you onboard as soon as we're able."

The Squirrel looked at him with sullen, bloodshot eyes. "Lovar's passing—"

"Is a loss we'll need overcome, like the others." Ivin tapped his horse's flank into a walk, his legs aching and fatigued. They avoided the docks by riding the edge of the city wall. Pensive guards stood their watches along the allure in numbers Ivin had never seen before, brave men ready to fight and die against an enemy they didn't know or understand. He wondered how brave they'd be if they fathomed the threat heading their way.

Every man here should be on a ship, standing in the water, swimming for the Watch if they knew how to paddle. They'd die in the frozen currents, but it was a fate better than what fighting held.

No. Ivin slapped his face, the tingle in his cheek revitalizing his mind as they rode into the Fost's castle. *An enemy we can kill is one we will defeat; find a way.* He may not survive to see the day Kaludor was free of demons, but his people would live. Hopelessness and fatalism were for lesser peoples, not the Silone Clans.

Ivin dismounted in front of the Keep and his eyes swung to catch a glimpse of Solineus, wide-eyed, pale, staring as if looking through the world instead of at it. He'd seen the man wade into demonic enemies without hesitation, but for the first time Ivin swore he saw fear.

"I'm coming," he whispered. Solineus shifted his weight and cleared his throat. "I need a fresh horse."

The man was strange, no doubt, but they'd need his swords and skill if the enemy reached them. "What the hells are you talking about?"

"There's a family of fishers, maybe six leagues down the coast… the Taken have reached them."

"If Shadows and Taken have pushed so far south, we need you here, Shadows could climb the walls—"

"I don't have time to explain!" The man didn't like his own tone, clenching his fists and speaking with more control. "I swore an oath to two girls. Get me a fresh horse or I'll ride this one 'til it's dead."

Ivin locked eyes with the man. He owed Solineus his life and more, and as a man of Emudar, Solineus didn't owe Ivin fealty. Ivin broke the gaze and pinned his glare on a guard. "Take this man to the stables and get him a fresh steed."

"Thank you."

"It damned well better be worth it. Stay alive." Nothing else mattered.

The man grinned. "I'll see you on the Watch."

Ivin turned to Eliles and Tokodin. He couldn't get lucky enough for the damned monk to leave. He took Eliles' hand as he led her through the great doors and walked a straight line to Choerkin Hall. Ivin expected warriors and sailors bickering over strategies and supplies, what he found was silence and a man alone.

Eredin sat at the head of a table seated for forty, the room aglow from the great fireplace and lanterns hung high. Behind his cousin hung the Crystal Sword, a weapon deemed fragile decor, but Ivin knew now its ability to slay Shadows. For five-hundred years the Choerkins had dusted the *zweihänder* and handled it as glass, afraid to break it, when it was a finer weapon than any might've dreamed.

Dirty prints covered the marble floors, attesting to busier times, but this afternoon their footfalls echoed lonesome in a hall built for hundreds. Ivin's cousin looked up without a hint of surprise or emotion, his mouth drooping.

"The Wolverine said you rode north, our only hope if he's to be believed."

"The demons are close; Merutven was ablaze last night. We need sail for the Watch."

Eredin's mouth opened to speak, but his lips morphed into a forced smile, and he waggled his finger. "You know… you know why I'm alive? On the Eve of Snows I got so godsdamned drunk the knives didn't find me passed out behind a sack of potatoes. Funny, you know, since everyone always said drink would be the death of me."

Ivin strode until eye-to-eye with his cousin. "We can share pity and tears on Herald's Watch."

Eredin thrust a sealed scroll in Ivin's face. "This will travel in my stead; take it to your father for me."

Ivin glanced at it, but didn't lay a hand on the document. "Kotin needs his kin, and the head of the clan. Doom faces the Fost and the whole of Kaludor."

"This will solve half that problem. If indeed we are doomed, the clan doesn't need a drunken boy for its leader; Kotin will lead the Choerkin."

"You are Lovar's heir—"

"Tregin is Lovar's heir! And he's dead, with my sisters between us gone, too, their flesh ashes in the sky to fall with the next snow. I will die seeing my enemy, if die I must, to ease the shame of living. More than my family got, their throats slit in the night."

"We will find a way to destroy the Shadows, live to see revenge."

Eliles touched Ivin's shoulder, fingers kneading. "Every warrior you keep here will die beside you, one may even kill you, taken by Shadow."

"I've not grown mad." Eredin leaned on the table, tossed the scroll to Eliles. "I accepted one hundred volunteers to be the last to leave, or to die guarding the docks until the last leave. I command no one but myself to stay and die."

Ivin's mouth opened but horns blew from the towers and robbed him of words. The bugle call meant an enemy at the gates. Ivin walked to the Crystal Sword and took it from the wall. "If you promise to take the last ship leaving the docks, you may use this for your battle."

His cousin laughed, and Ivin slashed the sword through the air, cleaving an eating knife on the oak table, the sword's blade sinking several inches into the wood. "Make sure this reaches the Watch; any weapon which kills Shadow is vital to the clan's survival. That responsibility is yours, by my command as Kotin's proxy."

Ivin didn't wait for an answer, he strode from the hall with Eliles close behind, and Tokodin trailing.

"You think he'll deliver the sword?" Eliles asked.

"He'll try. We need to get to a ship, get the Sliver to the Watch." The wailing horns continued as they reached the bailey, and when Ivin swung into the saddle of his horse, a scream came from the wall. A Shadow stood on the allure with its arms sunk into a guard, another warrior sweeping his axe through the thing's vaporous form, a futile blow.

They rode hard into panic-filled streets, the city's people clamoring to reach the docks. The blue Luxun banner with its array of moons drew Ivin's eye as they approached the docks and he forced his horse through the throngs of people. The deck of the Luxun caravel with its three masts bore the weight of hundreds, and Ivin didn't know how many more its decks would hold. Sailors had loosed the ship's ropes by the time they reached the dock, and the gangplank was nowhere to be found.

Terrorized voices roared in his ears, and to the west he saw a Shadow greater than a Colok, its massive arms grasping and crushing the people in its path. It didn't take bodies, it killed, and from behind this horror Taken leaped into the crowd.

"Jump!"

Eliles stared at him, frozen. He looked to the ship, its blue-skinned crew darting through the crowd, but Lelishen stood with her arms out.

Ivin kissed Eliles. "Jump."

The ship edged from the dock and she leaped, landing safe in Lelishen's arms. "Now you, Monk."

Tokodin shook his head. "Leave me to die with your cousin."

"I gave you the option to die once, not this time." Ivin grabbed the man and slung him on the count of three. The monk screamed but jumped, clinging to the rail and the Trelelunin's arm until he found his footing on deck.

A hundred or more people were swimming, or drowning, in the icy waters, unable to make the jump to fleeing vessels, or pushed from the crowded docks and decks. The giant Shadow loomed, and Taken ripped through the crowds, screeching shrill with every kill. Instinct wanted to fight, to kill, to protect these people, but instead he leaped into Eliles' arms, panting, terrified, relieved... sickened by his own relief.

The ship eased further from the dock, people careening through the air as they jumped, arms extended in desperate hope for a helping hand. Several folks made the jump at first, and Ivin leaned as far as he could while trying to catch one woman's hand, but his grip failed: she clunked into the side of the boat and dropped into the bay with a horrifying splash. Safe from the Shadows, but caught by the desperate hands of a drowning man, she sank into the waves, and Ivin could only stare.

The Shadow arrived on the end of a dock and raised its arms, a chant emanating from an invisible mouth, and the waters of the bay crackled into ice stretching from the pier, spreading toward their ship. Taken feared water, but leaped to the ice to give chase.

Ivin nudged Eliles, and she rose from tending a boy's broken leg. Flames swarmed the Shadow, disappearing in and out of its substance, but the Shadow didn't flee nor dissipate, it ignored the assault and ice crept closer to the stern.

"I come for you. I come. Always and forever." The voice reverberated through air with an unnatural temblor of power that rippled the waters.

Eliles trembled in Ivin's grasp, and said, "Ulrikt."

The ship's sails drew taut and snapped in the wind and the caravel separated from the encroaching ice.

Ivin's breaths came easier, and he hugged Eliles tight, kissed her hair. "Eliles!"

A man in monk's habit and bearing a broad smile worked his way through the crowd until he and Eliles wrapped in a hug. Ivin stared, the man wasn't a bad-looking fellow, and his familiarity with Eliles and a pang jealousy made him forget the pain all around him for a flicker.

"Jinbin, gods be kind, good to see you."

"You, too. I've seen so few faces from Istinjoln."

The hug tightened and Ivin coughed.

Eliles turned and took Ivin's hand, letting go of the monk. "Ivin Choerkin, this is Jinbin of Gules, a friend of mine from Istinjoln."

Ivin clasped forearms with the man, shamed over his interrupting the reunion. "Well met, Jinbin."

"Likewise." Jinbin glanced at Eliles. "Hand-in-hand with a Choerkin? Only One Lash." And he chuckled.

Lelishen interrupted. "Ivin, I'd like to introduce you to Captain Intœño."

Ivin nodded and drew Eliles in for a brief kiss. "I'll be back in a moment."

Lelishen guided him through the masses and they climbed the steps to the quarterdeck, a place onboard reserved for the Luxun command. It was a relief to find elbow space.

The captain stood with his first mate at the helm, his hands tucked behind his back. The captain's skin was the color of turquoise and his head was covered in long black feathers highlighted by streaks of blues and purples and greens in the sun. If Ivin didn't know better, he'd call it a fanciful headdress.

"You are the Choerkin." His voice was higher in pitch than Ivin was used to, but his Silone was easy to understand.

Ivin towered over the man by a foot and only came eye-to-eye when he bowed. "On behalf of the Clan Choerkin I thank you for use of your vessel."

The man's feather-hair fluffed and relaxed to lay on his head and down his neck again. "A small service to repay a debt, but I may ask a favor someday."

Ivin smiled. "Anything within my power."

The captain bobbed his head, green eyes capturing Ivin's attention until he felt uncomfortable, as if he were staring at this exotic man. "Do me the favor of knowledge. What is this enemy we faced on the docks of your Fost?"

Ivin inhaled deep, rocked on his heels, and began the story of the Shadows and Istinjoln, but in between breaths he couldn't help but glance to the main deck. Eliles and Jinbin still spoke, sharing sad faces over their words. Amid Ivin's tale of sorrow and horror and blood, he couldn't help but wish he stood by her side, consoling her losses instead of sharing his own woes with a stranger.

FORTY-THREE

Castles and Pearls

A child's mind, a child's heart,
sweet, sweetly, swine,
Wine-glazed pork to feed our souls the
Innocence of their odious self-centered nature
And the endearing evil of its perpetuation.
Show the child their bloody hand,
Not today's, tomorrow's.
Innocence destroyed is truth perpetuated.

—Tomes of the Touched

The Migu Tortoise looked Kinesee in the eye, but the peak of its mottled green-brown shell swelled three feet above her head.

"Shoo! Get! Go away you stupid turtle!"

She waved her hands in the creature's face with her only ally, a small but determined black goat. The fight would go poorly if it came to it. But old Fank, marked by teeth scars in the crown of her shell, wasn't out to pick a fight with anyone. Every year she came ashore before winter in search of a spot of sand to lay her eggs before swimming south. While she'd make enough stew to last a season, they let her go about her business so long as she stayed on the beach and didn't head for the family's garden.

The giant beast headed straight for the sand palace Kinesee'd been working on since morning chores, no small feat keeping it intact, considering a prancing goat, and adults with more important tasks to attend. "Alu! Help me!" She poked the turtle between its fist-swallowing nostrils, and Tengkur clunked its shell with her horns. The beast stopped, cocking its head with a cranky grin.

She retreated far as possible without stomping on her castle, preparing to leap on the creature's neck or back, or something, and whoop on it until it surrendered.

Alu sauntered into view carrying a stick. "What and by gollies are you doing?"

Kinesee struck a menacing pose, coiled her legs for a running start. "Saving my palace!" Alu shoved her and she tumbled in the sand, snarling at her older sister. "What's that for?"

Alu ignored her, strode to the tortoise and poked it in a nostril with the same stick Solineus used to save Kinesee from the rapers. Fank snorted, her head raising high, but not high enough to avoid a second poke in the fleshy soft of its throat. "You go on now, no tromping on the kingdom today." Fank pivoted, shying from the branch, and with another jab to its nostril, the animal's path spared the sandy walls and towers.

Alu eyed Kinesee, the crinkle in her eye similar to Papa's when she'd been acting a fool. "You were really going to jump on that thing, weren't you?"

Kinesee trenched sand with her toe, sheepish, but never answered. Screams came from over the dune, from home.

Kinesee's feet drove her homeward, but she lurched as Alu collared her. Their father's words echoed in her mind. *Young girls don't run to danger, they hide.* But where? The beach lay wide open, trees a hundred strides away.

"Come on." Alu dragged her, putting Fank between them and the noise. Another scream, cut short. Odet, she thought, but no time to consider before more screams.

Kinesee eyed the strait, no boats in sight. The fishers weren't due to return for candles, leaving Regir and old Dom the only men to help the women defend the home.

"Whata we do? Alu, whata we do?"

"We hide, we run. First chance we get make for your pearl hole. We'll come back after the raiders leave."

Kinesee nodded, peeked around the turtle as shrill cries grew louder. Odet sprinted toward the beach, her dress bloodied and shredded. An animal ran on all fours, coming for her from behind, but it was no animal. A man, his tongue flapping as it lolled from his mouth, and from here she'd swear his eyes were hollow.

The man-thing leaped onto the woman's back, ramming bloodied fingers into her throat and ripped so hard Odet's head flew from her shoulders, rolling into the lapping waves of the surf.

Both girls crouched with backs pressed to Fank, praying. Alu clamped a hand over Kinesee's mouth.

Kinesee's lungs surged, her thoughts whirling, shrieking for her to run but her legs were numb with terror. Uncle Dom wailed in pain, worse than when he'd lost a finger gutting fish. Her hands shook as she peeked around Fank.

The monster who murdered Odet paced the beach, staring at the head rolling in the surf, as waves came in and withdrew. The creature danced with the water, following it out, retreating as the waves came in, until it snagged soaked hair. Prize in hand it retreated inland to feed.

"They're afraid of the water."

"Shhhh. Maybe, and what, freeze to death while it stares at us? Waiting for Papa?" She held Kinesee tight. "We follow this tortoise inland, moment that thing's gone, we head for the pearls, hear? We run and don't look back."

Kinesee nodded, but she wanted to run now. Tengkur made a noise and they froze, but the feeding thing paid the goat no mind. She snagged the goat's horns and dragged her close to hug Tengkur tight.

The screams stopped, not a sound except the sand shifting beneath the tortoise and the surf washing the shore. Their escort moved so slow. She risked a glance around the tortoise's tree-thick leg. A Shadow stood on the hill like a soul missing its body and the man-monster loped to its side. Uncle Dom strolled to the pair, but the thing was no longer their uncle.

The girls took turns sneaking desperate glances to the crest of the dune, and one-by-one the evil things disappeared. Alu's breaths quickened and Kinesee tightened in anticipation, throwing hair from her face and focusing on the woods only thirty paces away.

"Keep low, go."

Kinesee ran hunched a few strides but pent-up terror released drove her into a sprint. Alu's feet came fast behind her, and Tengkur passed them both, bucking and bouncing. Oh, to be a goat right now!

They sailed over underbrush and hit a deer trail. The temptation to duck behind a tree, to see if a dead thing or a Shadow gave chase grew, but if they followed, she didn't want to know. Kinesee's feet knew every root and stone of the trail, a familiarity which saved her life when running from the bad men to find Solineus. In her mind she ran to him again; he waited at her cave to save her. This time he wouldn't wield a broken branch, but a sword, and he'd avenge Odet and Dom and the others. He had to come, he promised.

Alu screamed, and Kinesee glanced over her shoulder. A flash of Shadow in the distance, and Kinesee stumbled over a stone, her sister running into her. Alu clutched Kinesee's shoulders, able to hold her from hitting the ground.

"Run, Kinesee."

They bobbed and weaved through trees, leaped over a small creek, following the water. Leaves crunched and twists of grass and vine grabbed at her feet and legs. Kinesee stumbled through the growth.

The Shadow rushed from the opposite bank, floating silent across the turf. It halted at the running water, emotionless, still as stone.

Kinesee slid to a greasy stop on the soggy soil of the bank and Alu stepped in front of her, branch ready to swing. The Shadow didn't move.

Alu spoke between gasping breaths. "Get to the cave."

Kinesee trotted, legs gone weak from battling the last hundred strides of underbrush, but her tree lay straight ahead. The hoary oak stood at the top of a steep embankment, its ancient roots exposed by years of washouts to create a web of wood, and in its depths a small cave. She ducked over and between roots and slid head first through the mouth of the bank into darkness.

Alu slid in moments later, followed by Tengkur, and they crammed into the back. It had taken the sisters a year to expand the hollow into a cave, and their father badgered them about it collapsing and killing them, but it was their refuge after Momma died. He didn't have the heart to make them stay away.

Kinesee prayed the Shadow hadn't seen them as she fumbled through her bag of oblong pearls until she found the special one.

Alu glared. "Don't you dare make that glow and give us away."

Kinesee nodded, but she wanted to summon Solineus so bad. He said he'd come to her call of need, and she needed him now.

The Shadow arrived silent, a darkness darker than the oak's shade, and the girls wailed as its head slithered into the cave's mouth. Rabbits in a hole without a backdoor, the snake's meal was easy.

Kinesee rubbed the pearl in her palms, the glow surged, and the Shadow paused. Alu grabbed the goat and shoved the bleating animal at the Shadow, a sacrifice to save their lives, but furious, Kinesee yelled, "No! Tengkur! Alu, no!"

Alu forced the scrabbling goat into the entrance, hooves first. Kinesee expected the Shadow to grab her precious goat, rip it to black-and-blood pieces before her eyes. The thing lurched from the hole instead, waited. Alu pulled the goat to her chest, and the Shadow moved for the entrance until she stuck the goat in its way again. It receded to skulk beneath the roots of the oak. It waited a quarter-candle before gliding away.

The girls slumped into the cave lit by Kinesee's pearl. Tengkur's eyes glowed in its light as both girls petted her, rubbing between her horns.

Kinesee felt a presence, and the words came faint between her ears. *I'm coming.* She clutched her sister's shoulder and burst into tears at the sound of Solineus' voice.

"He said he's coming. But he sounded so far away."

Alu's arm tightened around her shoulder. "I'm sure he will."

"He will. He promised." Alu never believed in the pearl, not even after seeing it glow.

"Papa will know where we are when he gets home, he'll come for us, too."

But father didn't come, nor Shadows. The sky was black, and so was the cave, seeing as Alu hadn't let her rub the pearl since sunset. The fishers should've come home by now, to find what, their loved ones dead and haunting the shore? They weren't warriors, their best chance against Shadows and the Wakened Dead lay in their boats, staying at sea, fleeing. Everyone might be dead, or rowing to Herald's Watch. Papa could bring a ship and real warriors from there.

Alu stretched beside her. "We need food and water."

"We ain't eating Tengkur."

"Did I say we're gonna eat your goat?"

"You thought it."

"Sleep. Tengkur and me, we'll watch for Shadows, you can take the second watch."

Kinesee drowsed but sleep came difficult. Visions of Odet's head kept creeping beneath her eyelids to startle her awake. Sleep overtook her but the second watch never arrived.

Kinesee's eyes fluttered open, her sister and goat snoozing beside her. Dawn's light crept into the cave and she braved a peek through the entrance. A gurgling stream and bird song greeted her ears, and the remaining leaves on trees rustling in the breeze. The world appeared at peace.

She scooted back, pressing into her sister's warmth as her stomach growled. She jostled Alu's shoulder, but Tengkur awoke first, ears flapping her horns as she gave her head and body a good shake.

"It's morning."

Alu kept a straight face, but her sister was angry for falling asleep. She groaned and crawled to the entrance and after a few moments wormed her way to stand amid the tree's roots. "I'll be right back."

Kinesee poked her head out and watched the older girl go to the stream and drink with cupped hands. Alu sat on her haunches, surveying the woods before she waved an invitation. Kinesee shoved Tengkur out first, then trotted to the creek, relieving her parched tongue with fresh water.

"What now?"

Alu glanced at the creek, crystal clear and fishless. "We gotta find food, we should head home."

Home, everything Kinesee wanted, but it terrified her. "We could head down-coast, the Izlur family?"

Her sister gazed into her eyes, sadness and determination. "You might be right. If Papa and the fishers aren't home, we'll head south."

They traveled as quiet and quick as possible when followed by a pesky black goat, approaching from the south near the strait to take advantage of the same hills they fled the day before. They slithered on their bellies to crest the dune.

Odet's body still lay on the beach, but it was no longer alone. Corpses lay scattered around fishing boats dragged ashore. Kinesee leaped to her feet, but Alu's arm wrapped her and pulled her to the gritty turf.

"Papa."

"Quiet."

Kinesee's heart pounded the sand as she lay there, tears filling her eyes. Several boats were missing, so survivors may have fled. Chickens wandered the yard, but as far as she could tell, nothing else remained alive.

Alu grabbed her face, forced Kinesee to look her in the eye. "You stay here. Something comes for me, you run to the Izlurs, you hear me? And stick beside the water."

Kinesee watched as Alu jogged straight to the boats in the surf. She avoided getting too close to the bodies, and leaned into a couple boats, grabbing canteens and haversacks, slinging them over her shoulder. She edged closer to a body and snatched a fishing spear and a couple knives.

She trotted halfway back, turned to face home. She waved Kinesee over to her.

"Seen anything 'cept chickens?"

Kinesee shook her head. "Papa?"

"No, he's not on the beach." Kinesee wanted to be relieved, but it left the greater question hanging. "I think… we'd be attacked by now, if those things were still here. Come on."

Alu handed her two fishing knives and took the spear in both hands to lead them home. Shonu and Leeru, Regin and Lole, their bodies lay scattered and mutilated along the way. She pinned her eyes on Alu's back, determined not to be a baby and cry. She'd lost love ones before, to sharks and the sea, and even bandits. The past hardened her, but didn't prepare her for carnage.

They arrived and Alu poked the door open with the barbed steel point. Dark silence greeted them, and nothing moved. They stepped inside, closed the door. "Your pearl."

Kinesee held the precious glow in her palm, revealing the room. The only body sat crumpled against the stone of the hearth, and Kinesee couldn't hold back. She ran to Grandma Ielu, hugging her, sobbing.

Alu stood above them. "Come on, help me find supplies."

Kinesee shook her head in defiance, but stood anyhow. "Why kill Grammu? Why?"

"Why kill anyone? Grab some rope, flint and steel, anything small that might be useful, and stay quiet. I'll get some more clothes and blankets."

They gathered two havers full of gear and food and slipped into greased sealskin boots in case forced to flee into chill waters. No sight nor sound of dead or Shadow, but Kinesee knew they pushed their luck.

Alu said, "If we could shove a boat into the water, or wait for a tide... we should head for the Izlurs."

"And what if they're dead?"

Sis glared with a frustrated sigh. "Then we head for the Fost, or better, Herald's Watch. Hug the water, a boat might find us, everybody can't be dead."

What would ring as an obvious truth two days ago sounded optimistic today. They carried food and fresh water, enough for days, but gnawing on nothing but salted meats and dried berries made every-thing a little more bleak. "Eggs. We should grab eggs."

Alu smiled and tussled Kinesee's already unkempt mess of blond hair. "Now you're thinking. Let's check the coop."

Kinesee ran to a small ladder and climbed, opening a trapdoor. Hens clucked and gave her the evil eye as she scurried into the dust and straw-laden coop atop their home. "It's all right, ladies." She stood while Alu hunched to keep from knocking her head on the raf-ters. The nests held eggs a-plenty, and Kinesee grabbed a few before Alu clutched her mouth.

They stood silent and Kinesee followed her sister's gaze. Something crossed the ground outside, passing a door into the coop made for chickens returning to roost. Alu stepped to the trap door, the only entrance sized for a human and eased it closed before crouching in the dust-hazed dark.

Whatever cast the shadow was too big to be a chicken. She clutched her pearl and snuck to the wall beside the chicken door and peeped through a crack. A hen squawked and flapped into the opening and she squeezed her bladder to keep from peeing her smallclothes. She took several breaths and looked back at Alu, whose wide eyes and panting breaths vindicated her start.

She turned her eye back to the crack. Nothing, until a red-and-black rooster hopped by. Could the shadow have been a stupid bird? Kinesee nudged toward the bigger opening for a better look but froze. A man sauntered into view, and her thoughts rushed to Solineus come to save them, but he wasn't so tall, and gashes rent his wool cloak and the flesh beneath with deadly wounds. Black and dried blood, none fresh, and the flesh held the color of day old meat.

The breadth of his shoulders, his height, she recognized him as kin, but many of the men looked similar from behind. Uncles and cousins. She prayed the dead man a stranger, or at the least anyone but Papa. Carvings on the fishing spear in his hand suggested a darker truth, but anyone might have picked up one of Papa's spears. Hope disappeared when the dead man turned, driving Kinesee's eyes closed.

She scrambled to Alu, clutching her shoulder. "It's Papa. He's Wakened."

Both girls shook with tears and stifled sobs. The pearl warmed Kinesee's hand, and she focused her thoughts. *Papa's dead.*

She didn't expect an answer. The first time she'd rubbed the pearl, the morning Solineus departed, she'd heard his voice, and she'd tried to answer. She rubbed the pearl a hundred times since, sending her thoughts, even trifling ones, without a response until yesterday. In her greatest need, he answered, and she needed his words more than ever. She prayed for an answer. *Papa's dead and walking.*

So often the pearl brought comfort, feeling its warmth, seeing its light. She squeezed so hard the pearl might leave bruises, willing him to answer.

Hold tight, sweet girl. I'm coming.

"He's coming."

Alu whispered in her ear through choking sobs. "I believe you. I heard him, too."

"He's closer."

Alu nodded and held her tight, and Kinesee wanted to collapse into a heap. She counted on a man she'd only known a couple days and she needed him to kill her papa. And if there were Shadows, too, she felt as though she summoned her savior to die.

FORTY-FOUR

Safety of Barren Rock

Fly into cowardice, Craven Raven, fly and Fly, and Die,
preen glistening feathers black and green
until wings no more, and the fluff fills your beak
choking your words.
Walk into Eternity, Craven Raven, with a thousand-thousand eyes
no two agreeing on their Fate.
Here. Now. Never. Forever.
Clean your feathers of lice to make space for maggots.
Die. Peace.
But peace is not for the likes of you and me.
Envy the dead and able to die.

—Tomes of the Touched

The horns of the Watch sounded as the *Entiyu Emoño* approached
Herald's Watch. Ships at anchor crammed the island's undersized
harbor, ranging from traders to small fishing boats, but a narrow gap
remained clear to receive important ships.

Captain Intœño belted out orders in the rolling language of the
Luxuns and his people leaped into action with practiced alacrity in
preparation for docking, scooting between refugees and furling the

436

three lateen sails. Even after a day onboard, Ivin found it difficult not to stare at their blue skin and vibrant feather-hair.

The Luxuns were known as the lords of the seas. Far as Ivin could tell, it was a reputation earned, as the *Entiyu Emono* brought them to the Watch with uncanny speed, then eased through the tight waterway to dock with an agility Ivin would've thought required oars.

He walked the gangplank to the docks hand-in-hand with Eliles and Roplin snared him in a bear hug less than ten steps from the *Entiyu Emono*. "Thank the gods! Damn good to see you. How's the Fost?"

Ivin shook his head. "Under siege. Eredin stayed to fight." He wasn't of a mood to explain the scroll he carried. "Roplin, I'd like you to meet Eliles."

Eliles curtsied with a shy smile. "The middle brother. Nice to meet you."

Roplin appraised her with a smirk. "Leave it to my brother to fall for a priestess." He took her hand and plied a kiss, winked at Ivin. "Yes, it's that obvious. Father will want to see you immediately. He's at the tower."

"Aye, I need to speak with him, too." He couldn't bring himself to say why. "If a man called Solineus arrives, about my height… he's from Emudar, and might have a couple young girls with him, be sure to send them to the tower."

The press of bodies cleared as they made their way from the docks, but crowds swarmed the town as he'd never seen before. In the coming days it'd get worse. It would be hard to keep up with the supplies needed for so many mouths and bellies, even if incoming ships carried worthwhile cargoes to sustain the lives they hauled on deck.

Tokodin scrambled through the crowd and ran to them. "They almost didn't let me on the docks. I had to convince them I knew you." He panted. "I could really use a privy."

Ivin chuckled and slapped the man on the back. The monk irritated him, but it was too good to be home to complain. "Can it wait until the tower?"

"I'll make it that far without soiling my robes."

The trio climbed the winding streets and entered the warrior-ringed Great Tower, finding escort to the dining hall where a back-thumping reunion took place. Ivin's ribs hurt by the time Kotin, Rikis, and Pikarn finished greeting him, but the jubilation sombered when Ivin passed the scroll to his father.

The old man's eyes perused the vellum, and he handed it to Rikis. "Eredin is certain?"

"His body is sound, but not his spirit. Not yet."

Kotin flopped in his seat, the wooden legs squawking on the hardwood floor. He glanced to Pikarn and back to his youngest. "You men have seen this enemy, what hope have we?"

The Wolverine raised his hands and snorted. "A sword against Shadow, you might as well be fighting smoke. Fire, the same, unless it's a priest's Fire. In the end, they fared little better. How a man beats a devil, I ain't got no idea once steel and fire fail."

Ivin said, "Istinjoln is lost, and the Shadows keep coming, slower, but still they come. Prayers killed them, but didn't save the monastery. Steel is a waste of sweat. We recovered the Sliver of Star: that'll keep the Mother of Shadows from getting through the portal."

"Pikarn told me of this Star, can we use it?"

"We thought to close the portal, worked our way into Istinjoln, but…" Eliles raised her head from hiding in her cowl. "What the Sliver is, what it's capable of, it's impossible to tell. Not without using it, and after? We need be sure of how to use it before we ever do, or its power could end us all."

"What prayers have you for this thing?"

"None, I've feral magic."

Ivin was proud of how tall she stood with those words, and he wrapped an arm around her shoulder.

His old man eyeballed her, then laughed. "I like you better already, welcome to the family, my girl. Never trusted magic, prayer or otherwise, but the times are different." Kotin turned to Joslin, a scullery boy of ten whose parents served in the Tower. "Run to the kitchens and bring us food, thinking comes better on full stomachs. Everyone, sit." The boy trotted down a hall, and Kotin kicked his feet onto the table, something the Lady Pineluple would never have tolerated. "Where's Eredin now?"

"He's at the Fost seeing folks onto boats, or at least he was when we left. He'll raise sail to the Watch soon as he's able. A Luxun ship with a Trelelunin woman will sail back to get more survivors."

"Luxuns won't do us much good outside of their sails, but Trelelunin, are there more of her people?"

"No, leastwise not I know of. Eredin took the Glass Sword; it's able to kill Shadows."

Kotin believed in Shadows and Taken, but a glass sword killing anything furrowed his brow.

"It's not glass, it's Latcu. God-forged."

His father's crooked lips spoke to what he thought of the notion. "So, we have one sword and a piece of star we don't understand to fend off demons."

Tokodin made his way to a keg of ale and poured with his back to the table. "They're called Shadows of Man, because they only pray on humans. They won't touch a living creature unless it's human, and they fear water." He carried a mug to Ivin and sat one at his seat, before returning to linger over the spigot, filling three more mugs.

Joslin's cart of food banged and rattled, a bowl and serving spoon hitting the floor with a clatter, and all eyes turned to the wide-eyed boy. "Sorry! So sorry." He scrambled to collect the offending silverware.

Ivin said, "We saw the fear of water ourselves in the Steaming Lakes, and Lelishen, the Trelelunin, told us of the root of their name." Ivin didn't have the patience to explain the Touched, so skipped him.

Tokodin carried mugs of ale to Kotin, Rikis, and the Wolverine. "Excuse me, where's the nearest garderobe?"

Joslin said, "I can show you, sir." The two departed through a side door and a scullery girl ladled bowls of stew as the conversation continued.

Kotin spooned soup and guzzled ale, wiping his lip of froth. "But these so-called Taken, steel kills them?"

The Wolverine said, "Aye, as it were, but the Shadows seep loose from the bodies and rise. Take's them a half candle or so before they're free." Pikarn spooned his stew and ignored his drink.

Kotin snorted and drained his mug. "These Taken fear water too?"

Ivin said, "Shadows and Taken alike fear water; we don't know why."

Kotin sat silent, finger tapping the rim of his mug before he poked, tipping it with a clunk. "Fear. Fear, Meris scares me."

Ivin glanced at Kotin. The old man had passed from a snit into melancholy. He stared at nothing, his spoon in his mouth. Chewing his spoon. "Father?"

"That bitch killed your mother. And your little sister."

The brothers shared glances, and Rikis asked, "Who?"

"Meris, that holy whore. I can see my sweet Pineluple now, blood down her thighs, her eyes rolling white, the oracle muttering prayers to kill her."

"To save her, not kill her," Ivin said.

"My limp daughter in my hands, baby Usate, we'd agreed to her name before she was born and buried. You boys never knew that, no one does. Too beautiful a baby to become a seed for a headstone, and that bitch killed her." He stood with a start, stumbling as his heavy chair toppled across the floor. He lunged for his sword on the table and shook it from its scabbard. "I see you, Meris! I'm going to kill you, you god's-whore!" Foam trickled from the corner of his mouth as he lumbered around the table, crashing through chairs.

Ivin dove from the man's path, the sword swinging in an uneven arc over his head. Rikis and Pikarn rounded the table's end as Ivin knocked the blade from the old man's hand and wrapped his arms around him. Kotin was over thirty years his senior but still hard and powerful as a bull. Ivin's knitted fingers strained and burned as the man roared in a fury, struggling to break free.

Ivin tangled their legs and heaved, throwing his father to the ground. They crashed to the maple floor and Ivin's fingers unknotted, his father's elbow writhing to connect with Ivin's skull. He rolled across the floor from the old man, and as Kotin charged, Rikis laid a ham fist aside their father's head, and like a boar struck dead Kotin plowed into the floor planks, writhing.

Rikis said, "What the godsdamned hells? Poison?"

Ivin's head thrummed, his eyes blurred. He glanced to the bowl and Kotin's empty mug. "The stew. Where's Joslin?"

"Right here, sir." Terror stretched the boy's eyes, his fingers trembling.

Rikis lifted Kotin onto the table, his eyes on Eliles. "Can you help?"

"You need a healer, not me. But I'll do what I can." Eliles stood over the fallen giant, hands trembling as she touched him. "Poison. I can feel it burning. He needs a healer, fast."

"I'll drag one back." Rikis ran out the door.

Joslin cleared his throat, his voice meek. "The monk, I saw him pouring something in the mugs when I were cleaning—"

Pikarn ripped the scullery boy from his feet in a fury, lifting to stare him in the eye. "You said nothing?"

Piss streamed down the child's leg. "I thought it were whiskey."

"The monk that brought us the ale! Where's that godsdamned son of a bitch?"

"In the privy down the hall."

The Wolverine slung the boy into the wall and pulled an axe from his belt. Ivin ran after him.

Tokodin? No, it wasn't possible. Not after everything they'd been through. He wouldn't believe it, but still his sword was in his hand.

Pikarn ripped the garderobe's door open with a bellow and froze. The tip of Ivin's sword clanged on the stone floor.

Tokodin sat on the wooden ring with a trickle of blood from the corner of his mouth, eyes wide and staring, and a dagger thrust through his heart.

Pikarn spat on the dead man. "Cowardly bastard." He grabbed the monk by the back of his head and slammed him into the wall, then floor.

The Wolverine bellowed and stormed from the room but Ivin could only stand and stare. His eyes trailed to the floor where the single white pip of a die painted black stared at him. Ivin snatched it from the floor, shook it in his hand. The monk kept his dice in a deep pocket, they wouldn't fall out by chance. He knelt to the floor and stuck his hand in the dead man's robes, but the pocket was empty.

A scream from down the hall shook him from his folly: What the hells was he doing worrying about dice? He clutched the die and ran to the dining hall where Kotin thrashed on the table, Eliles fought the dying man and her own tears as several men held him down.

Rikis stumbled into the room, breathless, a priestess in tow. He slung the young woman at the table. "Save him."

Eliles stepped from Kotin's side and wrapped her arms around Ivin as the priestess prayed. Ivin wanted nothing more than to hold her, but he pushed her aside to help hold his father down, grabbing an arm.

Kotin's muscles relaxed as the priestess prayed, splaying her hands across the man's chest and stomach. Ivin hoped it was a sign the prayers fought the poison, saving his father, but when the young girl's eyes turned to him with tears, he knew the peace in his father's arm was the tranquility of the dead.

Ivin slumped and dropped to his knees, but the peace was broken by Rikis's roar and the ring of steel. His brother charged the priestess with his sword, a dirty froth trickling from his mouth. Ivin lunged, driving his shoulder into Rikis' sternum, the sword tumbling through the air as he drove his brother into the floor. Several men helped hold him down, and the priestess held her hands on the eldest brother's chest and prayed.

Ivin knelt, panting, pinning his brother to the floor until the Wolverine returned, taking Ivin's place by Rikis' side. Ivin stumbled to a chair, tears in his eyes and Eliles provided what comfort she could with her arms and soft words, but all he heard were distant whispers, senseless words he didn't bother to understand as he sat watching his eldest brother die by the hand of a man he'd brought into the fold.

Meris arrived on Herald's Watch among an early wave of refugees from Kaludor, and once on shore rode in a litter with no one giving Her Holiness a second glance amid the throngs. They carried her through the streets, horrific descriptions of Shadows and Taken assaulting her ears, but she put no faith in them. Small people and small talk, lies spread by the Choerkin to turn the people against the Church. For once, however, she didn't blame the Choerkin, because the truth was Holy War and the Church had returned to rule.

Her bearers carried her to Skywatch, where she crawled from beneath wool blankets to test her legs for the first time since Ulrikt died. Her muscles were stronger than expected, and she used her cane more from habit than necessity as she climbed into the stars. She stared to the sky and focused on the Twelfth Star blazing as the Eye of the Fire Lion. A terror seeped into her blood, but she denied the sensation. All would be well, the gods were wise and generous.

She slept the next two nights in perfect peace, falling into slumber with her stars cloudless and tranquil in her eyes. In her heavens the chaos spoken of in the outer world faded and she forgot Ulrikt and his Face for a blessed time. But whispers assailed her haven in the night sky: Lord Kotin Choerkin lay dead, poisoned by a monk. Choerkin's pyre would burn that afternoon, sending his remains to the world in the form of smoke and ashes, to honor the Choerkin before him.

Meris hadn't attended a funeral since Pineluple died, but this was one she daren't miss. Respect or guilt, the driving motivation didn't matter, and she didn't waste time over-thinking her need to be there. She slipped into the plain robes of a senior monk, pulling the hood over her face and tossing her cane to the side.

She blended into crowded streets, a thing she wouldn't have considered before Ulrikt healed her. His prayers were powerful beyond any she'd experienced before. For years she'd sought the finest healers to give her vigor to continue her duties, but she'd never dreamt of walking the steep streets of the Watch without agonizing pain again. She was hale with the energy of a woman decades younger. She smiled at the sun overhead, despite it blinding her star-accustomed eyes.

The gate to Herald's Abbey stood crowded with mourners, but in her robes she passed the guards without question. Meris made her way to a hill overlooking the grounds where a stone platform heaped with kindling stood. Folks often called it the Smoking Rock. She couldn't see the body, but knew Kotin lay amid the sticks, draped in pure white linen. She'd known him since his teenage years, but he was just another dead man on the list of hundreds to pass before her, despite their youth.

For a long time, watching those younger than her pass made her sad; how unfair it was that she lived while they died, and now she didn't know a single soul older than her. The pang of sadness sometimes turned to a jealous burn for the lucky souls who'd escaped this world with so few years of anguish.

She muttered a prayer to improve her vision in time to see Ivin and Eliles stride from the crowd after the Prayer of Stars was intoned by a young priestess, a healer named Izilfer. Ulrikt's prize priestess standing arm in arm with a Choerkin brought a cluck to her tongue. *The world's gone upside down.* It was amazing how life could still surprise her. Izilfer's presence made sense, street whispers spoke of her saving the eldest brother's life, although he remained ill and unstable from the poison, but she had to wonder what Ulrikt would think of Eliles standing proud on Herald's Watch.

The eulogies were too distant for her ears, but whatever the words she didn't care. There was nothing to say she hadn't heard a hundred times in her century of living.

Ivin's face remained stern as he spoke, but when he smiled, it sent a shiver of pain through Meris' marrow. Her mind turned to Pineluple, the boy's mother. The hair, the cheekbones, the set of his eyes, his cursed smile, maybe it was her imagination, but she never realized how much he looked like his mother. A dear friend and corpse on Meris' list of victims, more painful killing her than even the infant girl.

She had read the bones and their intent was obvious. Bontore spoke through prophecy, a Choerkin daughter would break the

Church and bring doom upon the people. Meris had eliminated both the threat of the first born daughter and any further children in one cry-stricken night.

Her eyes remained glued to Ivin's sorrowful smile. *I was wrong.* Cracks in a bone could be interpreted with mild but critical variances. The weight of failure was crushing, driving the breath from her lungs and a wave of vertigo struck.

A tug on her sleeve shook Meris from the spin of her world and she turned her gaze to a young boy, perhaps ten years along his life. The boy smiled at her with an innocence that gave her chills. "Do you know me, child?"

The boy let go her sleeve and watched as Roplin Choerkin lit Kotin's pyre with a torch.

"After all these years you realized your mistake, didn't you? And the child who most resembles the mother will break the Church and bring doom to the people."

"How the hells...?" Meris' throat seized as if she'd swallowed poison. She wanted to scream at the boy to explain himself, but she knew who she spoke to, even if the face was different, and she didn't know its real name. "I failed."

"Sweet Meris. Like Sundel of Mirest who broke his legs and pulled himself from the mountains with bloodied hands, the Church's bones will heal, and grow stronger. Doom, too, has more than one interpretation. No, you did not fail, nor did you succeed. You did precisely as the gods knew you might, even if misguided. But if guided correctly, what then? Murder Ivin Choerkin? Neither the gods nor I would have allowed it."

"Leave me, please." *I killed my dearest and only friend on this island because I misread a bone, and this thing allowed it.*

"I will speak with you again, soon."

Meris couldn't look the Face in the eye, she stared at the smoke until the boy walked away, then she descended the hill. She stood in the middle of Januel's Way dazed and numb, glancing up and down the cobbled walk. She turned uphill, making her way toward the Watch Tower.

She arrived at the entrance and contrived a fable of bringing herbs to the kitchens from the Slave Gardens to gain entry. The night she killed Pineluple was the last time Meris had set foot in the tower, but she recalled the halls with an acuity of wit worthy of a younger woman.

She found the central stair, unguarded, as it had few destinations except the roof. The climb was slow and arduous, but she pumped her aged legs and rested as needed. Hurried decisions most often became the worst ones, so she took her time on the journey to destiny's end.

Icy winds cut straight through the sky and her robes when she crawled through the trapdoor at the peak of the climb and stepped into the elements, but prayer warmed her skin and strengthened the feeble remnants of will and muscle. She eased her way to the parapets. Two hundred feet above the world, she preferred to look up at the sky, where rising smoke thinned before reaching the clouds, rather than the body-breaking rocks below.

A deep breath drained her fear and she surveyed the scene below. Hundreds of boats and scores of ships bobbed at anchor, surrounding the island's jagged shores and filling its harbor. So many people desperate to live, and she had had a small hand in their plight. She had served the gods and might make her way to the heavens with their graces, but she deserved the Traitor's Hell or worse.

Ulrikt had given her a choice in Istinjoln, to die or to serve Sol one more time. Her decision demonstrated a lack of wisdom and a hubris unbecoming in a woman so old. Meris' soul would be happier navigating the Road of Living Stars without having realized her error. She had one pathetic revenge and retribution remaining to her. Repay lives lost with her own, and take a sad, antiquated tool from Ulrikt's arsenal. Whomever they wanted her to kill, they would need find another assassin.

But as she stood on the edge of paralyzing heights, thrilling in the breeze and a rush of fear, she contemplated the lord priest's words and his healing. She wondered if Ulrikt knew the path she now took, wondered if he didn't heal her so she could overcome the stairs and take her own life. Maybe hers was the life they wanted her to take.

She stepped from the stone tower without a care for her mind's final conspiratorial amusement, exulting in the rush of blood to her head, the rush of air rising beneath the folds of her cloak, before excitement and terror careened into tranquility.

The sun disappeared and every star she studied for decades shown bright in a black universe. A twisting pattern emerged and she felt her soul pulled to the Road of Living Stars, felt the judging eyes of the gods on her soul. Perhaps she smiled, she wasn't certain, but if she did, it didn't last. Joy faded as a voice echoed from the mortal world, the intonations of a young boy muttering prayers for her passage along the Road of Living Stars.

Eliles had attended funeral pyres twice in her life when common folks died in Istinjoln and the ground was too frozen for internment, but she'd never stood so close as to feel the licking heat of the flames. She stood by Ivin's side with twined arms, fingers laced together. His touch was gentler than her own, despite it being his father turning to ash. His unflinching stare made her wonder how she'd handle her own father's death, the man who had called the inquisition when discovering her feral fire.

Would she have cried, or would she have set the fire herself with glee? She doubted he still lived and refused him even the small honor of thinking his name. But when she considered he might still walk, Taken, shame and sorrow crept into her mood.

Branches crackled and flames rushed, helping to disperse her thoughts from her family. The Smoking Rock was a chiseled platform standing in front of Herald's Abbey, ten feet long and charred black over centuries of sending Ivin's kin to the clouds and sea with fire. Priests declared it hallowed ground, but for her and so many others it was just another place of sorrow.

She gazed at the man Januel had chosen for her; Ivin hurt, but it didn't show with tears. Instead, he'd transformed into a statue, jaw clenched and his eyes more likely to bleed than shed tears. She leaned into him with a nudge. "May we leave?"

Ivin's expression didn't change, and she wondered if he had heard her. She couldn't bring herself to ask a second time, but he exhaled and muttered to Roplin, "I'll see you back at the keep."

They turned arm in arm and strode through the gathered crowd, several folks calling out their support for the clan. Ivin waved and nodded; Eliles stared at her feet, knowing her priestess' robes drew the ire of many folk, no matter who walked on her arm.

They passed through Sol's gate and onto Januel's Way, and her shoulders relaxed in their escape from the fire and crowd. They turned northeast, beginning the winding trek to the central tower.

"I watched my mother and baby sister burn on that same godsdamned stone. Twelve years ago, a year for every hell." She gripped his hand. "I mean, I knew someday I'd watch him burn, or he'd watch me..."

"You think he'd trade positions?"

Ivin grunted. "He'd die a hundred deaths for each of us boys. For a daughter he never knew."

"My father would've seen me burn." His brows knitted and she regretted her words. "What I mean is you had a loving father."

"The man was an unerring arrow in my ass."

She fought a grin. "With good intent, I've no doubt."

He snaked his arm from hers and draped it over her shoulders. Walking so close she could feel the gimp in his stride, the wound from Istinjoln still healing. "Any thoughts on the Tome of the Touched?"

"Was your father so obvious when changing subjects?"

"At least."

She leaned her head into his shoulder as they walked. "I've read his words a hundred times, and flipped through other sections in Silone, I know I'm missing something."

They took several strides in silence and turned a sharp corner that afforded a view of the bay below. Small boats continued to arrive despite the clutter of masts anchored in the bay, desperate folks struggling to survive. Rumors spread by sailors spoke of families pulling their fishing boats onto every small island along the coast, even if it was little more than a boulder stuck from the surf. Many survived like this, sailing to shore for fresh water, fishing for food, but Shadows, hunger, thirst, and a score of unknowns would trim the number of survivors day by day.

Eliles said, "I wish the book told us how to feed all these people."

"Our larders will grow thin too soon, fishing boats will be a key, raiders another." Ivin scoffed. "Reclaimers, more like. We'll send ships to scout the shores, row in, snatch supplies, get out. Rain might afford us better chances against the Shadows."

"How long you think we can survive doing that?"

Ivin stared at the cobbles passing beneath his feet. "Long enough to find a better answer." The tower's bells rang. "Gods be kind, what the hells could it be now?"

They raised their pace the best they could with Ivin's limp and arrived at the tower as the clamor of bells faded. Several armed men stood out front, but nothing appeared untoward. An older warrior stepped forward, his cheeks, chin, and eyes marking him as Choerkin even if he stood several inches shorter than Ivin, but she didn't recognize him.

Ivin said, "Artus… When'd you make it to the island, you old dog?"

"Came in on the *Xole* this morn and paid my respects to your pa from afar. Too much crowd at the pyre for my tastes. Headed up to see Rikis and found the tower is raining monks. Hellish weather you got 'round these parts." He cocked his head and lead them around the tower. "Nobody's touched the body yet, not much anyhows."

"A name? What was a monk doing on the peak?"

"Don't know to either. The guards at the door mentioned letting an herbalist in." He glanced back with a toothy smile for Eliles. "This the purty priestess I been hearing about?"

"I'm my father's son after all… This is Eliles, a finer lady I've never met; this is Artus, no finer Artus I've ever met."

The man guffawed. "This boy is my fifteenth favorite cousin, give or take a few."

They rounded a boulder at the southern base of the tower, the purple flowers of blooming monkshood scattered across patches of dirt and moss amid the stone. A twisted and broken body lay mangled on the ground, a sight Eliles might have choked on a couple weeks ago, but it felt tame after what she'd seen.

Artus said, "We sent word down to the holies, should have someone get him, her, soon," Artus said.

Eliles said, "A woman, I think." The hair was long and gray but she couldn't see the face until Ivin flipped the cowl. She didn't believe her eyes until Ivin said the name.

"Meris. Godsdamn. Who found the body?"

Artus shrugged. "Heard a boy saw her jump, no idea who."

Ivin leaned in, his nose curling. "Maybe the stars told her to do it. How'd that crone make it up all them steps?"

Artus chuckled. "Maybe your pa's spirit done carried her on up and gave her a toss."

"No doubt the tavern gossip will say so."

Eliles listened and stared, unbelieving. She'd assumed the woman dead in Istinjoln, and to find her here, crashed to the rocks, what gods were at work to make such a thing possible? "She was in Istinjoln days before the Eve of Snows. She broke the bone that killed Ulrikt."

Ivin cocked his head. "She traveled all the way back here just throw herself from the tower?"

Artus asked, "Ulrikt is dead?"

Ivin and Eliles answer together. "No."

"You done just said—"

Ivin said, "It's a story best left to warmth and indoors." He stalked the body's perimeter, kneeling for a closer look. "What if she came here, garbed as a monk, to tell us something, could be one of her own gave her a toss. We need to find the boy, see what he knows. Few things are simple as they seem these days."

"Aye, true, lad. You've a better head on your shoulders than ever I did."

Eliles said, "I only met her once, but there's no way I believe she jumped."

Rocks clattered, and she turned to spot two monks struggling over loose rocks to reach them. The men arrived without a word and loaded the old woman on linen stretched between two oak shafts without looking at her face. Whether it was fear to see someone they knew, or business-like duty, Eliles couldn't be sure.

They stood in silence as the monks placed Meris' arms across her belly, unfolded pristine white linen across her remains, and finished with prayers for her soul. Within moments they toted the high oracle away, leaving only her blood on the rocks.

Ivin spat. "I don't need to read no bones to recognize this ill tiding."

"Your pa is smiling right now, boy." Artus pulled a flask from his cloak and popped its top before taking a swig. He offered Eliles a drink, but the strength of his breath convinced her this would be unwise.

The silence grew uncomfortable as they watched the litter disappear. Ivin bent and plucked a stem of monkshood. "A piece of beauty amid the horror."

Eliles clasped Ivin's hand in hers, soothed to feel his warmth and the beat of his heart, but as she took the flower her mind wandered to the words of the Touched with the speed of gale winds: *A tower, a tower, an autumn flower, read the oracle's bones and find your tower, the first, the second build in kind. Find. In kind. Tear-blind build.*

FORTY-FIVE

Promises

In a life previous
I was a bear with buttons for eyes
and stitches down my spine
a sadly happy little thing
slumbering in the arms of children
until arrived a day I became the child
and ripped the eyes off mine own bear.
So is the Odyssey of these Spaces in time.

—*Tomes of the Touched*

Kinesee awoke with her head resting in Alu's lap, the rhythm of their hearts in cadence. Her stomach growled and she sat up. She grabbed salted chicken, a tad rude, considering they hid in a chicken house, but it was the first bit of food she found rummaging through her sack. Alu smiled and offered her an egg, more rudeness.

She cracked the egg and drank before taking a bite of meat. "Seen the dead?" She forced herself to not call it Papa.

"No, nothing but chickens and Tenkgur. Stupid goat."

They'd seen Tengkur bounce and prance right up to the dead things, and the dead didn't even look at her. Mighty odd, she figured, considering the stories told about the Wakened. The dead killed every living thing, man and beast. Never once in them scary tales did the dead fear water, neither. Maybe spooky stories didn't know as much as she thought.

She sneaked to the crack in the wall and peered outside. They'd seen four Wakened yesterday: Papa, an aunt, and two cousins, but no Shadows. The creatures wandered, disappearing now and again, but came back. Only a couple hens pecked and scratched in the yard this morning.

High tide carried a couple dories into the strait, three remained on shore. They entertained the notion of a heroic escape, but neither of them could row a boat far even if they made it to shore alive. They sat in dirty straw suffering the stink of chicken poop and dust, moving as little as possible to keep quiet.

Kinesee crawled to Sis and sat, gnawed on a chunk of chicken. Claws grated the northern wall, *skrit-skrat* echoing through the coop, and both girls tightened. Scratchy feet passed over their heads and flickers later two beady eyes and a pointy nose gazed upside down through the door. A raccoon. A no-good, stinky, chicken-and-egg-eating raccoon. The animal snarled as it flipped inside and met Alu's boot. She struck hard and fast, but the beast clung to sealskin and bit. Kinesee grabbed a knife and lunged, plunging the blade into its back. It screeched and let go, tumbling out the door.

If the Wakened saw or heard, or found the wretched critter's blood trail from the coop, their hiding place would become a trap. They sat stone-still in the stir of dust, staring at the door. Chickens cackled outside, otherwise, silence. Kinesee took her breaths slow, scrunching her nose to stifle a sneeze. Solineus wouldn't be far away by now, she promised herself, all they needed was to stay hidden.

Stories spoke of the Wakened being dim-witted, and by grace of the gods and holy prayer she hoped they proved right on at least this one thing. The coop had one exit they'd fit through, so if the dead came through the trap door, they'd need to fight their family or scratch their way through the walls of the chicken house.

Footsteps outside. Alu readied her spear, and Kinesee tucked her pearl in its pouch and took a knife in both hands. Ready to fight and kill, not to die.

Slow trudging steps, dirt scuffling under heavy feet until coming to stand beneath the chicken door. Wood creaked, the coop shook, and a hand latched onto the rail outside, pulling itself up. Uncle Dom's ripped face rose to block the sun, his gaze turning to the girls.

Kinesee went numb, muscles freezing under the dead stare.

Alu didn't hesitate, driving the spear clean through the Wakened's eye and out the back of his head. The thing fell backward, wrenching the spear, and Alu struggled with her grip, the hook of the point lodged in bone. Dom's collapsing weight slid her to her feet and rammed her into the wall. The shaft slipped from her fingers, leaving them with fishing knives to fend for their lives.

"Run, run to the water."

Alu ripped the trap door open and dropped through on faith, but Kinesee lagged behind.

"Jump!"

Kinesee stuck her feet through the dark hole but couldn't make herself let go. She climbed down, shaking, unsteady. The main door stood open and Alu stood in the meager light streaking into the great room. Kinesee handed her a knife.

"Now, follow me, run and don't stop."

They sprinted through the door, keeping low into dim sunlight. Dom lay dead in the dirt and sand, and Alu pushed Kinesee by. She ran before turning to look. Her sister stood prying the spear from the Wakened's head, strange tendrils of Shadow seeping from the corpse into the ground.

Kinesee spotted Medlin on the hill, a cousin on mother's side. "Alu! Run!" Kinesee pointed, and with a final tug Alu gave up on the spear and bolted.

Kinesee leaped from a small rise and landed on the beach, tumbling and rolling into a sand-spraying sprint. The pounding of Alu's feet gained on her from behind. She didn't dare consider it was somebody else. The boats lay straight ahead and one's bow broke the waves of a rising tide. Feet splashed chilling waters into the air and she turned, Alu plowed into the surf right behind her. They grabbed the bow of the boat and stared into Medlin's sunken eyes.

The Wakened shied from the water, but wasn't near as dumb as Kinesee hoped. Medlin grabbed the back of the boat and pulled, trying to drag their escape inland. The girls grabbed hold best they could as a wave lifted the boat's nose; they managed it farther into the surf as the creature screamed, water hitting its bare feet. Kinesee wailed and dug her boots into the sand, pulling with every bit of her strength as another wave washed ashore.

Another dead thing loped on all fours down the beach, a cousin with his tongue lolling from a face and missing so much flesh it was hard to put a name to him; best Kinesee could figure, it was Ito. Together the two cousins dragged the boat backward, defeating the girls' gains inch-by-inch.

A wave surged, driving the dead prancing away from the spray and froth, but they took hold of the boat, and heaved as the water receded. Kinesee's fingers slipped and she lurched backward before regaining a grip in this tug-of-war. The tide was their hope, until Medlin climbed into the boat, coming at them with bared and bloody teeth.

A wave rushed ashore, sending freezing waters as high as their thighs, lifting them from their feet as it rocked the dory. Medlin tumbled and fell as the boat shifted, scrambled to her feet, and with a flash which might as well have come from heaven, a blade severed Ito's head in a splash of black gore. A rush of gray blurred across Kinesee's vision with the muted thumps of hooves in sand.

The boat lurched seaward and Medlin tumbled over the starboard edge, a piercing wail as she hit the water. Smoke seemed to rise from her body, but Kinesee grasped the truth, it was Shadow escaping. Within flickers Medlin floated dead in the water, and the surf drew Shadowy tendrils into its frothing depths, dispersing its darkness as if the thing never existed.

The next waves caught the toes of a man's boots and Kinesee ran to Solineus with tears wetting her cheeks. He wasn't the man she remembered, clad in mail and with a curved sword in either hand, but his face and smile were everything she remembered and dreamed of.

"The coop was safer for you birds." He hugged her, then Alu, as she latched onto his other side. "How many more Wakened?"

Kinesee couldn't manage words through her tears, so Alu answered. "Papa and Aunt Oleu, best we know."

He stuck his swords in the sand and his hands slid under Kinesee's arms to lift, setting her into the boat. Alu climbed aboard, and Solineus shoved the dory into deeper water. "Drop anchor and wait for me, I've another promise to keep."

The girls struggled to lift the anchor, but managed to flip it over the edge. They sat bobbing in the strait, watching. Kinesee's heart thrummed a desperate rhythm. In a single day she'd lost everybody important in her life save for her sister and this stranger. Solineus should climb into the boat, row them to safety. The words dangled on her trembling lips, but she couldn't give them voice.

Solineus dragged Ito to the water, Shadow seeping from his body, stretching stringy like translucent strands of seaweed refusing to snap as tiny fingers clung to the sand. When a wave found the body the

Shadow struggled, but the water drew its wriggling essence until the black splotch in the water faded into nothingness.

Kinesee prayed without words, saying goodbye to kin, while thankful he no longer threatened the living.

Since first realizing the demons feared water, he'd wondered why. Now he planned on enjoying it.

Solineus dropped Ito's body in a rushing wave, fascinated as strips of Shadow leeched from the body, morphed into ink, and diluted from existence. The image forced the surreal recollection of his soul afloat in the blue sea of his dreams, but he hoped the Shadows met torment instead of tranquility. Demons didn't deserve a gentle exit when kind folk such as Dareun met tortuous ends with their souls trapped in a doomed land.

A shrill scream overpowered the rumbling surf. Solineus met the eyeless gaze of the Shadow rising above Dom's corpse and sloshed to shore.

Kinesee cried out. "Let's leave! Don't fight that thing."

He walked between the swords standing in the sand and grabbed their hilts. The murmur of the Twins' voices nudged into the background of his thoughts, goosebumps rising on his arms with the tingle of power the blades fed him.

He turned and smiled, reassuring. "No worries, sweet girls."

The Shadow squirmed free of the corpse but several tendrils remained lodged in the body. He stepped within a few feet and spit. The saliva struck and breached the creature clean through, pulling a thin streak of the monster's being to the turf. Its metallic shriek, the way it cowered and suffered pain made him smile.

"Gotta say, that's godsdamned funny."

He resisted the urge to open his canteen on the thing and instead crossed the twins through the hazy form. No resistance, but the blades left crisp lines of clean air in their wake. The Shadow went silent and unmoving, faded. Pathetic how quiet these creatures departed the world after wreaking bloody havoc. When Colok struck the Shadows, their anguish satisfied the yearning for revenge.

He scanned the perimeter for threats and sheathed his swords, took Dom by his feet and dragged him through the house door. The empty shell no longer felt a home, cold, dark, hollow. Plenty of split wood sat stacked by the hearth. In moments a fire stoked with skins of oil raged, sending smoke through the hole in the conical roof. In time it would be seen for miles. He lifted Ielu and placed her body in the flames, followed by Dom. As dignified an end as time allowed.

Blades sang from sheaths and whispers flirted with his consciousness as he drew the Twins, exiting the home with cautious steps. Oleu came from the woods, stopping to stare at him before eyeing the girls floating on the boat. She sat back on her haunches, waiting, a mop of hair turned dark with dried blood clinging to her lifeless face, but she wasn't his target, the next arrival was. Iku carried his fishing spear and Solineus found it more difficult than expected to separate his memories of a living man he called friend from a corpse given life by a demon.

The pair gazed at him, assessing him, perhaps. Unusual behavior for creatures who attacked without a second thought. Solineus nodded to Iku with a sullen grin. The Lady spoke to Iku in his dreams and told him Solineus would save his girls and free Iku. At the time he knew nothing of what this meant, but he swore to fulfill the Lady's promise. If the man's soul remained trapped within its shell, he wanted him to know he kept the first half of this promise, and soon he'd keep the second.

He turned and strode into Iku's home, nostrils assaulted by the acrid, sulfurous fumes of burning flesh and whale oil. The smoke burnt his eyes, but better for him to suffer than the girls. Whatever they'd been through, they didn't need the image of their father's death seared into their memories, even if dead already. He waited for the inevitable, staring at the open portal through the roiling haze.

The Taken strolled into the room impervious to the stench, blank eyes unblinking.

"The girls are safe, Iku. I will see them to Herald's Watch and do my best to see they reach old age." He hoped to see a reaction, a glimmer of recognition, but the man's sallow face didn't so much as twitch. He'd done what he could, now time to finish things.

Solineus raised the blade in his right hand to honor the sun and dropped his left to honor the lands and seas. The creatures rushed, Oleu on all fours and leaping, Iku charging through with his spear. A Twin struck the shaft of the spear, shaving splinters and fingers into the air while stepping beneath the soaring woman. The second Twin swept a gash clean from Oleu's neck to her pelvis, and she dropped into a flailing, hissing mass of innards.

He twisted to face Iku, the Wakened struggling to grasp the spear with a hand missing fingers. The dead's strength wasn't of flesh, it was of Shadow, and a thrust of the spear even with a single hand carried the force of two men, but it was too slow. Solineus slapped the spear to the side, a blade severing the man's arm before the second took his head.

Solineus stood, not knowing whether his tears were from smoke or sorrow. Over the span of the last two weeks killing had become a constant companion, but the agony of this death drove nails into his heart. The man had taken him in, fed and clothed him, bequeathed to him a sword passed down through generations. Bittersweet, knowing he killed a man already gone. Worse that the chore remained unfinished.

He tipped a stool upright and sat, wrapping a cloth around his nose and mouth, waiting for the Shadows to rise. When Shadows emanated from the dead, they blended with the smoke, and he didn't waste time with spit or water. He no longer concerned himself with revenge. The Shadows faded from the universe, split by the Twins, and he lifted the bodies into the fire.

Solineus strolled to the beach and watched thick smoke rise to mingle with clouds as he removed the saddle and tack from his horse, setting the animal free.

A blow to his calf came from nowhere and he looked down at a set of horns attached to a sneaky little goat.

He cocked an eyebrow. "Well, hello, Tengkur." He lifted the malcontent goat, strode through icy waters with oiled boots and set her in Kinesee's lap before climbing into the dory with the girls. The sisters stared mute as he pulled anchor and grabbed the oars. The girls' sorrow and his own guilt for not saving more of the family compelled him to say something, but it pained him to speak.

"Your father is free. Pray for his soul, so he may cross the Bridge of Living Stars in peace."

He couldn't meet their eyes. Oars struck water and he pulled, the exertion straining his shoulders, providing a focus for his mind and a release. The girls weren't so lucky, he needed to take their minds off the day. "We'll make for Herald's Watch, meet up with folks I know. Ivin Choerkin and his kin should be there by now."

The girls remained somber, but at least he'd given them something to think on.

"Your memories came back?" Alu asked.

He smiled and met Alu's gaze. "No, sorry to say."

"How you know the Choerkin then?"

"I only met the one, Ivin, up in Istinjoln. We had quite the journey, into the Treaty Lands, yonder yet to the Steaming Lakes."

Kinesee raised her head. "I heard the Steaming Lakes are filled with boiling waters and Wakened."

"You heard right. Quite a tale if you want to hear it. I'm betting you've a blanket in those sacks, so curl up with that stinky goat'n I'll tell you about it."

It took a candle for the girls to relax into slumber, but at last only the goat stared at him. The waters of the bay were peaceful, but the location of Herald's Watch, well, he didn't know where it was, so he kept within sight of land while rowing up the coast. After a brief nap at anchor he rowed for another candle until they chanced on a fishing boat.

He woke the girls and they shouted to the crew. The sisters pinned their hopes on the boat being family who survived, but turned out they were from a village several miles north of Iku's home, distant cousins at best. But they too sailed for Herald's Watch and didn't hesitate in making space on their boat for three plus a goat.

Kinesee and Alu sat with the Gerin family's surviving children, and Solineus relaxed his soul and shoulders, knowing at least he'd get the girls so far as an island refuge the dead and Shadows could never reach.

FORTY-SIX

Tower in a Tower

Every loss is a sadness but weighed against its End.
A Lover of me, of mine,
Lost in sleep by morn to mourn
A sadness certain with dead smile at dawn
But in balance a youthful demise happy
compared to the ancient living to die Forever.

—*Tomes of the Touched*

The harbor and surrounding waters of Herald's Watch were a forest of masts by the time Solineus arrived on the Gerins' boat. Vessels both great and tiny amassed around the mountainous island rising from the waters. Walls, streets, and buildings climbed the steep slopes with a fortress crowning its peak with a single great tower. A man standing at those heights might see twenty horizons or more out to sea, but for all its tactical uses, it was relegated to a refugee camp.

The talk among sailors Solineus hailed was that the island took few new arrivals ashore. Solineus might have sailors for kin, but the warrior in him wanted the hells off the creaking boat and his feet planted on steady rock. Solineus offered the Gerins every coin he had, and the matriarch agreed they'd sail in, to at least try the docks.

Their prow bumped a dozen other boats as they wiggled closer to the pier. A logjam of hewn planks bent and wrestled into fishing rigs would become a serviceable bridge if he got permission to disembark.

Solineus stood with the girls under either arm, scanning the docks for Ivin. "Choerkin! I'm looking for Ivin Choerkin!"

No one paid him any mind in the bustle, as men and women handed supplies to and from the docks, supplies traveling hand-by-hand to boats farther out in the bay.

"Ivin Choerkin! I need to speak to him!"

Alu glanced at him then shrieked loud enough a hundred eyes turned on her.

He grinned at her, a smart child with impressive lungs. "I'm look-ing for Ivin Choerkin!"

A burly bearded man in his fifties, armed with a sword and axe, passed him a scrutinizing gaze from the pier. "Who the hells are you?"

"Solineus Mikjehemlut of Emudar."

The man's face spread into a smile with a couple gaps. "With two girls, I see. Come ashore, we've been expecting you."

"Women and children?"

"Aye, sure. Alls you want. Drop anchor where yer at."

Solineus made certain the Gerins made it to the docks before he and the girls followed, swaying and tripping from boat to boat with a goat in his arms, with helping hands for balance from other fam-ilies. When they reached the dock he set Tengkur on the planks and Kinesee took the rope around the animal's neck.

"Artus Choerkin, Ivin's cousin." The man clasped his forearm and thumped his back with a hug. "Heard good things about you. I hope half of them are true."

Solineus laughed, by the gods it felt good to be off a boat. "Artus, these are Alu and Kinesee, my good friends."

The man knelt, shaking both their hands although they tried to curtsy. "Pleased to make the acquaintances of two ladies so lovely." His eyes turned to Solineus. "Last I heard Ivin was checking stores in the granary district, I'll show you there personal-like." The older man groaned as his knees straightened but he walked fast.

A path cleared, then filled in the man's wake, everyone on the streets knew to be out of his way. "It true you killed Dunkol Broldun or horseshit?"

"I slew what was left of him, whatever that's worth."

"Worth a bunch around these parts. Worth a drink, at least." Artus slipped a flagon from his waist and guzzled before handing it over.

A cedar-flavored burn slipped down Solineus' throat, making his eyes water, and he handed it back, hoping it never returned. "Word in the bay is several Choerkin were killed."

Artus' mustache drooped and he took a long pull of his drink. "Aye, all but Eredin in the Fost. Lord Kotin and his eldest were poisoned by a monk, and as I hear tell, he traveled with you."

"Tokodin? Gods*damn*…" Solineus' stomach sunk to his toes. Hard to believe a man would do such a thing after helping them. "You're sure?"

"Ah, hells. Who's sure of anything anymore? But they found him, stabbed himself on the shitter before they could take him, and he carried a flask done smelled same as the poison."

Solineus didn't love the monk and his piss poor attitude, but he'd never considered him an assassin. He lifted Kinesee to his shoulder and took Alu under his other arm as they walked, the goat trailing behind with leaping bounces. "Done is done, but wish I'd seen it coming. Would've killed the bastard myself."

Poison, it made a pathetic sort of sense. A coward's kill.

Ivin stood on a ladder built into the grain bin, staring into its gaping maw, distressed that it stood half empty. Even with fishermen plying the waters day and night, and several ships sailing east, there were so many mouths to feed that desperation would arrive at their door within a month. As more folks fled to the continent they'd be able to stretch food stores, but at the same time they'd lose fishers. The angst, stress, worry, combined with checking marks on scrolls would've been a horror weeks ago, now it focused his thoughts on something other than sorrow.

Ivin returned to the ground to find Artus grinning beside Solineus, two pretty young girls, and a small but irritable goat.

He trotted to the man and clasped forearms, all smiles. "By the gods, good to see you whole. Who do you have with you?"

Both girls ran their fingers through their knotted hair and curtsied as Solineus introduced them. "Alu here is the eldest, and her sister, Kinesee. My good friends. And Tengkur, she's the short black one with horns."

"Fine young ladies, horns not withstanding." The younger girl giggled. "Shall we walk? I bet we can find you food and drink." They strolled outside with Artus on their heels, heading for the Salty Frog, a tavern that had run out of beer days before.

"Any word from Lelishen? And the monk, it's true?"

"Seems so, Tokodin poured the ale and served… but didn't poison mine." He wanted to move on from this conversation, unwilling to face that he had brought his father's assassin to the island after saving his life more than once. "The Fost's under attack. Shadows climbed the walls, and Taken came through sewers from what I heard. They weren't in great numbers the last I knew, so priests are holding them back as ships travel back and forth, evacuating, but it's a matter of time."

"I heard the Fost's horns as I rode from the gates, sorry I couldn't turn back. My sympathies for your loss, these girls… So many have lost so much. Eliles?"

"She's safe in the Second Tower, she won't let the Sliver out of her sight, and she studies the Touched's book. She barely eats." They reached the tavern and unleashed the girls on the staff, but Solineus kept hold of the goat, who butted Ivin in the knee. "The girls' family?"

Solineus' eyes turned to the goat, and he leaned to rub the animal between its horns, all the answer Ivin needed. "I swore to their father I would see them safe."

The Watch's horn bellowed and Ivin cocked his head to listen: Twice low, twice high. "A foreign ship, might be the Luxuns." There would be no good news, the best he hoped for was word that things weren't as bad as they could be.

"You go, I'll keep an eye on the girls."

The *Entiyu Emoño* approached the docks, close enough for Ivin to see Eredin standing on deck beside Lelishen, the Crystal Sword rising above his shoulder.

Artus smiled and clapped Ivin on the back. "Our cousin lives."

"And the Fost is no longer in Choerkin hands." His family had held the Fost since the beginning of remembered time, over five hundred years. Demons and Taken owned those streets now, another agony heaped on recent pains. Inevitability didn't make it easier to accept.

Luxuns leaped from the decks to the docks, their feathery hair flashing in the sun as they moored the ship. Eredin disembarked the moment the plank lowered, with Lelishen and Captain Intœño by his side.

Ivin bowed to the Luxun. "My gratitude for all you've done."

"A pleasure to help your people. I will continue to do what I may."

Eredin clasped arms with Ivin. "I managed to get the sword back in one piece, although I tried to break it more than once."

Artus asked, "That hunk of glass?"

Eredin hugged the older man. "Turns out this glass is harder than you head."

Artus guffawed. "That's sayin' something, for sure."

Ivin said, "You're alive and safe. Best we could hope."

Eredin sighed, his bleak expression darkening behind his week-old beard. "Sorry to hear about the old man and Rikis, but we come with more ill-tidings."

Ivin locked his cousin's eyes and sighed. "How bad?"

"Ice grows across the bay, a bridge a hundred paces wide stretching toward the Watch. It's already farther than I'd have imagined. A hundred, maybe two hundred Taken sitting and waiting. We held the docks with the holy, if you can get a Taken into the water, it's their end. Rain helped our cause, driving the bastards back for the better part of a day. A host gathered on the ice bridge, they want your hide more'n mine."

Ivin's legs weakened and he wanted to sit, but instead leaned against a pier post. "Not me they're after. The gods have damned us all. How long we got?"

Eredin shrugged, but Captain Intœño spoke. "My spotters in the crow's nest have keen eyes; I'd count on four to five days, no more."

Lelishen said, "Your people need to leave this island."

"My people. How far can we run? Tek Brotna? Tek Hidreng? We'd be invaders with women and children, slaughtered."

Lelishen said, "There's no choice, everyone needs to sail to the continent, as far east as they're able. The Edan won't welcome you, but neither will they feed you to the dirt and worms. And the Hidreng can be more forgiving than you might imagine, with the proper diplomacy."

Ivin nodded, thankful his next words were true. "Roplin commands the Watch and the Choerkin; it isn't my decision to make." *This crack passes the Sails of Zinmil, you will be at sea.* Meris' words of prophecy came back to him, and right now his only joy came from knowing the oracle's ashes followed his father's.

Eliles studied the book Lelishen had claimed as a gift from the Touched, parsing every word for meaning and clues. Dame of Fire was not a name earned, not yet, despite his calling her such, and his reference to a tower caught her eye the instant she set foot on Herald's Watch, with its high tower rising from the peak of the island. They tied together somehow, the Watch was where she should earn her name, but she didn't know how. Bad news seemed to trickle in daily, sometimes hitting like a boulder.

Roplin had called for evacuation of the Watch within several candles of Eredin's arrival, but they didn't give up hope. Cogs fitted with rams attempted to break the ice bridge, but they were set upon by Taken. Catapulting flaming pitch damaged the bridge, but didn't stop it. Eliles made the journey once, when the ice bridge was a couple days from the Watch, and her Fire proved useless. Against the power of Ulrikt she needed the Sliver of Star, and she didn't trust herself to contain its energy a second time.

Longboats traveled the shores of Kaludor, alerting all peoples to flee as near to Eleris Edan as they could sail. They either manned the abandoned boats they found or burned them. No one knew if the Shadows and Taken would take to the waters, but it was a risk no one was willing to take.

Eliles wandered to the docks at least once every day, hoping to find Ilpen and his family, donkeys included, but no luck. Many ships bypassed the island on their journey east, so not seeing him didn't mean the worst, but she would've loved to have seen the dear man. Most faces she saw she didn't recognize, but one boat of refugees carried adherents she'd known from Istinjoln. She thought she caught a glimpse of Meliu in the crowd, but the girl disappeared before she could say hello.

Jinbin remained her only connection to her life in Istinjoln. It was bittersweet. As much as she hated her life there, it was disconcerting not having a home.

The dawn of the fifth day after Eredin's arrival revealed encroaching ice on the horizon. A lone ship remained in harbor. The Watch had swelled into a city of refugees before bleeding the population back to the sea until Eliles stood with her friends on the deck of the *Entiyu Emoño* as the last remaining people.

Ice crept across the bay with Taken swarming the tip of the unnatural peninsula. At the fore stood a great Shadow.

She leaned on Ivin, absorbing his warmth beside the heat of the Sliver of Star tucked in her robes. They all expected something from her, or so she felt. The bearer of the Sliver of Star should save Kaludor and the Silone people. In the memory of its power she found fear and exultation. If she dared bring its energies to bear she knew she could destroy the ice bridge, but she also knew she could lose herself and her soul, all while handing the Sliver to the enemy.

She gazed at Ivin's determined face as he stared into the distance with his arm around her. She could lose the man she'd come to love. Love, she hated to admit it despite having fantasized of these feelings since outcast as a child. Her dream of love came to her begowned in the trappings of nightmare. She didn't want to lose him, more so than even her soul. She snuggled close.

The Sliver and fire could defeat the ice, but it wouldn't destroy the enemy. It would slow them, but it wouldn't stop them. Ulrikt, or whatever the lord priest had become, wouldn't relent. If his powers stretched ice to the Watch, there was no reason to believe he would stop before reaching the continent. History spoke of years where the Parapet Strait froze over, forming a natural bridge to the mainland. Nothing would keep the Shadows from someday following.

Eliles recalled the raging power pulsing through her veins, the feeling of eternity, the rapture feeding her soul as fire circled them inside Istinjoln. Eternal Fire, the Dame of Fire, a tower. She stared at the Watch rising from the middle of the island.

The solution horrified her, but less so than letting the demons reach the continent. She wormed from Ivin's grip and hugged him. "You all need to leave, but I have to stay."

Everyone in ear shot stared at her, but the look in his eyes alone made her knees quake. "What?"

"The Sliver of Star, I can stop the ice."

"You said you couldn't."

"I was wrong." Eliles' heart pounded, desperate to explain, but it was impossible to define such a vague sensation. "The ice won't stop unless I stop it, forever."

"I can't lose you."

They'd both lost so many. "You can stay with me if you want. But if you stay, I don't think you or I will ever be able to leave this island." She stepped to the gangplank, determined but still not letting go of his hand. "But your people, they need you."

Solineus stepped beside them, shaking his head. "Whoa, girl. Whatever this idea, if you fail, Ulrikt gets the Sliver."

"If I sail from here, it's a matter of time. Either the ice bridge reaches the continent, or nature will do it for them, sooner or later. The only victory is to make sure these waters can never freeze."

Ivin said, "Too godsdamned risky."

Lelishen said, "We can't let you risk everything, not without some idea of your plan."

Eliles wanted them to understand, but all she had was instinct, of fire and power, of potential and terror. "When at Istinjoln I felt the bridled power of the Sliver, steered into flame by my... by my friends. Its power, me, drew the fire. If I hone those powers into the bay..."

Ivin pleaded, "No, no, no."

She grabbed his face. "The Touched told us I could find the answer to how the Sliver could defeat the Shadows... not destroy them, defeat. You, all of you, must trust me. The answer is there and I will find it. I am the Dame of Fire, and the Watch is my tower."

Sorrow and fury stretched his face, and tears came to her eyes as he pulled away and paced the deck. "Godsdamn it! I can't stay with you."

"I know, I don't blame you, but I'd love it if you did."

He wanted to cry, she saw it in his quivering cheeks, but he defeated his eyes. "If you do this thing, how do I know you're safe?"

"When this works, no force in the world will be able to harm me."

"Only the dead can make that promise."

"I will live, I swear."

Artus stepped to the gangplank. "I'll stay with the lady. Feels wrong to run from my home, anyhow. Whether a sword to protect her, or a voice to talk to, I'll stay."

Jinbin, too, stepped up. "I will stay." Eliles' nerves frayed, the monk was the last man Ivin would want staying behind, but she couldn't refuse his courage.

Several more stepped forward, then a second wave. Eliles recognized Seden from the Salty Frog Tavern. "I ain't fond of running m'self, and someone'll need to cook." She eyed Artus. "Someone with taste, that is."

Eliles chewed her lip, perplexed that so many would stay behind, and pained by Ivin's frown as he turned his gaze anywhere but on Jinbin. "I don't know what's going to happen, all I promise is survival."

Artus asked, "And what promises do the Parapet Straits and the continent make?"

Ivin came to her, wrapped her in his arms, his eyes soft, but he held her so tight she could feel both their hearts beating. "Don't stay, come with me."

"Ulrikt's Shadow brings the ice, if the Sliver can destroy him—"

"Drop the Sliver in the ocean, lose it forever."

"Even if… It wouldn't stop them from reaching the continent, us, our people, the Tek Nations, and how many more peoples? I can keep them from ever leaving Kaludor."

"We'll find another way."

"I can no more go with you than you can stay with me. Go, find a way to close the gate, then come back for me. I'll be here, always, waiting." Her words were neither a falsehood nor the truth, there wasn't a way to know for sure, but the grind in her gut felt like she lied. But his grip eased, her words maybe soothing his fears with hope. "Time runs short."

His lips pressed to hers, and he let go of her. "Any who wish to remain on the island, disembark now."

"Thank you."

Nineteen men and women walked the plank to the pier before Artus hugged his nephew. "Gods be kind and bring you back to us with good news."

Ivin nodded, and clapped the man on his back, but didn't say a word as his uncle stepped from the ship.

Eliles pulled the Touched's tome from her haversack, offering it to Lelishen. "This was your gift."

The woman smiled, staring. "You should keep it."

Generosity was in the Trelelunin's nature, but there was no doubting she wanted the book. Eliles shoved the book into her chest. "I can't read most of it anyhow."

Lelishen gave a curt nod and clutched the book.

Eliles held the rail, one foot still on the deck. She turned to Ivin, wanting to say "I love you" but instead she only mustered a smile before turning from his anguished eyes. She reached the dock and stood staring into the empty streets of the town, unable to look back until she knew there was no means to re-board the caravel. When the sails whipped in the wind, she faced the bay again, but turned her eyes to the oncoming ice.

Shadows and Taken drew close, giving her pause. The Luxuns needed to get the ship from the island quick or risk incineration. Artus and Jinbin stood beside her, everyone else meandering to the wharf to wait.

Artus said, "Well, girl, I hope you know what the hells yer doing."

Jinbin put on a smile, but his voice strained. "My life is on my faith in One Lash."

Eliles' breath quivered, and she looked to the older man. "Still got that flask?"

Artus beamed. "Do I? Always!"

He twisted the cap and offered her the first drink. The cedar burn constricted her throat, making her cough, but she managed a second swallow.

"Quality whiskey, made it m'self."

Her eyes watered. "You don't say?"

The third and fourth drink of the concoction went down easier and she no longer doubted its quality. The knots in her gut unwound, and she relaxed with a couple breaths, but had to pass on a fifth lest she wobble.

She sat cross-legged, closing her eyes, taking deep breaths, meditating her mind into focus, reaching out to her friends and stirring them awake.

When she reopened her eyes to the world, the Shadow of Ulrikt was no longer a blur in a wall of wriggling black, he was a being distinct from the crowd. She reached into her robes, grasping the warmth of the Sliver of Star and held it in her lap. Her eyelids flared in sparkling rainbows with every blink.

She could feel Ulrikt's hatred burning into her and she fed on the threat, the fear and hatred he bred within her, to speak to fire. Her friends swarmed around her and the Sliver swelled into a star of silver liquid-light.

The great Shadow roared, and she felt the man's mind forced into her consciousness, grasping for control of her will, of the Sliver. "Your world is mine, fool girl. Your soul, too."

The voice belonged to Ulrikt, and his power made her fingers twitch. In a lesser moment, in a time past, he would've frozen her every action and thought, but with her fury and fire amplified by the Sliver, his efforts were as a pup underestimating what comes from a badger's hole.

Silver light spread in translucent liquid waves, her friends of Fire diving and dancing in its energies, sprinkling every color of flame into its essence until the silver turned to waves of orange and yellow, streaks of blue and green. She raised her head and smiled at the Shadow, still several hundred strides away. In Istinjoln the ring of fire had threatened eternity, now she summoned it.

"Goodbye, Ulrikt."

Her hair lifted then fell flat, and her tongue dried with her next breath. Heat surged and flames hissed, and she called it from the skies in a great wheel, slamming the bay with a deafening roar and blinding steam that left her skin dripping with moisture, cooling in hot winds.

Ulrikt's Shadow disappeared in fire and fog, gone, but she didn't know whether she'd killed it. She would love to know she'd brought his end, but it didn't matter. The Sliver of Star would never be his, nor anyone else's.

Victory belonged to her, but she realized she had lied to her love, and she regretted the decision to give him false hope. These fires would burn until the end of days, more powerful than she had imagined.

The vague sense of Artus' hand on her shoulder gave some small comfort. "By the Gods, girl."

Jinbin kissed two fingers and pressed them to his forehead. "A prison of fire."

Eliles stood and wiped her face with the soaked sleeve of her robe, took a quaking breath, and stifled tears. The flames and fog were beautiful, and she found herself taking pride in her creation. *Breathing is hope.* She smiled. "I've never been more free.

I made the right decision. Ivin needed to believe that. His clan needed him, hells, the entire Silone people might need him. The island of Kaludor would be overrun within weeks, he couldn't even be sure the Colok would survive such a hostile world. When they reclaimed his home, he needed to be there, be part of the revenge. But his heart remained empty and lost.

The docks and the woman he loved shrank into the distance first, Eliles standing resolute on the wharf waiting for evil with Jinbin by her side, and as additional sails rose and filled with winds, the rocky island and its towers traveled into his past. Everything he had known in his life disappeared on the horizon. He clutched the rail, his sorrow turning to anger at himself. He should've stayed. He should strip his gear and dive into the waters, swim for the shore. Kick the smug monk's ass straight into the bay.

"The ice must be close, what is she waiting for?"

Solineus leaned on the rail, unflappable as ever, at least on the outside. "I trust her."

Ivin doubted the man's words. "And if she's failed? If Ulrikt has killed her, taken the Sliver, what then?"

"We fight that fight, but only when it comes."

The bastard picked his fingernails while Ivin's gut tore him apart. "You're a godsdamned—"

Fog rose from the waters of the Bay, and a warm wind washed over them in a rush. Everyone on deck stared, and several screamed. A concentric wall of fire fell from the heavens, slamming into frigid waters with a roar of steam from combative elements. Waves surged from the fire, roiling until lifting the stern of the *Entiyu Emoño*, lifting and shifting, the winds of the rush pushing them farther and faster from his love.

Ivin's heart collapsed, his fingers limp and numb on the rail. Flames mountain high engulfed the Watch, nothing could survive such an inferno. Eliles, Artus, and the others sacrificed for a failing cause.

Heat rushed over his face and hands, worked its way beneath winter layers, warmed the breath in his lungs.

He expected the fires to fade, to disappear, but they streamed constant as if given birth by the sun, a tower of oranges, yellows, and blues built from a foundation of gray sky to plummet into a steam-cloud of its own making, and a parapet of boiling waters. An inversion of reality that brought awe and terror to Ivin's heart. Through the flames he caught glimpses, flickers of the Watch deep within. A chill danced down his back. A relief, a hint of hope that might prove as false as so many before.

"Her second tower? They're alive, she's alive."

Solineus clapped him on the shoulder. "I reckon so. A sweet girl who might sacrifice herself, but did you think she'd kill those other folks?"

Hot winds filled the sails as unending flame plunged from the sky, striking the sea. "No."

Hope rushed with the beat of his heart, but the heat drying his skin and eyes as he stared brought despair while erasing any tears which might otherwise have fallen.

Lelishen stepped beside them, her eyes wide, and voice hushed. "Not since the God Wars have mortals witnessed such raw power."

Solineus asked, "The Sliver of Star, what the hells is it?"

"I'd wager only the First Dragons, or the Touched, could answer your question. The White-Eyes, perhaps."

Solineus quipped, "If only we could earn its name."

Ivin leaned on the rail until his chin rested on his knuckles, ignoring their conversation. They spoke of historical deeds, all he could think of was himself. Someday, somehow, he'd find his way back to her, he felt a certitude that the gods wouldn't deny him this one favor, but another piece of him squirmed and told him the gods were to blame.

Solineus clutched the nape of Ivin's cloak and lifted him from his thoughts, dragging him stumbling across the deck. They passed so many eyes looking to him, for what? For leadership, positive words, hope? He paused to meet their stares and staggered when Solineus smacked him in the back of the head.

"Keep them feet moving." The man led him to the forecastle where they stood alone. Solineus pointed to the open sea dotted with sails. "If you look to get back to her, this is your direction."

The breeze was cool, refreshing, easier to breathe.

Ivin wanted to scream, pummel the man, but he recognized the truth in Solineus' words. Kotin, the son of a bitch, proved himself right again. "Forward is the best way to get everywhere."

With wind in the sails, the future was coming fast.

Moztoko, Мурерар, Поибель, Emvikrobu, Tureviveven, Fatum, Omnare,

Doom is my Mood in the winter of my birth, the end of all.

Dance in the womb!

Dance amid the emotional Soul!

The blood of my mother steams upon my newborn brow, the witch of eternity and promise of potential unfounded and wicked, the single eye—my father if you need know, the swirl, the sworl, the whorl, father not of Dragons but of the dragon's Nest and me and you and her—incestuous whoremonger?

You misunderstand me, you, yourself, whores and mongering in general, mongrel mongering dumb monkey with a twitch you speak of as a mind.

If or when that sad, puny, pruney, and shamed, flickety-flash of lightning trapped within your skull is able to stand under understanding, of seeing, of feeling, of tasting the slick of the blood of Life, come again and speak to me, and I will tell you more, of when Doom is my Mood, in the summer of my Death.

My Sincere Apologies.

No, not you.

You. Dugnamtar?

—Tomes of the Touched

If you enjoyed this book, or hate it so much you want to read more, join my mailing list. As reward for your adoration or contempt for my writing, you will receive the short story *Hiding Fire*, which details how Eliles came to Istinjoln.

http://sunderingthegods.com/newsletter-signup/

Fan mail, hate mail, and requests to send me millions of dollars from Nigeria, may be directed to:

LJRice@SunderingTheGods.com

Gods of the Pantheon of Sol

In tales of heroism and war, the gods of the Silone are depicted by their adherents as human in nature and appearance, but it is well-accepted by theologians that their true dispositions are unknown. Surviving documents from the Age of God Wars describe them in idealized human terms, but also confirm the shape-changing abilities of these deities.

While pantheon canon teaches what follows as fact, scholars should note that most religions on the Sister Continents have creation stories. They can't all be right.

In the beginning there was war.
In the blackness of deep time two forces separated from one, swirling, a tide-pool of water and oil no longer able to mix. Tundeu (mother of the universe) came to consciousness, her hands locked around the throat of Kudarn (father of the universe), her own neck squeezed by this other. They twirled in a murderous dance, their living passions setting the universe ablaze. Two sparks arose: Sol and Rin.

Sol, King of the Gods, was born amid the Flames of War between Tundeu and Kudarn soon after the formation of the universe. He took the form of a Fire Lion in the name of his mother to battle Rin, the Ice Lion. Sol defeated Rin, and as the battle between his parents raged he recruited other gods born from their battle, bringing them under his rule to defeat Kudarn.

Sol rules from the Conqueror Heaven, his constellation is the Fire Lion.

Elinwe, Queen of the Gods, was the second created from the war between Tundeu and Kudarn. She is often called the Lion's Paw, and surviving accounts from the Age of God Wars suggest she was brutal in battle, but quicker to peace than her husband, giving rise to the saying "ask the Lion's Paw" when seeking peace with the pantheon.

Elinwe rules beside her husband in the Conqueror Heaven, but Sol also gifted her with the Loved Heaven. Her constellation is the Lion's Paw.

Burdenis, Lord of Winter, was third created, and at first he battled beside Kudarn, but Sol eventually won him over with the promise of taking on Rin's powers of Ice. His turning from Kudarn is spoken of as the most important point in the war aside from Sol's victory over Rin.

Burdenis is said to reside in the Wise Heaven, and his constellation is the Mountain Eagle.

Estenwile, Lady of the Sea, was fourth created simultaneously with Zinmil. She is depicted as a kind heart with a vicious temper. Sailors and fishermen pray often to her for deliverance from storms.

Estenwile's alliance with Sol earned her the Faithful Heaven, co-ruled with Zinmil, and her constellation is the Dolphin.

Zinmil, Lord of Winds, was Fourth created along with Estenwile. They are often spoken of as a couple, but this varies between texts. As Lord of the Wind, Zinmil is often included in prayers to Estenwile.

Zinmil rules the faithful Heaven alongside Estenwile, and his constellation is the Anchor.

Kibole, Lady of the Night, was Sixth created. She was slow to come to Sol's aid but her presence was vital in the end, blinding Kundar with Dark so that he might be slain. Her personality is conflicted, similar to the night which is beautiful and tranquil, but capable of concealing terrors. Kibole is also the creator of the Road of Living Stars.

Kibole rules the Serene Heaven, and she is represented by no constellation. Her symbol is the ring of fire surrounding the eclipsed sun. Eclipses are an important time for her worship.

Tulule, Lady of Fertility, was seventh created, and she never went to war with Kundar, but she is later instrumental in Sol and Elinwe's union bringing children into the universe. Farmers and midwives, as well as parents pray to her for fertility in the womb and the fields, as well as for healthy children and crops.

Tulule rules from the Provider Heaven, and her constellation is the Cross of Pearls.

Turzjen, Lord of Valor and Wisdom, was eighth created, and the god credited with the tactics that defeated Kudarn after eons of war. It is said that he charged Kudarn and was nearly killed in the effort, but it opened

Kudarn to Kibole's Dark and Sol's flaming teeth, striking such fear and pain that Tundelu was able to swallow Kudarn whole.

Turzjen rules the Wise Heaven, and his constellation is the Warhorse.

Erginle, Goddess of Life, is the first-born daughter of Sol and Elinwe. When Tundeu regurgitated the "head" of Kudarn (creating the world of the Sister Continents) and commanded it populated, Tulule first needed to discover the secrets of Spirit and Life. Erginle, and the fertility of the gods, was the result.

Erginle rules over the Wealthy Heaven, the only "born" god to control a heaven. Her constellation is the Tree of life.

Etinbin, God of the Dead and the Hells, is the first born son of Sol and Elinwe. He is often, but not always, considered a key god when praying for a soul to cross safely over the Road of Living Stars.

Etinbine is the overseer of all the Hells, and the Hell of the False Prophet in particular. His constellation is the Broken Skeleton.

Bontore, God of Knowledge, is the second born son of Sol and Elinwe. He begins his existence seeking understanding of the mortal soul, but after the Great Forgetting, his knowledge is converted into seeing the future and communicating with the pantheon's faithful through the oracles of bones.

Bontore oversees the Vainglorious' Hell, and his constellation is the Bent Spear.

Januel, Goddess of Love and War, embodies the protective aspects of Love and War; keeping your lover alive, protecting family, guarding the castle, etc. Also, if you pray for love in general with no one in particular in mind, you pray to Januel.

Januel oversees the Lustful's Hell, and her constellation is the Heart of Januel.

Anzelok, God of War and Love, is Januel's twin and embodies aggression in both love and war (particularly war). If marching to war, or praying for a specific person to fall in love with you (seduction), you pray to Anzelok. Anzelok oversees the Raper's Hell (seen as an abuse of "aggressive love") and his constellation is the Northern Axe.

Pintole, God of Storms, is seen as the partner of Tulule. At first this love was frowned upon by Sol, but Elinwe convinced him to ease his restrictions and allow the love to flourish. The price for this love was for Sol to erase his constellation from the sky.

Pintole oversees the Liar's Hell, and is without a constellation. His symbol is a circle of lightning.

Momemu, Goddess of the Harvest, is the first born daughter of Tulule and Pintole. She is seen as an arbiter of fairness and sound judgement in the defense of the innocent.

Momemu oversees the Hoarder's Hell, and is without a constellation. Her symbol is a Shaft of Wheat.

Koldun, God of the Slave Fields, is the first born son of Tulule and Pintole. Koldun tends the Slave Fields, where the labor of the slaves assists mortal crops. Part of his duties is judging whether a soul has served long enough in the Slave Fields to pass into the heavens.

Koldun is without a constellation, but his symbols are a sickle and chain.

Seleseu, Goddess of the Hunt, is the second daughter of Tulule and Pintole. She is credited with keeping the nets filled with fish and the livestock healthy, along with wild game being plentiful for the hunt.

Seleseu is overseer of the Malignant's Hell, and during the God Wars earned the constellation known as the Bull Antlers.

Rettinu, God of Wandering and Lost Souls, is the last known daughter of Sol and Elinwe. She is said to be of a kind heart for those who lost their way in sin, and those who unjustly fell into the hells.

Rettinu is overseer of the Coward's Hell, and is without a constellation. Her symbol is an eyeless face, but this can be inverted to eyes without a face.

Tezlonu, God of the Slave Forges, is the last known son of Sol and Elinwe, and like Rettinu is known to have a kind heart, despite his position as overseer of the Slave Forges. Sol placed him in charge of the Forges because Tezlonu sought justice not revenge, and so only the worst souls are accepted into the Forges. But so too, do they rarely find their way to freedom.

Tezlonu is overseer of the Slave Forges, his symbol is a Hammer and Tongs.

Seven Heavens and Twelve Hells

The heavens in the Silone religion are paradises earned by living well in some facet of life, but not necessarily all. In the course of a lifetime, a person might have earned a path to the Provider Heaven (as parent, merchant, ruler, etc.) but have failed in their faith to the gods in some way. Upon death and seeing the Road of Living Stars, there will be a path to The Provider, but also traps along the way which the soul may fall into, delivering them to a hell.

This is always a possibility, and there is a sense of "chance" involved in crossing the Stars. A worthy soul may slip, and a questionable soul might struggle their way safely across. None who fully deserves the hells will ever cross without penance. The soul has two benefactors in its journey: the prayers of mortals they've left behind, and if they lived an inspired life, they may receive the favor of a god in order to assist their journey.

A soul which falls into a hell is not lost, however. The hells are not seen as a final destination, they are places of punishment and enlightenment. With perseverance a soul may work its way from the hells and to the Slave Fields, and from there, they may find their way into the heavens.

Heavens

The Seven Heavens are depicted as palatial grounds with the Conqueror a fortress in the center. The Loved is a walled garden which surrounds the fortress. The remaining five heavens circle the walls, equally spaced, but the only entrance to the Loved is via the Faithful.

The Conqueror: The highest heaven is an indomitable fortress reserved for the gods and their most deserving adherents. On ascending the stairs to the Sun Throne, a soul found worthy kisses two fingertips of Sol's right hand, and he places them to his forehead. Forever more the soul is accepted as a Valiant of the Pantheon, destined to lead warriors to victory upon their return to the mortal realms.

The Loved: This heaven is a lavish garden in stark contrast to the fortress of the Conqueror, filled with flowers eternally in bloom and trees bearing the sweetest fruit. Not all souls who reach the Loved will earn the kiss of the Sun Throne.

The Faithful: The highest heaven an ordinary soul (not a priest) is likely to achieve on crossing the Road of the Living Stars. The Faithful is reserved for those who've proven their faith in the pantheon beyond an ordinary standard, through great sacrifice in the mortal and/or spiritual realms.

The Provider, Serene, Wealthy, and Wise: These four heavens are seen as equals in most church canon, but various doctrines will make arguments for the superiority of one or the other. Souls residing in one may visit the others, and attempt to enter the Faithful, but if they aren't found worthy their stay is limited. A phrase such as, "You're but a visitor to wisdom," owes its origin to these heavens, and means that while you are wise, don't over estimate yourself.

Hells

The *Book of Leds* details many of the sins which earn particular hells, but even this compendium is not considered exhaustive. In *Leds* every hell is accompanied by several tales of individuals who earned particular hells during the Age of God Wars.

A hell's name does not make them exclusive to a specific sin. Each bares a multitude of potential sins and variations, and a single sin may (and often does) make the soul vulnerable to more than one hell. What follows are simplistic descriptions of the hells, numbered as they are taught in Istinjoln. Each hell has layers, and the weight of sin adds density to the soul, taking it deeper.

The Liar: A white lie won't land you in torment, but broken vows, thievery, reneging on a contract, as well as dastardly untruths might.

The Lustful: Souls who put love of the flesh before the love of the gods will find themselves paying for their pleasures here.

The Coward: If a mortal finds themselves unwilling to risk wealth or life to serve the Pantheon, they might find themselves here.

The Heathen: Reserved for mortals who converted to the Pantheon of Sol in life, but who were unable to live to expectations, or whose soul already bore the weight of too many sins.

The Vainglorious: For those who set their own needs above those of the Pantheon.

The Hoarder: Mortals who hoard their wealth or knowledge from the Church, or actively use said assets against the Church fall here.

The Murderer: On top of the obvious sin, people who protect people from the Church's justice may also find themselves here.

The Rapist: While rape is considered a vile sin, souls who abuse the Church's influence or power for personal gain, or worse, to subvert the Canon, will suffer this hell for an extended time.

The Slaver: The Doctrine of Sol dictates that only the gods have the wisdom to enforce slavery upon the deserving. Those who break this doctrine are punished here, among others.

The False Prophet: Reserved for those who preach or lead falsely in the name of the Church, unintentionally, or with intent.

The Heretic: Souls who once prayed to the pantheon, but who turned to another religion may be found here.

The Malignant: Souls weighed down by sins worthy of multiple hells find themselves here. So to might a soul cast out from another hell, the Malignant being their last chance for penance before the Slave Forges.

Other

The Slave Fields: Souls found unworthy of the heavens or hells tend crops here, as well as souls having earned their way out of the Twelve Hells.

The Slave Forges: From here, there is no escape, earned or otherwise. The fortunate are doomed to pumping the bellows, powering the hammers, or other menial tasks, while belligerent unrepentant sinners are snared and used to fuel the fires. During the God Wars, sinners and true enemies of the gods were forged into weapons for the Maimers and Mercies.

The Seven Clans

The Great Forgetting left the Silone people in chaos, but compared to many other regions of the world, peace came quickly and with fewer lives lost. The clans are due much of the credit for this, because the memories of these tight-knit families were better remembered. Still, differences in recollections of leadership brought on more than two years of war, brother versus brother and clan versus clan.

The leadership of the clans wasn't settled until after the War of Seven Lies, but the seven original family names, if not all the members, survived.

Choerkin

In the Fourth Year of Remembered Time, Holkar Choerkin brought the clan to preeminence with the capture of Lord Priest Imrok Girn. Imrok's capture and subsequent execution ended the War of Seven Lies while boosting Choerkin status, but there are additional reasons for the continued influence.

Choerkin territory is more southern than all but the Emudar, providing longer growing seasons. Also, Choerkin Fost is a sheltered, deep harbor, which allows trade from the mainland of Northern Vandunez and other parts of the world. The third factor in their power is also a thorn in their side: Istinjoln Monastery. A disproportionate number of high and lord priests are trained here, and their loyalty to Istinjoln has spread across Kaludor.

Broldun

Broldun territory neighbors the Choerkin to the northeast, and these two clans haven't agreed on much after Lord Priest Imrok was set ablaze. Their first falling out came over a dispute over ownership of the Omindi Pass, one of the safest mountain routes into the Treaty Lands. Several pitched battles were fought in the north over this territory (also determining what clan would hold sway over Istinjoln, at the time was being rebuilt). The Choerkin struck a decisive victory in 75 R.T. and the Broldun were forced to relinquish all claims in a treaty signed and witnessed by the heads of the seven clans.

Through the generations, disagreements over trade and territory have been enflamed by the Brolduns' cozying up to the Church. In 463 R.T. Triwan Broldun wedded High Priestess Levelu of Devinlok, a move which Fermiden Abbey (headed then by Lord Priestess Iulo) hoped would escalate their standing above Istinjoln in the eyes of other church leaders. Unfortunately for Fermiden's plans, Ulrikt was already rising as a force in Istinjoln.

The marriage's first born son, Dunkol, was secretly trained in Fermiden, and when Iulo died under suspicious circumstances in 501 R.T., Dunkol was named lord priest.

Emudar

Headed by Lord Lidin Emudar, their lands are the southern most territory on Kaludor, and the most fertile. They are the most populous clan, and arguably the wealthiest, due to their growing seasons, and naval prowess. Despite these advantages, their influence has but rarely been on par with the Choerkin and Broldun. The clans north of the Ravinrin tend to see the Emudar as soft, an image the Broldun foster as the Emudar are tight allies of the Choerkin.

Of the Seven Clans, Emudar boasts the finest trading vessels to pilot the seas. While other clans venture no further than the Parapet Straits, Emudar captains venture down the mainland's western coast, crossing the Po-Homox Sea into the Gulf of Volgrahar. These are dangerous waters thick with ships of several Tek nations, but it opened unique trading opportunities.

Emudar territory shares one border with another clan: Choerkin. They fought by each others' sides in the War of Seven Lies often, and it forged a political bond between the two which has stayed strong for five centuries.

Ravinrin

Headed by Lady Tedeu, Clan Ravinrin rounds out the big four in clan politics. Tedeu is married to Findus Uolar (her second marriage, her first husband, Lanklin, died at sea) who is third cousin to Lovar Choerkin. This second marriage put strains on relations between the Broldun and Ravinrin, but Lady Tedeu isn't a woman to fuss around with appeasing folks she doesn't care for. Practicality is a Ravinrin strength, so while their relations with the Broldun are sometimes shaky, they never fall apart.

The wealth of the Ravinrin comes from the silver trade, but a substantial prestige is also found in their foundries, which produce high quality steel, and their smiths, who produce the finest arms and armor on Kaludor. The secret is a rare mineral which comes from a single mine in their territory.

Mulharth

Lord Borun rules the Mulharth as a staunch ally of the Broldun, his great-great-grandmother being Suemu Broldun, while maintaining a good relationship with the Ravinrin as well as the two more northerly clans. Culturally, the Mulharth-Ravinrin border draws the line between the northern and southern clans, with northerners seeing the southerners as "soft" and the southerners seeing the northerners as "crude"

Their territory is cold and sparse, but strong trade with the Broldun as well as a couple Tek nations on the mainland of Northern Vandunez, keep them well supplied even during poor fishing seasons. They have ample mines in the mountains, but weather and Colok hamper their productivity.

Bulubar

Lord Gorum leads this clan, but as he spends much of his winters fighting Colok in the mountains, and Tek raiders on the coast in the summer, his wife, Heshiu, is known as the political leader of the clan. She is a cunning woman who stays neutral in most clan politics in order to keep her people fed during brutal winters. The Bulubar also have more trade and cultural contacts with the Edan and Trelelunin, as adventurous explorers who brave the Treaty Lands can make fortunes by selling artifacts to the woodkin.

Most of this clan's population is coastal, with settlements becoming sparse the more inland one travels. They are a fisher folks, who live off stores of whale and seal meat for much of the year, while inlanders rely upon mountain goats and elk for sustenance.

Tuvrikt

Lady Lansdir leads this clan, and she has formed a tight relationship with the Broldun over the years, having married Yosif Broldun. The marriage alliance was formed in 485 R.T. due to a particularly brutal winter which threatened to decimate the Tuvrikt people. The Broldun stepped in with ships filled with supplies as part of a secret arrangement between the ailing Lord Tarm Tuvrikt and Lord Triwan Broldun, promising the lady's hand to Yosif. The deal forged a strong bond, for as luck would have it, Lansdir and Yosif turned out to be a fine match. Tarm walked the Road of Living Stars only six months after the marriage.

The clan's meager population hugs tight to the coast, relying on the sea and trade to fill their larders most years. The people are hard as stone, and dangerous in a fight, but tend to be strong individualists who don't take orders well.

Printed in Great Britain
by Amazon